Wolves around the Throne

S.J.A. Turney is an author of Roman and medieval historical fiction, gritty historical fantasy and rollicking Roman children's books. He lives with his family and extended menagerie of pets in rural North Yorkshire.

D1437583

Also by S.J.A. Turney

Tales of the Empire

Interregnum
Ironroot
Dark Empress
Insurgency
Invasion
Jade Empire
Emperor's Bane

The Ottoman Cycle

The Thief's Tale
The Priest's Tale
The Assassin's Tale
The Pasha's Tale

The Knights Templar

Daughter of War
The Last Emir
City of God
The Winter Knight
The Crescent and the Cross
The Last Crusade

Wolves of Odin

Blood Feud
The Bear of Byzantium
Iron and Gold
Wolves around the Throne

WOLVES
AROUND THE
THRONE
S.J.A. TURNEY

CANELO

First published in the United Kingdom in 2023 by

Canelo
Unit 9, 5th Floor
Cargo Works, 1–2 Hatfields
London SE1 9PG
United Kingdom

A CIP catalogue record for this book is available from the British Library.

Print ISBN 978 1 80436 433 8
Ebook ISBN 978 1 80436 434 5

This book is a work of fiction. Names, characters, businesses, organizations, places and events are either the product of the author's imagination or are used fictitiously. Any resemblance to actual persons, living or dead, events or locales is entirely coincidental.

Cover design by Tom Sanderson

Cover images © ArcAngel

Look for more great books at www.canelo.co

Printed and bound in Great Britain by Clays Ltd, Elcograf S.p.A.

I

For my parents, who introduced me to the historical wonders of France from an early age.

A note on pronunciation

Wherever possible within this tale, I have adhered to the Old Norse spellings and pronunciations of Viking names, concepts and words. There is a certain closeness to be gained from speaking these names as they would have been spoken a thousand years ago. For example, I have used Valhöll rather than Valhalla, which is more ubiquitous now, but they refer to the same thing. There is a glossary of Norse terms at the back of the book.

Two letters in particular may be unfamiliar to readers. The letter ð (eth) is pronounced in Old Norse as 'th', as you would pronounce it in 'the' or 'then', but in many cases over the centuries has been anglicised as a 'd'. So, for example, you will find Harald Hardrada's name written in the text as Harðráði (pronounced Har-th-rar-thi) but it can be read as Hardradi for ease. Similarly, Seiðr can be read as seithr or seidr. The letter æ (ash) is pronounced 'a' as in cat, or bat.

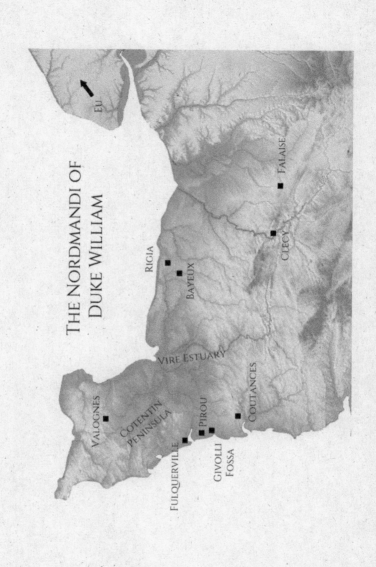

THE NORDMANDI OF
DUKE WILLIAM

EU

FALAISE

CLECY

RIGIA

BAYEUX

VIRE ESTUARY

COUTANCES

VALOGNES

COTENTIN
PENINSULA

PIROU

FULQUERVILLE

GIVOLLI
FOSSA

Part One

ᛈᚩᛚᚠᛗᛋ ᛟᚠ ᛟᚾᛁᛏ

Land of the Northmen

When passing a door post,
watch as you walk on, inspect as you enter.
It is uncertain where enemies lurk
or crouch in a dark corner.

Advice to a visitor from the *Hávamál*

Chapter 1

Autumn 1043

The wagon groaned and creaked along, the stocky horse in its traces huffing and snorting, the gentle crunch of gravel beneath the wheels almost hypnotic in its mile-eating repetitiveness. The same noises echoed from other wagons ahead and behind, joining the tapestry of sound, coloured threads added by the murmur of conversation all around.

Ulfr Sveinsson listened with a relaxed smile.

Before he'd left with the *Sea Wolf*, he'd never been beyond the lands bordering the cold, dark sea of the North, where everyone spoke variations of a tongue, and nothing was alien. Four years of travel with the young jarl, though, had opened his eyes to a wider and much more varied world. Now, he hardly noticed anything odd in the sound of Rus warriors, their accents tinted with Greek from years of service in Miklagarðr, deep in discussion with these new Northmen from the land beyond the Franks, their strange semi-Norse dialect tinged with an Italian fluidity.

The two groups had become closer and closer throughout the journey from Apulia, to the point where Ulfr had to remind himself that they had not always been comrades. The Wolves of Odin, survivors from the Byzantine wars and adventurers in the east, mixing so easily with the twelve-man Norman escort that William Iron Arm had assigned to guard his sister on the way north. Their leader, Thurstan, had become a good friend of the young jarl's, and the constant peril of their journey had brought them all closer together. It would be almost a shame when they finally reached Eu and the two groups went their separate ways.

Other voices trickled across the surface of that complex weave of accents: women's voices, and the honeyed tongue of a Rus among them. Ulfr had volunteered to drive the wagon of the women, and Halfdan had readily accepted. It would draw unwanted attention to have the wagon driven by Gunnhild, though she had offered. Leif had taken his turn here and there, but Halfdan had his own tasks leading this strange group, Ketil was too tall for the wagon seat – any attempt to drive was horribly uncomfortable for the Icelandic beanpole – and no one trusted Bjorn near women, of course. Even if he didn't try for an occasional opportunistic grope, his sense of humour tended to horrify the fairer sex. And, of course, with the oath Halfdan had given Iron Arm to make sure that his sister reached her home, it had to be one of the Wolves who took the responsibility.

Hence: Ulfr.

'Destiny is a hard mistress,' Gunnhild was saying.

'Destiny is of our own making,' Beatrix de Hauteville replied, her tone harsh, unyielding.

'Destiny is a road, a path, a journey.'

'Yet you defied it,' Cassandra put in.

'I did,' Gunnhild admitted, 'but I can feel the *Norns* weaving, more than ever, *closer* than ever. I fear that all journeys lead to the same place in the end. In stepping off the path, I have only found a harder road that will lead me to the same end.'

'You are a strange one, Gunnhild,' Beatrix sighed. 'But I tell you again, I will not be tied in matrimony to any man not of my choosing.'

Gunnhild, again, her voice calm, as though explaining basic logic to a child: 'Nothing is of our choosing in the end. It is all woven. We make the decisions, yes, but they are the decisions we are bound by fate to make.'

'Is that why you don't cast the bones any more?' Anna said.

There was an uncomfortable silence.

'Cast bones?' Beatrix queried, distaste in her tone.

'Gunnhild receives visions from the Divine Theotokos,' Anna explained, 'the Mother of God.'

'I have told you before that this is nothing to do with your nailed god,' the *völva* replied with a little irritation. 'Freyja gifts visions to those she deems worthy. And I do not cast for direction when I already know the way. Cease your prattle, Anna.'

'You should *cast* your bones,' Beatrix said with an air of defiance in her tone. 'You will find that I shall not be married to this man.'

'I fear you shall be surprised,' was Gunnhild's enigmatic answer, which set off a fresh round of discussion.

Ulfr smiled and leaned back, listening to the gentle debate. It had been going on for so many days that it seemed part of the soundtrack of their journey. Beatrix did not understand Gunnhild or their world, and seemed even deliberately ignorant. Anna and Cassandra were as close to the völva as ever, the three women like a coven, despite their insistence that Gunnhild was a tool of their god. They had argued and debated everything over the journey, and for all that this sounded like a new argument, it was merely a new angle on a well-tried one.

It amused Ulfr to see the reactions people had to Gunnhild, even Halfdan's. Those who followed the nailed god were almost universally shocked or repulsed when they learned of her gifts, while some became fascinated, and even accepting. Others, like the young jarl, or Ketil, brought up in widely Christian Iceland, treated her with a sense of baffled awe. Not so, Ulfr. He had been raised in the old way, and there had been a völva in the village, until the priests of the White Christ had come and burned her. She was mysterious, yes, and magical even, but no more beyond comprehension than a rock, or a tree. She just simply *was*.

'Hush. Travellers,' he called back into the wagon, and the women fell silent in an instant.

5

Indeed, most of the column went silent, barring the men under Thurstan's command, who began to chant slowly, their leader stepping his horse slightly in front of Halfdan's, taking point.

The travellers were only a man and his wife leading a cow on a leather rein, heading the other way, perhaps to their farm, perhaps to market. Nothing greatly alarming, but the Wolves had learned time and again on this journey to be wary.

Ulfr pulled at the itchy, brown woollen robe he wore, drawing the hood down a little. The Normans with them kept up their murmured litany. Whether they were doing it right, Ulfr could not say, but they certainly sounded like the monks of the nailed god that he'd heard in their journeys, and they seemed adequate to fool the general public. The couple with the cow crossed themselves and offered their respect to the 'monks' as they passed.

Was it normal to see a score of priests, some on horse-back, escorting five heavy wagons? It must be, for they had encountered little difficulty since they'd assumed the guise. It had been Leif's idea, of course, the clever little bastard.

The journey had been long and painfully slow, the pace set by the carts, and they had moved north through Iron Arm's lands under his protection until they reached the coast. There, they had travelled along the shore from city to city in the lands of the nailed god's highest priest, called 'pope', and then began to angle in a more westerly direction after the first sixteen days.

The first real trouble had come once they turned inland. Once pope's flag stopped flying over the cities they passed, there was less control. The roads became more dangerous and the population more suspicious. They had passed through the lands called Tuscany and there had been forced to fight or flee on several occasions, sometimes from opportunistic brig-ands, sometimes from the authorities of the lord of that region. As they moved into the lands of the Lombards, who were rumoured to be even less controlled, they passed a local priest on his travels and noted how even the soldiers simply bowed their heads to him respectfully as he passed, and that had set Leif the Teeth thinking. Within a few days they had spent a little of their mountain of hidden gold and acquired a number of very nailed-god-looking brown cassocks, some simple staffs, a number of wooden crosses on leather thongs, and had assumed the guise of a column of monks.

All trouble had stopped then. No one accosted them any more. Once, even, as they climbed into a mountainous region where deep, shadowed passes led them from the Italian lands into those of the Franks, they had even encountered a gang of vicious thieves who had leapt out, realised they were monks, crossed themselves, and even donated a few coins to the passing priests. That had been a source of endless amusement to the Wolves – once they were long out of earshot, anyway. The mountains had been difficult even in the autumn, and the going had slowed. They had been on the road something around fifty days by the time they left this high land of lakes and mountains and began to move slowly down once more to lowlands.

Ulfr had assumed that the Franks were similar to the Normans, being northern, but it seemed he was wrong. In fact, the King of the Franks apparently *hated* the Normans, and the two peoples were as comfortable together as Svears and Danes, which was to say: not at all.

'I am itching to get out of this cloak,' Bjorn said as they reached the hills and rivers of the Frank-land. 'And I'm itching in this cloak, too. I just itch. I'd rather drop the disguise and fight my way north.'

Halfdan shook his head. 'We are still forty days or more from Iron Arm's lands. We cannot fight for forty days.'

'*I* can fight for forty days,' Bjorn insisted. 'But I'm not sure how many more days I can wear this rotten Christ-robe without madness claiming me.'

Ulfr, taciturn, and not given to argument, laughed then. 'Any madness coming to claim you, my big friend, will be disappointed that he is late, for his friends took you years ago.'

7

They all laughed. All except Bjorn, who made a number of incoherent threats, and then went on to tell some tall tale about how he'd once spent the night with a *Valkyrja* and had had to fight her off when she wanted to take him to the Hall of the Slain while he was still alive. Some of the details of their night of passion were eye-watering, extremely unlikely, and made their guest, Beatrix, pale with shock.

Still, they had maintained the robes, moving on through these lands, which their Norman companions referred to as Burgundy and then France, two separate lands that seemed more or less identical to Ulfr.

'You drive a wagon well,' Cassandra noted one morning as they rumbled along, leaving the other women in an argument about gods, yet again.

'A wagon is easy. You should see me with a good dragon ship.' He smiled.

'Dragon ship?'

'The ships of the North. Not like the fat-bellied traders or the massive galleys of the south,' he explained. 'A good longship should be like an arrow, made to carve a speedy path through the waves. Whether for trade or for war, it is better to be fast than strong, for if Ran seeks to pull you down into her halls in the deep, no amount of heavy timbers will save you, but while you ride the whale road, there is much to be gained from speed.'

'You sound like a true sailor,' she said.

He smiled. 'A sailor, a shipwright, an artist. I have made the best ships in the world. You never saw the *Sea Wolf*, did you? She was taken by Harðráði when we left the great city. It still hurts, for she was a part of me, that ship. My best work.'

She left him, then, returning to the wagon and the argument, which was no longer about Freyja and Christ, but about the differences between Beatrix's and Anna's versions of the same nailed god. She left him feeling thoughtful, and slightly sad. Halfdan had been insistent, any time the subject came up, that they would find the *Sea Wolf* again, along with its glorious thief, and Gunnhild was of the same opinion, though finding herself with Harðráði again was a less than welcome proposition. Still, she insisted they would find the ship and its thief. But then they had also been insistent that they would find the treacherous priest Hjalmvigi, too, and that promise was no closer, even four years on.

He sighed. They would sail again. Halfdan had said so. The jarl had told them all that once Beatrix was safely with her kin, they would buy a new ship and take to the whale road as was in their blood, back into the North.

That would be good. He would like to feel the cold spray from the bow of a ship again. In a perfect world, it would be the *Sea Wolf*. He would be less pleased with the work of another shipwright, but even a slow scow would be better than these *land ships* he had piloted for so many days. Some mornings, he wondered whether he should be more outspoken and insistent, should perhaps demand of the jarl that he take them to find the *Sea Wolf* rather than these wide wanderings.

But it was not in Ulfr's nature. He was a quiet man. Solid, determined, but quiet and faithful. And whatever troubles they had met in their time, he could not deny that they had more gold in their wagons than any man could hope for, and that when he was a true greybeard he would never lack for a heroic tale to tell in a mead hall.

In the great scheme, he was content.

He would just be more content in a ship.

They passed around the edge of a city by the name of Orléans that afternoon, an ancient place with high walls of great antiquity. They kept their distance, though, despite their disguises, for the Normans among their number warned with low voices that this city was one of the Frankish king's most important and valued properties, and so it would be well guarded. One sniff of the Normans and they would bring down upon them the might of France.

And so they returned to the main road on the far side of the city and, as the light of their seventy-fourth day began to fade,

9

they left the metalled highway and moved off into the woodland south of the road to make camp for the night.

An old foresters' trail – from the looks of it unused for some time – led them into the woodland as the light glimmered here and there between the canopy, still bearing its summer greenery. They finally pulled up a good mile from the road, by a lake of shining blue-green, formed in the shape of a half-moon and with a wide grassy clearing at the curved side. They drew the five wagons into a circle, tethering the other horses as they had done so many times. As some began to prepare for the night, feeding the animals, extricating the bedding from the wagons and fishing out the food they had purchased from a village market the previous day, a group of men scoured the bone-dry woods and gathered armfuls of logs and brush, heaping them together at the centre of their little camp and bringing forth flames, the fire bursting into warm, golden life, fighting back the growing darkness.

'We are about three days from leaving French lands,' Thurstan said with a relieved voice as he sank to a tree stump and rubbed his knee.

'And then we're safe?' Leif asked.

Ulfr simply nodded, listening as he helped the ladies from the wagon.

'Safe is a relative term,' the Norman said with a humourless laugh. 'There is considerably less likelihood of meeting angry soldiers of the French king, but there are plenty of lords in our own lands who like nothing more than to kick the snot out of one another. For fun, sometimes.'

Bjorn roared with laughter. 'I knew these Normans had not lost *all* the North from their blood. No one likes a good fight like a son of rock and ice.'

Thurstan rolled his eyes. After so many days on the road, even the Normans had become used to the great albino. And after the first couple of fights, they'd stopped accepting his challenges, too.

'And how far to Eu?'

'Fifteen days, I would say.'

Ulfr, on some instinct, turned to look at Beatrix de Hauteville at this news, and noted her distaste fold into solid resolve, which was then swiftly replaced with innocence the moment she realised she was being observed. Trouble lay ahead there, and he made a note to keep a close eye on things.

In truth, he was surprised they'd had so little trouble. From what Iron Arm had said back in Apulia, they had anticipated having to keep the woman bound with ropes and locked in a wagon to prevent her escaping. But perhaps even she had realised that escape would only land her on her own in hostile lands, and so she had chosen the lesser evil of the Wolves' ongoing company. She *had* been extremely outspoken, challenging, and even hostile in the early days of the journey, but seemed to have found something of the kindred spirit in Gunnhild, Cassandra and Anna, and had settled in with them.

Still, Ulfr felt sure there was trouble brewing once more, as they neared her homeland and the point at which she would be forced to accept a fate against which she had railed many times.

'I shall miss this company,' Thurstan said. 'I have grown accustomed to your presence, our ancient cousins from the North.'

Halfdan laughed. It was mutual, all had become content. That the Normans – mercenaries by breeding – had known from the start that the wagons held a fortune in gold and had never yet made an attempt to claim any of it had come as a pleasant surprise.

'Tell us a little more of what awaits us?' the jarl asked of Thurstan.

They had not really discussed the land of the Normans a great deal thus far, concentrating more on the Hauteville family, their noble cargo, and the journey.

'In some ways it will remind you of Apulia.' The Norman shrugged. 'Every little lord wants to be a bigger lord, and every *big* lord wants to be the *only* one. The natural state for our people is to be at war with one another. It is only ever the presence of a mutual enemy that brings us together. Such was the case in Apulia, and the reason that a council was put together under Iron Arm, the most powerful of them all.'

Ulfr smiled at that. He'd liked Iron Arm. The man might sound like a southerner, but his very core had been iron and rock, like a Northman of old.

'And the same is true here?' Halfdan probed.

That made Ulfr smile again. The wily, Loki-born jarl had solid plans to finish this job and then sail away, finding adventure away from the twists and turns of these southern peoples, yet he knew they would have to pass through the lands of the Normans and perhaps spend a little time among them yet, and so he wanted to know all he could.

'After a fashion,' Thurstan said, 'or at least it was the last time I was here, a few years ago. The barons are all gathered under one duke, who keeps everything together. Duke Robert was a strong man, and under him most of the warring stopped. But he went east on pilgrimage to Jerusalem, and I hear he died there. He had no legitimate sons, and so I'm not at all sure what the situation is now. He had a bastard, but the lad will be quite young, and being a bastard, I'm not sure whether he could inherit such power unopposed. Still, heading to Eu we will be on the very periphery of Nordmandi, and should be able to stay clear of any trouble. Iron Arm's older brother is stronger even than he, and will navigate the currents of court well, I am sure.'

Ulfr was less sure. After seeing what the Normans were like down in Italy, he couldn't imagine them being any more straightforward up here.

'What took you away from here and down to Apulia?' he asked the man suddenly, as he helped Cassandra alight.

Thurstan turned to him, frowning. 'What?'

'You left your own home and went south. I wondered why.'

'Fame and fortune,' the man said with a shrug.

'Here's to that,' Bjorn bellowed, raising his jug of beer and tipping most of it into his mouth, only a little down his front.

'And not to be away from the dangers of your countrymen?' Halfdan said with a sly smile.

Thurstan coughed quietly. 'There may have been additional reasons,' he admitted.

The conversation went on in such a manner as they gathered around the fire, preparing dinner in a huge cauldron, Thurstan telling them what little he knew of current Norman lands, Halfdan asking questions, Bjorn making off-colour jokes and outrageous boasts, while Gunnhild threw acidic remarks at him. Ketil was off at the far side of the camp with one of the Normans, each with a bow, practising again and again. With his missing eye, it had taken the rangy Icelander a long time to become reasonably proficient once more, even with the help of another accomplished archer. He would probably never be the sure shot he had once been, but he was at least improving all the time.

Beatrix remained in the wagon, claiming a headache, and because no one was willing to leave their guest entirely out of sight for any length of time, Leif stayed with her. As Ulfr unloaded the last gear from the wagon for the night, the jarl called across to Gunnhild. 'Will you walk with the goddess and sing your songs for me, völva? We are close to our destination now, and I would know what lies beyond.'

Gunnhild looked as though she might argue for a moment, but Cassandra and Anna murmured something to her, and she nodded, tersely. Ulfr placed the pile of blankets nearby and sat, watching. As the völva began her song and her rites, he sensed that something had changed, something was new, and it took a while for him to realise what it was. Cassandra and Anna were singing *with* her, their gentle voices adding harmonies that had never been there before. When had *they* learned her song?

The melody rose and fell several times, before carrying Gunnhild to sufficient a height to see far, and when she cast her bones and beads and feathers and bent to interpret their shape, her two companions leaned close, still humming gently.

'There is much to see,' she said, 'but perhaps we are not close enough for detail. I see wolves and lions, a dragon swallowing men, Loki freed of his chains, and my jarl at the prow of a great ship.'

The Christians around the clearing crossed themselves, the followers of the true gods shivering at her words. Loki unbound was the opening of *Ragnarok*, the last battle between gods and giants, and the remaking of the world. That shock was enough that it took Ulfr moments to notice the last comment: the jarl on a ship. He tried not to focus on the worrying part, and found himself dreaming of ships once more as he rose to go about his work.

Ulfr moved around the edge of the camp, checking the wagons' wheels and traces, as he did every night. On his first pass, he nodded to one of Thurstan's men, who sat facing into the darkening woodlands, watching for trouble. His second pass revealed a cracked running board he'd not noted the first time, which he committed to memory as a job he would carry out before they hit the road in the morning.

The third pass turned up nothing, yet for some reason the hairs rose on the back of his neck. He turned. The man on watch wasn't there. His searching gaze scoured the area around him. There was no body in a heap, so it was highly likely the Norman had simply gone into the nearest trees for a piss.

But that shiver and itch of something wrong was still there, nagging at him.

He stopped, alert now, looking around.

The rear canvas flap of the next wagon was loose.

It should not be.

He'd checked them all, and on two passes he could not reasonably have missed that. He frowned. He almost put out a cry of alert, but bit down on it. Better he didn't alert anyone to trouble until he had more of an idea of what was going on.

Could that missing guard have climbed into the wagon? Maybe the proximity of so much ready gold had finally got the better of him.

Like the others, Ulfr had removed his monk's robe once they had settled into camp, and he carried only the sharp sax at his belt, his axe remaining hidden in the wagon, for it could hardly be concealed beneath the robe. His fingers closed on the cold hilt of the long fighting knife, and he drew it slowly, a steely whisper in the night, lost even beneath the faint sound of his light footsteps on the grass as he closed on the wagon.

His hand went slowly up to the flap, but instead of pulling it open, he paused, listening. Ulfr had learned long ago that sometimes patience and care were far more important than simply gaining the initiative. Any ship's pilot could tell you that.

He could hear rummaging. Whoever it was was rooting around in the wagon, and that meant someone who was not supposed to be there. The alarm needed to be given, then. He stepped to the side and drew breath.

'To arms,' he bellowed, and then enjoyed the benefit of his careful approach as a sword slammed out beneath the loose flap, right where he had just been. His free hand slammed down, grabbing hold of the sword's guard, preventing its owner from pulling the weapon back inside. Indeed, Ulfr yanked and the arm and the hand gripping the hilt were suddenly jerked out into the open. His sax came down then, the sharp tip plunging into the man's forearm so hard it came out of the other side.

The owner screamed and tried to pull back the arm, which only worsened the wound. The sword fell from the hand, and Ulfr pulled his blade free, drawing another shriek from his unseen victim. With his free arm, he thrust his hand under the canvas, grabbed a handful of woollen tunic, and heaved. He may not be as broad as Bjorn, nor as tall as Ketil, but Ulfr Sveinsson was barrel-chested and as strong as an ox, and the wounded man was jerked from the wagon with a panicked cry, where he fell in a heap, clutching his arm.

He was unarmoured, and Ulfr decided in that moment the man was probably just yet another forest-dwelling thief of the sort they had met so many times. The villain was going to be no threat, but Ulfr gave him a good kick in the head, just to be sure, as he pulled open the wagon flap and looked inside. Sure enough, the contents had been pulled aside, and the boxes containing the Byzantine gold coins they had brought all the way from southern Apulia were visible.

He turned. There were the sounds of combat across the clearing. Grunts, curses, cries, thuds and wooden clonks, metallic rasping, and odd, recognisable voices among them.

'I'm going to tear off your head and fuck the stump,' Bjorn yelled at some unseen enemy.

Halfdan was bellowing orders. An arrow thrummed through the darkness between the wagons, not a long way from where Ulfr stood, and buried itself in a tree trunk.

He heard a feminine voice cry out in surprise and, alert, Ulfr leapt around the side of the next wagon, into the circle of firelight. Here and there, men were struggling with assailants, but even Ulfr, no great leader of men, could see that the Wolves would be the easy victors. The thieves were fewer than they, and unarmoured, and were already trying to get away. Bjorn had some poor bandit by the leg, upside down, and was bashing his head on the ground, repeatedly, while telling the man what he intended to do to him.

A glance to the right showed that Beatrix was in trouble, and for a moment Ulfr wondered whether the attack had actually been a failed attempt to get to her, but then he reasoned that no one other than those in the column knew the noblewoman was there, so he quickly abandoned that notion. They were thieves and opportunists, and that was all.

One of them, though, had hold of Beatrix's wrist and was trying to pull her from the wagon. Even as Ulfr watched, Leif came running to help. Beatrix's free hand managed to fall upon a hammer somewhere inside the wagon, and came out into the open, swinging. Unfortunately, her assailant saw it coming and ducked, and the heavy flattened end connected with Leif's forehead even as he lunged to help. The little Rus went down in a heap instantly, as Beatrix yelled something furious and very unladylike. She had clearly been in Gunnhild's company too long. Or possibly even Bjorn's, given what it was that she said.

Her assailant cried out in triumph and gave a heavy tug at her arm, and Beatrix fell from the wagon, collapsing on the ground. Even as the man lowered the tip of his sword to the woman's chest, demanding that she lie still, she swung the hammer again. It struck the thief's ankle with an audible crack, and he fell with a scream, collapsing on his shattered joint. Still gripping his sax, Ulfr paused only to kick out twice, once into the man's head, and then a second time to kick his blade away out of reach. He grasped Beatrix's free hand, which was red raw from the thief's tight grip, and pulled her to her feet. She was so surprised she almost swung the hammer again, but Ulfr was already bending out of the way, unwilling to share Leif's fate.

As she recovered, Ulfr turned and took in the scene. The fight was over. It had only been a light scuffle, really, with a vastly inferior foe. Ketil was walking around the fallen thieves and finishing them off with a swift stab to the throat, while Bjorn was pulverising his latest victim, who, if he was still alive, was at least far from able to feel the agony any more.

The barrel-chested shipwright bent to Leif's immobile form. He checked the man's neck and mouth and nose, and was relieved to feel both pulse and breath, though there was a perfectly circular red mark in the centre of the little man's forehead. Ulfr gave a light chuckle. When he awoke, that mark would give Bjorn endless amusement in poking fun at his little friend. And probably poking the injury, too.

Satisfied that the danger was past, Ulfr dipped back between the wagons again and off to the edge of the clearing, where the darkness was becoming oppressive, only dancing golden beams periodically illuminating the world from between and beneath the circle of wagons. It did not take him long to find the unfortunate man they'd left on watch. His throat had been cut and the body dumped behind a tree.

Ulfr gave a huff of disappointment, not at the man's death, but at the fact that a man supposedly on watch had allowed himself to be jumped and murdered without issuing a sound. That damned the man as either a coward, an idiot, or asleep on watch, all of which were unlikely to elicit any sympathy. Odin would not save room in his hall for such a man. Still, for general tidiness – Ulfr was by nature a tidy person – he dragged the body back to the campfire circle, landing the blame for this squarely with the dead man.

A head count in his absence had turned up two injuries, neither of which were debilitating, and one other death: another of Thurstan's Normans, though this one had died more heroically, fighting off the biggest of the attackers.

In all, it could have been so much worse.

Ulfr heaved a sigh of relief and accepted a skin of wine from someone.

Three days until Norman lands…

Chapter 2

Days passed, their destination drawing ever closer, the autumn weather holding, thankfully. Bright days, with just a small chill in the air a reminder that cold times were coming. Finally, Thurstan announced that they had passed from French lands and into those controlled by the Norman lords, and even though that would not be the end of potential danger, and no one truly knew what to expect, there was still a tangible air of relief among the weary travellers.

One morning, as the sun blazed over the horizon at the small column, each wagon hooked up and ready for the day's journey, Ulfr found himself whistling an old tune in an almost jolly manner as he walked around the women's wagon and checked everything one last time. He could see Beatrix de Hauteville in some animated discussion with Thurstan and Halfdan by the lead wagon, and the murmur of the other three women issued from within.

He was not a man prone to eavesdropping, but it was hard not to hear as he climbed up to the driver's bench and checked the reins, preparing for the off, the occupants only a few feet behind him through the canvas flap.

'It was so vague. Have you tried again?' Cassandra was saying.

'No. That is the very point,' Gunnhild replied with strained patience. 'I am not sure that I need to.'

'So what is it that you have seen now, without casting?'

There was a pensive, uncomfortable silence, and Ulfr found himself willing the conversation to restart. It sounded interesting, important. Finally, Gunnhild sighed.

'It is not so much *seen*. I find it hard to describe, for I have not the words.'

'Try,' Anna urged.

'I have told you of the divinings. Of the bones and the beads. Of walking with the goddess and of the lifting of my being into the world of prophecy. Of how it feels?'

'Yes,' agreed Cassandra.

'This is not the same. When I cast bones, I will see a scene, or a tapestry of woven possibilities and certainties. It is rarely clear and requires some interpretation. But it is a visible thing, something that can be remembered and unpicked for the truth. This is different.'

Again there was a pause, and Ulfr wondered if he should be fetching Halfdan to hear this. But he didn't have time – he might miss something if he left. As if to accentuate that, Gunnhild chose that moment to go on.

'This is a feeling. A nebulous thing with no detail. But it is new. Something I cannot remember. All I know is that I have felt things and they have been borne out by events. Usually only small things of interest. I knew we would have a slow day, that day back in Burgundy when Ketil's wagon broke a wheel. And we hardly moved that day. And now, I feel a growing trouble, rising like a cloud to envelop us. More than that, I cannot say.'

'You are völva now,' Anna said, discomfort tinting the word in her voice. 'Perhaps this is because you have become something new?'

Again, a pause, then with a heavy breath, 'I cannot rule that out, but I wonder in myself if this is not my punishment by the Norns. I defied them in Miklagarðr. I turned my back on that golden bear as he sailed away, and in doing so I cut the threads they had woven me. I have known from that moment that something would come of it. I would pay for my arrogance. I had thought that not being able to hear the goddess for a time was that punishment, but I suspect that was Freyja's choice, not willing to walk with me in that strange southern world where

20

your nailed god is all powerful. I wonder if the Norns are now punishing me with a taste of the weaving. If, perhaps, I am seeing their work even as they weave.'

'Perhaps—' Their conversation stopped suddenly, and the reason became clear in just moments as Beatrix appeared, climbing up to the wagon.

'If you have no objection, I will ride here?' she said.

Ulfr shrugged an answer. It mattered not to him. Halfdan might argue, for it would look strange to passers-by to find a noblewoman amid monks, but even if that could not be explained, Ulfr reasoned that he could easily shuffle her back inside through the canvas flap before anyone saw her.

Her expression was dark. It often was. If they had needed a visual confirmation that they had crossed into Norman lands, it was writ upon Beatrix's face. The closer they came to their destination, the less content she became. She had been prickly these past few days, hard to deal with, much as she had been when they first left Melfi. Her darkening attitude had irritated Gunnhild sufficiently that the previous afternoon the völva had exploded and given the Norman noblewoman a piece of her mind, in very blunt and even insulting terms. Since then, Beatrix had kept herself away from the other women, and it was therefore no great surprise that she chose to ride up front.

Part of her decision might be Ulfr himself, though. He had, throughout the journey, found within himself an unexpected sympathy for her. Her plight was really none of their concern, beyond the business transacted between Halfdan and Iron Arm, and once they left her with her family, they would forget all about her. But enforced proximity over these months had led to an understanding of her situation for the middle-aged worker of wood who drove her wagon. She was not one of those shrinking, obedient wenches they seemed to like in the nailed-god lands of the south. She was proud and fierce, like a good woman of northern stone and ice, and yet her fate had been decided for her by her family. She was to be shackled in marriage to a man she had never met and did not want. There was nothing she could do to stop it, and the gods knew she had tried, so far even as to flee halfway across the world to the one brother she thought might intervene. And the Wolves were little more than her jailers, taking her back to face that fate. As such, Ulfr had made himself be as calming and as friendly as he could. Where everyone else became irritated with her, Ulfr had listened and nodded, soothing. It had cost him nothing, and he was a patient man. A shipbuilder *had* to be.

He listened to the general hum of the gathering as they prepared, Beatrix silent beside him. She almost radiated anger. Whatever she had been discussing with Halfdan and Thurstan had not pleased her – likely she had once again attempted to persuade them to a change of course. After a time, the call to move on was given, and the wagons began to roll and grind forward, those men on horseback walking their mounts steadily alongside. As usual, Ulfr's was the fourth of the five wagons, with the ones before and after containing, as well as the gold, Thurstan's soldiers. More of the Wolves brought up the rear. They may be dressed as monks, but each man was still armed in some manner and prepared for trouble. As well as Beatrix, they had another precious cargo, after all.

The morning wore on, with only occasional other road users, each time Beatrix ducking back into the cover of the wagon until they had passed.

Her anger slowly faded into the background irritation that seemed to be her natural state, yet whenever she turned to Ulfr, she managed a weak smile. She seemed to save them for him, which was perhaps understandable, given that he was the only one who seemed to hold a shred of sympathy for her.

'Have you always been a teamster?' she asked, out of the blue.

Ulfr's brow creased. 'Teamster?'

'A wagoner. You handle both vehicle and animals so well it seems you were born to it. I would not know how to begin.'

He shrugged. 'It's an easy enough thing. Any vehicle can be learned, animals or not. I have driven wagons in my time, but they are not my life, my passion.'

There was the oddest of pauses, and when he looked round, Beatrix was giving him a strange look, almost as though she were trying to unpick the stitches that held him together.

'What?' he asked.

'Men do not have passions, in my experience. Or, at least, they have only basic ones. I have noted in all men I meet passion only for food and drink, for women and for war. Four basic loves of men.'

Ulfr almost laughed out loud. If anyone had asked him to describe Bjorn, that might well have been the perfect match. It had been something of a sweeping statement, but in many cases, she was right. The quintessential man of the North lived for such things. But not *all* men were the same.

'You would not understand,' he said, although not unkindly. She had enough troubles.

'Test me, if you would.'

The road ahead was flat, straight, and of good quality, and the animal in the traces was content at a steady plod, so Ulfr wound the reins around the peg before him, anchoring them, and turned to her, folding his arms.

'Your people were once of the North, like us – sons of Odin and of Thor. Once, your forebears raided the coast-lines to survive, taking Hacksilver and thralls where you could. Wielding axes, and with beaded beards.'

She gave him a strange smile. 'It sounds almost... desirable, *poetic*, the way you say it.'

'There are few of us now who live that old life, and we cling to what made our people. And while we were born of grey rock and white ice, children of ash and elm, the whale road was our way, our path. We rode the ways in dragons.'

She frowned. 'Whale road? You mean ships?'

He nodded. 'You cannot understand. There is no feeling in the world like standing in the prow of a sleek dragon ship, the sail bellied with a following wind, skipping across the white waves, searching the unknown, hunting and journeying the whale road. It is a unique feeling, and one that cannot be found anywhere else, even if there is just the slightest echo of it in a wagon.' He smiled, indicating the tied reins.

Beatrix de Hauteville snorted. 'You think so little of us. You think that we are a weak and ordered people. That we have lost that which you describe.'

'Not weak,' Ulfr said. 'Never *weak*.'

'Still,' she said, folding her own arms, mirroring him, 'you believe truly that you are alone in your love of your whale road?'

He said nothing. He was a little lost with what she meant.

'Would it surprise you,' she went on, 'to know that I know the thrill of a face battered by sea spray? Of the lurch and buck of a ship in high waves? And not the wide merchants they use in the south. My people still sail, and we know a little of that ancient world you describe. I know sleek hunter ships.'

'You sail?'

Beatrix laughed, then. 'I was brought up at Pirou, one of the family's castles. Pirou is by the coast, built there to protect two harbours, to north and south. My father was always a sailor, even if his love of the ocean has been somewhat diluted among his sons. I spent my childhood with him at one harbour or another, at Fulquerville or at Givolli Fossa, and out on the waves. The family's demesne covers a number of coastal towns, and it was usually quicker to visit our various lands by ship than by wagon.'

Ulfr nodded thoughtfully. Perhaps he had underestimated this woman. He had known her to have strength beneath her spiky exterior, but it sounded as though she truly understood the call of the whale road. He flourished a cheeky smile.

'How do you lower the yard?' he said.

Her eyebrows rose, and for a moment he thought he had caught her out. Then she snorted and tossed her hair, the braid at the back flicking like a whip. 'Let out the halyard slowly. But there needs to be at least two of you, for your companion needs to keep on the other ropes and make sure the *rakke* does not spin, lest you be plucked from the deck and hurled into the water.'

'Shit, girl, you know your ships. As a boy I suffered that very accident. Almost did for me. Held tight to the halyard and was smacked into the sheer strake. Broke three ribs on the way down to the water. Fortunately we were in the harbour in Sigtun when it happened, and Ran's reach was insufficient to claim me.'

They fell silent, each contemplating the waves neither had seen for so long. As his thoughts wandered and struck upon the subject of her history once more, a thought occurred to him, and his eyes narrowed.

'Is that why you do not want your marriage? Is this Eu place inland?'

She shrugged, though her face had darkened again at the reminder, and Ulfr regretted raising the subject. 'I do not know,' she said. 'But the ring on my finger may as well be a shackle on my ankle. At Pirou I was never far from the water, and a week rarely passed without some sea journey or other. I cannot see that ever being my fate in Eu.'

He nodded. Again, it was really none of his business, once they had delivered her, but his sympathy deepened. He could not imagine any life in which he was taken from the sea and denied it. It would not be a life of any sort. If he were Beatrix, he, too, would have railed against such a fate.

He bit down hard on that, and forced himself back to a dispassionate view. He could hardly afford to be tied up in this. In just days, she would be gone and he would be looking for a new ship and a way back to the whale road.

They rode the rest of the day in silence, barring a few minor pleasantries. They stopped for lunch by a river, eating a simple snack of salted meat, cheese and bread. For the first time since the fight in the forest, Leif seemed back to his normal self. He had slept worryingly long and often, the first couple of days, and had even then been rather withdrawn, although the latter might be more the fault of Bjorn, who took every opportunity to prod the little Rus in his circular hammer wound and then waddle off, chortling. 'Seven days,' Thurstan estimated, until they reached Eu and the end of their journey.

There was a renewed sense of purpose when they rumbled on that afternoon. It had been the longest land-bound journey of their collective lives, and though they had made new friends along the way, in the form of Thurstan's Normans, and had a few small adventures, had eaten surprisingly well, and suffered few real setbacks, every one of them would be grateful to move on, to look for a ship and to head north again.

Indeed, there was something of a festive atmosphere that night as they made camp, their journey almost at an end. Wine and beer were broken out in larger quantities than usual, knowing that soon they would be able to resupply properly. There was singing around the fire, with Leif playing the pipes and Bjorn belting out a song that sounded like a dangerously unlikely sex manual in a thoroughly unmusical voice. They were careful, despite everything, the memory of that attack in the woods fresh. Two men would stay on watch, and they limited their drinking to remain alert. Farlof sat at the edge of the firelight to one side of the camp, and Leif at the other, the little Rus still recovering his wits and happy not to overindulge on this occasion.

The night's revelry ended later than usual, too, and it was easily past midnight when the travellers turned in. The men rolled in their blankets on the turf, Gunnhild and her women in their own little sub-camp, undisturbed by the men, Beatrix in the wagon, with Ulfr asleep on the bench seat as usual.

It was dark when his eyes snapped open, his hand going reflexively to the hilt of the sax at his belt. It stayed there as a cold hand closed on it and pushed the blade back into the sheath. He turned and looked up into the disconcertingly large and clear green eyes of Gunnhild. He blinked and, noticing movement out of the corner of his eye, looked past her to see Cassandra and Anna waiting, looking worried.

'Where is the Hauteville woman?' Gunnhild hissed.

Ulfr, frowning, thumbed at the wagon behind him, turning over. The flap was down, and Gunnhild moved then, like a wraith, fluid and strange, ripping open the canvas flap. Ulfr focused for a moment as he looked past her and felt his stomach lurch. The wagon was empty. Not *entirely*, of course, but certainly Beatrix was nowhere to be seen. Her personal bag, brought all the way from Melfi, was gone, as were two blankets, a cloak and a dagger. One of the caskets of gold had been levered open, too, and though there was no way to check swiftly, Ulfr would be willing to bet that a handful of coins had gone. The rear flap of the wagon was loose – her escape route, clearly.

He winced and rubbed his eyes as he sat up.

'How did you know?'

Gunnhild gave him a withering look, and he returned a weak smile.

'I have felt this coming for two days now,' she snarled. 'I have known there would be trouble, yet it was too vague for me, and I did not act upon it. Foolish. I should have anticipated every possible *type* of trouble. I should have scattered bones and walked with the goddess. I have been complacent.'

'How long has she been gone?' Ulfr said, stretching and looking about.

Gunnhild glared at him. 'Perhaps we should ask the man who was dozing happily not five feet from her? How should *I* know when?' she growled. 'Some time in the last three hours, once everyone was abed. The question is not how long, but where has she gone.'

Gunnhild left him, then, storming across to where the men slept, though many were already waking with the commotion. She went straight to Halfdan to warn him. Guilt filling him for not having anticipated this, and certainly for not noticing her go, Ulfr clambered down from the wagon. Beatrix would have left camp, surely, but if so, why had she not been seen? One glance and he could see Farlof coming back into the diminished light of the camp, joining the others, learning the news. With a sinking feeling, Ulfr rounded the wagon and moved out into the darkness, where the last embers of the campfire failed to illuminate the surroundings. There, with pounding pulse, he found the rock upon which Leif had been sitting, and spotted the heap of a body nearby.

Shit. And he couldn't blame Leif, as he had the Norman who'd failed to notice trouble in the woods a few days before. Leif had probably been perfectly alert, but would not expect to be jumped from behind by someone from their own camp. With an awful sense of déjà vu, he knelt over Leif and checked neck and nose. Breath and pulse were both present. The man was still alive – again. Lifting the unconscious man a little, he was aware of warm stickiness on his hand as he cradled the Rus's head. The back of his hair was matted. There appeared to be no fracture, Ulfr ascertained with a little probing, but he'd been given a good thump. Almost directly opposite the hammer wound on his forehead, in fact. Leif had always been too quick-witted. Were jealous gods trying to thump the brains out of the man?

He looked around, but could find no other marks or trail. It was too dark and dry for that. Lifting the little man with ease, he swung Leif over his shoulder and began to walk back to the circle of firelight. Chaos reigned as everyone demanded or shouted, blamed or questioned, all wondering what had happened.

'She has gone,' Ulfr shouted over the top of them, his call drawing everyone's attention. Anna turned and, seeing the shape on his shoulder, her hand flew to her mouth, eyes going wide.

Ulfr lifted his free hand, holding it out toward her. 'He's all right, Anna. Had his wits knocked clear again. He'll be out for a few hours and have a day-long headache, but he'll be fine. I think he was hit with a log this time, not a hammer.

'Count the horses,' Halfdan shouted, pointing at Farlof, then to Ketil. 'Go to Leif's position. Find her trail.'

As the two men hurried off to carry out those tasks, Halfdan, with Gunnhild at his side, stormed over to Ulfr. 'How could you not notice her leave?'

Ulfr fixed his jarl with a defiant look. 'You ask the impossible. Were there *two* of me, I could have slept at both ends of the wagon, I suppose. Perhaps a *wise* jarl would have assigned more guards?'

Halfdan, clearly taken aback by the vehemence of Ulfr's reply, nodded. 'Sorry, old friend.' He turned to Thurstan instead.

Ulfr grabbed his shoulder. 'Don't. They were no more expecting this than we were. She's a clever one. She's lulled us over the weeks into thinking she had accepted her lot, and she waited until the night we were all tired and beer-addled. She must have been planning this for days.'

Gunnhild cleared her throat. 'The fault lies with us *all*. We should have seen this coming, each of us. We can blame one another, but that does not solve the problem.'

'Where will she have gone?' Bjorn rumbled, joining them.

'Not to Eu,' Gunnhild said. 'Escaping her fate at Eu is precisely what caused her to run. As though fate can be escaped,' she added, with a hint of personal bitterness.

'And not back the way we came,' Halfdan added. 'Last time she fled to her brother, she probably went by ship, and she cannot possibly risk travelling alone through French and Burgundian territory. She likely made for lands with which she is familiar. She took gold?' he asked, looking across at Ulfr, who nodded. 'Then she can probably afford to take ship.'

'Pirou,' Ulfr said, suddenly.

'What?'

'Pirou. It's a family castle where she lived as a child, close to two harbours. She knows it well, knows the harbours, probably even the ships and their skippers.'

Halfdan breathed deep. 'Sounds most likely then.' He turned to Thurstan. 'Do you know of Pirou?'

The man nodded. 'It is on the coast on the Cotentin Peninsula beyond Coutances. A distance away, though. Eu is but sixty miles or so north, while Pirou must be over a hundred to the west.'

'And she is moving fast,' Farlof added, rejoining them. 'One horse missing. The fastest, too. *Your* horse,' he confirmed, looking at Halfdan, who quivered with irritation.

Ketil returned moments later, too, shaking his head. 'I found faint hoof prints in places nearby, but even when the sun is up, her trail will be spotty at best. The ground is hard as a rock from weeks of dry sun, and there are plenty of gravel roads where horses have left other tracks.'

'It matters not,' Halfdan sighed. 'We know where she is going. A hundred miles? Even resting the horse well, she could manage that in two days, even if she is not a good horsewoman.'

'More,' Thurstan said. 'Noblewomen are not habitually taught to ride. She will be lucky if she is not thrown in the first mile.'

'I don't think so,' Ulfr said. 'She's brighter and stronger than you think. She may be no practised horsewoman, but she will learn fast. Say three days.'

'And how long will it take *us*?' Ketil said, rubbing his missing eye out of habit.

'If we travel from before sunrise until it is dark once more, and do not stop for meals,' Ulfr said, 'we could cover a hundred miles in four days. And that is without suitable time to rest the animals and not allowing for unexpected problems. I would allow five days. If we left the gold somewhere and came back for it, we could shave that down to three.'

Ketil shook his head avidly, Bjorn mirroring him. 'No way we leave the gold.'

Ulfr nodded. 'Or some of us ride ahead. We split the column.'

'Dangerous in unknown lands,' Halfdan said. He looked to Gunnhild – a silent question. She sighed, closed her eyes, and prepared. This would be the first time in their journey she'd had call to seek the wisdom of Freyja, and though Cassandra and Anna, the latter still clutching her unconscious man, watched with anticipation, Thurstan's Normans crossed themselves and stepped back.

'Is this...? Is she...?' Thurstan tried.

Halfdan nodded as Gunnhild sank to a cross-legged position, issuing the most haunting melody in a quiet voice. 'She walks with the goddess.'

The Normans watched, worried yet fascinated, unable to look away as Gunnhild's song rose and fell like the waves of the sea, her arms winding shapes, her staff in one hand whirling glittering patterns in the dark. Suddenly she threw a handful of things across the dirt below her and her song wound to a close. Blinking, she gathered the bones, beads and silver, and dropped them back in her pouch, rising, using the staff for support.

She took a deep breath. 'We do not need to hurry. Her thread remains bound to us in some way.' She turned to Ulfr. 'To *one* of us, in particular. Travel on as we have been, it matters not. Destiny remains the same, no matter the road we take to meet it.'

Halfdan looked relieved, nodding. 'If need be, we will abandon her to fate. The gold and the Wolves are more important than the Hauteville woman. *They* are my prime concern. But I gave my oath to Iron Arm, and I do not like to break my oath. It is no small thing. If Beatrix can be retrieved and handed over, then we should do what we can to see that this happens.'

Everyone nodded at this. A man's word was of great value, after all.

'Pack everything. Regardless, we move as fast as we dare, and we may as well set off now, before the sun comes up.'

Men across the camp sprang to life, hurrying this way and that, preparing for the day's journey. Gone was the frivolity of

31

the past evening, each man consumed by the need to catch up with their quarry and retrieve her.

Ulfr sighed, and Halfdan gave out a few last-moment orders, watching as Farlof, Ketil, Bjorn and Thurstan hurried off to carry them out. Gunnhild had not moved, though.

'What is it?' the jarl asked her.

'There is more, Halfdan,' she said. 'More. I saw lions and wolves before, but it becomes clear that there is a *golden* lion in this land, and I see him surrounded by wolves. And the dragon. I see the dragon now, close. We have another destiny in this place, beyond the Hauteville woman.'

Halfdan frowned, wearing a worried look. 'And what of Loki?'

She shook that off. 'No. Loki's bindings hold for now. But the lion and the dragon await us.'

Ulfr watched as she walked off, considering her words. What was it with Gunnhild, Freyja and animals? Wolves and boars and bears in the east, but in the north, a lion. And dragons were not something he wanted to think too hard about, either. Surely the Byzantines and their dragon fire could not be at work this far north?

Whatever the coming days held, he felt sure they would be far from dull.

Chapter 3

Despite the lack of tracks for Ketil's sharp eye, in the end Beatrix's trail was not a difficult one to follow. Just after noon the next day, they passed through a village where a few well-placed questions turned up the fact that a lone, well-dressed woman on a horse had passed by early that morning. She had been moving at speed, as though demons harried her, and had not stopped even to speak to anyone. A similar story arose at almost everywhere they passed that day and the next. They had even found a ruined barn not far from the road that showed signs of having been used overnight as a campsite, though without a fire. Hoofprints and footprints suggested it had been the woman.

Ulfr cursed himself throughout the days of pursuit. It had hardly been his responsibility alone to make sure Beatrix de Hauteville did not flee the wagons, but he had been the closest to her, and when he thought back, he had recognised the warning signs building for days. He should have been prepared, and yet he hadn't. No one else blamed Ulfr for her escape, but Ulfr certainly did. At least he was not alone. From the few words they'd had from Gunnhild, she was experiencing a similar irritation, for she felt she should have known, too.

She, on the other hand, was at least calm, for she was certain that this was not over and that they would see Beatrix again, which at least assuaged much of her guilt. And Ulfr had known and trusted the völva long enough that he should have been comforted by her certainty. Still, he wasn't.

Two more days, and more signs of their quarry's passage as they gradually fell further behind with the speed of the wagons, and then came the news that they were approaching the town of Coutances, a sizeable place that lay close to their destination. There, as the sun began to slip from the blue sky and turn the horizon a dazzling gold, Halfdan brought them to a halt and called the Wolves together, with Thurstan in attendance, too, to represent his men.

'We need to change our guise now,' he told them.

'Why?' Bjorn asked.

'Because the monks' robes are all well and good passing along country roads and hiding in woods overnight, but we are now in the Norman lands of built-up towns. The closer we get, the more we are going to have to speak to locals and ask questions. We need to stay in the town tonight, too, as our supplies are low and we're all tired. We're not going to be able to hold up the guise of monks overnight, especially with giants and women among us. We need a disguise that will not draw undue attention and yet allows us to keep our armour and weapons on hand. Thoughts?'

'Can we not just be us?' Ulfr said. 'I mean, we're not wanted here or anything.'

Halfdan mused on this for a moment, but shook his head. 'Only Beatrix herself knows who we are and that we are here with her. Any Norman lord might take offence at armed foreigners in his lands. More ideas.'

'Can we not just pretend to be Normans like them?' Ketil put in. He gestured to Thurstan. 'They sound like locals. They can do the talking.'

'Better,' Thurstan said, folding his arms. '*We* can be ourselves. Men of the Hautevilles, returning from Melfi. This will be both believable and acceptable to anyone, as the Hautevilles have no ongoing feud with anyone. The rest of you will also have to be returning soldiers from Melfi. Just let me, as One-eye says, do all the talking.'

And so they did just that. The monks' robes went away into the wagons and they shrugged into their chain shirts with some relief. Though many kept their crucifixes, it was with almost glee that the core of the Wolves cast their wooden crosses away into the grass, replacing them with *Mjǫllnir* pendants that were tucked inside tunics for safety. Once more attired as warriors, they moved off, with Thurstan taking the lead. It said much about how close the two groups had become on the journey that the Wolves were content to let the Norman lead them without fearing betrayal, especially after the business with Fulk and Marc in Apulia.

As they closed on the town of Coutances in the last of the light, Halfdan quizzed their current leader.

'How far is this Pirou from Coutances, Thurstan?'

'A day at most. We have made excellent time.'

'And the journey there?'

The Norman grinned. 'Easy. Leave town in a north-west direction. Walk until your feet get wet and you're at Pirou.'

Halfdan laughed. 'Fair. When we are settled tonight, I need you to start up a conversation with some locals. You can confirm that you've not been back for years, and that news in Melfi is slow and late. Find out everything you can about the current circumstances in the area. Our prime concern has to be finding Beatrix and returning her to her betrothed, but we are strangers here and I don't want to walk into trouble unprepared.'

The column rumbled over a rough, old timber bridge across a narrow, sluggish river and approached the heavy gates of a fortification so old that the Byzantines would probably think it ancient. As they passed over the dark flow of water, once more Ulfr's thoughts were drawn to the open waves and the whale road. It seemed reminders were being set to plague him, and every time he thought of the foamy crests of waves he felt the closeness of the seashore in his bones and his blood. They were almost back to the water, which was Ulfr's land, as it were.

Two guards in blue and white livery, bearing the device of a white tower or column of some sort, closed in as they approached and demanded of Thurstan their business.

'We return to Pirou from the south, men of Hauteville,' the Norman replied, in a tone of voice that conveyed relief and weariness in equal measure.

Ulfr was relieved to see no sign of suspicion fall across the men's faces, and they waved the column into the town without delay, returning to their own banal conversation as a fortune in gold rolled past them, hidden in the beds of low-slung wagons. Ulfr examined the gates and the walls as they passed into the city. His love was ships, but it was not hard to appreciate good construction and fine workmanship in masonry. It was not *that* far removed from timbers and shipbuilding, in basis. The walls were centuries old. Back in Miklagarðr, he had heard of the Romans, who had built their stone worlds fifty generations earlier, before even the great white stone cities of Georgia. These walls, he suspected, were their work, and were testament to their skill, since they still stood and protected the town.

Then they were inside, rumbling and clopping through narrow streets between leaning houses, mostly of timber, some of stone, the last light of sunset vying with lamps and torches in windows that cast golden glows out into the increasing dark. Thurstan seemed to know the place, although he'd been away for a long time, and consequently he did take a wrong way once, cursing as they backtracked with difficulty, having to reverse wagons in streets too narrow for turning.

They passed a great church of the White Christ that was in the process of construction – a massive affair at the crest of the hill, bigger than the biggest mead hall in the world, as big as some of the grand churches of Miklagarðr. With yet no roof, the walls rose high and delicate, and the whole place was surrounded by masons' yards and carpenters' workshops and more. The place was a hive of activity even at sunset, but no one paid any heed to the five wagons passing by.

They arrived at a place called 'The Pen', and Thurstan led them in through a rickety wooden arch into a yard behind the inn, where they were greeted by a man older than the gods, with milky eyes, parchment skin and a voice that sounded like the wind scraping over prickly bushes. A short exchange, three coins changed hands, and the wagons were found a place in the large shed behind. Thurstan went into discussion with Halfdan, and the two men assigned guards. Many of them would use the bunk room of the inn and get a good night's rest in the warm with real beds, but five men would stay down below with the wagons. Their load was far too precious to deliver into the hands of strangers, after all. The old man did not seem perturbed by this. Likely, merchants who used the place would similarly have guards set on their wagons of wares, after all.

Three of the Normans and two of the *Varangoi* from the south were assigned, and Thurstan led the group toward the inn proper. As they did so, Halfdan collared Ulfr and Leif.

'While I trust our new men, and they've given us no reason to fear for the gold in all our journey, I would feel more comfortable if one of us was with them, just in case.'

Leif nodded. 'I quite agree.' He looked at Ulfr. 'Two shifts?'

Ulfr smiled. 'I could use a damn good meal and a drink. I will come and take over at midnight. That way, one or other of us can be awake all night.'

'Good. But send me some food and wine out, will you? Good stuff if you can.'

Halfdan patted the little Rus on the shoulder. 'We will send out food and drink for all of you.'

As they all turned to follow Thurstan inside, the assigned men sighing and moving into the big shed to guard the vehicles, Bjorn took the opportunity to give Leif a little poke in the forehead and issue a belly laugh before he walked off, leaving the Rus cursing and rubbing the mark on his head. It had faded somewhat, but was still visible and clearly ached.

Ulfr relaxed. He couldn't actually remember the last time he'd done so. Some parts of the journey had been less relaxing

37

than others, but at no point had he felt no real worries at all. That night, for the time being, he let go. Halfdan had the worrying to do, Gunnhild the planning, and Thurstan the talking. All Ulfr needed to do was collapse into a chair and order a bowl of delicious rabbit stew, turnips and bread, and a strong beer with a good frothy head. He ate, he drank, he relaxed, and he listened.

'So Duke William is unopposed in his inheritance?' Thurstan was saying to some local soldier who was off duty and enjoying hearing their tales of adventure in Apulia, carefully worked to avoid mention of Atenulf's missing gold.

'I wouldn't say unopposed,' the man snorted, taking a pull of his beer. 'The lad's only fifteen. Clever, mind, and vicious as a wounded badger, but still young. And he's a bastard. I mean, he was named heir by Duke Robert, but since the man died on his way back from the Holy City, it's all down to how well young William can hold on to his inheritance. He has a few strong supporters who are backing him, particularly some of the bishops, but there are plenty of lords who have openly declared their failure to recognise his authority.'

'Revolt, you mean? War, even?'

'There is yet to be war, but I certainly wouldn't rule it out. Some of the most powerful lords in Nordmandi have all but declared independence of the duke. Young William might have been able to come to terms with them and accept a much-diminished fief under his control without trouble, but there are others determined to cause a deeper rift.'

'Oh?'

'William's cousin, Guy of Burgundy, has made noises that he should have been the rightful duke, and there are plenty here who might prefer Guy. And the King of France has been interfering, too. He hated Duke Robert, and so now he hates young Duke William by association.'

The man sighed, took a swig of his drink, and sighed again. 'It's a mess. And I don't think it's going to end peacefully. All it will take is the wrong word at the wrong time and it will be a tinderbox in the hayloft, setting light to the whole region.'

'And what of the Hautevilles?' Thurstan asked, his voice apprehensive.

'Eh? Aren't they your lot?'

Their Norman friend snorted. 'I've been with William Iron Arm in Melfi. Allegiances are a bit different down there. We didn't know Duke Robert had died for over a year. We've been away a while now, and I could do with knowing where my own lord stands before I speak to him. And what of the lord of Coutances, too?'

The man nodded his understanding. 'Better for any man to know where he stands, I agree. A few months ago both Serlo de Hauteville and milord de Coutances were at the duke's knee, pledging allegiance. I doubt your lord has changed since then. In truth, most of the Cotentin Peninsula has remained loyal.'

'Good. Good to know. Let me buy you a beer.'

And the two men moved off toward the bar. Ulfr let himself relax just a little more at the news that the people they were likely to be involved with, both here and at their destination, were not rebelling. He had not realised that he and Halfdan were alone at their small table until the young jarl leaned closer.

'Ulfr?'

'Yes?'

'This place is dangerous. You heard all that?'

'I did. Sounds like it's heading for war.'

'A war that's none of our concern, and unlikely to be a lucrative one. If it's a place of rebellions and betrayals, a small group of foreigners with a large amount of gold are unlikely to fare well.'

Ulfr hadn't thought of it that way, and he felt his new-found ease evaporating rapidly. 'So?'

'So, I want to be out of here before anything critical happens. I certainly don't want a repeat of Miklagarðr, where we stayed too long and became tied up in their troubles. If we can't leave

39

immediately – Gunnhild seems to be under the impression that we will be here for a short time – then I at least want to be ready to leave at a moment's notice. This place we're bound for, this...'

'Pirou.'

'Yes, this Pirou. It is by the sea and guards two harbours, so I understand. When we get there, I will deal with Beatrix and the duke and our handover. I will even try to claim a reward. But while I am doing that, I want you to get us a ship. Buy one, hire one, steal one – whatever you need to do – but I want a ship and I want it soon, and ready to sail at a moment's notice. We'll not get caught again. Understand?'

Ulfr frowned, though in his soul he felt a surge of glory at the thought that they would soon be on the whale road again, and that the jarl had no intention of delaying. And then, Gunnhild's vision – the jarl at the prow of a ship once more. 'Perhaps you'd be better setting Leif to the task,' he said, uncertainly. 'Leif could argue the legs from a mule and would get you a ship for a cheap price.' Leif the Teeth's reputation was solid. No one ever argued money with him.

Halfdan shook his head. 'Cost is not an issue. One peek into the wagons should remind you of that. No, I don't care what we spend, but I want it to be the right ship. We have sailed in some poor vessels in the south, and we don't know what ships these Normans build. If this is to be a ship to carry us across the wide seas, it needs to be good, and it needs to be one you are happy to handle. That means it needs to be you who chooses it.'

Ulfr nodded his understanding – indeed, his agreement. He was fussy with his ships, and he knew it. He longed to be out on the whale road once more, but not in a big fat merchant scow. It had to be something sleek, fast, something old-fashioned but fresh and beautiful, with lines that took away the breath. He pulled himself together, aware that he'd probably begun to stare into the middle distance.

'If there is a ship worthy of the Wolves in this whole Norman world, I will find it for us.'

'And fast.'

'And fast,' he smiled. He doubted anyone in the world would make a ship better than the *Sea Wolf*, but when money was no object, he was determined to come damn close.

He listened on, or at least half-listened, as Thurstan and his new friend went back to their conversation. It was a little grating at times, trying to concentrate on the speech. He'd managed to become pretty used to the strange tongue of the Normans, which was what happened when the good old language of the North mated with that of the Franks, but in their homeland they spoke it a little differently. In truth, it was probably closer to his own tongue, lacking the Italian inflections, but they spoke it so fast and with such a drawl that he had to concentrate more, regardless.

The conversation picked up on the subject of the revolt of the barons, but became more embroiled in details that Ulfr neither understood nor felt he needed to know, and so he drifted a little as the names of unknown warriors and nobles floated past him. There was a brief worrying moment when Ulfr thought Thurstan had dropped them in it. They had been talking about the cost of maintaining troops, and at some point Thurstan impulsively opened his purse and tipped the contents onto the table to demonstrate his near poverty, but amid the copper coins, there were three shining gold Byzantine solidi, and they all heard the local's sharp intake of breath.

'Brass,' Thurstan snorted, pretending to bite the disc without marking it, and tipping the coins back into the purse. 'Cheap knock-offs they have in Apulia. Gotta be careful.'

The incident passed, but from that moment Halfdan involved himself in their conversation, steering it to safe waters. Before Ulfr knew it, the time had marched on and he had long since finished his food and drained his cup. Soon, the locals began to leave, heading home, with the visitors staying in the inn retired to their rooms for the night. Even some of the Wolves did the same, barring Ketil and Bjorn, who had engaged in some disaster-destined drinking competition, and Halfdan and Thurstan, who – their new friend having departed – began planning the coming days. Ulfr asked the jarl to wake him before midnight, and allowed his head to droop, dozing happily at the warm table.

He awoke without the need for Halfdan's warning, as the church bells tolled. Vespers had been called at sunset not long after they'd arrived in town, and so this must be Compline, he reasoned, blinking awake. The Allfather did not care when men prayed to him, or perhaps even *whether* they did. The gods of ice and stone were not so needy as the nailed Christ. And so Ulfr did not really care about their calls to prayer, but he did have to admit that having regular bells was hugely beneficial, purely in terms of knowing when to do things. With a smile, he took his leave of the others and crossed the room, making his way out into the yard and across to the great shed where the wagons were being kept and the horses stabled, and where he would spend the night.

The other lads were sitting, playing with dice and gambling small amounts of coin – just coppers. No grand gold coins from within the wagons. No one, other than apparently Thurstan, wanted to draw that sort of attention. Leif had remained in place, separate from the others, watching the door as he idly whittled away at a stick. Anna had stayed with him, but she lay in a pile of hay, on her back, eyes closed, murmuring quietly.

Ulfr wandered over to the Rus, nodding a greeting.

'Time?'

'It's time. Go. Get sleep.'

Leif smiled and thanked him, helped Anna to her feet, and the pair of them strolled off back out into the yard, letting the door clack shut behind them. Ulfr did not bother rising to bolt it. There was always the possibility that one of the others might come to see them at some point, and it was not as if Ulfr was going to take his eyes off the entrance, after all. After a while, becoming a little bored and not wanting to join the game across the room, Ulfr found a stick of charred wood he kept in the wagon and began to doodle on the timber side of the vehicle, drawing a ship, carefully, paying attention to every strake, every spar, every halyard. He closed his eyes and pondered. Opening them again, decision made, he marked ten oars along the side of the ship, doubled with the far side, naturally.

Having designed a beautiful ship, he sat back and smiled, then began to embellish the scene, adding waves, rocks, birds and so on. He was still doing so when the others finished their game of dice and wandered over.

'What's the plan?' one of the Wolves asked.

Ulfr had assumed that Leif had already issued orders, but it appeared not. He looked around the room. It was a large place, with two other wagons pulled up inside, both empty and open, and stabling for twelve horses, each stall occupied by a calm beast, ten of them by their own. There was a tack room and a storeroom, though both had been checked more than once, both devoid of living creatures, both sealed from the outside. That left only the main doors, which were a huge double affair with a small single door built into one side, allowing for the access of wagons or just men as appropriate, and a secondary door that led directly to the inn's main building via the kitchens and stores, but which was kept locked and had also been checked several times. He contemplated having the five men sleep next to the two doors, but it seemed unnecessary.

'Each of you take a wagon. Roll in blankets inside and stay there. I see no need for you to be awake all night. I will keep watch.'

With that, he rose, crossed to the main door and, for security, dropped the latch into place. The large room was secure.

He sat back again and listened as the five men each found a wagon and settled in. The melody of retiring began: the scratching, yawning, murmurs, curses, farts and belches; the jokes thrown lightly around; and finally, blessedly, the snoring. Ulfr smiled to himself as he listened, adding depth to the charcoal waves of his boat image. After a time, he retrieved his own pack from the wagon and began to check through it, organise it, and repack it. That done, he opened his coin pouch and found the nine gold Byzantine coins in it, laying them out on the ground and examining them, trying to translate the Greek inscriptions, identify the men shown on them, and finally to stack them in piles of similar types. He recognised he was faffing, but at this point it was important to stay awake, and any little game that helped was worthwhile.

An hour or so passed, and then a second, and Ulfr wandered into the storeroom and began to check through the boxes and bags, purely through boredom. It was more pleasant close to the tack room and the inn door, largely because the wall muted the snoring from the five wagons, and Ulfr could properly hear himself think. It was as he was thinking just that, and appreciating it, that he heard a quiet click from outside the small room.

He fell still in an instant, listening. The snoring had a sort of lulling background rhythm all its own, and was easy enough to dismiss, listening over the top. The click had been a lock, and he heard the laboured low creak of a door being opened very slowly and carefully. It had to be the door to the inn, since the main door was latched closed from inside. Carefully, on the balls of his feet, Ulfr crept toward the opening that led out to the main hall and paused behind a heap of grain sacks. He peered around them. The big shed was lit with two lamps that they'd kept fuelled periodically, and so he saw two figures pass the gap, but the two small golden flickers in such a large place made it impossible to make out details.

His hand went to the hilt of the sax at his side, and he thought hard. There was almost no chance these were friends or allies – they had to be up to no good. He contemplated simply jumping them. He could probably kill one in moments, and then he could hold off the other until the noise brought the other five running. He decided against it. He wanted to know both who they were and what they were doing. Consequently, as they moved out of sight, he slipped from the room, hand still on dagger, and ducked around the corner where he paused again, watching.

The two shadowy figures moved to the nearest wagon. His decision was made easy a moment later, as one of the pair unsheathed a long knife that gleamed in the golden light.

'To arms,' Ulfr bellowed.

The pair by the wagon froze, then turned. They looked at each other, and then clearly registered that the men in all the wagons, who they'd known were there from the snoring, were waking up. They knew in an instant they were outnumbered and, cutting their losses, they turned and ran. Firstly they ran the way they'd come, but then realised that Ulfr, broad and dangerous, with a sax in his hand, stood in the way.

As they neared, he finally recognised the pair. One was the local who'd been in conversation with Thurstan in the bar, the other one of the servants. Everything fell into place. The man had not been put off by the explanation of brass forgeries. He'd recognised gold coins for what they were, and where there were three, there were probably more. He'd come to raid their packs, and had enlisted the help of one of the inn's staff, who could access the shed through the side door.

The pair turned and ran for the main doors.

They stood no chance.

Before they could get near the door, one of the Varangian Wolves and one of Thurstan's Normans had leapt from their wagons and were in the way, blocking the exit. Ulfr chewed his lip. There was trouble here. He couldn't let them go. To do so would leave free someone who at least suspected them of having Byzantine gold, and rumour like that spread fast, as they'd seen in Apulia. On the other hand, killing a local soldier might land them in a lot of trouble, and killing one of the staff from the inn where they were staying even more so.

'We don't want trouble,' the soldier said, as the wide-eyed servant shivered with fear.

Ulfr sighed. He couldn't let them go. 'Then you shouldn't have come looking for it.' He nodded to the men between the pair and the door, who stepped forward. The soldier took on a look of forlorn understanding and turned, blade out, to face the Wolves, while the servant suddenly bolted, trying to skirt around Ulfr and head for the other door.

The soldier was good enough, but the others were better. Whatever the man had trained in and practised, the pair he faced were a Northman who had served in the wars of the Byzantine emperor, and a mercenary who had fought his way across half of Italy. They took him apart in moments, leaving a gurgling, bleeding heap.

Ulfr barely noticed this, though, as he turned, watching the servant running past. He lifted his sax – a nicely weighted one – and threw it. The blade caught the young lad in the bicep, knocking him sideways with a cry of pain. Ulfr walked over to him, picking up the knife where it had fallen as the lad lurched about. The servant whispered a single plea, eyes filled with tears, and moments later folded up with a sigh as Ulfr cut his throat with no small regret. Stupid decision, the boy had made. Shame it had cost him his life.

He turned to the others, to see the dead soldier. A thought occurred to him. He didn't like it, it wasn't nice. But it was a solution. He gestured to the men.

'Check outside, make sure it's clear. Then take these two out somewhere into a deserted alley. Should be easy at this time of night. Strip them down and leave their clothes in piles. Leave a knife with them.'

The men wore looks of distaste, but they recognised the need to solve the problem and gathered up the fallen, two more coming to help. In moments the four of them had taken the pair of bodies away. They would be found in the morning and a number of theories would arise over their demise, but none of them should touch on the Wolves or their wagons.

'And what do *we* do?' the fifth man sighed, wearily, once they'd left.

Ulfr walked to the shed wall and picked up a bucket and a mop, then pointed at the two pools of blood. 'Time to earn our coins with a bit of elbow grease.'

As they worked, he made a new mental note on his list. They were going to have to be a lot more careful with the gold in this place.

Chapter 4

Pirou was not what *he* would call coastal, Ulfr noted as they approached, with no sign of sea in sight. Oh, they were damn close, for he could smell the salt in the air, and the whale road called more than ever, deep in his blood, but not actually there. The wheeling gulls all across the blue sky told him just how near the shore was, but Pirou itself sat among green fields and scattered copses, largely of beech, elm and yew. Here and there, though, small stands of pine and oak did little to assuage his need for the open waves, for such timbers were good shipbuilding wood, and brought back memories of the old days in Sigtun – of snow-coated shipyards, angry craftsmen, and the *Sea Wolf*'s construction.

Over to the left – the west, Ulfr thought – there were distant hints of dunes, which presumably marked the site of the shore, but they were a walk away, while in the green was the castle of Pirou. The village they knew to be present must be further to the north, since they had approached from the south-east and the shore lay to the west. But then, the castle was not there to protect the village, but the harbours to north and south.

There had been much discussion that morning, as they'd departed on the last leg of their journey, over their specific destination, for the plan had thus far remained uncertain. It seemed unarguable that Beatrix had come back to Pirou, based on her conversations with Ulfr, and the trail they had sporadically picked up supported that assumption. But Pirou was, from what Thurstan told them, the home of the oldest of the Hauteville siblings, Serlo, who would reside at the castle and who, presumably, had arranged Beatrix's marriage in the first place. It seemed unlikely, therefore, that she would want to bump into him. More likely, she had gone to the village or to one of the harbours nearby, seeking either aid in some way or a ship away. In the end, they had decided that the castle had to be their first port of call. For a score of heavily armed men to arrive in the domain and start poking around uninvited might cause all sorts of trouble, and so they had decided to present themselves to Serlo de Hauteville, explain the situation, and then find Beatrix for him and finish their mission.

Ulfr heard the sound of hooves on timber and his focus drew back in, concentrating on their destination, instead of meandering thoughts about their plans and of the sea. The fortress loomed ahead. Whoever had built the castle of Pirou had done so with an eye not for comfort but for defence, and possibly with a touch of paranoia about their neighbours, too. The fortress itself was simple, a staunch timber palisade with a walkway, encircling a bailey that contained all the buildings of the castle. A single gatehouse of timber rose strong and impressive. But it was the moat that impressed Ulfr. The ringed fortress sat within a lake that was just regular enough in shape to suggest being man-made, wide enough that an arrow could just cross it, and breached only by a timber bridge that connected the gatehouse with the world outside.

It was not stone, like the old defences of the Romans or the Byzantines, but still Ulfr would not like to be the one tasked with taking the place from its owner. It would be a difficult proposition. For a moment he wondered when his perceptions had changed so. Once, back in the North a few years ago, a timber palisade would have seemed the apex of defence, the notion of stone towers a fanciful thing. Now he seemed to have a southerner's opinion woven into his own.

The gates opened on their approach, likely because Thurstan had removed from storage the banner of William 'Iron Arm' de Hauteville. It fluttered above the lead wagon, declaring the column's allegiance now that they were in family lands. The vanguard and then the wagons rumbled across the timbers of the bridge, above black, glassy water, and in through the stockade to Pirou's fortress. Scattered buildings, some large, some small, lay around the interior, as well as fenced corrals for horses and other beasts, small areas of vegetable garden, and workshops, some belching out smoke from solid chimneys. A good number of armoured men were visible on the walkway of the palisade and at the gate and, though people in ordinary dress went about their business within, moving from building to building, there were a number of soldiers in there, too. Even one of the workshops had freshly made chain shirts hanging from the eaves. The Normans took the business of war seriously.

Ulfr paid little attention to the exchanges between Thurstan, Halfdan and the officer who had crossed to meet them. Greetings were made – offers, thanks, directions for unloading and the like – while Ulfr wandered around the wagons, checking their condition. The vehicles were bearing up well after such a long journey, and he was satisfied with them. Halfdan and Thurstan persuaded the officer that the wagons were to be kept under the Wolves' supervision, and separate from castle stores, as they bore important cargo from Apulia. This being Iron Arm's elder brother's castle, he would hopefully respect that. The jarl then left the *Varangians* and their Norman companions with the wagons, under the supervision of Bjorn as someone that no one in their right mind was going to mess with, and then beckoned to his old shipmates of the *Sea Wolf*. Ulfr ambled over to join the others, grateful that such care was being taken with the gold. Since that little episode at the stable in Coutances, he'd felt a nagging worry that word of the gold might spread in the region.

'We are to be escorted to Serlo, the lord of this place,' the jarl explained as the officer led them off toward a huge structure at the northern end, rising above the others and sitting on a slightly raised mound.

The main building in the compound was a large timber structure on two floors. As they entered, Ulfr was impressed.

The place was almost as complex as the keeps they had seen in Miklagarðr and Apulia, formed of corridors and rooms, stairs and halls, just of well-constructed timber instead of stone. The place had been there long enough that it had lost all scent of timber, and instead smelled of burned-out fireplaces, food, and what could only be the three mangy hounds that were mooching around, begging.

Their host stood at a window in the largest hall of this large building, facing outwards, hands clasped behind his back in a proprietary manner. Serlo de Hauteville was an impressive man. Neat and well dressed, and with short, severe hair, he had the grey of age but the build and stance of a warrior in his prime.

'You come from my brother,' Serlo said without turning.

'Yes, my lord,' Thurstan said respectfully, not surprised that the lord would know given that they had displayed Iron Arm's banner on approach.

'A dozen of William's men and a rambling collection of Norsemen and Greeks, I understand,' Serlo went on.

That was a pretty poor summation, to Ulfr's mind. But as the man unclasped his hands and turned to face them, folding his arms instead, his features softened into almost a smile. The resemblance to Iron Arm was uncanny, though he appeared a little more serious and dour than his younger brother. There were elements of Beatrix's features visible in his face, too. The family resemblance held strong across the line.

'Not my words,' Serlo de Hauteville smiled. 'My sister's.'

Ulfr blinked. 'Beatrix is here?' he said.

The man looked past the jarl at Ulfr, frowning, seemingly surprised at being addressed by one of the warriors and not Thurstan or Halfdan. 'Yes,' he said, gleaming eyes locked on Ulfr. 'Beatrix arrived in the village a few days ago. She had no intention of visiting me, of course, and was attempting to gather what she needed for a journey. She had strange Byzantine gold with her, and was purchasing supplies for a journey. Fortunately the villagers respect their lord enough that they informed my men of her actions. We apprehended my frustrating sister in the church, and she is now my guest in the north block, here.'

'*Guest?*' Halfdan said with a knowing look.

Serlo nodded. 'Yes. Let us say, *enforced* guest, since she continues to defy my commands.'

'Frankly, I am on her side,' said Anna, drawing a strange look from the lord. She rallied. 'Beatrix is a strong woman, and enforced marriages to a stranger are rarely a good idea.'

Serlo de Hauteville sighed. 'Unfortunately they are a requirement in this world of ours. Alliances are made and broken with wedding rings. My own wife would never have chosen me, I am sure, and yet she has accepted her lot for the benefit of *both* our houses. I have always treated her well, mind. We are happier than most.'

'You need your sister for an alliance?' Halfdan said. 'I had heard of trouble in the region. Is this something to do with lords revolting against your duke?'

'My word, but you people are full of questions.' Serlo snorted. '*Insolent* ones, too. But yes, as it happens. Some years ago I had a little trouble at court and was banished for a time. I am back in the circles of the powerful now, but my credibility took something of a knock, and so I do what I must to bind the Hautevilles back to the duke. Most of my family are too busy stomping around the south, searching for fame and fortune, to do what is right for the family, and so it falls to me. And to Beatrix.'

He sighed again, unfolding his arms, stepping forward and gripping the back of a chair at the great oak table. 'In truth, I would spare her this if I could. She is a good soul, and a spirited one, and I fear that this marriage will dull that spirit. But Armand de Mortain will bring much needed power and authority to the Hautevilles. It has to happen. And we are still powerful enough that he will be good to her, out of fear of reprisals from me, if nothing else.'

Anna opened her mouth to argue, but was silenced with a look from Gunnhild. 'Sometimes our woven fate is not to our liking,' the völva said, 'yet it remains our fate, whatever we might wish.'

Anna almost exploded at this, her mouth opening and closing, until she managed to get out, 'But you, yourself—'

Ulfr knew full well what she was going to say – how Gunnhild had defied her own fate, and was being the very soul of hypocrisy – but fortunately Halfdan this time interrupted, addressing the lord.

'I gave my word to your brother that we would see Beatrix back to her husband-to-be. We escorted her safely from Apulia to the edge of your lands, as Thurstan will avow. She ran from us just a few days from here, and we were fully prepared to hunt her down even to the sea, and return her to you, but it is fortunate that she has been secured already. Strictly, we should continue to escort her, taking her from here to the count at Eu, though I recognise your authority in this matter, and that perhaps our task is complete now, ending here?'

Hauteville nodded. 'I relieve you of further responsibility with regard to Beatrix. In truth, it is impressive that you managed to get her that far without incident.' He chuckled. 'You have had a long journey and, knowing my sister, a complicated one, and it would be remiss of me not to offer you my hospitality for a few days while you rest and recover, and perhaps resupply for your return journey?'

'I cannot speak for Thurstan and his men,' Halfdan replied, gesturing to the man at his side, 'but *we* will not be returning to Apulia. Indeed, we seek to secure a ship, for we are northward bound. I understand there are ships here? We are on the coast?'

Serlo smiled. 'Nearby, but not here. There are harbours both north and south a few miles distant, though here there is nothing but beach and dunes. Pirou was built between the two harbours to guard them. But I am afraid I doubt that you will find a ship available at either harbour. The few good warships there, which are built for open sea, belong to either me or to the duke, and with the current political situation I'm afraid we cannot risk decreasing our military strength. The duke may call on me for ships at any time, should he face stronger insurrection. There will be small, rickety fishing vessels, and the odd fat merchant coming in and out,' he gave Halfdan a sly smile, 'but looking at you and your men, somehow I cannot see you in a fishing boat.'

Halfdan turned and looked back at Ulfr. 'I'm sure we will find something,' the jarl said, meaningfully. Ulfr nodded, then Halfdan looked to Gunnhild, who mouthed something to him. The jarl frowned for a moment, then turned back to Serlo. 'We would be pleased to accept your hospitality for a few days, then, while our pilot here seeks the best vessel we can find. Might I ask that our wagons be stored away under our guard and locked away?'

The man smiled. 'I'm sure that can be arranged.'

'I shall be interested to meet your duke,' Gunnhild said.

Every pair of eyes in the room turned to her, most frowning.

'I doubt that will happen,' Serlo said. 'The duke is off to the south-west on some errand or other, and his fortress is at Falaise, to the south-east. We are out of his way here. He rarely spends time in the peninsula, concentrating instead on the lands of the barons who oppose his rule.'

Gunnhild fixed Hauteville with a flat look. She said nothing, but her silence left Ulfr with the impression that there was no doubt in her mind that they would meet the duke. He wondered whether it would be acceptable to ask Serlo if he could speak to Beatrix. She may have caused them trouble, but he still felt a little sorry for her, and she was being held against her will, awaiting her fate. He decided against it, in the end. Perhaps it would be better to draw that chapter to a close and concentrate on ships. Halfdan had made it clear that he wanted a good ship to get away, while Serlo was sure no good ship was to be found, but if there *was* a usable ship within a day's travel, Ulfr was the man to find it.

He looked up as they started to move and realised he'd not been listening to the end of the conversation. He nudged Ketil. 'Where are we going?'

'We've agreed to stay a few days.'

'I heard that bit.'

'The Norman's going to show us around.'

Ulfr nodded as they made their way out of the keep. Across the bailey, Bjorn was overseeing the wagons being unhitched outside a palisaded compound that had, from the liberal spray of muck, been a cattle pen until very recently. As they walked, Ketil stepped across in front of Ulfr, forcing him to halt suddenly and then change his footing. The lanky Icelander kept doing things like this, unintentionally, a symptom of limited vision courtesy of his missing eye, yet he still had a quiver at his belt and a bow slung over his shoulder. He'd been practising regularly, trying to regain his mastery. He was almost there, not quite the legend he had once been, but certainly still the best of them.

Serlo de Hauteville led them up a timber staircase to the gatehouse, the highest place in the castle and the location with the best view. Thurstan seemed as interested as any, and Ulfr realised suddenly that although those men had served a Hauteville, he had been a different brother. They might well have never been to Pirou in their lives, and might not even have met this Serlo before.

Atop the gate, they came to a halt, and the lord of the place began to point out individual buildings, explaining their use, naming certain important personages in the castle, especially the priest. The lord's eyes flicked to the Mjǫllnir pendants brazenly hanging around their necks whenever he mentioned the priest or the chapel, though he seemed more interested than offended. Ulfr listened attentively until the man had identified the building they would use as their own during their stay, and heard Halfdan offer to pay the lord a small fee for his hospitality, then his attention trailed away. Instead, he began to use the lofty viewpoint for more important things. The gatehouse was on the southern edge of the castle, and so he shuffled past Thurstan and looked off to the west, along the line of the timber palisade, and off into the distance. Sure enough, with the added height, he could see the dunes he'd identified earlier, and a beach, perhaps a mile to the west, and a thin, dark ribbon that marked the shore. His heart soared at the sight. It had been half a year or more since he'd seen the waves, and it felt like putting on a familiar, comfortable garment just to know how close he was.

Serlo had been right, though, looking across that mile. There would be no ships, not with such a wide, shallow beach. He would have to be more inventive, and to search wider, even though the Norman had already said there would be nothing suitable to find in either of the nearest harbours. Perhaps there were other harbours, a little further along the coast, that might suit.

He glanced at Serlo de Hauteville, standing at the far side of the platform, waxing lyrical about the chapel, the only stone building in the compound. The Norman stood in the small open space granted by the gathering in deference to his position as lord of this domain. Again, Ulfr's gaze wandered, and it was quite by chance that he spotted the figure. A single man standing on the other side of the moat, not far from the bridge. It took him just a moment to register the fact that the man had a bow in hand, drawn back, arrow nocked.

He bellowed something, though he was far from sure what it was in the heat of the moment, as he hit Serlo de Hauteville in the midriff with his shoulder, slamming the Norman to the floor hard, winding him. Even as the pair tumbled to the timber deck, the arrow whirred through the open air where Serlo had been and buried itself in an upright timber, vibrating with the impact. It had been instinct that had set Ulfr moving. The moment he'd seen the bow, he'd known who the arrow was meant for, since everyone else was a stranger to the place.

An uproar broke out as the guards, whose attention had been on their master and his guests, and not on the far side of the moat, began to react. As Ulfr pulled himself up from the fallen lord, grasping the timber fence, he looked over and realised that the castle guards would never catch the archer. He'd had a horse beneath a nearby tree and had already vaulted into the saddle and kicked the animal to speed.

Even as Ulfr watched the man ride away, a shaft whipped past him and the would-be assassin suddenly lolled in the saddle, then slipped to the side and fell from the horse. Ulfr turned to see Ketil lowering his bow, with an aura of smug satisfaction.

Thurstan was helping the lord to his feet, and Hauteville was clearly sharp, his darting eyes taking in the arrow close to his head and then turning to see the dead man and the rapidly fleeing horse. He looked to Ulfr and nodded. 'My thanks for your timely intervention.' Then to the jarl. 'I would say you have already paid for your accommodation.'

'Who was it?' Halfdan asked.

Serlo shrugged. 'Any one of a dozen local lords might be responsible, let alone distant ones and foreign kings. It is not the first attempt on my life, not even this month.'

Ulfr frowned. 'Because of your loyalty to the duke?'

'Because of my loyalty to the duke, a number of rebel lords are set against me, but there are also those *within* the duke's court who hold a grudge over past grievances, and who would also be more than happy to see an arrow in my heart. I have more enemies than friends, by quite a margin. Balancing my allegiance has always been a thing of difficulty.'

'You're taking this very casually,' Leif said, his brow creasing.

'Death is a daily hazard,' Hauteville said. 'I have been luckier than most. Perhaps we are done up here, though,' he added, gaze strafing the countryside outside in search of other archers.

As Serlo began to lead them back down from the gatehouse, Halfdan delayed and joined Ulfr.

'I stand by what I said. Gunnhild thinks we are here for a time, but this Nordmandi is as dangerous a place as we've ever been. I think we want to be ready to leave in a heartbeat. Take whatever gold you need and get us a ship. I don't care how you do it, just do it. Bribe one of the lord's warship captains if you have to, but we're not getting caught here.'

Ulfr nodded, and then, as they brought up the rear of the group descending from the platform, Thurstan joined them, tapping Halfdan on the shoulder.

'Yes?'

'You will need a crew for your new ship.'

Halfdan frowned. 'We have fifteen. It is light for a crew, but we'll manage.'

The Norman's lip curled up at the corner. 'Three of them are women, though I acknowledge your witch is probably more than a match for any man. It is not enough, and even with the women it would still not be.'

'Your place is here,' Halfdan replied. 'You are of the Hautevilles.'

Thustan snorted. 'My lord was Iron Arm in the south, not these lords. I have not even been to Nordmandi for a decade. And you know what Apulia is like. The borders change weekly. We've been away a month and a half and it'll take the same to get back, so there's a good chance Iron Arm will be dead and the Byzantines ruling Melfi by the time I get back. No, I don't think our future is in Italy.'

'And not with this lord?'

'You said it yourself not a moment ago. This place is as dangerous as we've ever seen.'

'You are not sailors.'

The Norman shrugged. 'How long does a man need to learn to row a ship?'

Ulfr frowned at that. 'To do it right, a while.' He'd seen desperate skippers take to the waves with untrained crews before. One oar out of time could fuck the whole thing up spectacularly.

Thurstan shot Ulfr a look and then turned back to Halfdan. 'Give us a share of the gold and we'll crew your benches for you. You want to get out of here fast, you'll need enough men for your ship. You can't afford to turn down ten warriors.'

Halfdan's face was already twisting into that expression he habitually used when he was trying to let someone down without offending them, but Ulfr's mind was racing ahead. Say he did manage to find and secure a warship of some kind – even a small one, the size of the *Sea Wolf* or smaller – it would still need more than fifteen of them at the oars. And really they were eleven, not fifteen, because Anna and Cassandra would never manage, no one would ask Gunnhild to row, and Ulfr would need to steer. But with ten more backs bending at the oars, they would stand a chance. Ulfr clapped his hand on the jarl's shoulder.

'He's right.'

Halfdan turned that furrowed brow on his ship's skipper. There was a question in the look, not spoken out loud in Thurstan's presence, but Ulfr had known his jarl long enough to read the question plain. His answering look confirmed that he trusted their Norman companions. They had never given the Wolves a reason to doubt them, and the simple fact was that if they had wanted to, they'd had endless opportunities during the long journey to turn on the Wolves. They'd numbered a dozen to the thirteen of Halfdan's crew. One surprise attack from within during the night and they'd have killed half the Wolves before anyone shouted the alarm. They could have had the gold and been off, but they hadn't, and that spoke a lot for their loyalty.

Of course, both Ulfr and Halfdan knew that such a thing would never have happened, for Gunnhild would have given them warning, and they had been pretty careful and alert. But Thurstan could not have known that.

'All right,' Halfdan said. 'A share in the gold, equal with the other Wolves. And it starts now. If you're Wolves of Odin, you are Wolves from the moment you agree. And you relinquish your command. You and your men are all Wolves, free men in service to your jarl – me.'

59

Thurstan nodded, though there was an element of doubt writ on his features.

'What?'

'I'm not sure about the Odin thing. My priest would haul me over coals for allegiance to a pagan god.'

'Is your priest here?'

Thurstan frowned. 'No. In Apulia.'

'Then what are you worrying about?'

The Norman chuckled. 'Wolves of Odin it is. But we wear a cross still.'

Halfdan shrugged. 'So do many of ours, the ones from Miklagarðr. But we don't care. Odin is a sensible god. He takes for his mead hall those who are worthy, no matter what trinkets they might wear.'

Ulfr laughed, then. 'Besides, it will give Bjorn someone new to argue with.'

That set the jarl laughing, too, as they walked off in Hauteville's wake. Ulfr found himself at the back, then, as they descended, his jarl and the head of the Apulian Normans in deep conversation about their plans. The big sailor took a deep breath. Twenty-two of them. That would just be enough. All they needed was a ship.

Chapter 5

Beside Ulfr, the Norman grumbled a little about not being a horseman. He wasn't. That much had been clear when he'd fallen from the saddle within two hundred paces of leaving the castle. But Ulfr was no great master of the beast himself, and so was inclined toward sympathy. He was at home on a deck or, at a push, a wagon bench, not really a horse, although he'd had to do it often enough that he had become pretty competent. Galfrid clearly was not. And from the repeated comments, he was breaking all records for the number of blisters on his arse.

They'd only ridden four miles.

Ulfr thought back over the morning, trying to blot out the complaints. The Wolves had been at Pirou for two days, with no further assassination attempts or dangerous incidents. Halfdan and Serlo seemed to be getting on well, and everyone was comfortable. The Wolves' wagons were kept separate and, as they bore Iron Arm's colours, no one dared even ask about them. And there were never fewer than three men in the compound watching them, too.

Agreements had been reached with all of Thurstan's men, none of whom had looked forward to the long return journey to a land that might have closed against them again by the time they got there. Every man had taken the ancient oath to a jarl with apparent enthusiasm, though with varied attitudes toward the part where the oath was given with Odin as a witness. Some had swallowed nervously then, but all had done it, regardless, and they were part of the crew. Indeed, the Wolves were as strong and numerous as they had been any time since they'd first landed in Miklagarðr, anticipating great wealth. They had that great wealth, though they had acquired it in a different land, and even sharing it among the new crewmates, it was still a fortune for each. There had been a few grumbles from the Varangoi among them at having their share reduced to spread it out, but when challenged by Halfdan they had quickly folded.

'What was your share beforehand?' he'd asked of the dissenters.

They had looked at one another. 'We don't know,' a spokesman admitted. 'The gold's never been divvied yet.'

'So you're quibbling over a figure you don't even know.'

That had more or less ended the argument. Bjorn's statement that the jarl's decision overrode all, unless anyone felt like challenging him for command through Holmgang, had sealed the deal. Everyone was aware that the last man to argue with Halfdan's command had lost an eye and come crawling back chastened. No one fancied Ketil's fate.

Thus, at Pirou all had been relatively comfortable and easy, but there remained the nagging knowledge that danger lurked never far away, and the need to move on pressed on them. Halfdan had even voiced it the night before.

'We will soon have outstayed our welcome,' the jarl said to his closest over the evening meal. 'We need to move on before trouble finds us.'

It had been, as usual, Gunnhild who had made the decision. 'No. We stay here. The lion comes, and lion and wolf will walk side by side.'

The lion, they had all decided, was Duke William, for it was said his banner bore two golden lions. Serlo de Hauteville remained sceptical that the duke would ever visit him, but Gunnhild was rarely, if ever, wrong. Ulfr had decided it was time to move on the plan. The first step had been to ask to see Beatrix. It was, he'd admit, partially to be sure that she was all right and not being kept like some languishing prisoner. But it was also the fact that she was the only person he knew from this region with an interest in ships and the sea. Her viewpoint might be incredibly useful. Hauteville had not been keen on his sister receiving visitors, noting how easily she could twist men round her finger and how readily she was able to escape. Still, with persistence, the lord had agreed, and so Ulfr found himself admitted to the house that was Beatrix's temporary home. Word had been sent to Eu, and the Count de Mortain would come to collect her in due course.

The unhappy lady was slumped in a chair that morning when Ulfr entered. The house was locked from the outside, and the window shutters barred, but she had two maids who were permitted in and out, and seemed to be being looked after better than most ordinary folk could hope for. Before her on a table lay an uneaten breakfast.

'Have you come to gloat?' she hissed as he entered.

'No. I am glad to see you are well.'

'I am *not* well. I am a prisoner and a condemned woman. Condemned to be shackled to a brute.'

'Mortain might not be a brute,' he reminded her. After all, neither of them had ever met the man. 'I don't think your brother would marry you to a brute, even for an allegiance.'

'I might have known you'd take Serlo's side, just as you did William's.'

'We did our duty and you know that,' Ulfr replied stiffly, irritated. 'We gave an oath.'

She softened visibly. 'I will escape before they shackle me, Ulfr,' she said, leaning forward and placing her hand on his wrist. 'You know that.'

He resisted pulling back his arm. Her hand was cold. 'Good luck to you. You're no longer our concern.'

She rose and stepped a few paces to the side. Behind her, Ulfr noted, the wall was painted with a colourful map of the area. He tried to take it in for a moment, noting the little tower that represented Pirou. Beatrix's eyes narrowed.

'I *could* be. I know you have gold, but there are other prizes to be had than Byzantine coins. If a man could see a way to helping me leave Pirou, I could be very generous.'

Ulfr frowned. He was not at all sure whether she was promising him riches, ships, or her body. None of them would buy his aid, sadly, though he still felt for her. He patted that cold hand. 'If I could help, I would. I will speak to your brother and see what I can do to persuade him of your need for freedom, but I will not defy my jarl, even for you.'

She sagged back. 'Then what use are you?'

'I came for your help.'

She laughed acidly, tossing her braided hair. 'You need something knitting? You're hungry? Anything else and I'm powerless.'

'You're not. Of all the souls in Pirou, you are the only one I know who understands the call of the open sea. You know the coasts, the tides, the ports and the ships here.' She sat up slightly, interested in spite of herself, and Ulfr leaned against the wall nearby. 'I need to find a ship. Not a fishing boat and not a merchant scow. I need a warship, fitted out for maybe twenty to thirty oars. You've told me of the two harbours nearby, but your brother tells us we'll not find a vessel there, for all the warships belong to your family or the duke.'

She nodded. 'He's right. There are half a dozen other harbours in the Cotentin, too, but the same story will greet you at each one. Every ship around the peninsula will be jealously guarded by its lord at this time of troubles, whether they stand for or against the duke. The only great port on the peninsula is Carisburg,' she explained, reaching out and tapping a finger at the top of the peninsula on the painted map, 'and that is under the control of Neel de Cotentin, lord of Valognes, who would not even grant the use of his ships to a foreigner. In fact, you might not even be allowed to the port in the current circumstances, for it is my private opinion that Neel is a dangerous and untrustworthy man.'

Ulfr nodded. Clearly the main port was out. So, if she was to be believed, were all the small harbours of the peninsula. Small harbours would be unlikely to support the kind of ship they would need anyway.

'Where are the nearest major ports where I might be granted access?' he asked.

'East, the nearest is Diva, the port of Duke's William's domain, but that is seventy miles as the gull flies, and through lands belonging to Ranulf de Bayeux, the Viscount de Bessin, another strong figure who is no friend of the duke's. West, there is Mallou, which is in Breton lands, in the hands of the French king, where your kind, like ours, is far from welcome. And that must be seventy miles or so from here, too. There will be no ship for you, and no friendly port for days in every direction.'

'Mercenaries?' he tried, a hint of dejection creeping into his tone. 'Pirates?'

She shook her head. 'Any mercenaries in the region have long since been brought under the banner of one lord or another. And there are no pirates here. There is no cove on this coast where they would be welcome, and any who dared to come from other regions were taught not to do so by Duke Robert. My brother was right. You will find no warship within reach of Pirou. Not unless you are willing to take the duke's wage and fight for him.'

Ulfr thought of the others back in the keep, and Halfdan's assertion that they needed the ship to get away before they got caught up in troubles. Signing on for those very troubles seemed a poor way of doing that. He sighed and sagged.

'You are a shipwright, are you not?' she said suddenly. He frowned, and she snorted. 'You told me you designed your *Sea Wolf*. That she was the best ship you ever built. You will not find a ship to hire or buy in this land. So, *make* one.'

Ulfr blinked. The very notion seemed at once simple and ridiculous. Even as his mind began to whirl with ideas, he stamped down on it. Halfdan wanted a ship immediately, not in half a year.

'We don't have time. It takes a long time to build a ship, even with all the equipment, components and labour. I have none of those things.'

'So *get* them. You'll find it easier to acquire them than you will a ship.'

And at that, he'd felt a twitch beginning, a small frisson of excitement, of a sort he hadn't felt since the day he'd run his hands along the glorious carvings on the sheer strake of the *Sea Wolf*. He hardly dared breathe at the thought. It took a lot to stamp down the excitement.

'No. We don't have time. I wish we did, I really do, but we don't.'

He'd pressed her then for any more information about local ships and shipping, their owners, harbours, tides and coastal conditions, and she had been relatively forthcoming, though every now and then she had dropped in less than subtle hints that, were she to be a free woman, she might be a great deal more help. Though she'd not said it overtly, she'd even hinted that she might be able to secure them a ship if they could get her away from Pirou. He'd considered that as the conversation dwindled to a close and he left the building, but had decided that even if she were capable of doing such a thing, Halfdan would be unlikely to agree to it. It would be nice to have a ship to take them away from any danger, of course, but to turn the local lord and all his allies against them by betraying his trust would rather diminish the value of that deal.

As he'd sat over a beer and a bite to eat afterwards, he considered his next move, though he continually had to fight down the idea that he could build a ship. There simply was not time. Just in case, he asked Halfdan how long they were likely to be staying, and the jarl had retorted with, 'Until you get us a ship and Gunnhild is happy we can leave.'

Ulfr didn't know how long that was, but it seemed unlikely it was going to be half a year, which was the length of time the *Sea Wolf* had taken, and that was with a good staff. He'd asked Thurstan, then, if any of his men were sailors. The man had singled out Galfrid as the only one with any experience at sea. A little questioning of the man had turned up that he'd sailed much in his youth, and had even lived and worked in a harbour on the other side of the peninsula. It had not taken much persuasion to borrow Galfrid and two horses. Before he made any further decision, he needed to see for himself the situation in the local harbours, and whether Serlo and Beatrix had been straight with them.

The pair had left the castle just after noon. First they rode into the village to get the general lie of the land there. Pirou was far from large, but it did have its own carpenter and smith, as well as farmers, millers and a nailed-god priest. They seemed perfectly ordinary, but there was no one there who would be any help to him, he decided, though even as he left, riding toward the shore, his eyes had been drawn to the carpenter working at his lathe, a sight that took him back to the shipyards of Sigtun.

They'd crossed the dunes and reached the long, shallow sandy beach, and the sheer joy of the lapping waves sent a thrill through Ulfr, bringing with it the determination that he would do whatever had to be done to succeed, and to get them out to sea once more.

For a time, he'd even been able to block out Galfrid's complaints with the crash of waves and the hiss of water retreating across the sand before the next barrage. He enjoyed riding with a mind empty, for a while, of worries and thoughts; he surrendered to the rhythm of the whale road. Then, finally, a few miles from Pirou, they approached a built-up place, and he was forced to bring his thoughts back to the present and their task.

The harbour was far from great. In fact, it was little more than a huge tidal lake formed by the mouth of a river that wound its way off inland, a collection of buildings huddled on the northern, far shore. At least the town was bigger than

Pirou village, and he could see a slipway where a small team of men were working hard at caulking a twenty-foot fisher's boat. If there were caulkers, then there were other trained workers. Two large warehouses nearby probably held stores and other workplaces. Not a shipyard as such, but certainly a dock for repairs.

As they approached the harbour, he could see two merchantmen, grounded on the sand below the town, waiting for the tide to come in so that they could sail once more. It would be a while. By Ulfr's estimation, the tide was still going out, some of the harbour's ships having only recently arrived on the last high water. The merchants were not large, and not in good condition. A score of fishermen's vessels were mostly either empty and idle, or being unloaded of the day's catch, all far too small for their purpose.

And there were two warships.

Ulfr's breath caught in his throat.

They were proper ships. These Normans may have lost a lot of what it meant to be a child of stone and ice, but it seemed that the way of the dragon ship was still in their blood. The two vessels were each forty- or fifty-oar ships, a little larger than the perfect fit, each with a good mast and a furled square sail. Even at first glance, though, he knew that although they were a familiar design, they were not of the very best quality. They had been built by a craftsman who knew what he was doing, but who was working to order. A man who was churning out exactly what the client asked for, and no more. They were good enough, and certainly closer to the ships of home than anything he'd seen since Miklagarðr, but they could be better.

As the men rounded the south side of the harbour and closed on those two vessels, he became aware of movement aboard each. Despite their temporarily being stranded by the tide, their captains had been sensible and careful enough to leave a small force of soldiers on board the ships.

The first thing that went through Ulfr's head was how hard it might be to steal one. Any attempt to make off with one of these ships would be limited to when the tide was in at sufficient depth to allow the rowing of the vessel. Their owners were careful enough to leave at least a dozen men on board, and the ships were close enough together that any attempt to take one of them would probably bring in reinforcements from the other. And if the skippers were careful enough to make sure they were left manned, then there was a good chance that the rest of the crew were close by. Close enough, probably, to involve themselves in any fight quickly. He identified three long, low buildings with shuttered windows and single doors, hemmed in by warehouses, and decided they were almost certainly bunk-houses for the sailors. Close enough to the vessels to spit at them.

Taking a ship was, he decided, unlikely. It *was* possible – if they could take everyone by sufficient surprise, and somehow seal the bunkhouses to prevent the occupants rushing to join in. They could feint by attacking one ship, and then when the other crew came to help, perhaps they could spring a second attack on the poorly defended ship. It would take a lot of planning, the luck of the Loki-born, and no small amount of effort in blood and steel, but it might just be possible.

He sighed. It was, of course, a foolish thought. To steal a ship would be to turn not only its owner, but all the allies of that lord, against them. From what Beatrix had said about the pirates, if they made enemies here, they would have to sail directly out into the open sea and hope for a land-bound course to fall into their lap, for it seemed the coast would be forbidden to them. It seemed impossible that they might be able to buy a ship, but perhaps they could buy passage on one to somewhere less troubled, where they would have more time to plan.

He reined in before the first ship, and two of the men on board hurried to the bow and looked across at him.

'Where is your skipper?' Ulfr asked, raising funny looks from them, given his non-local accent.

The men looked at one another, and one called, 'At the Widow's Lamp,' pointing across to the town on the far side of the harbour. Thanking the man, Ulfr and his companion rode on around the southern side of the harbour. Crossing the river was not difficult, for once they reached the tide's furthest extent, the flow was but thirty feet across and as deep as a horse's belly. They forded it without trouble, then turned and rode back along the northern shore.

'Perhaps we might stay for a few drinks?' Galfrid said hopefully. 'Whether we find the captains or not? My rump can't face the ride back without a rest.'

Ulfr nodded. 'A drink or two. No more. I'm not familiar with the tides here yet, and the last thing we want is for that river to fill up and us to be stuck on the opposite bank to the Wolves.'

The Norman nodded wearily, and the pair rode into the village – no great place, but perhaps twice the size of Pirou and with a few more amenities. The church looked old enough to have been there before the rest of the village, but they found the tavern, the Widow's Lamp, without trouble. It sat on the shore, a sign of peeled paint showing a miserable-looking woman holding a lamp and looking out to sea. They dismounted and tethered their horses to the rail there, then walked inside.

It did not take much looking around to spot the skippers of the two warships. There was something about a ship's skipper that, while it did not show like an emblazon, left no doubt in the mind of a peer. Ulfr knew the look of a man who led and steered a vessel, and the two such were seated near a roaring fire, their feet up on a table as they talked, beer in hand.

Ulfr decided that there was no better way to approach this than being direct and honest. 'Direct' was usually the best way with a man of the whale road, though 'honest' could be more of a challenge. He approached their table, with Galfrid at his shoulder.

'You are the skippers of the two dragon ships in the harbour?'

The two men frowned at each other, apparently unfamiliar with the term, then turned back.

'Yes,' one confirmed, 'if you mean the warships.'

'My companions and I are looking for a ship, a warship. For preference we want to buy one, but for now, at the very least, we are seeking passage from the region, toward the North.'

There, it was out. The two men looked surprised.

'You should try a *merchant* ship.'

'No. There are around thirty of us, with a large amount of cargo. There is no ship in this harbour large enough to take thirty men, barring your warships. If you are masters of your own ships, I can offer you a price of which you could rarely dream. I don't even need your oarsmen, either.'

'We are for neither sale, nor rent,' the second man said.

'Name your price.'

'There is no price,' the man replied irritably.

'Name your price and I'll double it,' Ulfr said.

For just a moment, one of the men's eyes sparkled with greed before he shook his head. 'We are oath-sworn to Hauteville. Not for sale.'

'Triple it.'

But that light of greed had been momentary, and it had passed. Ulfr knew they were not to be bribed or argued with. In truth he'd expected as much, but he'd had to try. Leaving the two men, he deposited Galfrid with a beer while he went for a walk and a think. Outside, he wandered along the shore until he reached the workmen caulking the ship. The ten of them were not doing a bad job. Ulfr had had seventy men at the height of work on the *Sea Wolf*. His notion of perhaps building a ship retreated from possibility just a little further. He would never find the manpower, even if they could spare the time, which, of course, they couldn't.

As he watched, he ran through the calculations. With fifty ordinary men or thralls, a ship like the *Sea Wolf* would take six months, with the workers working three weeks in every four, for a good day's shift each day. Given a hundred men, he could get it down to maybe four months. *Maybe*. If he worked them hard, for a level of pay way above the norm, with only an occasional day's rest, and working daylight hours, he might get it down to three months. Might. More workers than a hundred would not make much difference, as they would get in one another's way. And it was no good trying to create a masterpiece in the dark. Two months. No quicker than that, he felt sure.

He wandered around the outside of the storehouses and work sheds and reappraised the area. No place for the sort of shipbuilding the merchant vessels required, but they'd probably constructed the fishing boats there, and done repair work, and there seemed to be plenty of personnel and equipment, though he did not want to intrude too deeply and risk offending the local shipwright. It was, really, just out of interest that he was perusing the work area. Once again, he reminded himself, there simply wasn't time to build a ship.

He paused as he passed the newly caulked hull on his return journey, and looked around it. He'd seen similar vessels back home in his time, though the builder here had not thought to nail down the decking planks. Perhaps he wanted easy access to the space beneath, but in Ulfr's experience, loose-laid decking had a tendency to shift in rough weather.

He returned to the inn and waited patiently for Galfrid to finish his drink, not at all sure why he'd brought the man in the first place. He'd had visions of lively debate over potential vessels or new ideas, rather than a sullen Norman, drinking beer and complaining about his horse, and nothing to see but disheartening confirmation that the summation of Serlo and Beatrix was true. There were no ships to be had in the region.

They left the inn and unfastened their reins, mounting once more and making for the river to cross. Ulfr couldn't say what it was that had made him turn back as they passed the last house, but he did, and was surprised to see the two ships' skippers in front of the inn, watching the riders leave. There was something about them that made him uncomfortable. They were oath-sworn Hauteville men, so they should be safe, yet they had taken an interest in the visitors. He brushed the feeling off. The sailors had not known who Ulfr and his companion were. Perhaps they thought them men of an enemy lord.

A short while later they were across the river and riding south once more, hugging the coastline, where the tide was at its lowest.

'What harbour did you work out of?' he asked Galfrid as they rode.

'Place called Ouistre,' the Norman replied. 'On the far side of the peninsula, not far from Diva, where the river Orne empties into the sea. It's tidal, a little like the one we were just at, but maybe twice the size. Lost most of its importance to Diva under Duke Robert, though. That's why I went south. Work dried up.'

Ulfr nodded, noting that this was the most the man had said the whole time, with the exception of complaints about the horse.

'Would you remember the tides, the coasts and the rocks if we went to sea again?'

Galfrid gave him a look that suggested he would forget where his own nose was first. 'Years of sailing the coast back and forth. Yes, I remember it well.' He pointed out to sea, back past the harbour they had just left. 'There's a dangerous area. Close to the shore are tidal banks and submerged rocks, called the "Lucky Banks" for some reason. Beyond them is a passage heading north-west. Many unwary try to sail east around them and find themselves grounded.'

Ulfr nodded again. *Good.* The man was actually useful after all. 'When we do get a ship—'

'*If.*'

'*When.* When we get a ship, I will be skipper and steersman for the jarl, but I will want you to hand as my navigator.'

Galfrid smiled. 'Almost makes the bruised arse worthwhile.'

For the first time, Ulfr actually laughed at the man's comments. They rode on, heading south at a steady, gentle pace. They were not pressed for time and could afford to take it easy for the horses, and as they rode, they compared their experiences at sea. Ulfr was further heartened to find that while these Normans had changed somewhat since leaving the North, of all the things they held on to, their ships and sailing seemed to be the strongest, almost as natural as that of the Svears and Geats, and the Norse. It would make things easy when they did finally get back on the whale road.

They passed Pirou a few miles later, a mile or so inland as they rode along the beach, and continued on south to check out the other location.

It turned out that the other local harbour, Givolli Fossa, was considerably less impressive than its sister to the north. The settlement was no larger than Pirou village, with no sign of ship repairs or construction. Just a smaller tidal harbour, mostly low and muddy, waiting for the tide to come back in and fill it. One poor quality merchant ship lay deserted, and half a dozen small fishing vessels sat at angles, waiting for the water once more.

That was it. Just to be sure, they crossed the river as they had done to the north and had a look at the village, though it proved truly unspectacular. Ulfr reined in near a water trough. Three cows were drinking from the trough in the street in the middle of the village, which lent the place a certain backward rurality.

He sighed. They'd exhausted everything. There were no ships to be had nearby, and the only places such vessels might be found were either in enemy hands, forbidden to them, in foreign territory, or on the other side of the lands of rebel nobles. He'd spent half a day out with Galfrid, and the net result had been only that they had confirmed everything they had been told before they left.

'What now?' the Norman said as they walked the animals back to the narrow river to cross.

Ulfr straightened. 'We can't leave this place by land. West are these Bretons, who apparently don't like Northmen. East and south are the French lands, and we know their king's not friendly. So it has to be out to sea. We can't get to any of the major ports, and only a few minor harbours have suitable ships, and even then those ships are held ready and not available to us. We cannot buy or hire a ship, and though I thought through plans, I do not think that stealing a ship is feasible.'

'That rules out everything,' Galfrid said with a sigh as they neared the crossing.

'Everything but one option.'

The Norman's brows arched in the middle as he turned in surprise. 'Oh?'

'There is only one alternative. We have to *build* a ship.'

'I've worked in harbours,' Galfrid sighed, 'but not building ships. I'd not know where to start.'

'But I do. And I can do it. I can make a new *Sea Wolf*. It would take six months back in Sigtun, but I have three advantages here that I did not have then.'

'What?'

'Firstly, the timber we need, oak and pine, is all close and available, and we should be able to pick up most of what else we need, either from the workers at Fulquerville or the smith and carpenter in Pirou. Saves having to do a lot of manufacturing. Secondly, money is no object. It's amazing how doors open and people say yes to requests when that's the case. I've never been able to build a ship when I'm not working on a tight budget. And thirdly, we're desperate. Desperate men are often capable of feats that the comfortable would never manage.'

'So we can do it faster than your six months?'

'Definitely. Four, maybe. Maybe less, if we get everything we require. Now all I need to do is persuade Halfdan that we need that long.'

'I'll back you up.'

'Good.'

Ulfr fell silent and gestured to the Norman, and to a stand of trees close to the road. As they disappeared into the shade of the copse, the noise that had alerted Ulfr became louder and clearer. Pounding hooves and the jingle and clonk of armour. As they waited, half-hidden, eight men rode past and to the river, armoured in knee-length byrnies of chain with long sleeves, helmets with wide nose guards that cast their faces into shadow, lances held high with pennants snapping from them, teardrop-shaped shields bearing bright designs. They rode across the river, heading north, but they were not alone, for more such noises were approaching yet. Ulfr's heart pounded. *Could the war have broken out already? It would be dreadful luck to be out here when an enemy force surrounded Pirou to besiege it.*

Another half a dozen riders pounded past, very similar to the last lot, and then a cavalcade emerged around the edge of the trees: a nobleman riding in his rich clothes, but similarly with helmet and lance, as though prepared for battle. Then his bannerman came into view, and Ulfr felt relief wash over him.

Two golden lions.

William the Bastard had arrived.

Chapter 6

Ulfr sat at the great table in the long hall, tearing a leg off the chicken on the platter before him and looking around the table, sizing the other diners up. He and Galfrid had made themselves known to the duke's column at the harbour and had been allowed to ride alongside, though not close enough to pose a threat to Duke William. The questions thrown at the pair had been brief, to the point, and apparently satisfactory enough that they were under no immediate suspicion. It seemed that the duke's enemies generally announced the fact rather than hiding it, and by extension the two travellers were warily trustworthy. So, they had ridden the two miles back to the castle with the column of heavily armoured men. Halfdan's eyebrows had risen in curiosity to see his friends clop into the fortress in the duke's company, but Gunnhild simply wore her usual inscrutable expression. She was always hard to surprise, naturally.

Initially, there had been a huge round of pleasantries, non-conversation and platitudes, but Ulfr had watched them all with interest. The duke was fascinating. It was not just that he was grown beyond his tender age, though he clearly was. After all, back home in the North, if a lad couldn't swing an axe, trap an animal, sail a boat and throw a punch by the time he was fifteen, he would *never* be a man. William the Bastard, though, at fifteen, had already gone beyond such things. There was a shrewdness to his eyes, a complexity to his manner, and an aura of power about him that made Ulfr itch to be near. The duke was not just clever; he was Loki-cunning, a match for Halfdan.

It played out, too, as they sat along the huge, U-shaped dining tables in the hall with Serlo at the head and William beside him. Serlo was no idiot – he was a bright, clever, careful man – but he seemed unsure and almost foolish beside the duke. You had to concentrate to have even a clue what the man was thinking. Some people said one thing with their mouth, while their eyes said another. William, he quickly realised, also said one thing with his mouth and one with his eyes, but they were both constructs and deliberately delivered, so that his true meaning was deeply hidden beneath two layers of façade. Serlo clearly knew this, and so his conversation was as carefully constructed as possible.

'Avranches,' William was saying as he replaced his cup of wine, in answer to Serlo's question of where he had been.

'Avranches has always been loyal, my lord duke,' Serlo said.

The duke smiled. 'Loyalty in men is like water over stones. On every visit the stone remains, but the water has changed.'

Was that a dig at Serlo, Ulfr wondered? A question? The duke's eyes were smiling, but did they mask suspicion? Odin, but this man was hard to read. Halfdan had clearly noticed something in the phrasing, too, as he looked across from where a pinch-faced man with an impressive bald spot was busy trying to monopolise him in conversation.

'Thorstein le Goz has *always* been loyal,' Serlo frowned. 'Of all the lords of Nordmandi, surely he is the *most* trustworthy?'

William gave a light chuckle, with as much humour as a pestilent grave. 'Loyal even unto death, our favoured count of Avranches. Thorstein is no more. His son Richard commands in Avranches now, and he is something of an unknown quantity. It suited me to visit him on my rounds and look into his eyes.'

Was that what William was doing here? Looking into Serlo's eyes? Testing his loyalty?

'Fortunately,' the duke went on in a benevolent tone, 'it would appear that Richard lacks even his father's minimal guile. His face displays his heart, and I would be highly surprised if his heart was not true. It was something of a relief. Avranches is important.'

Another one. William's thought processes made Ulfr's head hurt. Did that mean that Pirou was important, or did it mean that Pirou was not? It had to mean one or the other. Ulfr was sure there was at least one more meaning hidden in this conversation, and probably several.

'You will find only allies in the whole of Cotentin,' the lord of Pirou said.

'Of course,' William said dismissively. 'Yourself included, dear Serlo. Since the day you returned to court after your little... trouble, you have been the very soul of loyalty. I *almost* didn't come.'

Ulfr chewed his lip, trying to decide whether that was a suggestion that Serlo was loyal enough not to require checking up on, or perhaps quite the opposite.

'Might I ask what *does* bring you here, my lord duke?' the lord of Pirou asked, seemingly casually. 'We are not on the route from Avranches to Falaise, and, I might add, you have a rather small entourage for such a tour, even in the safe Cotentin.'

The duke smiled. 'A twin-pronged attack of words, Serlo. I have a smaller entourage than you might expect because that entourage has divided. At Avranches I received word that there has been something of a build-up of troops in French territory, in the region south of Falaise. I dispatched the greater part of my force to my home. I would hate to see it fall to my enemies because I had drawn too many men west.'

'Does that not leave you unprotected here?' Halfdan asked, causing both lords to turn to him. The squat courtier with the thinning hair beside the jarl threw him an irritated look for interrupting his monologue.

The duke's gaze darted back and forth between the jarl and Serlo. 'But is the Cotentin Peninsula not the most loyal and safest of lands?' he smiled. 'Why, I brought twenty-four men-at-arms with me. More might be seen as an occupational force.' He laughed a laugh that made Ulfr shiver, wondering if there was an intimation of just such a possible occupation in that sentence. 'As it happens,' William said, 'Neel of Valognes is hosting a hunt and I am to be his guest. The guest of honour, in fact. And the route to Valognes naturally takes me by Pirou.'

Ulfr frowned. Neel. That name was familiar, odd enough to stick in the mind. He dredged his memory for it as Serlo spoke next.

'It still unnerves me that you travel with a minimal guard, my lord duke. Perhaps you will permit me to assign some of my men to your escort.'

'Thank you, good Serlo, but I believe I will be safe without.'

Again, Ulfr wondered whether that was a simple dismissal, or perhaps a suggestion that Serlo's men might add to the danger rather than reducing it. Neither the duke's eyes nor voice gave anything away. Gods, but Ulfr would hate to play dice against this man. William was not only utterly inscrutable, but, despite there being no direct evidence, the shipwright would be willing to bet that the young duke was also utterly ruthless.

'You will be safer with the Wolves,' Gunnhild said suddenly.

The top table fell silent, all eyes turning to her. William's face was fascinating, and not just because a man in his position was unused to ordinary women addressing him directly. He was clearly used to sizing people up at a single glance, and apparently could not make out Gunnhild at all, and that intrigued him.

'Wolves?' the duke said, finally.

'Our company,' Halfdan put in. 'A crew of Svears, Icelanders, Gotlanders, Rus, Byzantine Varangoi and Apulian Normans.'

'Heavens,' William laughed, 'but you must pay extremely well to draw half the world to your banner.' His laughter stopped, and solemnity dropped across his face once more like a lead curtain. 'Thank you, my Northern friend, but if I am in danger, then a few extra men will make little difference, even brave Norsemen of old. And logic dictates that I do not take an unknown force along with me, of course, for the security implications, even if they *are* foreigners and therefore outsiders to our local disputes.'

Gunnhild leaned forward. 'You misunderstand, William of Nordmandi. I was not making a suggestion. I was stating a fact. You will be safer with the Wolves.'

This settled the table into silence again as the duke looked at Gunnhild once more, his brows knitting. Before anything else could be said, though, a new voice piped up, a little further down the table – a rough one, full of barbs.

'The witch must be mistaken if she thinks the duke could trust these ice-born *animals* over good, loyal men of the Cotentin.'

The silence that returned after those words was tense, loaded, and Ulfr's gaze swept around, waiting to see who would break it. To his momentary relief, Duke William smiled warmly and opened his mouth to heal this awkwardness, but that relief was dashed a moment later as, with the scrape of chair legs on stone, Bjorn rose to his feet. To say that Ulfr had a sinking feeling would be to underestimate the disaster he could see unfolding.

'Perhaps,' the albino giant rumbled, 'this *loyal man of the Cotentin* might be more comfortable if he took the big stick out of his arse. It seems to be long enough to press hard on his brain. The ugly fuck,' he added, just in case the insult had been too subtle.

'Careful,' the Norman said, rising to face him, his expression contorted with anger. 'In my experience, big men fall hard.' He might not be as big as Bjorn, but the man was no waif either, and was lined with battle scars.

Serlo started to his feet, face angry, ready to stop this, but Ulfr was interested to see the young duke's hand close on the lord's wrist, gently but firmly guiding him back down to his seat. The two warriors were glaring at each other across the room, both standing.

'I've forgotten more about how to be *vikingr* than you ever knew,' Bjorn snapped, then frowned as he ran the sentence back over in his head to make sure it had been insulting to his enemy and not himself. Satisfied that it worked, he grinned. 'I've shit out better fighters than you.'

'Care to put your blade where your tongue is?'

Bjorn rolled his shoulders. 'Happily, but be careful not to do that yourself, with your tongue so far up the duke's arse.'

'I challenge you, Norse animal,' the Norman spat, 'to combat.'

'Holmgang!' Bjorn roared with delight. 'And stop calling me Norse, you dickhead. I'm no more Norse than you are French!'

Ulfr was impressed to note Gunnhild immediately close her hand on the pouch of the compound used by both her for her sight and warriors for their berserk. She was not going to let Bjorn go too far, remembering the last time.

Ulfr half-expected the nobles at the top of the table to put a stop to the matter, but Duke William was clearly interested, and Serlo was not about to overrule his guest. As Bjorn stepped back from the table, Ulfr rose and crossed to him.

'Don't kill him,' he said to the big white warrior.

'Fuck him.'

'Don't do that either,' Ulfr advised, which just made Bjorn grin and grab his crotch suggestively.

'No,' the Norman was saying at the far side of the hall, as two of his friends spoke to him urgently, trying to hold him back.

He shook them off and stormed around the table, gripping his weapons. Until then the open space at the centre of the U of tables had been the home only to the mangy hounds that lived here, chewing on what pieces of food the diners deigned to cast their way. The dogs scattered as the Norman stepped into the open space, settling his teardrop-shaped shield on his arm, coloured with bright blue and red stripes, and then drawing a heavy-looking sword. Bjorn grinned, accepting a small, round shield offered up by Leif, and pulling out his heavy axe. He, too, rounded the tables and moved into the centre, boots squelching and crunching on the meagre food remains left by the dogs.

Ulfr tried not to laugh at the momentary flash of doubt that passed through the Norman's eyes as he and Bjorn closed on each other and the stranger realised just how big the albino was. He recovered well, shaking out his arms, readying the muscles.

'First blood, or death?' the Norman said, more casually than Ulfr expected.

Bjorn grinned and kissed the blade of his axe. 'Same thing. If I draw blood, you'll be dead anyway.'

'Death it is, then.'

Ulfr seriously expected Halfdan, Serlo or the duke to call a halt to this, but all three seemed content to let the fight continue. Halfdan, he could understand, for the jarl had to believe that Bjorn would kill this Norman in the blink of an eye. Serlo, he could understand, too, for there was a certain amount of pride at stake in his men. As for the duke...

Ulfr frowned as he looked at William. The young lord had put his feet up on the table and was leaning back in his chair with a platter of food, ready to enjoy the bloodshed. *Yes, definitely ruthless.*

'Try to make it quick,' Serlo told his man, 'and tidy. Not too much cleaning up.'

'Don't die,' was Halfdan's advice to his man.

Both nobles looked to the duke.

'Who do you favour, my lord duke?' Serlo murmured.

William sucked on his lip. 'The clear physical advantage lies with the giant. I would not match a man against him without careful thought. But your man is unafraid, and that in itself is telling. I have seen men bluster over the fear of combat, and this is no such thing. He is clearly good. One of your best, I would say, and certainly one of your bravest, to take on the giant willingly. He may die in the process of proving his might, but I do not think even the giant will walk away with this easily. I think that neither will win.'

'My lord duke?'

'Either both will live, or both will die. Neither of them will accept anything less than victory. If both live, we will know we are in the presence of powerful men, but also of God's divine intervention. If both die, we will at least have had an excellent evening's entertainment.'

Ulfr winced. The duke was far too clever for his own good, but Ulfr was reassessing just how cold and dangerous the young man was.

'Fight,' William commanded with a flick of his forefinger.

Someone around the table hammered a fist on the timber rhythmically, and a moment later, it was taken up by many others, drumming a steady beat that filled the room, drowning out almost everything else.

Bjorn and the Norman circled each other slowly, only just out of weapon range, for the space between the tables was limited. To Ulfr's surprise, it was the Norman who attacked first. Changing footing deftly, he backtracked on his own circling and lunged with his sword. Bjorn dodged out of the way only just in time, the blade whispering past his midriff and clattering jugs and dishes on the table behind. Half a dozen spectators hurriedly moved back out of the danger area as the two men circled once more.

It was the Norman who attacked again. This time, he swung his sword backhanded. Bjorn leaned back and the tip passed within a hand's breadth of his nose. Still, the giant did not react. The circling resumed and Ulfr began to frown. Why had Bjorn done nothing so far? His big friend was many things, but careful and thoughtful were not generally two of them. Bjorn tended to size people up and then react in a single blow.

Then Bjorn struck. He'd been so oddly passive thus far that the move took Ulfr completely by surprise. The fact that it seemed to do exactly the same to his Norman opponent suggested that perhaps this had been Bjorn's intention all along – a move of subtle enough strategy that it seemed totally unlike the big albino. Perhaps he was learning from prolonged exposure to Halfdan's Loki cunning. That heavy axe almost cut the Norman's arm clean off just below the shoulder, and it was only through a mix of luck and effort that the defender managed to lift his shield enough to turn the blow in time. As it was, the weight of the strike sent him dancing away, trying to keep his feet.

The Norman recovered as Bjorn made some loud and unlikely speculations on the man's parentage, and looked to the teardrop-shaped shield that had saved his arm, and probably his life. Bjorn's single powerful blow had ruined it. It had smashed through the edging in two places and wrecked the frame between, easily cutting through the hide and laminated panels. The Norman gave the shield a light shake to test its efficacy, wincing at the pain the movement brought, and what was left of the shield fell into two pieces, clinging to his arm with difficulty.

Bjorn was turning slowly, grinning at his audience. He barely had time to spin back as the Norman came once more, only alerted by the expressions on the gathered faces as they looked past him. The Norman's next strike was another lunge, the blade coming straight for Bjorn's middle. Instead of ducking or leaning away this time, though, the giant leapt forward. In a single heartbeat he was inside the range of the Norman's sword. Simultaneously, he'd dropped both axe and shield as he jumped, and was empty-handed as he reached his opponent. The Norman was utterly surprised by the move, though perhaps not as much as he was when Bjorn reached under the man's chain shirt, his hand disappearing up to the forearm.

The Norman's eyes bulged.

'Drop the sword,' Bjorn said quietly.

If Ulfr had not already surmised that Bjorn held the Norman's manhood in his enormous grip, the speed with which the man dropped his sword made that clear. He was breathing in short, tight gasps, eyes wide and horrified.

'Now the shield,' the big man said.

The Norman let go and shook what was left of the shield from his arm, the straps troublesome. Too much shaking caused a knock-on effect down below, and he issued a few short squeaks as he did so.

'Now tell all your friends that the Wolves are better than you.'

'The... Wolves are better...' the man gasped.

'Than who?' Bjorn prompted with the slightest squeeze.

'Than *me*, than *me*,' the Norman gasped urgently.

'Say "Bjorn is a better man".'

'Bjorn is a better man.'

'Bjorn has a bigger dick.'

'Bjorn has a bigger dick.'

'I would like to buy Bjorn a whole evening of drinks.'

'I would... What?'

With a snort, Bjorn let go of the man's genitals, then held that same, sweaty hand out for the Norman to shake. The aching combatant stared at the hand, making small squeaking noises, and then finally, wincing with every movement, reached up and took the hand.

The weird silence that followed was broken when the Norman suddenly laughed. It was not the biggest belly laugh, for his privates hurt too much for that, but it was enough to calm the situation.

'I think you misread the fight,' Halfdan called to the duke.

William's brow arched. 'Did I? Or did both men live after all?'

As Bjorn helped his former opponent back to a seat – the most unlikely pair – William took his feet from the table and leaned forward again.

'Despite any misgivings some might have over your past, Hauteville,' he said, gesturing to Serlo, 'I seek good men in my council of nobles, and of the lords in the Cotentin, you are certainly among the best. I would have you sit on my council. And because I realise that, in the current situation, that makes you something of a target for any potential rebel, I will sweeten this deal with the offer of a substantial stipend. What do you say?'

Serlo, to his credit, covered his surprise well and bowed his head graciously. 'I was hoping to find a way to bring myself into your better graces, my lord duke, but I suspected there would be much work to do yet.'

'Good,' Duke William said with a nod. 'That is settled. I intend to hold council within the month to lay plans to end this growing insurrection against my rightful accession for good. The meeting will, of course, be held at Falaise, but I will make sure to give you adequate warning to make all necessary arrangements. I shall have appropriate documentation drawn up by the Bishop of Bayeux, who is attaching the seals to all such agreements.'

The duke looked around the room. 'It seems that while your own men are brave and strong, Serlo, these visitors of yours are wily. I *like* wily. Wily wins wars.' The duke gestured to Gunnhild. 'To return to our conversation prior to that little demonstration of martial and genital prowess, you were asserting that I will be safer with your Wolves.'

'Yes.'

'You are neither retainers of my own estate, nor of any of my vassals, if I am not mistaken. I get the impression that you are but recent visitors to Pirou. As such, wily and strong or not, I cannot command your loyalty, and I am not in the habit of paying mercenaries. In my experience, mercenaries are only as loyal as the highest offered wage, and more than once I have heard of sell-swords changing their side for a few extra coins. Thus, I am not inclined to hire your Wolves, my good lady, I'm afraid.'

'I am not your lady, good or bad,' Gunnhild replied archly. 'And we are not mercenaries. We are Wolves of Odin, hungry and rapacious. Raiders and traders. Adventurers and children of the gods. We fight for who we like and go where the winds take us, and we have no need of your coin, Bastard of Nordmandi.'

There was just a flicker of annoyance in the duke's expression at that appellation, but he quickly pushed it aside. He was still fascinated by this woman he couldn't work out.

'Then why come with me?'

'It is what must happen,' Gunnhild replied.

'You speak in riddles.'

At that, Cassandra rose at the far end of the table, clearing her throat. Her accent was thick and her use of the Norman tongue stilted, for she did not have the natural grounding in it of a Northerner. Still, she did well.

'My lord duke, the lady Gunnhild is favoured of the Divine. The Theotokos, the Mother of God, gives her sight beyond the natural. If she says we will go with you, then be sure that we will.'

William's frown only deepened, but he looked across as Halfdan nodded. 'I lead the Wolves,' the jarl added, 'but I have learned through experience many times that when Gunnhild says a thing must be, then it must be. She says we go with you, and so we will go with you, and neither you nor I will be able to stop it.'

'My lord duke?' One of William's men leaned forward and looked along the table at him. '*We* are all the protection you could need. To bring a score of warriors of uncertain allegiance with you does not *improve* your safety, but rather *diminishes* it.'

The Duke of Nordmandi chewed his lip as he looked back and forth between them all, his gaze finally settling on Bjorn and the injured Norman. The latter was massaging his bruised manhood, while Bjorn told him an appallingly off-colour story and poured more beer for them both. William laughed at the sight – genuine humour, perhaps for the first time.

'It is my impression that these Wolves are trustworthy, or at least for now.'

'My lord duke, look. They wear the symbols of pagans. They are godless heathens!'

William gave a small smile. 'They have yet to find the love of Christ. We were all there once, Ancel. Do not forget that but five generations ago our families came raiding from the North with pagan hammers and curse magic.' He turned to Gunnhild. 'I understand what I might gain from your presence, that being my ongoing safety, but I am at a loss as to what you and yours gain from the deal.'

'As yet I have only the shadow of an idea,' Gunnhild said. 'But in due course the shadow will clear, and I will understand. I know, though, that wolves will walk with lions.'

'Then I will take you with me to Valognes,' William announced. 'I shall tarry here two days to enjoy the hospitality of the newest member of my council, and then I must away to the domain of the lord of Valognes for his hunt, and after the hunt I will return to Falaise, and all will be well.'

Halfdan, Leif and Ketil took the opportunity of the surge of resuming conversation then to shuffle down the hall and meet with Gunnhild, gesturing on the way for Ulfr to join them. Bjorn was best left to himself, clearly, but as the room devolved into laughter and planning, a musician tootling on a pipe in the corner, Halfdan gathered his crew.

'Where is this Valognes? Do we know?'

Ulfr thought back over recent conversations – he'd heard of Valognes before. As the others shrugged and discussed the matter, he dredged his memory, back through meeting the duke at the southern harbour, then the meeting with the warship skippers at Fulquerville, and finally to his first conversation of the morning.

'Shit,' he said suddenly, silencing the others.

'What?'

'I spoke with Beatrix this morning. She had a map, and told me of many places in our discussions over ships and harbours. One was Valognes. It is further up the peninsula, maybe twenty miles from here.'

'Twenty miles is not too far,' Halfdan murmured, concerned at Ulfr's worried tone.

'But she also mentioned its lord, Neel,' the shipwright said. 'She does not trust him. And that is where the duke is bound for a hunt.'

Halfdan looked to Gunnhild, questioning. She shrugged. 'It is where wolves and lions walk together.'

The jarl looked back to Ulfr. 'Can you get us a ship?'

The shipwright sighed. 'I have searched for four miles north and south, so far, to the nearest harbours, but the simple answer is no. There is no ship suitable for the Wolves within reach, unless you are willing to attempt a dangerous theft from beneath the nose of its lord. And if Beatrix is correct – and I have no reason to doubt her – we will find the same problem all along this Norman coast.'

'Then we are trapped.'

'Not quite. I've been thinking.'

'Oh?'

'With sufficient manpower, I have everything I need here. Good oak and pine in abundance, caulk and tools and rope and canvas at the harbour of Fulquerville, and even trained manpower – carpenters and smiths and labourers. I have everything I need.'

'To build a ship?'

'To build a ship.'

'How long?'

Ulfr sucked air through his teeth. 'Therein lies the problem. I have worked out the numbers every way I can, and even with unlimited gold, a professional crew, ready-made oars, sails and the like, and timbers on hand, I cannot get the timing below two months. And even two months will be pushing it, with very hard work.'

Halfdan glanced back along the hall at the duke and Serlo, deep in conversation. Then he looked to Gunnhild, who scrutinised Ulfr, turning back to her jarl and nodding.

'I do not know how long we will be with the duke and his men,' she said, 'but you and I both know that no man in this whole land better knows ships than Ulfr. If he says the only ship we will get is one he makes, then let him make the ship. And if it takes two months, we will have to bare our teeth and survive in this place for two months.'

'You've still not actually told me why we're going?' Halfdan said to her. 'Why we must stay with this duke? Why we don't simply leave, ride along the coast and find a new place that *does* have a ship? There must be more, beside wolves and lions together?'

Gunnhild rubbed her temple, then looked around, conspiratorially, as though anyone in the hall might be listening in with a care for what she said. 'There is a great deal more. I see a queen, and a dragon. And in the great weaving of the Norns, this Bastard is a thread of gold. But somewhere in the weaving in days to come, that thread becomes tied to another much the same. I have, in all my castings and all my dreams, only ever seen one other golden thread.'

Haldfan blinked, straightening. 'Harðráði.'

Ulfr was suddenly alert. 'And Harðráði has the *Sea Wolf*.'

'Quite,' Gunnhild replied, though there was something else in her tone, too. It brought to Ulfr's mind that time in the great city of the Greeks when she and the golden bear had been more than a little close.

'So we must stay with this duke, because through him, we might find Harðráði,' Halfdan breathed, a tinge of excitement in his voice. The decision suddenly made, the jarl nodded, jabbing a finger at the shipwright. 'All right. I will take most of the Wolves with me to this Valognes, but I will leave a small force with you, Ulfr. Farlof will stay, and we will leave three of the Apulians and three of the Varangoi with you.'

'That's not much of a workforce,' Ulfr said uncertainly.

'That's not a workforce at all,' the jarl said. 'Those men have no skills in such things. They will stay to guard the wagons, for all those wagons and their contents will have to stay with you. We will not take such precious cargo into the unknown.

But that means that you will have ready access to the gold. Use as much as you need to hire men, to buy goods. Spend like a waterfall if you must, just get that ship ready as fast as possible.'

Ulfr nodded and couldn't help a small smile creeping on to his face. Early this morning, Beatrix had implanted the idea in his head, and he'd dismissed it as simple fantasy. Now, his jarl had not only given it his assent, but he had thrown every resource they had into Ulfr's hands to make it work.

Hafldan would take the Wolves north and pry the knowledge they all sought from the Bastard duke, while Ulfr would stay at Pirou…

…and build a ship.

Part Two

ᚠᛟᛚᚠᛗᛋ ᛟᚠ ᛟᛁᛏ

The Bastard Duke

Never walk away from home
ahead of your axe and sword.
You cannot feel a battle in your bones
or foresee a fight.

On *Caution* from the *Hávamál*

Chapter 7

Valognes castle was impressive, if in a different way from the one they had left that morning at Pirou. Where Pirou had been moated and sitting alone in wide countryside, a solitary stronghold, Valognes was larger, but crowded in by the town that had grown up around it, sprawling out across the flat land. Its ramparts were of timber on an earth bank that raised them above the streets, but the gatehouse was a recent formidable stone construction, and even from outside the walls Halfdan could see a massive, squat grey tower that had to form the main block of the complex. That, to Halfdan, spoke of the lord of this place having more power than Hauteville. Such was always the case in the North. A jarl sought to have a better hall than his peers, to prove his superiority.

He looked away from the looming fortress at the end of the street and back along the thoroughfare to the distant greenery with just a hint of concern. They had passed through thick forests for much of the journey, which had made the young jarl wary, watching for potential enemies among the trees, but which William had greeted with a smile, proclaiming it excellent terrain for the hunt. In the coming days, then, they would be in those woods with many armed men and a limited quantity of trust.

Along the walls and above the gates of the fortress stood men in glittering chain byrnies with shields emblazoned with stripes of blue and red, bright in the autumn sunlight. The gates were closed, but as the visitors emerged from among the streets of the town, the locals cowering back into doorways and side streets out of the way of this noble and his procession, the great gates swung open to admit the Duke of Nordmandi.

The first to pass through the gates were a small group of William's own knights, including the man whom Bjorn had fought in the hall, who had been making uncomfortable groans and squeaks throughout the ride every time his balls slapped against the saddle leather. The vanguard were clearly wary, as was their master, but the men of Valognes were scattered around the place rather than gathered for trouble, and so the van dismounted with increasing ease, as a small party emerged from that stone keep and strode across the grass.

There were four figures, one a blond man of a height almost to challenge Ketil, pale and with a drooping moustache but with short, severe hair, who had to be the lord of this place, if not from his clothing, which was rich velvet but also of blue and red, then from his manner, which was haughty and entitled. Halfdan took an immediate dislike to the man on sight, an impulse supported by the fact that the Loki serpent marking on his arm began to itch at that moment. As he scratched it, he took in the other three: a bulky warrior in the same dress as the men around them, but with additional frippery that suggested some sort of commander; an old greybeard with a staff; and a weaselly looking little fellow in the robes of the White Christ priests.

Behind him, Halfdan could feel some sort of seething discomfort, and he turned to see Gunnhild looking at the lord, her lip curling. Good; if she agreed, then his instincts had been right. He turned to Ketil, Bjorn and Leif.

'Be on your guard. This place is dangerous,' he hissed, not loud enough to carry to their hosts.

'My lord duke,' the tall, blond man said, wearing a wide smile as he strode over, reaching out a hand.

William looked at it for just a moment, as though expecting to find a dagger in it, then took it and shook.

'Master Neel. Thank you for your invitation. It comes at the perfect time, for life has been fraught and troublesome, and a

96

little relaxation and enjoyment is to be welcomed. You have excellent hunting grounds hereabouts.'

Halfdan was not fooled by the duke's easy manner. That momentary pause had been enough to show that the duke was equally ill at ease in this place. Halfdan nodded to himself. Many a man would not have come, knowing the danger such a move held, but it was the lot of a jarl to avoid peril. No man who hoped to command unchallenged could show fear or weakness. Indeed, walking into the bear's den and laughing all the way was the only choice for a true jarl. The Duke of Nordmandi might only be fifteen summers, but many a jarl in the North could have taken lessons from him.

'I apologise,' Neel de Cotentin said with a flourish, 'for not having met and greeted you with more ceremony. I was otherwise engaged with a small matter of local troubles.'

'Oh?'

'Some of the local barons have been reticent in paying their taxes, not clearly stating their intent to rebel, but suggestive of such. I have sent men out to urge them back into line, and one such baron has been captured and brought to Valognes. I was about to pass judgement on him, but perhaps since you have arrived, you would prefer to administer justice directly?'

William nodded. 'Of course.' He gestured to the head of his guards. 'See to it that the horses are stabled and the men quartered well.' Then, as Cotentin's men scurried around to organise everything, the duke gestured to one of his soldiers. 'Ancel, bring your two best men.' As he and the three Normans gestured for the lord de Cotentin to lead the way, Halfdan used a series of hand signals to Thurstan, telling him to keep the men together, alert, and out in the open, while he and his close companions moved with the duke.

William turned a frown on them, neither he nor their host having invited the Northmen along, but accepted their presence by simply turning away and not commanding them to stay put. As such, five of the Wolves followed the duke and his men into the keep on the heel of the lord de Cotentin. Like most Norman fortresses Halfdan had seen, like Pirou, Acerenza and Melfi, this keep was one great stone block split into rooms and passages, and the soldiers of Neel were in evidence in alcoves and doorways throughout.

Halfdan mused on the danger of their situation as they walked. He already did not trust this Neel de Cotentin as far as he could spit a rat, and considered the very real possibility of betrayal at any moment. There were enough men in the fortress to overwhelm the force the duke had brought, but the Loki cunning that had kept the jarl alive for so long was at work, and so he reasoned they were safe, at least for now. William was accompanied by five of the Wolves and three of his men. With the duke himself, that made nine, all alert and armed, many with shields. In the castle, any gathering of Neel's men large enough to overwhelm them would be very visible and would put the duke on the alert in time to react, and any individual archer was unlikely to get past so many prepared shields. No, Neel de Cotentin was not foolish enough to make a move against the duke while William was prepared, at least. Yet there was little doubt in Halfdan's mind already that this lord was ready to turn on his master. He was just wily enough not to state the fact until he was ready. *But when would he move?*

The hunt seemed the obvious answer, something he'd already half considered during their approach through the forests. During the hunt they would be in open countryside and dense woodland. There was a good chance that William's men would be scattered and unable to gather to defend him at short notice, while Neel could already have planned routes and prepared positions to trap him. *Yes, the hunt would be the most dangerous time.*

Of course, if Halfdan realised this, then probably so did the duke. And knowing these Normans, it was quite possible that Neel *knew* that William knew, which would put the hunt out of the question and meant there would likely be another, more insidious move coming.

His musings were cut short as they strode into a large hall draped with hangings of red and blue. A huge carved wooden seat on a raised step at one side marked the lord's throne – worthy of a great jarl, Halfdan noted. He wondered what William thought about it, but as usual the duke's expression was unreadable. The far side of the room held a number of long tables pushed against the wall, ready to bring out for feasts, while off to the right side a shallow apse held what appeared to be a nailed god chapel, for some sort of altar stood there, bearing a large cross of heavy wood decorated with silver plates. *Worth a little pillaging, that.* Halfdan noted his friends register the value of the cross at the same time as him, and that made him smile. *You could take the warrior out of the North, but you couldn't take the North out of the warrior.*

The open space in the centre of the hall was home to a different tableau. Four of Cotentin's soldiers stood at the corners, but the centre place was held by a man in rich green and yellow clothes, his face bloodied, two of the prisoner's green and yellow soldiers standing morose close by, equally battered. All were unarmed. A man of middling height in a near chain byrnie, with salt-and-pepper hair and a neat beard, stood with his sword tip close to the captive noble's throat. He was some minor lord himself, judging by the fact that he had two of his own guards present in black and white livery.

Halfdan chewed his lip. The duke and his men, Neel and his men, this other noble and his men, the captive lord and his men – this land had so many factions to keep track of, a man could tie his mind in knots trying to stay on the right side of the right people.

'This is your rebellious lord?' the duke asked their host, coming to a halt, looking at the prisoner.

Neel de Cotentin nodded as his seneschal, priest and sergeant came to a halt behind them. 'Yes, and this is Geoffroi, a vassal of mine who brought the man in, at no small cost to his own retinue, I believe.'

Halfdan looked into the eyes of this Geoffroi, the man with the sword held out. In them he saw no immediate deceit, just plain exhaustion. That, at least, was refreshing in this place.

'You are required,' William said calmly to the prisoner, 'to pay taxes to your duke, through his higher nobles. It is one of the conditions of maintaining a fief in this land. I take a tithe of gold, and you supply men when we must make war. It has always been this way, not only under my father, but even back to the days when our ancestors came ravaging along this coast in their longships from the North.' His eyes slid to Halfdan. 'In the days of jarls and longships, even then, this was what we did.'

Halfdan did not want to disabuse the duke of this notion, but he could only imagine what the Wolves would say if he tried to tithe their own shares of the loot. He would not stay 'jarl unchallenged' for long, he suspected. At the very least, a broken nose and enforced poverty would head his way swiftly – neither Bjorn nor Ketil liked to be short-changed.

Silence fell across the room.

'What makes you think you are exempt,' William asked the battered nobleman quietly.

'I do not recognise a bastard as rightful duke,' the prisoner said, head high and defiant, even though his eyes darted nervously, betraying his true state.

William nodded slowly. 'Then you are remorseless?' No answer was forthcoming, and so the duke continued to nod in the silence. When he stopped, he looked across to the man with the levelled sword. 'I am inconvenienced in that my taxes have not been paid, but the gold is still there, and that can be rectified. Cotentin here is inconvenienced by having a man in his domain refusing orders, but that fief can always be granted to a man more loyal, so that problem can be resolved. You, though, Geoffroi, lost men in the taking of this rebel?'

The knight bowed his head in acknowledgement.

'How many?'

The man's brow creased. 'Eleven, my lord duke. It was a brutal assault.'

William nodded again. 'Eleven. And where my gold can be found, and Neel's man can be replaced, your corpses cannot be brought back. In my opinion, it is you who has truly lost out here, thanks to your valour and your loyalty.' His gaze swept across to the prisoner. He folded his arms. 'Hang him for eleven repetitions of the Pater Noster, one for each of his victims. If he lasts his punishment, he can go free with God's grace. If not, kill his men, too.'

The captive lord stared in horror, and Halfdan pursed his lips. He'd seen men hang for several times, and even the greatest struggle had not lasted that long. A hanging that long was a death sentence anyway, but without the convenience of a snapped neck to speed the process. Still, Halfdan held that the world was always open to possibilities, and just because something had never happened before did not mean it could not happen at all. Had not Odin survive nine nights hanging on the tree, after all? The jarl stepped closer to the duke as the captive lord started to backtrack, offering allegiance and gold for his life, while his men whimpered in panic, looking for a way out.

The three ducal men moved to intercept Halfdan, but William waved them aside. 'What is it?'

'This punishment. You are making a mistake.'

At this, the various faces in the room turned to Halfdan in a mix of surprise and shock. It was unexpected enough for a stranger of no apparent rank to even *address* the duke, let alone argue with him, and with no sign of honouring his position. William, though, just frowned.

'I had you marked as a hard man of the North, and a bright one, too, Halfdan the Gotlander. I am surprised to hear you suggest a path of mercy.'

The jarl frowned for a moment, wondering what the duke was talking about, then realised that he had been misunderstood, probably something to do with the subtle difference between their natural languages.

'No. Not mercy. I mean you are making a mistake giving him such a chance.'

The duke chuckled. 'No man survives a hanging for eleven pater nosters,' he said, which brought a fresh wave of begging from across the room.

'Because no man has done so, does not mean that no man *cannot*,' Halfdan countered.

William frowned, thinking this over. He turned to Halfdan and gestured to his side. 'Your sword.'

The jarl looked down at his hip. Despite everything that had happened to him, he had managed to hold on to that excellent eagle-hilted blade he had taken from the Alani warrior in the east – a Roman blade by all accounts. It was a good deal shorter than any other sword on show, but more decorative.

He nodded. 'Yes?'

'It is an unusual piece,' William said. 'Might I see it?'

To the background babbling and moaning of the desperate men across the hall, Halfdan shrugged and drew the sword, lifting and holding it so that the duke could see it clearly. William held out his hands to receive the sword, but Halfdan held on to it, showing the blade without relinquishing it. William seemed to consider this for a moment, and then gave a strange smile.

'This, I favour, is an ancient blade, from before the light of Christ graced the world, and suited to your godless leanings. Kill the prisoner for me, my pagan friend.'

Halfdan looked at the blade for a moment, then to William's eyes, then to the prisoner. The duke said nothing more. A test, Halfdan wondered? The captive lord was still begging for his life, promising anything he had. Christians, Halfdan remembered as he walked across the room, were ordered by their god not to kill. An odd thing, really, since they seemed to kill for the slightest reasons, regardless. Halfdan did not, for Odin imposed no such rule. Sometimes he preferred not to kill, not because he was squeamish or peaceful, but simply because cleaning a used sword was messy and dull, and he would rather not bloody his blade unless there was a reason. Here, though, there was a reason: a way of securing the duke's trust, and in this land, any ally could be of value.

The captive shrank away as Halfdan stomped over toward him, but Geoffroi's blade prevented the prisoner from backing out of reach.

'No,' William said suddenly. 'Wait, Gotlander.'

Halfdan stopped a few feet from his victim and looked around. The duke had a very unpleasant smile.

'Step away. I have had a change of heart.'

Shrugging, Halfdan sheathed his blade once more and moved aside, finding himself in that small chapel apse and wondering when he had become comfortable enough with Christians not to recoil at such a thing. William had folded his arms once more and strolled around the room, arcing a path toward the captive, his pace steady. He finally came to a halt in front of the man.

'Do you think you could survive eleven pater nosters?'

The man stared. He shook his head.

'Would you prefer to die now, or to try?'

Panic gripped the man and he began to babble again, this time largely incoherently. William moved then, so fast that Halfdan had not been prepared for it. Indeed, the move seemed to take the whole room by surprise. The duke's arms unfolded, and the gathering only realised there had been a small, sharp knife concealed in the fold when it whipped through the air, coated with a watery crimson and spraying droplets across the hall.

Halfdan was impressed. The blow had been half a heartbeat in the action, and from folded arms, but the small blade had caught the prisoner's neck at the side and cut through the blood vessel there. It was not a deep wound, and not enough to spray wildly, like some Halfdan had seen on the battlefield. Instead, it was a wound that issued a steady flow of blood that quickly ran down into the man's rich clothes, soaking them. The noble shrieked and clapped a hand to his neck, trying to staunch the flow. Definitely impressive. Many a fifteen-year-old would baulk at doing such a thing, even if they were capable.

'Hang him,' William said, turning away. 'Eleven minutes. No more, no less.'

Though the noble was clearly done for – for even had he managed eleven minutes without breathing, he would be bloodless by then – the other two captives lurched into action, knowing that their fate would be quicker, but no better.

One tried to run, but two of Geoffroi's men got there first, slamming him to the ground and pinning him there. The other, though, had a different plan in mind. He leapt for the duke, whose back was turned as he began to walk away. Perhaps he planned to wrestle the knife away and kill William. Perhaps he meant to take him hostage and use him to escape the castle. Whatever the case, the duke was his target.

Halfdan reached for the only thing within easy reach and threw it. The heavy cross whirled through the air and struck the escaping Norman on the shoulder, sending him staggering sideways and to his knees, where Geoffroi's men swiftly surrounded him. The duke turned in surprise, first to the downed man who had almost been on him, then to the Northman in the chapel.

Halfdan looked at his hand, then at the cross lying close to the prisoner. Worth every silver penny.

'Brought down by the cross of the Lord in the hand of a pagan.' William laughed and gestured to the leader of his guards. 'See, Ancel? This day is full of surprises. The Lord appears to work even through your dreaded pagans.'

He gestured to Geoffroi with a thumb across his neck, and the knight's men cut the throats of the two captive soldiers, while another brought a rope and threw it up to a beam, over and then down, positioning it so that the noose at the end hung some five feet from the ground. The noble let go of his wound, fresh panic taking over as he turned this way and that, trying to find a way to get out, blood pumping from his neck, until Geoffroi's men grabbed him and dragged him toward the rope.

'Where was this man's fief?' William asked.

Neel de Cotentin was close again, and cleared his throat. He looked disgusted. Perhaps it was all the blood staining his hall floor, Halfdan mused.

'Close to the north coast, my duke.'

'Then I bestow the dead man's lands upon this Geoffroi. May he prove more reliable than his predecessor.'

While he spoke, three men were busy trying to force the condemned man's struggling head into the noose. Cotentin bowed his head in acknowledgement of the appointment.

'I should like to relax for a time,' the duke told him, rolling his shoulders and holding out the bloodied knife so that one of his men could take it away and clean it. 'I presume you have appropriate quarters for us until the evening meal?'

Behind them, there was a rhythmic slithering sound as the rope was pulled tight over the beam. Halfdan turned only long enough to see the captive noble hoisted three feet from the floor by his neck. It was faintly possible, he acknowledged, that the rope around his neck had staunched the wound and prevented further blood loss, in which case it would come down to whether he could last eleven minutes. Halfdan didn't particularly care, but as he turned and walked away with the others, he did decided that, had it been him, he would just have killed the man there and then to be sure.

'I shall make all arrangements, my lord duke. The hunt is planned three days hence, for there are other noble guests invited, and we await their arrival. In the meantime, my house is yours. I will have your men quartered in the inner bailey. There is an empty bunkhouse there. You and your noble friends, of course, shall be in the keep.'

As Cotentin gestured for them to leave the hall, William's man handed back the clean knife, and the duke sheathed it as they climbed a set of stairs in the tower and entered a long corridor with windows along one side. The other interior wall was hung with a tapestry of great length, formed of several sections. William's brow rose when he saw it. Cotentin smiled.

'A history, begun in the time of my grandfather. It tells the tale of our family.'

The duke nodded, smiling. 'These works fascinate me. The very idea that a story can be told in the warp and weft of cloth is astounding, is it not?'

Halfdan looked around at Gunnhild, who was rolling her eyes, given her own opinion on that. William examined the tale as they walked. Halfdan, too, found himself immersed in the history of Neel's forebears, how they had come here in their longships like good men of ice and stone, of the building of the castle, the subduing of the lands, and their bowing of heads to a man that he suspected was William's father, the former duke. The whole work was made up of many separate panels woven throughout the years and then stitched together to form a whole, their patterns kept close enough to blend when combined. A masterful piece of work, to be sure. The duke came to a halt suddenly toward the end.

'What is this? The tapestry hangs unfinished, and not at the present day, either, but some years ago, I gather.'

They noted the figure of a youth, who had to be Neel, which meant that nothing had been added for at least a decade.

Cotentin shrugged. 'It is said that my grandfather and my father encountered a dreadful sea monster off the coast near the Mont Tombe island. My grandfather was injured during the voyage and died shortly thereafter, and my father never spoke of the voyage again, and so no description of the monster remains. The weaver of this work faltered at the depiction, and superstition has grown around the absent creature, so the tapestry has never been restarted.'

'I could tell your weaver of the monsters in the deeps around Iceland,' Ketil said knowledgeably, but Bjorn was leaning in a moment later.

'Did I ever tell you of the beast I fought in the waters off Hróarskelda?' he said. 'I thought it only had three heads at first, but—'

He never got any further through his story, for Ketil and Gunnhild between them pulled him back away from the duke, amid some deep-voiced swearing and complaints.

'I used to wonder,' Neel said distantly, looking down the length of the hall's tapestry, 'what the future would hold for me. I used to look at this and wish that the weaver had gone on ahead and told me what was to come.' He seemed to pull his distant musings back to the present and straightened. 'It would certainly make the difficult decisions of adulthood easier.'

The duke nodded his agreement, despite his own tender years, and Halfdan found himself wondering what difficult decisions Cotentin was dealing with at the moment that were causing him trouble. A glance at Gunnhild made it abundantly clear that she thought such prognostication was at best a double-edged sword.

As they walked on, Halfdan noted their host's hand occasionally hovering near the hilt of the knife sheathed at his belt; once when he did so, Neel's eyes fell upon the little blade at the duke's belt with which he had so efficiently dispatched the prisoner. Halfdan suspected even now that their host might have made an attempt on William's life in the corridor, had he been more sure he could do so without the duke's own blade finding its way to somewhere fleshy in the process.

They were shown to rooms, that fellow with the staff apparently some sort of house thrall leading the way. At one door, the duke was escorted inside, one of his men heading back down to bring a couple more friends. The room was sumptuous, as befitted a jarl of power, with its own antechamber lying between the main chamber and the outer door, with room for several servants or guards. The Wolves were led further, along another corridor and to a separate room. This was a simple chamber, done out with a number of bunks, which went some way to illustrating the differing opinions Cotentin had about his visitors. There were eight bunks in the room, which were clearly not going to be enough, for in their entirety the Wolves who had come with the duke numbered a grand seventeen.

Leif looked about.

'Not much room. Do you think the others are being kept out in the outbuildings?'

Halfdan nodded. 'That will be the plan. They assume we are just the duke's men, I think.'

He stepped out into the corridor once more, where the staff man was busy striding away. On a whim, Halfdan moved to the next door and tried it. It came open and revealed a room very similar to the one they were in. He waved to the retreating figures.

'There are more than eight of us,' he called. 'Have this room made up for the rest of my men.'

The thrall gave him a surprised look, folded it into a frown, and finally left with a curt nod. The jarl returned to the room.

'I do not like having our men divided. I do find myself wondering whether the duke's room is so far from ours by design.'

Gunnhild nodded. 'This Cotentin is a wolverine.'

'You mean he stinks out of his arse?' Bjorn grinned.

She rolled her eyes at him and focused on Halfdan. 'He cannot be trusted. He is vicious and malicious, but he is also careful and a user of others. I think he means harm to the Bastard, and also to those who travel with him, but I do not think he will openly declare war. Like the wolverine, he wants to feed off the Bastard's corpse, but he would like a bear or wolf to come along and do the dangerous killing first. That, I think, is why for now he remains polite and apparently friendly. I think he is waiting for something – perhaps for the hunt, or these other guests. But that does not mean we are safe. Though he will not move until things are ready, the time is close. I think we need to be on our guard day and night until we leave this place.'

Halfdan nodded. He'd intended as much anyway.

Chapter 8

Halfdan had been dreaming, and it had been a god-sent dream, he was sure, even as he lived it behind flickering eyelids. The skies had been red as blood and shaking and booming, as though being torn apart. A black crack had loomed above him as he stood, sword in hand, watching his enemy emerge from the doorway of the stone hall. The man was tall, in a glittering shirt of silver. His eyes shone almost gold in the reflected light of the dreadful sky; in his right hand he held a sword that was the death of men, and in his left was a beautiful and terrible horn. It was that which transfixed Halfdan, even deep in the dream, for the very sight of the horn made the Loki serpents on his arm burn, as though he were aflame with the war-fire of the Greeks.

He woke with a start, his hand going to the hilt of the sword that he had left beside the bed the past few nights, ready to grasp at a moment's notice. It closed on empty air as his eyes blinked into the darkness and his mind reeled, trying to reconcile the dark of the true world with the blazing red of the dreamland.

His heart was thundering with the realisation that he had been seeing his own death, for the golden-eyed giant with the horn could only be Heimdallr, watchman of the Aesir, and that horn could only be the herald of Ragnarok, which accounted for the sky above him. He was Loki, and Loki was doomed to die with Heimdallr, perishing together on the field of battle at the end of the world.

Loki unbound…

He was having real trouble pulling his mind back from the dream, even as his conscious mind shook him again and again and told him to concentrate, for there was seemingly just as much to worry about in this black existence. His sword was not there.

His eyes were open properly, and he turned to see in the gloom that his sword had gone, though not far. Someone had moved it by two feet, placing it just out of reach. He became aware then of another shape nearby, a black within the black, and as he turned to focus on it, it gradually resolved into the shape of Gunnhild. She had a finger to her lips.

'What?' he hissed as quietly as he could, as he sat up and his sweat-soaked back peeled away from the sheets.

'Trouble,' she replied in a whisper. A redundant explanation if ever there was one, for surely she would not have woken him in the middle of the night with a whisper because she had thought of a new poem.

'What trouble?'

'I do not know. I can sense something. A noose closing on us, just as one had closed on the traitor in the hall.'

Halfdan was becoming properly alert, almost all his senses in this world and just vague tatters of the dream remaining, flapping in the background. It had meant something, and something important, but it could not have been this, could it?

Loki unbound...

He reached out and grabbed the sword that he realised Gunnhild had moved out of reach to prevent him killing her in simple reaction when she roused him.

'Wake the others,' he hissed. She nodded and moved away from the bed, heading for the next bunk.

Halfdan rose and reached across for his shirt, pulling it on, feeling it cling to the sweat as he dragged it down into place. For now, he left the chain shirt where it lay. Some occasions called for subtlety rather than force, and until he knew which this was, he might be better moving without the shush and clink of armour. As he became fully accustomed to the gloom, he realised that Anna and Cassandra were already up and helping Gunnhild rouse the others quietly. He felt a little put out that it appeared the völva had woken her women before her jarl, but he brushed the annoyance aside. This was not the time for such things, and, besides, there was some sort of sisterhood growing between the three that he could barely begin to understand. Instead, leaving the others to rise and ready themselves, Halfdan crossed to the single shuttered window of the room. Carefully, and as slowly and quietly as he could, he opened the right-hand shutter just a little, not enough to be noticed by anyone watching from outside, but enough to put an eye to, with a limited range of view.

The castle looked eerie. The sky was mostly clear with a narrow sliver of a moon, but scattered with fast, high, scudding clouds that cast small areas of the world below into high-speed shadows that tricked the eye. He wished that he'd paid more attention to the layout of the castle over the few days they'd been there, but their host had kept them busy and entertained in the keep most of the time, with the promise of the hunt to come.

The window of this room looked out into the main outer bailey, across to the stable blocks and storerooms below that heavy palisade wall. He closed his eyes for a moment and imagined the place from above, as though he were one of Odin's ravens looking down. One main stone gatehouse in a great oval circuit of timber palisade. A stone chapel, workshops, storehouses, stables and the like, all in clusters within. Then, off to the southern edge of the compound, the great stone keep on two floors, heavy and wide. From the outer bailey, a gate in a dividing palisade led into the smaller inner bailey, from where the door to the keep led off. The keep formed part of the barrier between baileys, but opened only into the small one. There was another gate in the inner bailey, but it was well protected, just a small postern in the rampart.

A movement caught his eye, and he focused, spotting the man on the wall-walk. He couldn't make out colours in this strange light, but the man was clearly one of Neel de Cotentin's soldiers patrolling the wall, which they would do all night with a lesser garrison than during the day. That did not seem amiss – that was all he could see.

Frustrated by the lack of view, he pushed both shutters and leaned forward, looking this way and that. He could see more guards on the wall. Quite a heavy tally for a night watch, but perhaps that was the norm, given the unsettled and potentially rebellious nature of the land. It was enough to draw his attention, but nothing to worry about especially, and had Gunnhild not been so sure, Halfdan would have been content that nothing was amiss, and would have gone back to bed.

Instead, he stood there for long moments, counting the men on the wall, trying to remember where everyone was. Cotentin's men were all over the castle, of course. The Wolves were all together, either in this room or the one next door. He'd made sure of that. William's men had been assigned appropriately. Three were in the antechamber of his room for protection. Others were in that bunkhouse within the smaller inner bailey, and a couple had been left with the horses in the larger, outer bailey.

The serpents on his forearm were itching again. Nothing was amiss, and yet *everything* was, even if he couldn't see it. Gunnhild had been absolutely right.

He noted one odd thing in passing, just as the action began. The guards on the walls were all facing inwards, looking into the bailey, not over the wall into the town. *Shit.*

At that moment, the door of the stable opened. What happened did so in the blink of an eye, and had Halfdan not happened to be looking at the building at the time he would have missed it entirely. The door jerked open, and a man emerged in a desperate rush, but before he found his way clear, arms grabbed him and dragged him back inside, the door closing behind them.

There was no sound but the general night-time murmur of the town, yet in his mind, Halfdan could almost hear the sounds of butchery from within the stable, and the muffled gasps of the man trying to scream through hands over his mouth. The duke's men down there had just been killed, and it had been done quietly and subtly – an assassination rather than an assault. And had he been under any illusion that this was not the work of their host, the fact that Cotentin's men were watching the castle's interior clarified it all.

The danger came from within the castle, and they were part of it.

He turned back to the room. Everyone was awake.

'The rebellion against the duke has begun.'

'Which side are we on?' Bjorn asked as he shrugged into his chain shirt.

Halfdan blinked. What a damned good question that was. It had taken someone as plain-thinking as the albino giant to realise that they still had the option of taking sides. Halfdan and his men had given the duke no oath or promise, and their future lay wherever profit and fame was to be found. Maybe that did not mean with the duke.

But there were four problems with that. Firstly, Gunnhild had tied their future to William with the hope of learning more of Harðráði and their missing ship. Secondly, Ulfr and the gold were back at Pirou and in the hands of loyalists. Thirdly, Neel de Cotentin would already have them labelled as William's men, and was unlikely to accept their offer of help. And fourthly, most of all, Halfdan did not like Cotentin at all.

'We are on the side of the Golden Lion of Nordmandi.'

'Who?'

'The duke, you great idiot,' Ketil grunted from across the room, where he was testing the string of his bow.

'Oh. All right. Just point me at some fuck and tell me to kill him.'

Halfdan smiled. That was all he *ever* needed to do with Bjorn.

'Gunnhild, go next door and stir the others.'

'Where are you going?' she replied.

'To warn the duke.'

With Ketil and Bjorn at his shoulder, Halfdan passed his sword and belt to the tall Icelander, grabbed his chain shirt and pulled open the door, glancing this way and that. There was no movement in the corridor and no sound he could hear. Then he caught the distant murmur of voices down below. They had very little time. Cotentin's soldiers would already have been within the keep. They would have dealt with the men out in the bailey first, and then closed the noose.

As he crept out into the hall and moved along toward where he knew the duke to be quartered, Halfdan did a little calculating in his head. William had twenty men with him, but two would be corpses out in the stables. There were three in the antechamber, guarding the duke, and the other fifteen were all quartered down in the small bailey.

Those fifteen men had to be assumed dead. If Cotentin had betrayed the duke, he already had control of the whole castle, and that would mean the inner bailey, too. If they were closing the noose, killing the men in the outer bailey and blocking off access to the main gate, they would have done the same in the inner bailey. They would have killed the duke's men down there before moving into the keep.

Once again imagining the raven's-eye view of the castle, he realised that at the next window he would be able to see across the inner bailey. Behind them, Gunnhild opened the other door and went to wake the others. Thank Odin that he'd had the sense to make sure all his men were quartered together – their presence was probably the only reason the enemy had not flooded the keep already. They were wary and were making sure to remove all other trouble first.

As Halfdan shrugged into his chain byrnie and accepted his sword back from Ketil, belting it on, he thought about it all. Seventeen Wolves. Three of the duke's men, and William himself. Twenty-one men. There would be at least four times that in the castle. There was, therefore, no realistic hope of holding them off.

He reached the next window and pushed open the shutters.

Down below, in the inner bailey, he saw the demise of the rest of the duke's men beginning. They were in a solid timber building, but half a dozen men in the livery of two different lords had blocked the door with barrels and beams, and even now they slopped pitch across the lower timbers of the building. They'd been working quietly, and the duke's men inside would still be asleep, blissfully unaware of the horrible fate that awaited them. He turned away as two men with lit torches approached, but not before registering the colours of the livery now that the glowing fires illuminated the men. Cotentin's blue and red stripes he recognised, but there were other men in blue and yellow quartered colours. His suspicions were confirmed. This was not just Neel de Cotentin making a play for power, but the strike of more than one revolting lord – the opening move of a rebellion. He had thought Neel had been hanging back for something – the man had been waiting for the reinforcements of a fellow rebel. The other guests had finally arrived, and their hunt was on.

Gesturing to the others, he ran, rounding a corner and heading for William's room. Thus far everything had been quiet and subtle, but any moment, it was all going to become loud and active – the moment that fire woke the men within and the screaming started. The rebels would have to be ready to move by then.

He approached the next corner, around which William's room lay, and stopped dead. He could hear the very subtle sounds of men trying not to be heard around the corner. Slowly, quietly, he drew his sword from its sheath and used his other hand to draw a finger across his throat and then point to the corridor ahead.

The others nodded, weapons at the ready. Ketil had his axe out, bow over his shoulder.

Halfdan ran around the corner and charged at the men outside William's door. In that blink of an eye, he registered that these men were all in that new blue and yellow livery, and wondered whether Neel had found it too distasteful to kill his lord in his own castle and had left the job to his ally.

Then the Wolves hit them. There were five of them, but more a little further along, just arriving at the top of the steps.

'*Odiiiiiiiiin!*' he bellowed as he drove the nearest man against the duke's door.

His sword found its way above the collar of the Norman's chain shirt and slammed into muscle and cartilage, half-decapitating the man in a single strike. Blood gouted out and coated both attacker and victim, as well as others in the corridor. Ketil's axe bit into another man's face, the Icelander cursing as the gleaming blade caught on the Norman helmet's nose guard and picked up a chip that would take hours of polishing out. The ruined face within sprayed blood and worse as the Icelander pulled the axe free and the dying man fell away. Bjorn's strike was the most brutal of all, for the man simply ran into the others, flattening one back against the wall, with an elbow to the gut, as the other went down with a cry under the great albino's heavy boots. Bjorn had seen the other men in the stairwell and was determined to have them all to himself. Bellowing eye-watering things, the giant hit them like a boulder from a catapult.

Halfdan turned his attention back to the matter in hand. Ketil was moving about, axe in one hand now unused, dripping gore, as he used the sax in his other to cut the throat of every remaining figure there.

All subtlety was gone. Halfdan could just hear the screams of William's men burning, various shouted commands outside, the cries of the men Ketil was finishing, and the bellowing from Bjorn and his opponents at the stairs. He could also hear the rest of his men emerging from their rooms and catching up. Good. The Wolves were equipped, alert, moving, and together.

Halfdan hammered on the door.

'Who goes there?' bellowed a man from inside.

'Halfdan Loki-born. Open up.'

There was a click, and the door crept in a little. Halfdan, knowing time was of the essence, pushed it open and burst into the room past the surprised Norman guard. The three men were all armed, yet not armoured, woken and alerted by the struggle outside.

'Get your shirts,' Halfdan snapped at them. 'We're leaving.'

They might have thought to argue, but looking past the jarl at the pile of bodies outside the door, Ketil moving among them like a *draugr*, slicing into windpipes, galvanised them into obedient action. They didn't even move to stop Halfdan as he reached the door to the inner chamber and pulled it open. Some instinct made him step aside as he did so, and he noted with satisfaction that little knife favoured by the young duke hurtle through the place he would have been, perfectly weighted and perfectly thrown. He ducked back to see William already dressed, booted, upright and armed.

'You?' the duke hissed.

'The rebellion has started,' Halfdan said flatly. 'We are outnumbered. Time to leave.'

William frowned for just a moment, and then nodded. 'Four to one, I reckon?'

'More,' Halfdan said as he moved past the duke to his window and pushed open the shutters. 'Your men in both baileys are dead, and Cotentin is not alone. He has friends.' He pointed back at the corridor, and William took in the blue and yellow figures in the doorway.

'That looks like the colours of Bessin.'

'Is this Bessin a short but heavy man in his twenties?' Halfdan said, peering out of the window.

The duke ran across and looked out next to him. From this room they had a good view of the inner bailey. The wooden building housing William's men was fully ablaze, and

118

the screaming was deafening. There was little chance of the fire spreading. Common sense in the castle's design had forced Neel to place his buildings far enough apart to prevent any sort of ongoing conflagration, so he could sacrifice just one building to disarm the duke. Soldiers in both colours were flooding into the keep's doorway, but across the bailey, standing in the open, were five men. One was Cotentin, another the leader of the blue and yellow men. They were accompanied by a priest, a third man in green and in rich armour, and one figure that made Halfdan's heart lurch.

'That is Ranulf de Bayeux, Viscount of the Bessin,' William snarled, pointing to the man in green. 'The traitor.'

'This goes deep and wide,' Halfdan said, pointing at the fifth figure, a gangly man in very nondescript clothes, but with a pinched face and a bald spot amid his black hair gleaming in the firelight. A man he had last seen when he'd sat next to him at Pirou.

'Who is it?' William frowned.

'He is one of Serlo de Hauteville's courtiers. I don't see Hauteville's men among the warriors, but that one's presence is enough to cast doubt on Serlo.'

The duke nodded. 'We are surrounded. What do we do? Where can we go?'

Halfdan ground his teeth. They were caught like rats in a trap. There was only one door to the keep, and it was on the ground floor, leading out into the inner bailey, from which men were pouring, intent on their deaths. They couldn't realistically get out there. And up was clearly out, too. That left…

Halfdan stepped back and looked at the window. It was big enough for a man – even one in armour – to fit through, at a push. The architect had known there was little need for defensive windows this high up. The jarl looked forward and down again. The drop to the grass below was at least twenty feet.

'We have to go out of the windows.'

William blinked. 'That's a long drop.'

'Easier than the front door,' Halfdan pointed out. 'The Wolves are outside in the corridor. Go with them. Get to our room. The window there opens out into the main bailey.'

'And what then? On the assumption we survive the fall without broken legs?'

Halfdan was already thinking that through, and a Loki grin reached his lips.

'There is only one way into the keep, and your enemies are flooding the door, trying to get to you. That means they're concentrating in the inner bailey. The outer bailey should be fairly clear. Get out there and to the stables. Break out horses for twenty-one, and we'll rush the main gate.'

William clearly knew better than to argue. It was a fairly ropey plan, but it was also the best one they had. The duke nodded and gathered his three men, running out into the corridor. Halfdan looked past them to Ketil and Gunnhild who, between them, were leading the Wolves.

'We go out of the window from our room. Get to horses and gather there.'

'Where are you going?' the völva asked.

Halfdan pointed at the stairs, from which they could hear the sounds of furious fighting, punctuated by crude insults being roared.

'To retrieve Bjorn.'

'I'll help,' Ketil said, and joined him as Gunnhild began to usher the Wolves, the duke and his men back along the corridor to the rooms that looked out over the outer bailey. As the bulk of them disappeared around the corner, Halfdan looked his friend in the one eye. 'This might be a last stand.'

Ketil snorted. 'The day the Loki-born walks to his death, we might as well *all* give up, as Ragnarok will be here.'

That sent a shiver up Halfdan's spine and brought back that vision-dream in horrible detail. He shuddered.

'If I fall, get out.'

But in that moment, somehow he knew he would not fall. In a moment of clarity he realised he had been handed a gift by the gods, albeit a double-edged one. He had seen his death, which was not something to look forward to, especially given the circumstances of it. But that also meant that until he found himself face to face with Heimdallr, surely nothing else could kill him? He made a mental note to speak to Gunnhild about this when he had the chance, but for now he had other things to deal with. Just because he could perhaps not die here did not mean the same held for Ketil and Bjorn.

In moments he was pounding down the stairs toward the sound of furious fighting, the rangy Icelander at his back, jumping three steps at a time, avoiding the trail of human destruction Bjorn had left behind him. At the bottom, they rounded the corner and found a wide corridor filled with fighting. It seemed in an instant that the Normans were busy fighting among themselves while Bjorn, somewhere in the midst of it all, was merrily chopping bits out of anyone he could reach.

Then the jarl's sharp eye picked out the details. Men in the colours of the two rebel lords were coming in through the door from the huge hall beyond, while Bjorn was fighting them back with the aid of another Norman and his men. He recognised the bloodied, tired face of Geoffroi from the previous afternoon, and nodded to himself. He'd recognised the man's quality in the hall immediately, and it seemed he held to it. In the face of the rebellion, even against insurmountable odds, Geoffroi had clung to his oath to the duke.

'We have to get that door shut and barred,' Halfdan bellowed.

Geoffroi turned at the voice and focused on him. 'Where is the duke?'

'With my men. We're getting him out.'

'Then go,' Geoffroi shouted. 'Save him.'

For a moment, Halfdan considered arguing, rushing to help and close the door, but common sense took hold of him. With the door barred, the enemy would spread out, fill the baileys and look for other ways in, which would make their own exit that much more difficult. Geoffroi and his men fighting at the door would keep them busy long enough, hopefully, for the Wolves to get William out of there. With just a nod to Geoffroi – who didn't see it, for he was already back to the fight – Halfdan and Ketil reached out and grabbed Bjorn.

It took both of them to drag him out of the fray, such was his desperate desire to fight. All three of them were slippery and sticky with other people's blood, and in Bjorn's case, some of his own, too. There were several moments when their hands slid free and the great white bear had another chance to struggle with the Normans, but finally they managed to drag him free.

'Come on,' Halfdan snapped at his big friend, and ran for the stairs, leaving Geoffroi to fight his desperate rearguard. Ketil followed him, and Bjorn, after one longing look back at the fight, sighed and made for the staircase.

Moments later they were pounding along to the upper floor.

'I was enjoying that,' the albino grumbled. 'Haven't had a proper fight since we were down south, fighting with Fuck.'

'Fulk,' said Ketil automatically, as he urged the big man on.

'We need to get William of Nordmandi out of here and to safety,' Halfdan said as they reached the upper corridor.

'Why?' Bjorn said.

'Because we need him if we ever want to find the *Sea Wolf.*'

This seemed to satisfy the big man, and he nodded and thundered along the corridor behind them. They passed the carnage at the door of the duke's room and found their own two chambers. Both doors were open, with men and women gathered around the windows. Even as Halfdan glanced into the first chamber, he saw Anna throw herself from the window. He gestured to Ketil.

'Go into the next room and bar the door. We need to hold them as long as possible.'

Ketil nodded and ran to the far room, while Halfdan dragged Bjorn into the nearest, then turned, shut and barred the door.

He then hurried over to join the others at the window. Five were yet to leave, and one of them was one of William's Normans. The rest moved aside as the jarl approached, and Halfdan took a quick look outside.

The enemy were aware of their escape already. Those men who were still on the ramparts were bellowing warnings and pointing at the escapees, yet they did not seem to be running to help, held in place either by orders or by fear.

Below, one of the first to jump had had the wisdom to reach a cart of grain sacks nearby and push it up to the wall. Grain sacks would still form a hard landing, but it brought it a good six feet closer, which also minimised the risk of injury as long as the jumper hit the cart centrally. The other window was a straight jump to the turf, and already one of the Wolves was rolling around, cursing and clutching his knee.

Halfdan's attention went out a little further, and he could see two small fights going on. Some of his men had reached the stable block and were struggling with the men there, while two more of his Wolves had run for the gate that separated the two baileys and were busy fighting to hold it.

Halfdan stepped back, and another jumped from the window, landing with a thud and a curse.

'Go,' he urged, pushing someone else into the aperture.

He had no idea how long Geoffroi could hold the room downstairs and how long these chamber doors would hold, but that was immaterial if they were slow enough in their egress that the enemy had time to move and bring their forces back out into the main bailey.

Breathing heavily, racing through what he could remember of the castle, the town beyond its walls, the forests beyond that, and the general geography of the peninsula, Halfdan waited impatiently until Bjorn, the second to last in the room, climbed up to the windowsill.

'This was not made for a big man,' Bjorn grumbled, trying to fit his enormous bulk into the opening.

'Jump.'

'Easy for you to say, Halfdan Loki-born. You're the size of my thigh.'

As Bjorn swore and shifted, scraped and struggled, Halfdan turned sideways, rolling his eyes, and slammed his shoulder into the big man's back. Bjorn popped from the window like a cork from a bottle, bellowing something about bastards as he fell. Halfdan grinned and climbed up in his wake.

'Best get out of the way,' he shouted to the huge albino.

And with that, he jumped.

Chapter 9

Halfdan hit the sacks of grain, rolled, and dropped from the cart, landing on his feet in a crouch, looking about. The Wolves and their Norman charges were scattered, and he wished he'd given more explicit instructions before sending them out. The four Normans were gathered together, looking determined, their young leader squinting into the darkness, taking in the situation. Halfdan took a deep breath and began shouting out orders.

'Ketil and Bjorn, go for the gate to the inner court. Take the cart and use it to block the gap. Take two men to help, and when you're done, run for the main gate.'

It was perhaps a tribute to how undisputed he was as jarl that neither man blinked, let alone argued, as they grabbed two of the biggest Wolves, grasped the cart by the traces and the sides, and began to move it. They were large, strong and fast men, and the cart, though heavy and slow to start rolling, was soon creaking across the grass, and picking up pace as they angled it toward where a small group of Wolves was currently holding back an increasing tide of garrison men trying to get out to catch them. There wasn't a lot more he could do than that. It would hopefully slow the enemy sufficiently.

One man was leaning against the wall, wincing, unable to put down his leg, while another was still rolling around on the floor, cursing and clutching his knee.

'Can you walk?'

The two men turned to Halfdan. Both nodded, for both knew the ugly truth. There was no time to take care of the wounded. They had to be gone, and anyone who couldn't make it would have to be left behind. The young jarl wasn't convinced, the way the two looked, but he had to give them a fighting chance.

'Make for the gatehouse now. Be fast and meet us there.'

As the two men hobbled off, he looked at the others, counting off to be sure he had everyone. Six men at the inner gate, blocking it and then running. Three at the stables. Not enough to handle twenty-one horses. Two injured hobbling off toward the gatehouse, and that left... Yes, ten of them, including the duke and his men.

He looked at them all and pointed to the three leanest-looking men left – a Wolf and two Normans.

'Go for the gatehouse. Secure it if you can. Try to stay alive.'

The Normans looked to their duke, the orders having been given by a stranger, but William nodded to them, and the three ran off, making to overtake the injured and seize the gate from its guards.

Thank Odin that the rebel lords had been so focused in their planning. They had cleared the outer bailey, and then pulled the bulk of their forces into the inner bailey and removed the loyalists there, assuming they could trap their prey in the keep. Now, those prey were in the outer bailey, and it really was quite sparsely manned – presumed secure and no longer a priority.

That left him, William and one of his men, the three women and Leif.

'The stables,' he said simply.

The men on the outer bailey walls were moving, some toward the main gate and some toward the stables.

They pounded across the grass of the bailey then, racing for where the warriors they'd sent earlier were already bringing horses out of the stables, some saddled, some not. As they approached the huge wooden structure, it became apparent that the fighting was not yet over. Two of the Wolves were leading out horses and letting them go to wander loose, while the sounds of furious combat raged inside. Without the need for words, Halfdan pointed to William and the women and then to the horses, and they moved to take control of the wandering beasts.

While they worked, Halfdan, Leif and the other Norman ran into the stable doorway. One of Halfdan's men, beleaguered, was fighting off two opponents. Only one was armed with a sword, the other a young stable lad thrusting with a pitchfork, but the need to divide his defence between the two meant the Wolf was permanently on the defensive, picking up small wounds as he fought, and yet unable to finish them off.

'Leif, get the rest of the horses out.'

The Rus nodded and turned, beginning to urge the beasts to movement, while Halfdan and the duke's man ran to the ongoing struggle. Halfdan leapt, pushing his troubled man aside out of danger, his own sword catching that of the Norman's and turning it aside. The parry required some effort, for the Norman's sword was much longer and heavier than his short Alani blade, but he managed, and that was when the smaller blade's advantage came to the fore. While the Norman grunted and lifted the heavy sword ready for another attack, Halfdan was already moving, the light weapon in his hand swift and easy to manoeuvre. He dropped and rolled, lashing out. The Norman was wearing one of their usual chain shirts. All the ones he'd seen were long-sleeved, thigh-length, and divided at the hem to allow for riding, and some had chain hoods built in. They were protective and bulky.

But they did little for the knees.

Halfdan's blade snicked through the man's hamstrings as he tumbled past and leapt to his feet once more, nimbly. The Norman soldier screamed and went down like a sack of grain on his ruined leg. The jarl turned to look for more trouble, but the duke's man had swiftly dispatched the stable boy now that he was alone.

The enemy were down. He didn't bother wasting time finishing off the maimed man. The guard could hardly chase after them, anyway. Instead, he and the duke's man turned and helped Leif usher the horses from the stables, out into the open.

He cursed as they emerged, and he counted. Twenty-one of the fugitives, and there appeared to be seventeen horses, only thirteen of those saddled. He reached back in through the door to where he'd seen saddle blankets and grabbed a few, throwing them to his friends.

'Anyone who can ride bareback, do it now.'

The Wolves and their Norman companions were climbing onto the horses, favouring the ones with saddles. The duke went for an unsaddled one, but one of his men grabbed his lord and turned him toward another, taking that one for himself, and so William climbed into a saddle with surprising skill for one so young. Halfdan smiled to himself. He'd not been a whole lot older himself when he'd left Gotland in search of a murderous jarl. When had *he* taken such a step toward being a greybeard?

A roared curse drew his attention, and he turned to see Bjorn and Ketil racing across the turf from the inner gate toward the outer gatehouse, two others close behind. It was a saddening sight, for it meant that two Wolves lay dead at that gate. Looking past them, he revised his estimation. One dead, one still struggling, fighting like a hero of old, wounded in a dozen places, but standing on the upturned cart and fighting a hopeless rearguard to let the other four escape.

Halfdan directed his people to leave four horses, and then took the others and rode for the gate. The two men with leg injuries from the fall were only two thirds of the way across the bailey. The three he'd sent to the gate had passed them and were in the recess of the gatehouse, fighting fiercely with a number of men, others joining even as their companions fell, feeding down from the ramparts. One of the men from the walls turned, seeing the small, mounted group – six figures herding thirteen horses toward the gate – and hurried toward them, shield up and sword out. It was brave. Stupid, but brave.

It was the young Duke of Nordmandi who veered out to ride the man down, and with a thunder of hooves left the broken soldier groaning his way to death in the trampled turf.

One of the men at the gate was down, but they had taken down an impressive number of guards between them, using the recess of the gate to limit the number of Cotentin's men who could approach them at any one time. Still, now they were down to two, they would not last long.

The six riders reached the gate swiftly, and those guards engaged with the pair fighting for control of the portal were caught between them and the new arrivals, and swiftly dispatched. Again, Halfdan paused for just a moment to take stock of the situation. The gate was just about theirs, barring four men running from the walls to help. Another four, this time their own Wolves, had reached the horses Halfdan had left for them and pulled themselves up on to the beasts, riding for the exit. They had almost done it. He pointed to the men in the gate, who were breathing heavily and recovering from their struggle.

'Get the gate open.'

As they, with the help of Leif and Gunnhild, lifted the heavy bar and began to haul the gates inward, Halfdan and the others rode to take on the men leaving the walls. It was short work, for Cotentin's guards were not enthusiastic in their task, and held back as much as they could. By the time Halfdan had delivered a deep chop across a man's neck, almost decapitating him, and another had fallen to one of his men, the remaining two ran for safety.

The gate was open, and freedom beckoned. William was already riding into the gap, and the others followed. Thanks to their three losses, they were only one horse short, and in a heartbeat Anna jumped clear and ran over to Leif, who hauled her up in front of him. By the time Ketil and Bjorn and their friends reached the gate, even the two men with the injured legs had arrived and were climbing on to horses with a lot of cursing.

Then they were gone. As they rode away from the gate, into the streets, men appeared on the ramparts behind them, and arrows began to fly, clacking down to the streets and off walls, none able to reach the fleeing riders. Halfdan looked around at his companions. There were eighteen of them on seventeen horses – the Wolves of old, with their two Byzantine women and two former varangoi, accompanied by Thurstan and four of his Apulians. And William and three Normans, of course.

Halfdan shook his head. He had to stop thinking of Thurstan and his men separately. They were Wolves now. In truth, as the duke had noted that first night, the Wolves were drawn from so far afield that they were far more than a dragon boat raiding party these days, even if their numbers had diminished a little. And even Cassandra and Anna had become an integral part of the crew. He smiled as he looked at the two women, wondering when they'd begun to braid their hair in a northern manner, as though taking their lead from Gunnhild. No matter who they were – Norman, Apulian, Byzantine or true Northerners – they were *all* Wolves.

As they took several turnings in the streets, putting them out of sight of the castle gate, they slowed. Some were clearly pleased, struggling to control mounts with only a blanket to ride and a mane to cling on to.

'What now?' Halfdan called to William.

The duke rubbed his scalp and yawned. 'Preferably sleep. But plenty to do before that. If Bessin and Cotentin have rebelled, then nowhere in the peninsula is safe. And if that was truly Hauteville's man you saw back there, even Pirou is barred to us. And to think I offered him a place at court and a stipend.'

Halfdan chewed his cheek in thought. 'I am not sure Hauteville has rebelled yet. Before you reached Pirou, he was still being hunted by rebels, or so we believe. I think he is doing what Normans do best,' he added, drawing on experience from Apulia. 'I think he is playing a game of self-preservation. He openly acknowledges you as his jarl, but he has a man in the rebel camp, negotiating, ready to change sides if it is to his advantage.'

The duke nodded. 'Still, this does not mean we can trust Serlo. We cannot ride for Pirou, lest we find ourselves stepping into the bear's den. And south there is only France. There may be ways I can persuade King Henry to my cause, but not if I meet him as a beggar and a fugitive.' The young duke pulled himself up in the saddle. 'There is only one course. We must ride south and east, make for my castle of Falaise, where my army awaits. Once there, I am again in a position of strength.'

'Is it far?'

William nodded wearily. 'A dreadful journey, in fact. As the crow flies it is more than seventy miles, and that is if the river Vire is at low tide when we reach it. If not, that pushes it to over a hundred miles via the nearest bridge.'

'A hundred miles is not *too* bad by horse,' Ketil put in.

'*This* hundred miles is. For the first stretch we will be in the lands of Cotentin, and once we cross the river we will be in the lands of Bessin and his allies. Sixty of those seventy miles are strongly controlled by my enemies.'

'One of the first things we will need to do is find somewhere we can acquire reins and saddles for the other horses,' Halfdan said. 'We cannot make seventy miles with men riding bareback. And we will need food and supplies.'

The duke nodded. 'There are places—' he began, but was interrupted by a triumphant shout.

They all turned and cursed their lack of foresight. A man in a chain hauberk sat on a horse at a junction fifty paces away, sword levelled in their direction, bellowing to others. Clearly the rebel lords had no intention of letting their quarry escape, even now he'd managed to slip through their grasp in the castle. And they would be better prepared.

'Ride,' Halfdan barked, but even as they started moving, he realised they were in trouble. With so many unsaddled horses that were causing their riders difficulty, they were not moving at high speed, while their pursuers were expert horsemen on their own mounts, fresh and ready to give chase. The Wolves and their Norman companions would be overtaken and ridden down in short order.

William seemed to have come to the same conclusion.

'We need to buy time,' the young duke shouted.

Halfdan nodded and pointed to some of their companions. 'I will hold them off for a while and catch you up. Get the women and the unsaddled to safety.'

The duke gestured to his man Ancel. 'Stay and help our pagan friends. Run when you have to. Meet us at Saint-Cyr.'

His sergeant nodded and hauled on his reins, turning the beast and urging it over to join Halfdan. The jarl watched the rest leave – those without saddles and those he sought to save first. Five of them would stay and hold the line to allow them time: Halfdan, Ancel, Ketil, Thurstan and Bjorn.

'How long do we hold?' Thurstan asked, an edge to his voice.

Halfdan glanced at Ancel. 'It will take five minutes to leave town completely, and in another five they will be vanished into woodland and hard to follow.'

'Five minutes, then,' Halfdan said. 'Make every minute count.'

Even as they drew themselves up in a mounted line, facing that street along which a second man had joined the one who'd spotted them, Halfdan heard a stretching noise and turned to see Ketil lifting his bow, an arrow nocked. In half a heartbeat the arrow thwacked off into the night. Halfdan tried to watch its flight, but it was impossible, the dark-fletched shaft vanishing into the dark distance. Nothing seemed to happen.

'You missed,' Ancel said. 'Must be that eye of yours.'

Ketil said nothing, simply watched. After what seemed an eternity, the enemy's horse suddenly collapsed beneath him, buckling and falling to one side, scattering the Norman across the street, where he'd had the sharpness of mind to unhook his feet from the stirrups first.

Another came around the corner, pointing and yelling.

'How long can you keep that up?' Halfdan asked.

Ketil reached down, counted the few arrows in his quiver and drew one out.

'Five more times,' the Icelander said, lifting, nocking, raising and releasing.

Again, in the night gloom, they never saw the arrow hit home, but the second rider suddenly swayed in his saddle, lolling.

'One more,' Halfdan said.

Ketil nodded and loosed a third shot. This time, the arrow seemed to hit the man's horse, but after a moment of rearing and whinnying, the rider managed to get his mount back under control.

'All right,' Halfdan said to the Icelander, 'here's what I want you to do. Take the most direct route from town and into the woods. Get beneath a tree and prepare. The moment we come into sight, take down the first three men following us, yes?'

Ketil nodded and turned, urging his horse away.

'That leaves us a man down,' Ancel said.

'But when we have to run, he will cover us and give us a chance.'

The four of them settled into their line, listening to Ketil clattering away behind them into the distance. More and more mounted Normans were gathering ahead, at the junction.

'Why don't they come?' Ancel breathed.

Halfdan grinned as he looked to each side. He had to look up to see the massive, eerily white bulk of Bjorn Bear-torn at one side. The solid, unyielding shape of Thurstan sat, heavily armoured, to the other.

'Would you?'

Ancel looked left and right, and shuddered.

Finally, some sort of officer appeared with the Normans down the street, and orders were bellowed. Four men were sent for them, their commander matching man for man. It was a sensible tactic. The street width would negate any advantage they could count on from numbers, and man for man would give the officer more of an idea of what he was dealing with.

Bjorn plucked a throwing axe from his belt, looked at it for a while and frowned.

'What's the matter?' Halfdan asked.

'Don't want to lose a good axe,' the big man answered, and reached down to the other side of his belt, lifting a bottle of something and popping the lid away with his thumb before taking a huge swig. Ancel looked at the big man as though he were mad, then settled his teardrop-shaped shield into place, proudly displaying the twin golden lions of the duke, and hefting his sword ready.

The four riders came on, strong, confident. Three of the defenders braced themselves, ready for combat. Bjorn shrugged, and upended his bottle, tipping what remained mostly into his mouth with just a small amount across his face and into his ears. Finally sated with drink, the great white warrior gripped his reins with his left hand and, as the enemy closed, flung the bottle with his right.

The empty vessel, spraying odd droplets, spun through the air and struck an impressive blow right in the face of the man charging at Bjorn. Halfdan had to put the blow down to luck. Ketil could pull off such a manoeuvre and expect success, but Bjorn was no archer. Thor was with the big man, just as Loki watched over Halfdan.

The man the missile had hit was out of the fight straight away, the bottle having smashed on the brow of his helmet and sprayed the man's face with shards of glass. The rider barrelled off to the side of the street, yelling in pain. The other three came on, preparing for the collision and combat. At the very last moment, Halfdan reached across to Ancel and grabbed his reins, hauling on them, pulling the horse over toward him. The Norman shouted in alarm, stunned, with no idea what the jarl was doing, but blinked in surprise when he realised Halfdan had saved him from their own companion. Bjorn, roaring and with his big axe out, pushed his horse across in front of Ancel, jealously choosing a second target now that he'd felled the first.

In front of them, as their enemies hit and crowded in, Bjorn swung his axe in a massive arc, over the head of his horse. The nearest man lifted his shield, full of professional confidence, preparing to take the blow and then stab out with his own long sword. He had clearly not counted upon the sheer weight and brutality of Bjorn's blow. The massive axe cut through the shield as though it were parchment, taking a huge piece from the man's arm, and then continuing almost without slowing, tearing a chunk of the man's side away, chain links scattering, wool and flesh following.

The man bellowed in shock and agony, and immediately fell away in the opposite direction to the blow, where he fell against the next man.

By the time any of the others could strike, their four opponents had dropped to one. Thurstan's blade thunked from the last man's shield, but he managed to turn his sword and knock aside the man's counterstroke.

Bjorn tore his axe free and struck again, sending the wounded Norman to meet his god with the second blow, following which he pushed forward, making for the man with the glass in his face, who was still reeling at the side of the street.

As Thurstan continued to deal with his own man, Halfdan leapt forth in his saddle, not giving the last Norman a chance to recover from where he had been knocked sideways by his friend. The man was armoured in hauberk with coif, conical steel helmet and shield. The way he was leaning, lurching this way and that, meant there was little chance of a blow to the face or neck landing without meeting iron links. Consequently, the jarl struck the only clear blow he could. The tip of his sword plunged into the horse's eye, and he ripped it back out sharply, knowing just how easily he could lose his blade if he were not swift.

The horse screamed and reared to an impressive height, and Halfdan and Ancel backed away from the flailing hooves. Its rider tried his hardest to stay in the saddle, not entirely sure in what way his horse had been wounded, but try as he might, finally one foot came free of the stirrup and, with that, he fell, toppling from the far side. His other foot remained anchored, and even over the screaming of the horse, Halfdan heard the man's ankle break in the stirrup. Halfdan had no need to do more, for the moment the horse dropped back, panic gripped it and it turned and cantered away along the street, making horrible keening noises and dragging the rider behind it by his broken leg, bouncing along the stones.

As Halfdan calmed his own horse, he looked around the street. A little further along and at the side, Bjorn was merrily carving the last echo of life from the man with the face full of glass. Two horses were further on, one dragging its doomed rider, the other with a dead body leaning, wobbling in the saddle. Thurstan remained locked in combat with the last man, but it was clear he had the upper hand. For a moment, Halfdan considered helping, for simple speed if for no other reason, but decided against it. He didn't know the man that well yet, and some Northmen – Bjorn being a prime example – could become quite offended if you intervened in a fight. Instead, he peered off to the end of the street. Quite a gathering was building at that next junction, and he could hear the distant, muffled sounds of angry shouting.

The next riders were in no hurry to follow the fate of the first wave, while the officer was clearly insistent that they do so. Even as Thurstan finished his man off with a blow to the face, Halfdan narrowed his eyes, peering away into the dark, suspicious.

The argument seemed to have ended, and to his eye there looked to be fewer men there, though still quite a number.

'Bjorn,' he called.

'What?'

'Back here.'

The big man frowned, but knew better than to argue with his jarl.

'Brace yourself for a second run,' Ancel advised them.

'I don't think so,' Halfdan said quietly as Bjorn rejoined the line.

'What?'

'They're trying something new. I think their officer has sent men off to come at us from other sides. I think now's our time to run or we're going to be surrounded.'

Ancel frowned, but then bowed his head to the man who was in charge. Flicking a gesture for them to follow, Halfdan clopped his horse backwards a dozen paces and then a little more. There they reached a crossroads, and he looked this way and that. He could see no one yet, but it seemed almost certain if they waited there, other riders would come from both sides in an attempt to trap and overwhelm them. He came to a halt.

'The moment they come, stick with me. We ride for Ketil's position. As soon as we pass the Icelander, we ride like the wind. Ancel, you know where this Saint-Cyr place is?'

'Yes.'

'Take us in a different direction for a while, and once we've laid sufficient trail, Ketil will cover our change of course while we turn back and make for the meet-up. It will be hard for them in the countryside to locate our tracks in the dark, especially without a good hunter. With luck they'll not pick up our trail until dawn.'

It did not take long. Perhaps thirty heartbeats later there were shouts ahead, and away at that other junction a fresh wave of riders started to hurtle their way.

'This is it. The other two pincers will close at the same time.'

Sure enough, once the riders ahead were moving, the fresh sounds of heavy horse came from both side streets.

'Now. Ride.'

The others turned with him and put their heels to the flanks, snapping the reins in their fists, though Bjorn looked faintly regretful. They raced away, following the most obvious route, the one Ketil would have taken. As they neared the edge of the town, the riders of the rebel lords racing at full speed behind them, hungry for victory, Halfdan began to vaguely recognise places. This was the route they'd come along when they arrived at Valognes.

As they reached a straight stretch of road, he looked back over his shoulder and could see the wave of men and horses pouring along the thoroughfare behind them, the scudding clouds casting moving dark patches across street and occupant, making it hard to gauge their strength. Too many to face, for certain – and this would only be the vanguard. There was nothing in this whole damn land that the rebel lords would want more than to have William either dead in a ditch or unconscious in their grasp. Halfdan and his companions had to get away now, and then they had to stay ahead until they met up with the duke's army.

In moments they were passing the last buildings of the town of Valognes and disappearing into the countryside. The road to Pirou crossed an open stretch of field and then entered woodland – that very woodland where Halfdan had expected to fall foul of Neel de Cotentin's betrayal. The man had been wilier, though, launching his attack the night *before* the hunt, prepared and planned, and had it not been for Gunnhild's *Seiðr* and her intuition, it was very likely that they would all have died in the darkness in Valognes.

As they rode out across the open ground, he judged that they'd perhaps ridden too fast and left their pursuers a little further behind. That would be useful, but only *after* Ketil. With a gesture to the others, he slowed his pace very slightly, allowing their hunters to gain just a little pace. Then, satisfied that the distance would be just right, he led the other three toward the woodland. Their pursuers gave cries of urgency, knowing that there was a chance of losing them once they reached the trees. The enemy picked up the pace.

So did Halfdan and his friends. They were perhaps twenty paces from the trees when the first arrow thrummed from the woods, hurtling past Ancel close enough to startle him. A quick glance over his shoulder, and Halfdan saw the lead rider of the Normans topple forward, dead in the saddle. As they passed the edge of the woods, a second arrow shot from the shadows and plunged into the next nearest horse, sending it tumbling, broken. The other riders were forced to pull up or change course and ride off to the sides to avoid collision.

The third arrow they never saw hit, though it clearly did from the cries of alarm back in the open. Then they were riding and Ketil was catching up, pounding along the road in their wake. At the next corner, where an old stone cross stood over a shallow bowl full of brown water, Ancel led them off to the right.

All they had to do was meet up with the duke and get him safely back to his castle. And hope beyond hope that Serlo de Hauteville did not turn rebel, kill Ulfr and the others, and steal all the gold.

Chapter 10

Saint-Cyr was not what Halfdan expected, though he had to acknowledge that was probably a good thing. As a meeting place chosen by the duke, he'd presumed it to be some sort of town or important place, but it was actually a hamlet of half a dozen houses scattered around a church, with a small mill, its wheel turning with a half-hearted languidness in the dark, the water burbling gently beneath it. The horizon was largely hidden by small stands of trees, and it was this very obscurity and unimportance that made it useful. With no tracks to follow, the men of the rebel barons would likely make for the nearest place of any importance, not this backwater.

There was a second reason, though, Halfdan realised as they reined in their sweating mounts close to the church, spotting William and his men gathered together. Saint-Cyr had a stables, and in the short time they'd been waiting for Halfdan and his companions, some sort of deal had been struck. A weary-looking man was busy bringing saddles, blankets, bits and bridles from a storehouse, while his wife packaged up bread and cheese in a basket. One of the duke's men was busy stacking a pile of coins on their windowsill in payment. The locals showed appropriate deference to the lord of their land, eyes lowered or averted whenever speaking to the duke, and then only in reply to his own queries. Otherwise, they spoke only to his men.

As the four of them rode up, William turned, eyes narrowing, looking first past the new arrivals and then at them. 'No pursuit?'

Halfdan shook his head. 'There *will* be, as soon as they locate the trail, and in the meantime, they will send out men along every possible road. We cannot delay.'

'Yet we will move faster with everyone appropriately equipped.'

This was true, and so Halfdan moved close to the duke while the bareback riders had their mounts saddled and prepared for the journey. In the pause while they worked, Halfdan looked at the young duke. Their whole reason for being there with William, and not back in Pirou helping Ulfr build a ship, came down to an unknown and tenuous connection with Harðráði and their missing ship, and some other nebulous belief of Gunnhild's, about which she was being cagey. Thus far they'd not had time to bring up the subject, and, in truth, while on the run from a dangerous enemy, hiding in a forest, was probably not the time. But as they'd ridden from Valognes, it had occurred to the jarl that the danger they were all in was great enough for William to die any time, and with him would die any useful information. Halfdan had to try his luck, while there was time.

'What do you know of Harðráði?' he said quietly.

William frowned. 'Harðráði?'

There was a moment of doubt then for Halfdan. The duke seemed to be unfamiliar with the name. Halfdan thought back over what he knew of the man – nuggets of information gleaned from their time in Miklagarðr.

'His brother was king in Norway, Óláfr Haraldsson. Harðráði was in the south with us, serving the Byzantines, but he came north once more.'

William shrugged. 'I am not familiar with the man. This Óláfr Haraldsson, though… this is Saint Olaf, yes? His son Magnus sits on the throne in Norway now, and his daughter rules with her husband among the Saxons. I did not know that Saint Olaf had a brother, though I find that remarkably interesting. It is always worth knowing everything about one's peers, for one never knows what information might end up being useful.'

The jarl felt his spirits sink. Had Gunnhild been mistaken in seeing any connection between this man and the lunatic who had stolen Halfdan's ship in Miklagarðr? But then she was always vague, and she had said 'in the days to come'. How far had she seen? He turned to the völva to find her watching him with slitted eyes, deep in thought. He shivered. No. She was always right, and he'd learned to his peril not to discount her advice. Whatever the duke said, whether he knew it or not, there was a connection there. He would have to ask her to go deeper, to seek more, when they had the chance, but in the meantime, it was important to keep this man alive. Besides, he had a dream tale of Loki and Heimdallr to ask her about, too.

He waited with growing impatience as the last horses were saddled, and then, finally, the duke led them from Saint-Cyr.

'Where now?' Halfdan asked, as they trotted in double file along a farm track between stands of poplars that rose, stately, into the night sky. The scudding clouds still raced on high, dappling the land with patches of fast-moving shade, yet down at ground level there was little more than a gentle breeze.

William turned to his senior man. 'Ancel?'

The knight looked across at the two nobles. 'We must pass carefully around Montburc. Undoubtedly the lord de Cotentin has sent men there to locate us, and may even have already had a garrison there. It is one of his fiefs, after all. From there we have a choice, my lord duke. The most direct, and fastest, route takes us south-east to the Vire's tidal crossing. Speed is important, not only to outrun our enemies, but also to catch the low tide, or we add a great deal to the journey, and the tide will be coming in already, so that is something of a race. But that road is also the obvious route, and so the one most likely to bring your enemies upon us. Also, there are woodlands that can hide dangers, and we will have to make our way around the Sancte Marie Ecclesia, where there is a village, and very likely a guard post under control of Cotentin's men. Fast, but dangerous.'

'And the alternative?' William asked, drumming fingers on his saddle horn.

'Moving further inland would only increase the troubles, but it is possible south of Montburc to cut across to the coast, five miles east, and from there ride along the shore. That would add five miles or so to our journey and increase the risk of missing the tide, but it is also much less likely to be patrolled by the enemy, and the settlements there are all just minor villages. It is also open coastland, and visibility will be good, with little chance for ambushes. The choice seems, to me, too close to call. What say you, my lord duke?'

Before William could answer, though, Halfdan leaned across. 'Follow the coast. Better to be able to see our enemies coming. Five miles will make little difference, and Ran will provide, when we reach this river.'

The duke frowned, perhaps wondering who Ran was, but nodded his agreement. 'Given our numbers and the distance we have to travel, I think it better that we minimise our risk of trouble. Lead us to the coast, Ancel.'

The man smiled grimly, then trotted back and passed the news to the others before rejoining his lord. As they closed on the main trade road from Valognes, and the small town of Montburc, Ancel rearranged the column, setting himself and the other two of William's men out front as a vanguard, keeping Halfdan, Bjorn, Ketil and Leif around the duke, they having proven their loyalty in the escape from Valognes. The rest followed as a rearguard, with Thurstan at the back, keeping a watch in their wake.

Emerging from the edge of the woodland, they moved carefully and slowly, Ancel ahead looking for trouble. Montburc was small by comparison with Valognes, yet large enough to cause concern. Halfdan looked up at the sky and tracked around until he found the moon. It was already low. He guessed they had perhaps three hours until the sun began to show. The high clouds chose that moment to pass across the silvery light, and the world went surprisingly dark. They hugged the edge of the woodland, crossing the main road as swiftly as they could, and then staying close to the cover of the trees as they passed the small town, relying on the night, the shadows of the clouds, and simple luck to see them away and into the countryside once more.

Something set the hair on Halfdan's neck up, and he shivered. In response, he looked about. It took him moments to spot them, and in that moment the clouds shifted once more. Suddenly the jarl was sitting in a patch of silvery light, his chain shirt glimmering like a beacon, just as were the two riders sitting astride their mounts upon a small wooden bridge over a minor stream on the dirt track leading into town.

The two riders saw them at the same moment. It had to be a split-second decision, whether they had time to chase down the men and stop them reporting in, or whether it would be better to run and put time and distance between them. He came down in that single heartbeat on the side of caution, reasoning that by the time those two men found their masters, the riders could have broken into a gallop and be close to the sea. Unfortunately for Halfdan, before he could open his mouth and give the order to ride, Bjorn had turned his mount, given out a whooping sound that would attract attention for half a mile, and put his heels to the horse's flanks, racing toward the two watchers.

'Shit,' Halfdan snapped, the decision having been taken out of his hands. Others were turning, ready to join the big man, who was already pounding across the turf toward the two men. Halfdan waved a hand at the others. 'No. Take the duke. Get him to the shore. I'll bring Bjorn.'

And with that, he left the column and urged his horse to speed, racing off in the albino's wake. Ahead, the two Normans had turned and begun to ride back for the town. Bjorn was racing away, the desperate urge to reach them and perpetrate his particular brand of violence driving him to surprising speed. Similarly, Halfdan managed to push his mount hard, trying to put things right. Now that Bjorn had committed them to this course of action, they had to catch the men, and fast.

The two riders reached the edge of the town itself first, some way ahead of the pursuing Northmen, disappearing into the shadows of a night-time street. Through sheer will and the strength of his mount, Halfdan managed to almost catch up with the big man, whose own steed had to be struggling with carrying such weight and bulk at such a speed.

'Idiot,' was all he could think to say as he pulled close.

Ahead, they could see the Norman riders, but more importantly, could *hear* them clattering along the street. The Wolves pushed hard, increasing their pace, desperate to catch them, though Halfdan was also horribly aware that they were exhausting their mounts at the very beginning of their journey, which was never a good idea.

Ahead, the other riders burst into a town square, the light illuminating them clearly. Then, they stopped, turning. Halfdan had only moments to wonder at their behaviour before he and Bjorn broke out into the open themselves, and all became clear. In truth, it could have been much worse. Had it been a proper trap, this square could have been filled with rebels, and there would have been little chance of the two Wolves leaving the place alive. As it happened, there had been no such plan. The two riders had turned to face them only to buy time. Beyond them, on the far side of the square, Halfdan could see another Norman wheeling his mount, ready to race away. These two would hold them off, while their friend rode for their superiors with news of the fugitives.

'These two are yours,' Halfdan barked at the big warrior. 'When they're down, ride for the duke.'

Leaving Bjorn with a grin of satisfaction that he had the strongest urge to slap from the man's face, the jarl forced yet more speed from his galloping mount, veering out to his left.

The nearest Norman made to swing at him as he passed, but Halfdan was fast and far enough away that leaning back kept him out of the way of the blade's passage. In a heartbeat he was past and hurtling across the square. The third man was starting to move. Behind him, Halfdan could hear Bjorn tackling the first two, without a care who heard. If there were other riders in this village, then there was little chance that they would miss anything. Nothing the jarl could do about it, though.

He had his own problem.

The rider ahead pounded along, picking up pace, but he'd been slow starting, and perhaps had underestimated Halfdan's speed, for the jarl was closing on him as the pair approached the edge of town. Halfdan looked at the man, at his muscular steed, then down at his own tired mount, and trusted to the cunning of Loki and the luck of all true warriors when the gods were with them. He removed his feet from the stirrups and, letting go of the reins, grasped the saddle horn and pulled himself up so that his feet were on the saddle, slipping here and there. He was almost on the other man.

He jumped.

He almost missed, and his heart lurched, cold, as he hit the Norman in the back and bounced, almost falling into the path of his own horse. Then, his scrabbling, desperate fingers found the back of the Norman's chain collar and gripped tight. The man made an 'urk' sound as he was almost choked, and inadvertently yanked the reins. Even as he found stability, Halfdan's other hand whipped the sax from his belt. This close, no sword, even his short one, was going to be much use. He lifted the sharp, narrow dagger and plunged it down just above his grasping fingers. The blade sank into flesh, then struck rib and vertebra, and grunting with the effort, Halfdan pulled the collar down, risking being thrown from the horse. He changed the blade's angle, slamming it in between the ribs, the spine and the shoulder blade – a narrow target, but a deadly one.

The Norman cried out, the horse reared, and Halfdan was almost thrown, only his double grip on the man's neck keeping him on the animal. Then they were back down, and the man was flailing ineffectually. Still gripping the collar, Halfdan let go of the dagger and leaned down, gripping the Norman's leg at the knee, below the chain hem, and pulling. In a single swift move the man's foot came free of his stirrup, and before he could recover in any way, the jarl gave him a hefty push, letting go of the collar and reaching down fast to grab the saddle's cantle. The Norman, already taken by surprise, grievously and painfully wounded, with a sizeable hole in his lung, had little chance of recovery. Unbalanced, he fell from the far side of his mount. At least his foot came free of the other stirrup and he fell away, rather than being dragged along by the horse.

Halfdan looked around, even as he pulled himself forward into the saddle and slid his feet into the stirrups. His own horse had simply come to a halt, exhausted, and breathing heavily at the side of the street. For a moment, he wondered whether he could manage both horses, but quickly changed his mind. This one was fresh, while his own was spent, and thanks to their sudden departure from Valognes, there was nothing of value of his on the animal.

He had to make sure the rider was dead, though, buying them some time. Rather than dismounting and approaching the writhing man to administer a killing blow, for simple expediency he walked his new horse back and forth across the man a few times, until the whimpering and thrashing stopped, and all that remained was a pulverised mess.

Satisfied the man was dead, he took his new horse three dozen paces further along the thoroughfare, keeping to the more shadowed side of the street. As he came to a halt near the edge of town, he could see another pair of riders on the road some way out, in the direction of Valognes. Thank Odin, for they seemed as yet unaware of the trouble in town, despite all the noise. He hoped that the pair would sit there, oblivious, for some time yet, and turned his horse, trotting back into the centre of town. Bjorn was mopping up – quite literally –

gripping one of his victims by the ankles while still in the saddle, dragging the man across the cobbles so that his skull bounced against every stone, while it looked to the casual observer as though he were trying to use the man's hair to clean up the substantial amount of blood.

'Stop playing,' the jarl snapped, still angry at Bjorn for his careless and unexpected attack. As he passed, the big man let go of the body and gripped the reins, turning and following Halfdan back out of town.

The jarl had to slow to let Bjorn keep pace with him, for the albino's horse was shattered.

'Next time, check with me before you decide to chase someone down.'

Bjorn looked irritated. 'Thor was in my blood. It had to be done.'

Halfdan sighed. There was something to that. Just as Loki sometimes took a hand in Halfdan's decisions, so the big man was truly one of Thor's children, and asking him to avoid a fight would be akin to suggesting he stop breathing for a day or two. Besides, in retrospect, it might have been the right decision; had the two men reached that rider unchecked, the man would have alerted the whole region to their presence. As it was, they would have a head start as long as that other pair stayed at their post and did not ride into Montburc to find their dead friends.

As they reached that little wooden bridge, Halfdan gestured to Bjorn and the pair came to a halt.

'Swap horses.'

'What? Why?'

'Because mine is fresh, and yours will collapse under your weight before we even see the sea.'

Bjorn did just that, clambering down from his sweating mount as Halfdan did the same. They swapped horses, and Halfdan realised with some irritation just how exhausted this one was, as it sagged even under the jarl's weight. He would have to be careful. *Damn the big bastard for his unanticipated actions.*

'You need to lose weight. You've fucked your horse.'

'Did I ever tell you about the time I—'

Halfdan winced. 'Now is not the time,' he interrupted, heading off what promised to be an eye-wateringly unlikely tale before it could see light.

They rode on in silence, going as fast as Halfdan dare with his exhausted horse, and after perhaps three quarters of an hour, a ribbon of silver came into view ahead. Gradually, as they rode, that ribbon resolved into a line of low, rough-grass dunes, a short beach, and then the glittering waves of the sea. Halfdan was no land-man himself – he was born an islander and was master of his own ship – but until that sight came into view, he'd perhaps never understood the longing that seemed to grip Ulfr throughout all their interminable journeys by cart or by horse. This tantalisingly close to the waves, though, it was impossible to ignore the call. He felt it in his very bones, in his blood, an almost unbearable need to be at sea, feeling the spray of salt water and the buck and roll of the deck, the groan of timbers, the slap of a sail filling, the rhythmic groan and splash of oars.

Ulfr would do whatever it took to put them back out among the waves. Halfdan had to trust his friend, but also he had to get word to him, to warn him of what might be happening among the Hautevilles. He tried not to let selfishness weigh in, but it was impossible to forget the large amounts of gold also at stake.

Shaking his head to free it of such thoughts, he and Bjorn turned and rode south along the coast, at the edge of the dunes, feeling a freedom he'd not experienced in a while, even as they rode for their lives. As they rode, largely in silence, there were times when he fancied he could hear shouts back inland, beyond the trees, though he told himself that was unlikely, and concentrated on plunging ahead.

They passed a farm after a couple of miles, and Halfdan's eyes played across the livestock in the scattered patches of moonlight. He spotted a horse grazing happily in a field and made the decision. It would not be a warhorse – probably more a farmer's carthorse – but it would be well rested, and they would never catch up with the others as long as he rode this weary beast. A quarter of an hour later, they left the farm with Halfdan on a fresh horse, having transferred the saddle. He left his own steed as a replacement, not through sympathy – a good Northman kept sympathy for people he cared about – but simply because it would probably not manage another mile anyway. Bjorn had begun to tell a joke as he worked, but the look Halfdan had given him had shut him up better than any command. The big man had already caused enough trouble, and they really didn't want to wake the farmer.

Soon enough, though, they were pounding across the turf near the dunes once more, and before long they spotted other riders ahead, in a crowd, moving the same way. It felt good to catch up with the others, and the duke greeted them with surprising warmth, asking after their escapade, eyeing their change of horses with interest. Halfdan explained what had happened, and they rode on, the last hour or two of night rapidly diminishing with every mile from Valognes. As they closed on their destination, Duke William set one of his men to ride just out of sight at their rear, looking for fresh pursuit after the debacle at Montburc.

Finally, as the night sky moved from true black to that odd glowing indigo of pre-dawn, the coastline began to curve around in front of them, marking the end of the peninsula. Halfdan looked ahead in the growing light and could see the Vire. He felt a sudden moment of doubt, then. Even now, at a relatively low tide, the crossing was over a mile wide. Still, he kept his worries to himself as the duke's man led them on, to the river and then along it. It did gradually narrow, but the level of the water was rising at an alarming rate. By the time they reached the width of a normal river, it would be deep enough to drown two horses standing one atop the other.

Ancel clearly knew the area, for he selected their crossing point with purpose and confidence, and they rode down to the riverbank with a growing sense of unease. They would cross maybe thirty paces of sucking muddy sand before they even reached the water, and the surface was rising at a rate Halfdan could only equate with a sudden winter thaw in mountain streams.

Somehow, in this early, purple light, the crossing seemed all the more daunting, the waves continually racing in and then pulling back out to sea, leaving a little more river with each flow. He was actually considering suggesting that they ride upriver for this bridge, when he heard the drumming of hooves behind. He turned in his saddle, but the dunes hid the land beyond. Then William's man suddenly crested the rise and pounded down into the sand, waving behind him.

'They're coming. The rebels.'

'How many?' the duke asked.

'All of them, I think.'

'Everyone into the water, now,' Halfdan called, for there was no longer a choice.

Without preamble, the entire group plodded as fast as they dared into the deep mud, the newly arrived rearguard joining them fast. Halfdan was somewhere mid-crowd as he began the trek.

'What do we do if they have bows?' Leif asked from his right, throwing fearful glances back.

'We die, until we're out of range. So just hope they don't.'

With that, the jarl pulled his attention to the business at hand. The going was extremely hard work, and this was just muddy sand. His horse was not happy, and he had to issue soothing sounds to it, while urging it on with heels, knees and reins, just to keep the animal going forward. He looked up and felt his pulse quicken. He had ridden the dragon boat's prow out across the icy northern sea and the Svartahaf of the Greeks, and yet no expanse of water had ever seemed as broad and as unforgiving as the stretch ahead of him. The very idea of crossing it on a horse seemed horrifying.

At the head of the column, Ancel and his man led the duke. Halfdan urged his own mount on, but watched what was to come with no small amount of trepidation. The lead riders were in the water, and it came up terrifyingly swiftly. One moment their horses were knee deep, the next, the riders themselves were submerged to the thigh. Ever since those dreadful days with the Alani fire throwers, it had been the conflagration of liquid fire that had haunted Halfdan's dreams, but now, he acknowledged with appropriate fear that the prospect of disappearing under that surface was no more pleasant.

His fears were made all the more real and immediate a moment later. Even as the cries of their pursuers became audible back beyond the dunes, the lead rider, one of the last of William's own guards, suddenly gave a cry of alarm. His horse had missed its footing somehow, and plunged into the water with an equine scream of panic. The animal reappeared moments later, swimming hard, desperate to make it to land, but there was no sign of its rider. His chain shirt, helmet, belted sword and heavy wool clothes had pulled him down into Ran's dark halls. The man was gone, and in moments, thanks to the next incoming wave, not even ripples marked his grave. Halfdan prayed the man had clutched his sword hilt as he sank, and that the battle maids of either Odin or Freyja would find him. It occurred to him then, oddly, how the *Valkyrjur* might manage to raise a man already in Ran's domain. He shook his head, aware that he was just trying to keep his mind from what lay ahead. Such thoughts were for women like Gunnhild, not him.

Fresh noise behind drew his head round, and he saw armoured horsemen cresting the dunes and riding down toward the river. Surely they were even more daunted than he had been? Halfdan was perhaps a third of the way across, the worst still to come, but it would be worse for anyone who followed, for the tide was coming in all the time.

Ahead of him, William and Ancel were forging through the waves, and he had to hand it to the young duke. The lad was truly fearless, for the pair were so deep that only the tops of their saddles and their horses' heads and necks remained above the surface. Surely they would drop further, and that would mean drowning?

Neel de Cotentin appeared behind them, haranguing his men, demanding the duke's head, urging them on, into the water. Despite the lord's power in this land, his men were less than ready to plough into the rising waters in pursuit. Finally, with some threats and more promises, he managed to get three men into the water, and the trio of knights pressed on, incredibly bravely, moving as fast as their horses could manage in the awful conditions.

Not far from Halfdan, a rider hauled on his reins. The jarl turned to the man.

'What?'

'I go no further, my jarl,' the man smiled sadly. He was one of Thurstan's, a former Hauteville warrior from Apulia. 'My horse hates the water, but my sword thirsts for blood.'

And with that, he was turning and wading back the way they came.

'That way lies death,' Halfdan called after him.

'Then I will meet God with pride, as one of your Wolves.'

'May Odin take you for his hall,' the jarl bellowed back, raising an odd smile from the man.

Halfdan ploughed on into the water. His panic was slightly abated when he looked up and realised that Ancel and William were slowly emerging from the surface, rising as they moved. They had crossed the worst and were almost safe. He looked back. The rider, whose name he didn't even know, had reached the rear of the column and was waiting for the three Cotentin men. Though it was difficult, Halfdan kept his mount moving forward with the others, making for shallower water and safety, yet kept his gaze on their rearguard. It was with no small regret, as he watched the Apulian fight for his life, that he wished he had learned the man's name, to honour him for what he'd done.

He'd ask Thurstan when he could, and raise a rune stone to the brave man.

The Apulian saw one of his opponents dead and beneath the surface of the rising waters, and another injured and pulling back to safety, before he finally fell, a heavy sword blow smashing his chest and crushing his organs, sending him lolling in the saddle until he fell beneath the waves.

The remaining rebel rider looked out at them across the now deep and wide water, and made no move to follow. The noble and his men were pulling back from the dunes and riding south, racing for the nearest bridge.

They had done it. At a cost, but they had done it.

Chapter 11

'What now?' Halfdan asked of the duke, as their horses clambered up over the grassy dunes and away from the river. Of the enemy riders on the far bank there was no sign, they having moved off south, seeking the bridge to cross the ever-deepening water. The sun was just casting a first ray of light between the trees on the horizon; there were no hills in this flat land to block its glow.

'We have left the lands of Cotentin,' William answered wearily, scrubbing his short hair with one hand, 'but the vast majority of the lands between here and safety belong to Bessin, so we are far from safe. Moreover, Bayeux, the heart of Bessin territory, lies almost directly in the path to my home at Falaise. There are a few lesser lords upon whom we can rely, though, so it is my intention to make for one and enlist his aid. Without friends, we will not get far.'

'We've done all right so far,' Ketil argued, drawing a look of strained patience from the duke.

'That is because our enemies were focused upon Valognes, with only small outposts elsewhere. Mostly, we were moving away ahead of them, keeping our foes behind us. Now, though, those same forces will continue to pursue us. With our crossing here, we have bought an hour's grace, perhaps two, but be sure Cotentin will continue to hunt me down. Now it has begun, he cannot let me go, and you are now seen as my people. There are men I can enlist against the rebels, and the King of France continues to play a game of advantage, so I may even be able to bring him in with appropriate promises, but that all relies upon me surviving to get home. The rebels cannot afford to let me reach safety in Falaise.'

He sighed. 'But now there are also enemies ahead of us and all around, in addition to those following us. Bessin will have taken only a small force to add to Cotentin's at Valognes, so most of his men will still be on this side of the river in his lands, and he has a much stronger force than Neel. They will be everywhere.'

Ketil, argued down, simply glowered as the duke went on.

'So, we make, I think, for Rigia, where Hubert will aid us. Along with my uncle Walter, Hubert spent much of my youth looking after me, playing more the role of father than did my actual father. I know beyond question where his loyalties lie. Rigia is perhaps twenty miles from here, to the north-east of Bayeux, so we will have to approach carefully. But Hubert will see us onwards safely.'

'That's still twenty miles through enemy territory, and with hunters chasing us down,' Halfdan pointed out.

'Then we had best get moving.'

With that, William moved out with Ancel, leading the way. Halfdan watched the whole group fall into step and realised with a sinking feeling that they were not going to be moving fast. They had been riding these beasts for hours, alternately cantering and trotting to save their strength as much as possible, but there had been no real break for them, and the river crossing had used much of what energy they still had. Every horse was tired, some worse than others, and they were going to move at a steady pace at best, with periodic pauses. Conversely, he surmised, the enemy ahead were perfectly well rested and the enemy following them were in friendly lands and could probably arrange to change mounts regularly. He had the distinct feeling that the worst still lay ahead.

The party trudged on, all eyes scouring the landscape for trouble.

As they rode, Halfdan found himself alongside Gunnhild, and sat silent for a moment, wondering how to frame the question that was nagging at him. In the end, he decided that straight was the only way to play it.

'Gunnhild, the duke does not know Harðráði.'

The völva simply shrugged, and Halfdan chewed his lip for a moment, wondering how to repeat the question without simply annoying her. Gunnhild could be prickly when she was annoyed.

'We are endangering a lot of our people for a boy we have no connection with. And if he does not know—'

'If he does not know Harðráði, then he *will*.'

Halfdan sighed. That was just vague, and did little to answer his worries. He risked that prickliness a little more. Her attention was elsewhere and he reached across and tugged on her sleeve, drawing her gaze.

'Gunnhild, there must be *other* ways to find Harðráði. The man is hardly subtle. If he's been within five hundred miles, there will be wailing former virgins, missing gold and angry princes. We could drop the duke with his friend at this Rigia place, where he reckons he will be safe, and then circle wide to the south and head back to Pirou. I don't like leaving Ulfr and the gold, and my trust in Serlo has been shaken at best.'

'Do not tie all your hopes to one mast, jarl Halfdan,' she said in flat tones. 'There is more to this yet. We are the wolves walking with the lion now, but there is a dragon to come, and I see you in a ship yet. This is far from over. No matter your fears, our path lies with the duke.'

'You've seen more?'

'From time to time. I will try to commune further with Freyja when we have the leisure. But now is not the time to discuss it. We have more pressing matters.'

'There is something else,' he added uncomfortably. She simply arched one eyebrow, and he steadied himself. 'You saw Loki unbound.' She nodded. He took a breath. 'I had a dream. I faced Heimdallr. You know what that means.'

She gave him a look that suggested he might be an idiot. 'Do you profess to walk with gods now, Halfdan? Not content with being our jarl, you must try to be völva?'

He felt irritation touching his fears, then dulling their edges. 'I cannot help it if the gods wish me to see something.'

She softened. 'Halfdan, everything in the sight of gods is too great and too vague for the ken of man. This is why völva are trained so. All things we see must be interpreted, and few things are as they seem on the surface. Loki unbound could be many years from now, or I could be seeing something that needs to be interpreted a different way. Your dream may have been a warning, or a truth, but even if you met the great watchman, do you truly claim to *be* Loki, and if so, where have you been bound?'

He frowned. He could think of plenty of places he'd been imprisoned or bound, but for everything there would have to be a level of interpretation, which then opened up the fact that the rest of it needed interpretation, too. Suddenly, he felt a vague headache coming on. He sighed. 'You are sure?'

'I am. As we come closer to events, my visions always come clearer. When we stop for an hour somewhere, I will sing the song and walk the way for you.'

He nodded. He could ask no more. And while he was no more certain of anything than he had been before, he felt somehow comforted. Gunnhild's certainty had that effect. He was so pleased that those days of her vagueness after Miklagarðr were gone, and that she was once more herself. Or perhaps even more than that. His gaze took in Anna and Cassandra following close by, listening with interest.

He returned his attention to the way ahead. William gestured to him, and he rode a little ahead to join the two Normans.

'I am torn,' the duke said. 'We are in a similar position now to when we left Valognes. It is perhaps twenty miles to Rigia direct, but we pass dangerously close to Bayeux on such roads. By the coast it will be perhaps five miles further, but also further from the heartland of my enemies.'

Halfdan nodded. 'Settlements on the coast?'

'Fishing villages. Three of them, if memory serves.'

'Garrisons?'

'In fishing villages? Likely none. But there will be coastal patrols from time to time.'

'Then it is worth the extra five miles. We are moving slow, and staying further from your enemies makes sense.'

William nodded, and he and Ancel led them on.

The light gradually increased as they rode, and clouds began to roll slowly in from the sea to the north, leaden grey and promising a downpour. On most occasions, Halfdan would pray to Thor to hold such weather back when riding in the open in armour, but today, he urged it on. Torrential rain, dark clouds and inclemency could only help hide them from their enemies, after all.

They passed through the first village perhaps an hour after the river, a sleepy little place where the only movement at this time had been fishermen out by their boats, discussing the clouds and considering whether it would be safe to put to sea this morning. Halfdan had not been the only one bemoaning their speed, for he could hear the murmurs among all present at the plodding pace they maintained by necessity. They could, perhaps, push the exhausted animals to a little more speed, but then if they ran into trouble there would be nothing left to give.

They were just out of sight of that village when the rain began. It came of a sudden, an instant blatter of heavy drops falling in a sheet along the coast in that way that soaks a man within moments. The grey clouds continued to roll south across the land, with no relief in sight out to sea. Back in the village, undoubtedly the fishermen had abandoned their day and settled in with their wives.

For a while, they rode with cliffs dropping some hundred feet to the water, and, given the rain and the wind, stayed a healthy distance from the edge. They stopped for just a few minutes in the lee of an ancient, overgrown hedgerow, and there Halfdan shuffled the riders around, taking the better rested mounts from those who applied the least pressure, such as Leif and Cassandra, and swapping them for the strained horses of larger men like Bjorn and himself. It would buy them a little extra speed and edge.

Another hour, and another village, this one clustered around a slope that led down through a ravine in the cliffs to sea level. As they passed through the place, where the only sign of life was worried pale faces peering out between shutters, watching the armoured men passing through, Halfdan caught a sign of what looked like distant movement up ahead. Where the coast climbed once more to the clifftops, just for a moment in the wall of driving rain he thought he saw figures.

He blinked and wiped away the excess water from his eyes and peered again.

Nothing.

Then the rain shifted once more with the wind, and there they were: three figures on horseback.

Halfdan looked around. The best rested and fastest horses were those bearing him, Ancel and two of the Apulians. Bjorn had a fresh horse, too, of course, but his sheer bulk was already wearing out the new one. Four would have to be enough. He couldn't risk laming the others.

'Riders,' he shouted through the downpour, pointing.

They all squinted, and the figures appeared again, briefly. The Wolves and their guest had the advantage. They would be much harder to spot in this weather, within the cluster of houses, while the three riders were alone on the cliff. He glanced a question at William, and the duke nodded, the answer clear. The only men on horses here, and in these conditions, would be enemies. Halfdan pointed to the other three with the better rested mounts, and then gestured onwards.

'With me,' he cried, and began to ride a little faster.

They had to take the three men down, and fast. If any got away, they could carry tidings of the duke to somewhere more important, like Bayeux. The others joined the jarl, and Halfdan, content that the enemy would not be able to see them clearly in the village, kept at a steady pace until they reached the last houses, and then put heel to flank and rode hard.

With Ancel and the Apulians, he raced up the slope toward the clifftop. Such was the angle of climb that they lost sight of their prey for a while, but in a few more moments the ground began to level out, and the four riders spotted their three adversaries. The patrol had clearly not been expecting trouble, and looked miserable and bored. They were taken utterly by surprise, and it took them precious moments to realise what was happening. By the time the senior of the three was reining in and barking orders, Halfdan and his men were already closing in.

'*Odiiiiiin!*' the jarl bellowed, ripping his short sword from its sheath.

Behind him the others similarly drew their long blades, though with no cry to old gods. They fell upon the three-man unit with brutality and speed. Halfdan took the leader. The man was in a full hauberk of chain, sleeved and with divided skirt to the knees, a ventail pulled up to his nose that, with his simple conical helmet, left only his eyes visible. His shield was a bright painted teardrop. The lead man lacked sufficient time to fully prepare for Halfdan's attack and, as he tried to bring his big sword to bear, he threw his shield out in the perfect place to stop a swing from a heavy long sword. The mistake cost him dearly. Halfdan did not wield such a sword.

There being no clear striking point for Halfdan's short Alani blade, he instead struck the man pommel first as they met, the heavy hilt smashing into the man's face, a foot higher than the shield that had been protecting him from a straight swing. The Norman's head snapped back and, giving him no time to recover, as he passed by Halfdan reversed his weapon and slammed pommel first once more, this time into the man's back, over his spine. The pain must have been intense for the rider, for it numbed the jarl's hand.

By the time Halfdan had wheeled his horse and come round ready for a second strike, the Norman was lolling, not far from losing consciousness, both sword and shield drooping in weak grips. Aware that his blade was not going to find an easy way into the man's chain shirt, Halfdan simply hammered at the face once more with his sword pommel. This time he hit the man's nose guard, which further numbed his hand, bent the guard into the man's face with agonising results, and, irritatingly, dented the pommel rather noticeably.

The Norman was done for. Blood was gushing from his face, and he was losing consciousness fast. The jarl looked up. The others had taken down the two remaining riders, three to two giving them plenty of advantage. Under his direction, they tipped the dead or wounded riders from their horses. By the time the rest of the party caught up with them on the clifftop, the four men had thrown the bodies over the edge into the wall of water, and a few minutes saw another shuffling of horses, making use of three relatively fresh mounts.

The encounter over, and with only a few bloodstains in the grass to mark it, all of which would wash away in the rain, they moved on, heading east once more. The weather had clearly set in for the day, but it no longer bothered any of them. There is only so wet a person can get, and so they resigned themselves to discomfort in return for the tactical advantages it offered them.

Another hour or so, and the duke and his men finally gestured for them to leave the coast. As they headed south, inland and on the far side of dangerous Bayeux, the weather became easier. Though the rain came at the same pace, the further they rode from the exposed clifftops, the less the wind drove it sideways. The sense of relief, as William pointed ahead and announced that he had sighted Rigia, was felt all along the column of riders.

The place was not large. Little more than a village, Rigia sat amid flat green fields, a cluster of houses close to a small stone chapel to the nailed god. It was not to this small settlement, hiding away from the weather, that the duke led them, though. Perhaps a quarter mile further south, across another two rolling fields, sat the home of William's childhood guardian. As they closed, Halfdan nodded his approval of the place. It was not merely the grand dwelling of a jarl showing off his power, but also a working place, as was clear from the form. The house itself was of stone, as impressive as any Norman keep, if on a smaller scale, but it was connected to other structures, barns and farm buildings, all of expensive and hard-wearing stone, the whole thing forming a defensive perimeter, any gap between buildings closed with a strong wall. The only entrance was a single strong gate, which stood open, and lights blazed in windows, holding back the gloom of the storm.

Halfdan let the duke take the lead, for clear reasons, and followed close behind as William led the way through that gate and into the wide grassy court between the many buildings. The place was part farm, part smithy, part fortress, but very well made, and a similar impression of its owner struck Halfdan as the house's door opened and Hubert de Rigia emerged with two men at his back. He was unarmoured, dressed in simple if well-made clothes, and a cloak against the weather. He was clean-shaven and his hair was shaved up the back of the head like many Normans, suggesting that he, too, had adopted the fashion for the expediency of their conical helmets and chain hoods and veils.

He was broad and tall, a strong man, made for war, but his skin also bore that ruddy, leathery look that a man only gets from hard work in the open air, year after year. Hubert de Rigia was a man of the land, and even Halfdan, who had never set eyes upon the man before, and whose trust in strangers was hard-won, found himself feeling safe in the big landowner's company.

'By the grace of God, if it is not young William,' Hubert grinned, striding over toward the horses.

The duke slid from the saddle and moved forward. The pair threw themselves into an embrace, and the familiarity and love there would have been impossible to fake. Halfdan could see why William had chosen to come here, of all places.

'Hubert, I am in dire need.'

The big man laughed. 'You are *always* in dire need, William, and occasionally it is of a slap to bring you to your senses.' He sobered suddenly. 'I know. Bayeux. I am aware of the troop movements. I sought to get word to you, but you were way out west at Avranches. I had hoped you would stay there, safe. Where is your army? Surely this is not all that is left?'

The duke chuckled. 'These are but my personal guard and a few friends who have proved their worth in the worst of times. My army is safe at Falaise. Sadly, *I* am not. I could do with following their example.'

'It will not be easy,' Hubert sighed. 'This whole land is swamped with Bessin's men now, and he has declared an open opposition to you. No longer is there any hope of the barons widely accepting your inheritance. The dissenters will need to be brought under control with steel. Bessin has approached me on numerous occasions, attempting to sound me out for his cause. I am loyal to you, of course, but I am also no fool, so I play the undecided advocate as long as I can, to save my lands.' Hubert looked up. 'This rain is dreadful. Step inside. Your guests are welcome, too. Arthur,' he said to one of his men, 'the stables are full, but the lesser barn is clear. Have their horses quartered there.'

The man nodded and went among the others, gesturing for them to follow. Halfdan left them to it and stepped forward to join William and Ancel as they followed the lord back into his house.

He felt immense relief stepping into the dry, for the warmth of the house was soothing, every fireplace burning bright, all windows shuttered and walls hung with tapestries and drapes. The place was so well appointed that even the floors were made comfortable with woven mats, something he had not seen since the imperial capital. Hubert was a man of means, clearly.

'How may I reach home safely?' William asked, as he shook off the worst of the wet in the doorway and slapped across the floor toward the fire.

'The best I can offer is a distraction,' Hubert said. 'I do not have enough men to go to war. The way from here to Falaise is some thirty miles, but the further you get from Bayeux, the safer the journey will become. If I can draw your enemies away, it will open your path somewhat. More, I cannot do. I hope you understand.'

'Of course I do.'

At that moment, another door opened, and three young men, not more than a few years William's senior, entered at speed. One glance made it clear they were Hubert's boys, for they bore his looks and build, and their smile at seeing William was genuine. Halfdan's eyes narrowed, though, for he could sense something wrong. Indeed, the momentary grins as the three boys saw William quickly disappeared again as they turned to Hubert.

'Father. Riders. A quarter mile out, passing the church.'

The lord frowned. 'Colours?'

'No idea in this rain, Father, but there are too many to be good news.'

'Damn it all to Hell,' Hubert snapped. 'This is inconvenient timing.'

The duke shook his head. 'It is more than that. We are pursued by Neel de Cotentin and Ranulf de Bessin and their men. I fear they have anticipated my movements and come in search of us. I had them marked as persistent, but never as particularly bright.'

Hubert gave a dark laugh. 'God in Heaven, William, but how are you of such tender years? I see so much of your father in you.' He turned to his sons. 'Be quick. Arthur settles their mounts into the lesser barn. Make sure they are shut away and all is secure. Bring all our visitors in here, quickly, before the lords arrive.'

As the three boys went about their duties obediently, Hubert placed his hands on the duke's shoulders. 'I shall do everything I can to distract them and lead them away. You take all your men upstairs and stay quiet. Do not draw any attention. I put my sons at your disposal. They will help, guide and defend you, my young lord duke. Now go.'

As the visitors began to hurry inside, sodden, from the yard, a servant directed each upstairs, while another led William, Halfdan and the others to the upper floor. As they settled into various rooms, directed by the servant, Ancel gestured, telling everyone to stay away from the windows. Such orders did not apply to the commanders, of course, and so Halfdan joined William at an upstairs viewpoint, the shutters left just far enough apart to allow a restricted view of the yard.

'If our horses are discovered,' the young duke said, 'even Hubert will not be able to explain them away.'

Halfdan nodded. 'But the enemy should have no reason to search every barn, and the rain is hard enough to cover the noise of horses. Odin will provide.'

'And if he doesn't, I shall ask Christ.' William grinned.

Somewhere in another room, Halfdan heard Bjorn cursing, and quickly changed rooms to jab a warning finger at the big man and then put it to his lips. He returned to the window in time to see the enemy enter the courtyard. He recognised Neel de Cotentin, though there was no sign of Bessin. Likely the man had diverted to Bayeux to rouse his garrison. The lord had six heavy cavalry with him in the courtyard, but Halfdan could see scores more outside the gates. Enough to make any engagement more or less a foregone conclusion.

Hubert de Rigia appeared in view, striding through the rain toward them. Two of his men were at his back. The rebel lord looked around the courtyard, and once again Halfdan was immensely grateful for the weather. The rain hammering down deadened most sound, and this being a farm, the churned turf under their feet could easily be recent land work, the pooling water making it impossible to tell how old the hoof prints were.

Cotentin pointed at the stables and said something. Hubert shrugged, and one of his attendants went to open up and show the rebel's men. They seemed to be satisfied with what they had seen, and after a lengthy exchange, Arthur hurried over and came out with a saddled horse, which Hubert swiftly mounted, accepting a cloak from his man. Over the following tense minutes, a dozen of Hubert's men emerged from the house, all armoured, and each retrieved a horse from the stables. Then, in a moment of immense relief to the observers, the entire group – Hubert, Neel and every rider – cantered out through the arched gate and into the open countryside.

The two men in the upstairs room remained silent, almost breathless, until one of the lord's sons came bounding up the stairs and into the room.

'Father has led them away, laying a false trail. He claims you visited, and then continued east, bound for Hunefleth. He takes them along that road in pursuit, while we must escort you south for Falaise.'

William smiled. 'Hunefleth. A loyal vassal. Quite believable. Excellent.' He turned to Halfdan. 'One last push, and we shall be at my home.'

The jarl nodded, rubbing the bridge of his nose. One last push, and he'd be ready to sleep for a week.

Chapter 12

The rain did not let up until late afternoon, when the sun – had they been able to see such a thing through the grey – would have been sliding toward the horizon. The going had still been slow. Once Hubert had led the enemy far enough from Rigia to be well out of sight, his three sons had hurried around, preparing. The weariest of the horses were swapped with those that could be spared from the stables, a full day's rations were packed, and everyone was given a fresh cloak, though the value of such a thing on top of sodden clothing was questionable.

Even though Hubert had conceived such a helpful diversion, there were plenty of enemies to watch for in this land, and so their journey was a tedious one, following back roads known only to the boys, being locals, through hamlets that never saw a nobleman's colours except on tax day. Twice, even before noon, they spotted in the driving rain small groups of men that their three guides said were Bessin's soldiers, and each time they were led in a circuitous route around them.

'Why do we not kill them and save time?' Bjorn had grumbled on the first occasion.

The duke had rolled his eyes. 'This is Bessin heartland. A death here will draw too much attention. Kill one, and within the hour there might be a hundred on our trail. Better slow and careful.'

Halfdan couldn't agree more. The majority of the group were his men, and he was less inclined to risk losing a Wolf to a fight that could be avoided for the good of an outsider, even one as important as William.

They had paused in a small woodland to eat their lunch, the trees so compact that they kept the very worst of the rain away for the short pause. Then, once more, they'd set off on their journey. During the afternoon, they had to bypass three more such gatherings of Bessin's men, and Halfdan became increasingly suspicious that every house they passed kept eyes on them, and only waited until they were out of sight before running off, reporting their presence to someone of importance.

Yet as the light started to fade, and they were some way from their destination, still they had avoided all encounters, and no one had challenged them.

'We will not make Falaise tonight,' William announced wearily, as he looked up at the last few spots of rain falling from a sky that remained threatening.

'Even if we ride at night?' Leif asked.

'Riding at night is dangerous at the best of times, especially with enemies looking for you. No, we should find somewhere to hole up until dawn and then make the last press for home in the morning. We still have over ten miles to go. The important thing now is finding somewhere suitable.'

'There,' Gunnhild said in a commanding tone, turning and pointing off to their right.

The others peered into the gloomy grey. The landscape was almost perfectly flat, a uniform patchwork of stubbly, recently harvested wheat fields, with small farms here and there. They could see nothing that stood out.

'Where?' William asked, frowning.

'Can you not feel it? Does your devotion to the nailed White Christ so blind you to the real world?'

William looked faintly irritated, but no more blessed with understanding.

Halfdan looked off into the distance. He *could* feel something. Just faintly. He was pragmatic enough to admit that it might be simple suggestiveness, given his knowledge of the völva's power, but he was also willing to believe, regardless.

'Tell us.'

'I can feel the Seiðr from even this far, perhaps half a mile away. It is an old place, and the nailed god has yet to claim it. There, I have strength. There, we will be safe.'

William looked doubtful, still, but Halfdan reached out and grasped his arm. 'If she is that sure, then she is right. Believe me.'

With that, he gestured for the others to follow, and they moved off across the open fields, shunning the road and following the direct path laid by Gunnhild's pointing finger. After a quarter of a mile, he no longer harboured any doubt. Even he could feel it, and it was no simple suggestion of the völva's. Judging by the looks on the other faces, the Christians could feel it, too, though with less delight than Gunnhild, who wore a look as though she were coming home, and whose pace continued to pick up as they neared her destination.

They passed the first ruins, little more than low walls with a few broken columns – some sort of house, perhaps, once upon a time, laid out in ordered squares around a garden. There was a small, round building, and then larger walls, which were also broken. Halfdan, interested, diverted slightly to ride through the middle of the ruins. The place was made of rooms with tanks sunk into the ground, some rectangular, some half-moon-shaped, of various sizes, all either filled with stagnant, algae-filled water or growing weeds and grass.

He'd seen enough of the columns of the style that abounded in the area to know the place had been of the Romans, abandoned when they fell centuries ago, and never yet built over. The nailed god priests seemed eager to place their churches over old places of power, but some, perhaps, were just too powerful for them to be comfortable with.

He rejoined the others, and they moved on.

It had been a town; not a great city like lofty Acerenza or golden Miklagarðr, or white-walled Kutaisi, but a town of some means, and larger than the villages that seemed to have supplanted such places in the region. They moved past build-ings, some little more than low rubble and shattered stumps, others more intact, some even with portions of roof remaining. With each great echo of bygone glory, Halfdan found himself trying to guess what the places had been.

Then, as they came to the centre, he needed no one to tell him about the buildings they approached. The town centre was some form of open square, surrounded on all sides by ruined shells. Several of the buildings were temples. The Seiðr was almost visible, writing across the bricks and marble like the liquid fire of the Greeks. He glanced at Gunnhild. She was in her element. This was her place more than anything else, for she felt the power of old gods, not dampened by the ever-growing wool blanket of Christian thinking.

'What was the name of the ship that carried us safely from Miklagarðr?' Gunnhild said as she reined in at the centre of the square.

William frowned, no idea what she was talking about.

'*Tyche's Arrow*,' Halfdan replied, the feeling of awe growing as he looked about him.

'And Tyche was…?'

'A goddess of fortune,' Leif answered, 'of luck.'

Gunnhild stepped her horse forward to one of the square ruins overlooking the square.

'Tyche continues to guide us,' she said, dismounting.

She left the horse where it was and strode into the place. It was one of the few surviving buildings with a roof, and she disappeared into the dark. William threw a worried look at Halfdan.

'She knows what she's doing,' the jarl replied, slipping from his own saddle.

He followed her in, and William was close behind, others dismounting, someone taking charge of the animals.

'Here is where we stay,' Gunnhild said from the darkness.

Someone behind Halfdan struck sparks a dozen times, and then a glow began that slowly lit the room. The jarl had seen places like this in Miklagarðr; they were ancient temples. In that great city they had been converted to churches or other buildings, but retained their form, and there could be no doubt what this place had been. And at the far end, next to the suddenly very imposing figure of Gunnhild, was a statue of a woman, almost twice life-size. She was beautiful, of perfect marble, unstained by weather in this place and even retaining stains of her original paint. In one hand she held some sort of container of fruit and flowers, and by her foot stood a wheel.

'Tyche,' Gunnhild said.

Halfdan nodded.

'I will walk with Freyja,' she announced.

Cassandra and Anna arrived, crossing themselves as they passed the threshold, but doing so with confidence regardless. Others entered, though when some saw what was happening, they hurried back out. William did not. He approached Halfdan.

'What is Freyja?'

'You Normans have lost too much Northern ice from your soul,' Halfdan grinned. 'Freyja is the goddess. The gatherer of the slain, the boar mistress, the hunter and the heart of the world. If among the Aesir and the Vanir there is even one to match Odin, it is she.'

'You talk like an epic of old,' the duke laughed.

'And you talk too much. Settle.'

Halfdan dropped to one of the stone benches that ran along the sides of the temple, William doing so beside him, and watched. He had seen Gunnhild do this many times, and he knew what to expect, and yet every time he felt somehow that it was new, and private, and special. Also, it seemed that Anna and Cassandra had become part of her weaving, for they sat with her, one to each side, as she began. Their voices joined hers in a haunting harmony as the ancient melody that he could never remember the next day rose and fell, rose and fell, then rose, and rose and rose. He had not seen her use the powder that she kept safely hidden from Bjorn, but he could only assume she had. When she was stretched high, on the balls of her feet, arms swirling, staff whirling, finally she dropped the handful of beads and bones, and more than she had held hit the stone flags of the temple floor. She sat for a time, cross-legged, as the melody faded, and then opened her eyes and looked down.

'This place is powerful,' she said. 'And so is the duke, for all his youth.'

Halfdan and William both frowned, leaning forward.

'I sought only to know more of what awaited the Wolves, and for what it is that we stay here, but I also see the duke's thread, gold and powerful. Kings and emperors have rarely had a brighter weaving than this Duke of Nordmandi.'

A strange smile crept across William's face. Gunnhild seemed to sense it. She looked up.

'Do not feel so content, William of Nordmandi. Do not be complacent. Your future may be great and long, but it will not be easy, and every ounce of success must be earned with sweat and blood.' She looked at Halfdan. 'He and the man who stole your ship both have a destiny far from here. They have yet to meet, I think. But now, here, there is great danger for all of us. Men come with swords, but they will regret it. They are sheep, while we are wolves and lions, and if we hold true, we will take the night. Then, tomorrow, we will find refuge at the duke's home. Someone waits for us there, their thread binding to ours. Someone whose very presence is a sign to point us onwards. Someone through whom the Wolves will grow strong once more, as we were when we left Kiev, and even more so. Theirs is a white thread, pure and bright. I do not understand what that means, but it will become clear in time. The dragon still comes. That, too, is yet unclear.'

Halfdan nodded. Whatever it all meant, it sounded more positive than he'd expected.

'What of Ulfr and the gold?' he asked.

She turned an arched brow at him. 'I told you before not to worry about Ulfr. He has his own business. For now, we prepare. This night we will be tested, and if we are successful, we will win through to Falaise.'

For the next hour, as the light began to fade, they worked. From Gunnhild's words, it seemed the enemy was coming for them here, and the better prepared they were, the more chance they stood. Some of the Christians were a little sceptical, but the general danger of the region was enough to goad them into doing their part anyway.

They scattered across the town, exploring the ruins, and at the centre, as they met time and again, they drew a map in the dirt. The horses were all quartered together in buildings off the square, blockaded in with scrub and branches. Then men worked with axes, cutting timbers, pulling long nettles and stripping them of their leaves, or peeling ivy from the trunks of trees, both to knot together as makeshift cords. By the time the darkness truly closed in, they had a fire burning in one of the roofless temples and were cooking the food Hubert's household had packed them off with. Pickets watched at the edge of town on the four main roads that led in, and they were changed hourly so that everyone could rest a little.

As they sat or lay in repose around the temples, William, propped up on one elbow, sighed. 'It seems a decade or more since I slept.'

'Then go to sleep,' Ketil grunted, wrapped in his cloak close by.

'It has been almost two days,' William added, 'and there looks little chance of making it up tonight.'

'Not next to you, anyway,' the Icelander complained.

Halfdan smiled. 'When we first came across the dark sea from Hedeby to the Rus lands, seeking the man who killed my father, I was so plagued with the need for revenge and yet so thrilled with the feel of the whale road, that I hardly slept the whole voyage.'

'I know,' said Ketil. 'In those days you yapped as much as he does.'

Bjorn rolled over in his cloak. 'I fell asleep on a waterfall, once.'

Ketil grunted, and Halfdan, despite knowing Bjorn's tales, found himself intrigued. It sounded more plausible than most of his fabrications, and the phrasing was odd.

'*On* a waterfall?'

'Yes. Back home, when I was young, before I was the Bear-torn and I knew which end of a woman to do what with, I had been climbing a mountain with two friends. We had heard that a dragon had stored its treasure there. Looking back, I think the elders were telling tales of Fafnir and we misheard and misunderstood. Obviously we never found dragon or treasure, so we decided to climb back down, but it was getting late, and climbing mountains is tiring. We found a pool, where a short waterfall fell from above to fill it, and from it, a huge waterfall fell to the green lands below. We drank the cold water, and we used rocks to part-dam the in-flow, so that there was space nearby to sleep. We slept.'

'That's not on a waterfall,' Halfdan said.

'*While* we slept,' Bjorn went on, 'the rocks we had piled started to move and come free, and the flow opened up again. Bjarni and Floki were fine, for they were a little higher than me, but the water picked me up and carried me, and I was so tired, I didn't wake. It carried me right to the edge of the great fall down the mountain, and there I was, lodged against a rock and kept stable.'

Halfdan found himself rapt. Bjorn's tales were *never* believable.

'And?'

'And just as the light came up, I woke, before the others, and opened my eyes, and I was looking down a thousand-foot drop.'

'And?'

'And I fell,' Bjorn grinned. 'It's how I got this dent in my shin.'

Halfdan rolled his eyes. It had been too good to be true. 'Go to sleep, unless you want a matching one on the other leg.'

But despite his urging and the tiredness of a two-day escape, few drifted off easily. The knowledge that they were only ten miles or so from safety, but that it seemed inescapable that they would be attacked during the night, preyed on every mind.

Halfdan was still awake when it happened.

One of the Apulians, who'd been on watch at the northern edge, came running into the centre, and every shoulder was shaken, men woken with quiet words of warning.

'Where?' Halfdan murmured, rising and reaching for his chain shirt.

'Half a mile out, across the fields. Maybe fifty of them, and coming slow, careful.'

Halfdan frowned. That meant the approaching enemy knew their prey was here, otherwise they would be moving speedily, trying to get somewhere for warmth and comfort. And if they knew the Wolves were here, then that meant that Halfdan had not been mistaken in his fear that every set of eyes in every window they'd passed had watched for them, and then hurried to report in.

Somehow, Gunnhild seemed to be up and prepared without anyone ever seeming to have approached her. The last time he'd looked, she'd been rolled in a cloak, chest rising and falling rhythmically, yet she was up and moving, hand waving, emphasising her words as she laid out strategies and directed people.

'From the north,' he shouted across to her. She nodded to him, though he wasn't sure whether that was 'thanks for the information' or just a slightly irritable confirmation that she knew that already.

'Positions,' he told them. 'Hold the north and concentrate there. Two-man pickets on all other approaches.'

As he belted his sword on over the chain shirt and rolled his shoulders, stretching out muscles tight from the lengthy repose even without sleep, he ran the numbers through his head once more. Fifty of them, the picket had said. Duke William and the Wolves numbered nineteen in all, with Hubert's sons. That was still more than two to one, which was the golden number that no sensible general went above if he held out any hope for success. But Gunnhild was confident. And she had said they would come, here, tonight.

He hurried through the town as men dashed around, finding the places that had been assigned using the map in the square's dirt that evening. They'd been well prepared, with four different plans, depending upon the direction from which the enemy approached. The north, in Halfdan's opinion, was their strongest, which was good.

'If that Neel de Cockpinch goatfucker is with them,' Bjorn said as he joined his jarl, 'he's mine.'

'There are plenty to go round, Bjorn. Just find them and kill them. You're on goading and killing, with the other three of us. We leave all the clever stuff to the others.'

It was really quite masterful. These Normans seemed almost as desperate to fight as good warriors of the old North, and so they shouldn't have been too hard to push into combat. The four men Halfdan had assigned as bait were exactly the four men to drive the enemy into a blind attack: Bjorn and Ketil, both of whom excelled at being provocative; Halfdan, for he was known to be a leader; and William, for one look at the duke would undoubtedly have them champing at the bit.

As the enemy approached the northern edge of town, where two men sat amid ruined buildings flanking the road, watching, Halfdan smiled. There lay the first line of defence, and, as long as it all held and worked, it should be excellent.

He could just see the enemy, approaching in the darkness, moving at a walk, their horses careful, slow, the riders scouring the ruins, sword in one hand, shield in the other. They were being far too careful. They needed a push.

'Ready?' he called to the men ahead.

Both of those he could see held up a hand, acknowledging that they were. He turned to the others. Bjorn and Ketil were looking hungry, excited, and – of course – unpleasant and brutal. William was stoic, his face unreadable. No fear in evidence, though, which was both a surprise and a relief to Halfdan.

'Let's get to it.'

The four of them stepped into the centre of the street, facing the approaching riders, and Bjorn and Ketil, flanking the two nobles, each retrieved a burning torch from the doorways at the street sides. The blazing torches were lifted, allowing their golden light to illuminate the four men. William wore his mail hauberk, of course, but over it he had his red tabard with the two gold lions on show, making him rather hard to miss, even in the dark.

'Come on, fuckers,' Bjorn called loudly through a grin. 'The *Bear-torn* is waiting!'

The shout, along with their clear presence and identity, did exactly what they'd hoped. The riders, little more than thirty yards from the edge of town already, started to call to one another and point ahead. An order was shouted, and in moments the enemy were kicking horses and slapping reins, pushing their horses into a speedy attack.

The riders, goaded into foolishness, raced into the edge of the town past those buildings, and as the first half a dozen passed, the trap was sprung. The men in the ruined buildings pulled on the ropes they'd spent a solid hour weaving from ivy and nettles, all bound together almost to the thickness of a wrist. The rope rose to between four and five feet from the ground, and the rest of the horses ploughed into it. For a moment, Halfdan thought the cord would not hold, for he'd been sceptical about the strength of the plants from the start, despite Gunnhild's insistence. The weight of even one horse was a lot of strain, even for a thick rope, after all.

Yet it held. The men who'd yanked it taut had immediately pulled it round beams to either side of the street and wound it there to hold it. The first horse struck the rope and skittered to a sudden halt, the next ploughing into his flank, the whole advance snarling up in the gap between the two buildings. Halfdan had only enough time to see that much before he had to move to deal with his own problem, but he knew exactly what would happen. The rope would break soon enough, but it had held long enough to stop the charge and unhorsed several men.

While the two rope-men fled their position, out of danger, others would appear above, having climbed onto the ruined walls to gain height. Each man carried a sling around his shoulder made from a cloak, containing half a dozen heavy cobbles taken from the ruins of the buildings. These would be liberally thrown among the snarled-up collection of men and horses. Where they struck humans, they would break bones and put men out of the fight. Where they struck horses, they would do less direct damage, but they *would* panic the animals into rearing and turning, where they would inevitably cause further casualties.

It would be carnage.

Still, they would fare better than the six poor bastards who'd made it through and were cut off. Those riders issued triumphant cries as they sped up, bearing down on their prey.

Halfdan and the others bolted, racing down the side street next to them as planned. Barely had they turned out of sight, though, when they stopped and scattered, two to each side of the street. The Normans turned the corner in their wake at a charge, hungry for victory. They stood no chance.

Two of the horses ploughed into the sharpened stakes that had been set at an angle into holes in the ground every couple of feet across the road. A third only just stopped short, rearing and throwing its rider. The other three did well to pull up short of the trap, but it did not save them. Instead, as they whirled in panic at the realisation of the trouble they were in, Thurstan and his men struck, emerging from doors at a run, swords and axes already out. They were not aiming for the men, though. The Wolves were outnumbered, so this was about bringing down the odds as fast as possible. They broke the legs and slit the bellies of the enemy horses and then leapt back out of the way as the thrashing, leaping and rolling began. Meanwhile, Halfdan and the others stepped forward to the three who'd been caught by the trap. One man was entirely hearty and recovering his shock, his horse impaled on a spike and shuddering wildly as the rider tried to extricate himself from saddle and stirrups in the chaos. His shield had gone during the disaster, fallen somewhere, and, though he still held his sword, he could not bring it to bear usefully in his current predicament. Halfdan watched as the young duke walked over to the man, head tilted slightly as though trying to understand something, and then calmly reached up with that small knife of his and expertly slashed the man's inner thigh under the hem of his chain shirt, stepping back quickly as the rider desperately tried to bring his sword around. Blood sheeted from the wound immediately, a constant torrent down the leg.

Once again, Halfdan found himself re-evaluating the duke. He was clever and brave, but he was also efficient and utterly ruthless.

The man died swiftly in the saddle, the strength sapping from him as he struggled, leg soaked through with his own blood.

Halfdan went to deal with the others, but found Bjorn and Ketil arguing over who got to kill the last survivor. The wounded rebel was staring wide-eyed and making pleading sounds even as the two big Northerners came to an agreement and struck him at the same time, one to each shoulder, almost beheading him.

The four of them melted away into the buildings just in time. The blockage at the rope had been cleared and a fresh wave of riders entered the streets, looking right to the sharpened stakes and the carnage there, and then moving on. Halfdan found his chosen position quickly: a nice little viewpoint where a flight of ancient stairs led only to open air but granted an excellent view of the ruins.

Even as he climbed, he heard the rumble of the next trap. It had taken only two men to push the unstable wall, which had been close to collapse. As the riders passed by, the wall fell on them, twelve feet of bricks and stone. Fresh ruination. Other screams across the town announced other traps being sprung. From his viewpoint, the jarl could spot odd little encounters, and when he turned to look north, he could see that there were no more than a dozen riders outside the town, including a nobleman who might well be Neel de Cotentin. The lord waited for some time as the crashes and rumbles and cries of panic issued across the ruins, and finally threw an arm out, at which his man produced some sort of horn and blew a short, desperate cadence.

At the sound, all across the ruins the rebel knights disengaged from their struggles and tried to depart with varying degrees of success. Many managed to put their heels to their mounts and race away. Others were less lucky, either unable to break free or already dismounted and finding themselves cut off and trapped.

It made Halfdan smile to see fourteen riders emerge sporadically from the ruins and converge on their master. Cotentin had lost half his force in the space of half an hour, and clearly had no intention of losing any more. Out in the darkness, the Norman lord retreated with his survivors, disappearing into the night.

Despite Gunnhild's insistence that there would be no further attack that night, as he returned to street level, Halfdan called out instructions to every figure he passed, ordering that the dead be stripped of anything of use or value and then moved out of the way, clearing the streets, any traps that could be reset having that done, in preparation, and all men back to their positions. He then returned to the square at the centre, where Gunnhild was in deep conversation with her women.

They started to settle once more, watchmen in place making sure Cotentin's men did not return unexpectedly. A headcount was taken, and it transpired that they had lost two Wolves: one a Hauteville man they'd picked up in Melfi, the other one of Maniakes's Varangians. A third man was nursing a wound, but both he and Gunnhild were confident that it would heal in good time. Two men was a high price for the Wolves to pay, but to fell two dozen enemies, it was an acceptable one, and no one complained over the death toll.

The rest of the night passed in peace, and the morning dawned damp but bright. The Wolves and their Ducal guest prepared themselves and emerged from the ruined town with a sense of hope. Falaise, and with it William's army and safety, lay little more than ten miles away, and there seemed no doubt that they would reach the place before noon. Gunnhild was sure their immediate troubles were behind them, Cotentin had scuttled back north with his tail between his legs, and William was content that they were in safe lands from here on.

The revolt had begun, but at least the duke and the Wolves would be safe... for now.

Part Three

ᚠᛟᛚᚠᛗᛋ ᛟᚠ ᚨᚾᛁᛏ

The Whale Road

He is truly wise who has travelled far
and knows the ways of the world.
He who has travelled can tell what spirit
governs the men he meets.

On Experience from the *Hávamál*

Chapter 13

'Are you sure the jarl's not going to be angry?'

Ulfr looked up from the latest consignment and frowned. 'What?'

'This is eating into the gold quite a bit. I swear we could fit it in one less wagon now.'

Farlof looked worried, and the shipwright tried to throw him a look of support and confidence to reassure him. 'We have Halfdan's full authority to spend whatever we need to in order to make this ship happen.'

'I just don't know whether he anticipated quite how much that would be.'

'It will be fine,' Ulfr said, catching sight over the other man's shoulder of a commotion at the edge of the beach. 'Just go and direct that wagoner.'

As the Varangian wandered off, thumbs tucked into his belt purposefully but still with a worried expression, Ulfr straightened and looked about himself. The beach had become a makeshift shipyard in less than three days. All it lacked was a half-constructed hull in the middle, where a conspicuously ship-sized tract of empty sand awaited. He already had most of the materials in place, though, which pleased him almost as much as it surprised him. In one small way it annoyed him, too, but he had to try and push that down and ignore it.

In a *perfect* world he would have begun by walking through the forests and woodlands, feeling the bark beneath his finger-tips, studying the arc of branches high up, selecting the trees for his work, using that innate skill of the lifelong craftsman to know, without needing to check, which trees were not perfectly suited. Of course, there was no time for such craft here. Two months, he'd assured Halfdan. This was a matter of speed, and so he was restricted to using materials that others had chosen and pre-cut, but there were at least two small reliefs there to counterbalance the irritation. Firstly, because his funds were more or less unlimited, he was able to select absolutely the best of everything on offer, and secondly, it seemed that these Normans had shipwrights who remembered the old ways and still had the grain of the oak in their very soul, so while he would have despaired of timbers purchased from a Byzantine shipbuilder, these ones were not so far from what he would have chosen himself. It was not perfect, but it was as close as a man could hope, and almost like being at home. And what he lacked in time and flexibility with his work, he more than made up for by having anything he needed to hand in an instant.

And so the beach was covered with stacks of timber in neat piles by size and shape and wood – oak and pine for the most part, mostly delivered from the shipyard at Fulquerville and, through a useful contact there, also fresh from the lumber yards of Coutances. If there was something he wanted that they could not provide from Fulquerville, he had only to send a description to Coutances, and the next day he would have either it, or the closest they could come to it. He had been through every single delivery, one piece at a time, with his expert eye. Seven timbers only had he sent back as substandard, or with barely noticeable faults, in each case even having slipped past the notice of men who should have been able to spot such things. But the vast majority were good, and he could almost see the ship taking shape in his mind's eye.

There was more than just timber, though, among the supplies stored around the beach worksite. Sacks of bast fibres from the trees sat in huge piles under waterproof canvas, waiting to be formed into good, strong ropes. Sacks of sheep's wool and barrels of heavy pine tar sat ready to be formed into caulking –

nearby, an experienced shipyard worker was delivering a lecture on caulk properties to a dozen new hires. A dizzying array of brand new tools was stored in a small, hastily assembled shed, enough tools to keep sixty men working at once. He had yet to source a sail, and to make one would add many precious days, but he yet had hopes he could track one down, and the oars might take some work, but they could wait a while yet.

'She's a thing of beauty,' he smiled, closing his eyes and picturing the finished work on a cradle in the middle of the yard, sixty workers cheering as they prepared to launch her. She would be slightly different from the *Sea Wolf*. She would be a little heavier and bulkier, with a few more oars. She would not be a dart, but she would be a sword, cutting the waves and heavy and powerful when it struck. Not a wolf. A... bear? No, that didn't feel right.

'What is?' murmured one of the workers, as he busily numbered timbers with a charred stick.

'Can you not see her?' Ulfr smiled, eyes still closed, hands running along the imaginary lines.

'You Northerners are mad,' the man grunted and walked off.

Ulfr just laughed again. Some people lacked imagination, which was fine, but which was also why they would never make a shipwright. Sixty men launching the... stag? No.

Sixty men he had, and more besides. The shipwright at Fulquerville had been argumentative, not graciously willing to lend out his men to a single job for the space of a couple of months, despite the work at his own yard having partially dried up for the season thanks to the threat of war. The exchange of a number of handfuls of Byzantine coins had soon changed his tune, and now that harbour ran on a skeleton crew while the bulk of the workers and even the master shipwright himself worked with Ulfr on the new ship. Along with the remaining Wolves to serve as unskilled manual labour, and a number of local craftsmen in Pirou who had signed on for good pay, including the village carpenter and blacksmith, Ulfr reckoned he would have more than a hundred souls working on the beach at any one time. It actually looked possible that he could have a new ship ready within two months.

As if reading his mind, Farlof, returning from storing the next load of timber, huffed in the cold air.

'Can it be done?'

'It can,' Ulfr replied. 'And it will.'

'Have you a plan?'

The shipwright frowned. Who needed a *plan*? If you knew how to build a ship, you knew how to build a ship. This one was the one he'd sketched on a wagon side before they'd ever reached the coast.

'No,' he answered. 'Why?'

'Because I know that *you* can see it all in your head, Ulfr, but it will save you endless troubles if *everyone else* can see it, too, if they have some idea of the schedule. Otherwise, there will be misunderstandings and delays. I worked for an armourer who hired unskilled labour. You have no idea how troublesome your workers are going to be.'

Ulfr's frown remained, but he could see the man's point. Back in Sigtun, his workers had been familiar with the long-ships of their forefathers, and had been able to work almost on instinct. Things might be quite different here.

'All right,' he said. 'Here's what we do. We begin by assembling the keel in the sand. Once we have that, we construct the cradle and then position the keel in it. Then we build up from there at bow and stern until the full keel's complete, short of figureheads. Next, we begin the strakes from keel upwards, caulking as we go, gradually building up and out, completing the shell of the ship. Before we get as far as the sheer strakes, though, we start to reinforce from the inside with the ribs and then the crossbeams. *Then* we finish the sides. Once that's done it's the body of the ship complete. Then comes the mast, and after that all the various fiddly bits, before we can start on rigging, sails and oars.'

'You make it sound so fast.' Farlof grinned.

'It won't be. I want each stage completed with absolute precision, and I will be checking every last plank and peg four or five times until I'm satisfied. It matters not whether it's a hundred-oar warship or a twenty-oar courier, no ship of mine will ever kiss the waves if I am not content that the job could have been done no better.'

'Will you decorate it in the old style? I have heard the tales of what your *Sea Wolf* looked like. Your friends say it was art, not just a ship.'

Ulfr was surprised by the question. He'd been thinking about that on and off himself, but it hadn't occurred to him that anyone else cared.

'Not for now,' he admitted. 'Eventually, when we have time, I'll look further. If we spend some time beached, perhaps, but for now it is too important to get the ship finished and launched to spend extra time on details. Sad, but there you go.'

'I'll have your plan relayed to everyone, if I can remember it all.' Farlof grinned again. 'When do we begin?'

'Today. This afternoon, in fact, my friend. I have to head back to the wagons now and release another payment to our people at Coutances, but when I return, I intend to begin laying down the keel. I want the basic structure ready by night-fall today, timbers selected and in place. Tomorrow we will construct the frame to hold our ship during construction and go through the selection process on the timber piles, deciding what to use for our first strakes. If we have enough men on site, I want the caulk manufacturing to begin, too. Better to get ahead on that one as soon as we can. For now, while I head to Pirou, I need you to go through the oak piles, and use chalk. Mark the ten longest and heaviest pieces and then try and lay them out separate on the sand so I can have a look at them when I get back. We'll compare them then and make our selections for the keel.'

Farlof nodded and then stood and looked around, taking in the activity all across the beach. Men of the Wolves, both those who'd been with them since Taranto and those who'd joined them following the journey, stood with a proprietorial look, keeping watch. There was, after all, considerable financial investment in this work, for the funds used to supply all these goods were taken from a treasury that affected each one of them, though it did also give them a financial interest in the ship. They were watchful, which was good, but soon enough the number of watchmen would diminish, for they would be required for work parties.

Ulfr left Farlof to it, and crossed to where his horse stood munching on the lush grass just up from the sand's edge. He untethered it from the iron hoop driven into the ground and mounted. He was not the greatest lover of horse riding, but the journey between the beach and the castle was just a mile, and so it was hardly worth hooking up a wagon each time. Moreover, any cart that became available was habitually sent for more goods straight away, with rarely a vehicle free for more than an hour.

The first quarter mile was little more than coastal scrub land, an easy ride, but as he neared halfway, he was riding through good arable land and past fields with pens of sheep and pigs, then along a farm lane and past the farm itself. Rosy-cheeked Mariot was out feeding the chickens, and she waved happily at the shipwright as he passed. Ulfr gave her a friendly smile and waved back. She had good reason to be happy. With rumours of revolution and war coming, all suppliers of goods across the region were facing an uncertain time, and yet Ulfr had done a deal with Mariot and her husband for all their produce over the next two months, and had paid well, and in advance. In fact, he'd done the same deal with four other farms. Keeping a workforce well fed was a good way to keep them working hard. Indeed, the brewery at Givolli Fossa was now working hard to turn out enough beer to keep the workers happy, too, as was a local winery. He had a brief moment of worry that Farlof had been right, and that Halfdan would be horrified when he saw how much gold had vanished. But then, periodically, the Wolves were poor men anyway, but poor men *with* a ship stand a much better chance than rich men *without* one.

Leaving the farm behind, he could see the castle ahead, and made for the northern edge, the nearest one, where he would round the moat and close on the gatehouse. His eyes picked out something unexpected and he slowed, suddenly.

Two riders were approaching Pirou castle, and there was something about them that put him on the alert, though he couldn't quite put his finger on what it was. His free hand went to the head of the axe slung at his side and his fingers danced there, tense. He was no coward and no small man, but he was also suddenly acutely aware that he was alone and that something was wrong.

Still, he walked his horse on, focusing on the two riders. As he closed, he could see more detail. They were Normans, and warriors, both in knee-length chain hauberks, split-hemmed for riding. Neither had a helmet on, and both had that common Norman haircut with the back shaved and the front short and neat. Neither man carried a shield, but one had a tabard over his chain bearing some colours with which Ulfr was not familiar. Strangers, then.

His tension mounted as he came closer and the pair registered the presence of another horse. Both heads snapped his way, and their hands went to their sword hilts, hovering there. In a show of peace, Ulfr carefully removed his own hand from his axe and returned it to his reins. The other riders relaxed, if only slightly. As he neared, though, Ulfr spotted another warning sign. The rider in colours had damaged chain, and patches of dried blood here and there. The man with him may have reached for his sword, but he would probably not be able to swing it. His other arm was folded across his front, and there was more blood there. These men had been in a fight, many hours ago, maybe more than a day. From the look of them, it was clear they had lost.

And they were coming from the north…

Ulfr tried to do a quick calculation, but it was fruitless. It had been four days since Halfdan and the others had gone north with the duke for Valognes. *Anything* could have happened in that time. Yet something nagged at Ulfr, suggesting that if blood had been drawn anywhere within a day's ride of Bjorn, the big idiot was likely to have been involved in it. His suspicions were just too strong to ignore.

Before he could interact with the pair, though, they were approaching the castle's bridge, and men on the gatehouse were shouting out warnings for them to stay where they were and to identify themselves.

'My name is Geoffroi de Petronilla,' called the man in the coloured tabard, 'and this is my companion Brenier. We have ridden hard from Valognes with important news, and we seek an audience with the lord de Hauteville.'

There was some conversation at the gate, and Ulfr, having heard this, closed on the riders and pulled up close by, though not close enough to spook them.

'You've come from Valognes?' he murmured.

Geoffroi nodded.

'There was trouble?' he asked, perhaps a little redundantly.

The man frowned, clearly uncertain who this stocky rider was, but before he could ask, someone at the gate called for them to enter. The two wounded men rode through the gate, grunting with each movement of the horses that shook their injuries. Ulfr followed them in, being such a regular visitor passing in and out that no one bothered even mentioning him. The two strangers came to a halt inside, making no effort to dismount as yet. As Ulfr slowed and reined in not far away, Serlo de Hauteville emerged from the keep, his attendants at his heel. He hurried over, soldiers flocking round, the eyes of the people in the castle bailey darting his way with interest.

'What has happened?' Hauteville demanded.

Geoffroi rocked a little in his saddle. 'There is war, my lord. The baron de Cotentin has betrayed the duke, in collusion with milord de Bessin.'

'How fares the duke?' Serlo asked, and Ulfr frowned. There was a nervousness in Hauteville's voice that might not be entirely fear for his lord. Was there something more? The shipwright filed that away to think on further later.

'The duke escaped the clutches of his enemies,' Geoffroi said, sagging slightly. 'Most of his escort fell to a wicked betrayal in the castle, though a group of mercenaries secured the duke's flight and, from what I heard, managed to get him at least to the Vire and across before high tide. They were bound for Falaise and the duke's forces there, but whether they made it I cannot say.'

'And you?'

'We fought a rearguard in the keep at Valognes to allow the duke to escape. Two of us survived, left for dead when Cotentin took his men away in pursuit. We waited until the place was more or less empty and fled, stealing horses. We did not know where else to come. The rest of the peninsula is crawling with the duke's enemies.'

Hauteville chewed this over for a moment. 'Duke William will be damned lucky to reach Falaise. The path will take him directly through Bessin's lands. If you think *this* peninsula is crawling with the duke's enemies…'

Ulfr cleared his throat, and all turned to look at him in surprise. 'If those mercenaries you are talking about are the Wolves, then they will find a way to get him to safety. Be sure of that.'

'You know them?' Geoffroi said in surprise, turning to him.

'We *are* them,' Ulfr replied. 'Halfdan is my jarl. We are the Wolves.'

'*You* are *Ulfr*,' the wounded man said, a smile cracking his face for the first time. 'Your jarl worries about your safety. I see he worries for naught. He describes you well, though.'

Serlo de Hauteville was drumming his fingers on his crossed arms. 'I will send riders to Falaise to determine the situation. Both Bishop Herbert of Saint-Lô and the baron Robert de Clécy are solidly the duke's men, so as long as my riders stay far enough south to avoid Cotentin and Bessin lands, they should reach Falaise and can return with tidings for us. If the rebellion has truly begun, we would be foolish to even leave Pirou until we know more.'

He seemed to realise for the first time that his new visitors were injured, and straightened. 'I will have your wounds looked at. Please, come in, be my guests. I will have appropriate quarters made ready.'

Other men hurried over and started to help Geoffroi and his man down. Ulfr made a mental note to try and come back and speak to the man as soon as possible, at least once he had been made comfortable. Anything he could learn about Halfdan and the others could be important. One thing was already certain: Ulfr had heard of this Falaise place several times, and it was both far to the east and deep inland, which would make access by ship difficult should any kind of rescue be required.

Turning his back on the matter, he walked his horse across the wide bailey of Pirou, between small groups of people who had gathered to find out what the excitement was, and made for the large shed that was being used to house the Wolves' wagons. A flutter of concern rippled through him as he realised there was no one at the front of the building. The two great doors, each large enough to admit a covered wagon, were both solidly closed, at least, but it had been Ulfr's orders, as the Wolf left in charge by Halfdan, that there should be a man on watch at all times. That he was not there was... concerning, to say the least. The wagons did hold an immense amount of gold, after all. Closing on the place, he slipped from the saddle and left the animal to wander and graze, knowing that it could not go far. His hand fell to the axe by his side once more, but he did not pull it free. Not yet. He was ready to, though.

He checked the doors; they were closed and barred. That, at least, was a relief. There was a third door, though, a smaller one, for men, not wagons, and he rounded the corner. The large building was close to the palisade that ran around the castle edge, and there were but six or seven feet between the two, the shade they combined to create looming quite dark. His gaze fell first on the door, which was blessedly closed, and then upon the watchman.

The Apulian Wolf lay in front of the door, and for a moment all sorts of questions assailed Ulfr, for the man's trousers were around his knees, while the man lay face down in the dirt. Had he been taken from behind? For a moment, Ulfr wondered whether he was dead, but then noticed the ribs rising and falling slightly with each breath. Drunk, then, perhaps? That was the next most likely option, and if the man had been drunk on watch, Ulfr would have him beaten until he couldn't remember his own name. Then, as he leaned closer, sniffing, the truth became clear. He'd thought to smell beer or strong wine, but what he actually smelled was blood.

He found the matted patch of hair on the back of the head with ease, and then felt around the scalp. Sure enough, there was a lump the size of half an egg on the back of the man's head, from a blow that had broken the skin but fortunately not the skull beneath. Reaching down, he turned the man over gently, carefully.

The Apulian blinked, then again, and his eyes remained open the third time, though they spent some time completely defocused as he made odd, mumbled sounds.

'What happened?' Ulfr asked, though he was already pretty sure of the answer.

'Wen… fra piss,' the man said, wincing. He reached up to touch the back of his head, but Ulfr pushed away his hand.

'I wouldn't. Not yet. You came here, in the shadows, for a piss?'

The man nodded, and then clearly regretted it. Ulfr approved. There were assigned latrines in the castle, but the man had had the sense to simply slip around the corner into the shadows rather than abandon his post. Unfortunately, he had clearly chosen exactly the wrong moment.

'And someone hit you on the back of the head, in mid-flow?'

He helped the man up so that he could recover his clothing and pull it up into place, and as soon as he knew the man could stand without swaying, let go and crossed to the door. He hammered on it.

'Yes?' called the other guard, the one he kept *inside* the sheds.

'It's me, Ulfr.'

There was a pause and then the sound of the latch being lifted before the door swung inwards. Ulfr stepped inside, past the man, and looked about. The wagons were all as they should be, and the man looked confused.

'Any trouble?'

The man shook his head. 'No.'

'You're sure? You've heard nothing?'

The guard frowned, then scratched his head. 'Nothing of note. There was some scraping noises around here maybe an hour or more ago, but nothing else. And to be honest, chief, this place is old and creaky. It makes weird noises at the best of times.'

Ulfr nodded. 'That scraping, I reckon, was someone a little too interested in what it is we're keeping in here. Enough to whack your mate out there over the head, anyway. I'm starting to think the castle isn't a safe place to store the wagons any more.'

'But most of us are still quartered in the castle,' the man said.

'Not for long, I think,' Ulfr mused.

'Boss?'

'It sounds like this rebellion everyone has been expecting has started. I think it sounds like they tried to strike fast and bring the duke down in one night, but they missed, and it's turning into a war. Halfdan and the others are caught up in it with the duke, but I reckon they're safe out east for now. I don't think *this* is a safe area, though. Serlo seems all right, but he's in the minority out here, and when wars start, men tend to be less trustworthy around another man's loot. Things just go missing. I think we need to be protecting *ourselves* now, rather than relying on Hauteville. I think I'd feel safer on the open beach on our own than inside another man's walls.'

'You want us to sleep on the beach?'

Ulfr gave him a hard look. 'You won't melt, man. The weather's not even bad. Not yet, anyway. I think we bring all the Wolves at Pirou, and all our wagons, down to the beach, and all our temporary workforce, too. We'll camp there, in the construction site, with the wagons and the gold right under our noses. I'll get hold of some tent material this afternoon. That merchant from Coutances is coming again in an hour or so to collect his money. I'll put in an order with him. We might have to sleep under the stars tonight, but tomorrow we should have tents for everyone.'

'Can I stay on duty here?'

Ulfr snorted. 'A man who can't tell the difference between settling timbers and someone trying the door? I think I want you on the beach. Stay here until the others come to move the wagons, then we'll all head to the coast.'

Leaving the chagrined man, he walked out past the other guard, who was busy recovering, rubbing the back of his head. Past his grazing horse, he strode toward the keep. The Wolves were being quartered in a building close by, and he stopped there first, dipping into the door and spotting one of the few men still in the residence at this time.

'Gather your gear and pass the word. We're moving to a new location, camping at the beach. Get anyone else here and take them to the sheds. Have the wagons brought out and fitted, ready to go with us as soon as I join you.'

The man looked at him in surprise, but nodded hurriedly and shouted for his mate. Leaving them to it, Ulfr strode from the bunkhouse, across the grass and in through the doorway into the keep. There was no sign of Geoffroi or his man, the pair having presumably been moved to a room where they could recover and where a healer could look at them. It was not Geoffroi for whom he looked, though, and Ulfr found Serlo de Hauteville easily enough, in his great hall. The lord of Pirou appeared worried and tired, and looked up as Ulfr entered.

'Yes?'

'We have imposed upon your hospitality long enough,' the shipwright said, which made the man's eyes narrow suspiciously.

'You are leaving?'

'The castle, yes. We will continue to build our new ship. We cannot stop now, for we've already brought in all the parts and retained workers. I ask your indulgence that we continue to occupy your local beach until that is done, when we shall put to sea and be out of your hair entirely. In the meantime, we shall not be especially intrusive. It is but a wide stretch of sand, after all.'

Hauteville looked less than impressed with the idea, but apparently could find nothing about it to argue with. In the end he gave a curt nod. Within a few minutes, Ulfr was back down in the bailey, retrieving his grazing horses and watching as the few remaining Wolves who'd occupied Pirou castle brought the wagons out of the building, heavy kitbags on every shoulder as they guided horses into the traces. Soon enough they would be on the beach. Such an exposed location should feel considerably less safe, yet oddly, to Ulfr, it currently felt more so. As they began to make their way from the bailey, across to the gatehouse and the way back to the beach, Ulfr found himself worrying about Beatrix, and about the new arrivals, the wounded knight, Geoffroi, and his man.

He was leaving, but he would be back.

Chapter 14

Ulfr was up early, and he knew it; he was probably the first one awake. Silence lay like a blanket across the beach, broken only by the lap and hiss of waves, and the gentle aural tapestry of many people sleeping. He opened his eyes, half expecting to see sky, but, of course, they had tents, so all he saw was thick, off-white fabric. He rolled to the other side, and could see through the tent door out into the early morning. It was still dark. Very early, then.

On the other side of the tent, Farlof rasped quietly in his sleep. The tents were all makeshift, pulled together from canvas sheets and rough-hewn poles, the ones used by the workers shared by anywhere between five and a dozen men, even three to each tent for the Wolves, though by general consent, no one had expected Ulfr – as their leader – to share a tent. He'd offered Farlof, though.

The sound out there was faintly hypnotic, and he almost found himself drifting off again. But that would be a waste of such an early rise. Instead, he lay, comfortable and warm, the blankets insulating him, the sand beneath moulded to his shape, and let his mind drift back.

It had been a productive week. The ship was properly under way, and they should have everything they need on the beach to complete it, barring oars and sail, and he was content they could source those by the time they were ready. The local harbours had a sort of network of gossip, spread by local traders and fishermen, and he'd put out a call for what he needed. There were tantalising messages of a sail available somewhere in the north of the peninsula, and a local sailmaker who already had a backlog had given them the option that he would have a spare ready in roughly two months. That might be a little late for Ulfr, and so he kept searching, but it was a good fall-back to have. In the perfect world he'd have had the sail made on site, too, but the shipyard workers from Fulquerville were not trained in such things, for they always bought from local craftsmen, which explained the backlog – at least that and the fact that every ship of war in the region had been refitted over the past half year in anticipation of trouble.

The oars were another issue. There were actually sufficient oars of good quality at the local harbour, but they were already spoken for, and since the speaker was a captain of Hauteville's, Ulfr was not ready to try and argue that one yet. But there were rumours reaching him of others.

Certainly work was going at a satisfying pace, and if everything continued the way it was, they would hit their two-month target, and possibly even complete early.

Which might be a good thing; he had a distinct feeling that they had begun to outstay their welcome. Serlo de Hauteville remained polite and courteous, and still came through when Ulfr needed anything, but there was something in the man's manner that suggested he would pay money for the Wolves and their work to be gone from his land. Of course, Serlo was probably trying to prepare for the coming trouble, and that would be made more difficult by the fact that all the farms and craftsmen in his fief were busy working for Ulfr.

At least, as something of a relief, Hauteville's riders had returned two days earlier with word from Falaise. William and the Wolves had made it to the ducal fortress and safety in good time, and though there were rumours that the whole of Cotentin and Bessin lands, as well as mercenaries from Burgundy and a number of lesser lords, were mobilising to move against William, there was no need to worry yet. The duke had not been idle. He had sent out messengers to loyal lords, calling them to his banner, and had sent overtures and offers to the King of France, whose own army was gathered not too far from the border. War was coming, but for now, the messengers said that Halfdan was safe, and if Halfdan was safe, the others would be, too.

There was one odd thing there, though. The duke had sent plenty of information and instructions to Hauteville, yet the jarl had sent nothing to Ulfr, not even a 'hurry up with the ship'. It seemed odd for Halfdan not to have contacted him. Still, there was little Ulfr could do from here.

He had managed to speak to Geoffroi, at least.

He liked the quiet-spoken knight. The man was a little lost at the moment, for his original fief, a rather small one, had been in Cotentin's lands. The larger fief he had been granted by the duke during some incident the previous week was also of Cotentin's. Yet that lord had rebelled and shown himself a traitor to the duke, while Geoffroi remained loyal. He could hardly go home and rouse any man in either land, right under the nose of Cotentin, and so he remained a refugee in Serlo's house at Pirou. At least his wounds were healing, and he was about ready for the world again, though his companion would be some months before he could comfortably fight or ride a horse again. Still, for now, Geoffroi and his man were safe.

Beatrix was oddly silent. Ulfr had only secured permission to visit her once, and had expected her to be railing against her imprisonment, throwing things and shouting. Instead, she was quiet.

'My brother will not send me to Eu at the moment, not with the land in such turmoil,' she said. 'So I am saved the pillory of matrimony for a time.'

'Can he not send you by ship?' Ulfr had frowned. 'Or with sufficient escort around the south? He sent riders to Falaise that way.'

'Serlo is no sailor. He will not commit something as valuable as me to the sea, as he does not know what is happening further along the coast. And by horse? Falaise is but sixty miles distant. Eu is almost three times that, at the very eastern edge of our lands. No. I am too useful as a bargaining piece, so Serlo will hold on to me until he can use me without risking my loss.'

And that had been more or less that. He'd stayed with her for a time and listened to her woes, but in the end he had left and returned to his work.

Ulfr rolled over again. For some reason, moving had changed the lie of the sand beneath him, and something was uncomfortable, digging into him just under his left shoulder blade. With a sigh, knowing that he was done with sleep, he pulled away his blankets, folded them, and dropped them onto the locked chest of Byzantine coins that he was currently using to pay various bills. He stretched, changed tunics for his favourite mustard yellow one, and retrieved his belt. No armour, just clothes. Pulling on his boots, he spent a moment with his bone comb, raking it through his hair and then his beard before tying a bead into the bottom. Finally presentable, he took a quick look at Farlof, considering whether to wake him, but decided to let him sleep and, stretching once more, crossed the tent and emerged into the night.

It was true dark, without that first pre-dawn glow. The camp was completely still.

He looked about. His makeshift shipyard was perfectly organised; he had divided the camp into two sections. The local levy workers varied in habit, some sleeping in their own homes with their families within a few miles of the camp and coming to work at first light, others preferring to stay on site and live a life with late evening camaraderie. The latter occupied six tents to one side of the work area, bounded by piles of timber. The part-built ship lay between them and the Wolves.

Three tents occupied the Wolves' area on the other side of the ship: one for the two leaders; one for the three Apulians; and one for the three Varangians. Each night, two of those tents would each supply two shifts of watchmen, the third having a full uninterrupted night's sleep. In some ways it was not the best arrangement; mixing the two groups, Wolves and locals, would have made for more of a sense of community and equality in the work, and would improve both morale and work speed.

But the decision had been made for expediency and safety. They had a small fortune in gold to keep secure, and while Ulfr felt he could trust any man on this side of the yard, the local levies were not even aware of the vast treasure that lay so close by. The Wolves had carefully secured the gold from the wagons without being observed.

Ulfr stretched. No one else was up.

The fire from the previous night had died, and the only light was that strange silver shimmer that the sea seemed to offer up from its heart. The ship stood in the middle of the camp, the one thing that rose proud and immediately visible. The frame was solid and complete and sat sturdy in the sand, with the keel atop it. The work so far was excellent, and even Ulfr was satisfied. The timber was smooth and well worked, the joins barely visible, so neat were they. The bow and stern rose to challenge the night sky. The first strakes were in place, too, and soon the whole ship would start to properly take shape.

He spotted the figure of the man on watch up there, seated on the keel below the prow, the highest point in the camp with the best view, leaning back against the timber, wrapped in his cloak. He gave the man a nod.

Nothing.

Frowning, Ulfr moved toward the ship. As he closed, he realised something was wrong. He could see it – the glistening on the timbers from all the blood. Hurrying, sensing disaster, he reached the work and clambered up the frame toward the watchman. It surprised him not at all when he saw the arrow. The shaft jutted from the man's chest, driven so deep that only a couple of inches showed before the flights. The arrow had come at short range, and from an expert. An instant kill, for the man had not been wearing a chain byrnie. It had happened maybe an hour before at most, for the blood was fresh enough to glisten, but the man was grey and cold.

Alert, Ulfr dropped back to the sand. If one watchman was dead, there was every chance that the other had gone, too. His mind raced as he dodged this way and that, making for the edge of the camp, where the other man would be watching the beach.

An arrow. That meant a professional. A soldier. Or potentially a hunter, true, but what hunter would risk such an attack? No, this was the work of a soldier. And a soldier would not do such a thing without good reason. After the bollocking Ulfr had given them all following that incident in the castle sheds, there was no way any Wolf was going to let anyone sneak up on them. And so the only way anyone was going to overcome Ulfr's watchmen was silently and from a distance. The whole thing *did* suggest that this was a repeat of the wagon house incident, probably by the same man or men.

Clambering across a pile of wrapped lengths of pine, he found the other watchman, an arrow in his throat. He cursed. He could not afford to lose men at such a rate. There had only been eight Wolves staying here in the first place, and they'd dropped by a quarter in one night. Fuck it, but this was why he never wanted to be a jarl. He was happy with his ships. Responsibility only on the water.

Swearing loud enough that he could hear men in the other tents starting to rouse, he climbed to the top of the pile of planks and looked about carefully, with an eye to random disturbance. And he could see it. Whoever had taken out the watchmen had been here, but only for a short while. Once the dying eyes had glazed over, someone had searched the camp for maybe a quarter of an hour, as quietly as they could.

There were signs. Plenty of footprints in the sand, things overturned, others moved. One of the Varangians appeared at his tent flap, frowning at Ulfr.

'Help me,' the shipwright hissed.

Though he'd no idea what had happened, the other man was out in a moment, his tent mate following on swiftly. They soon took in the man slumped at the prow of the ship and seriousness infused their expressions.

Careful that they were not being observed by either the ordinary workers on the other side of the camp or by anyone lurking at the periphery, Ulfr scurried across to the boxes of treenails they had managed to source from Fulquerville, heavy wooden pegs used to hold the timbers together. Normally Ulfr would have his men make such things during the work, but buying them in saved so much time, and it was hard to get treenails wrong, really. They were only sporadically needed for the work, and so Ulfr and his men supplied them a box at a time as required, while the rest remained in a corner of the camp, out of the way.

Perfectly out of the way. Reaching down, the three men moved one of the big boxes with heavy grunts. The footprints of strangers circled around the area, but there was no sign that they'd made an astounding discovery.

Ulfr felt huge relief as he reached a hand deep into the sand under where the box had stood and found the canvas sheet. He peeled it back and scraped into the sand beneath. There, a moment later, he found the lid of the chest of gold coins... undisturbed.

Good. It seemed hard to imagine that their latest incursion had been about anything other than the gold. They'd drawn attention on first arrival at Coutances by the heavy wagons they so jealously guarded, and clearly the same had happened in the castle at Pirou, leading to an attempt to gain access. This time, though, the would-be thieves had gone a step further, far enough to actually kill two of the Wolves in an attempt to search the camp and find the gold.

Ulfr had been too smart for them, though. Apart from the one chest of coins in his own tent, for which the only key was at his waist, all the rest of the gold was so hidden. Upon arrival they had buried it three feet down in the sand, covered it with canvas, scattered fresh sand atop, and then placed heavy boxes there to discourage easy searches.

It had worked. The thieves had scoured the camp, but only the bits they could do easily without rousing the other sleepers.

He looked across at the two Varangians.

'All right, bury the dead, and then rouse everyone, Wolf or craftsman or peasant. I want them all ready to listen to me when I get back.'

'Where are you going?'

'To have a word with the lord of Pirou.'

He helped them move everything back into place and scatter fresh sand, then left them to it, sure that there would be no further attempts to infiltrate and search the camp so soon. In mere moments, still in the dark, he was mounted and riding across the dunes, making for the castle. Even the farmers were yet to put in an appearance, so early was it, and when he arrived at the castle gate, a tired and bored-looking Hauteville guard frowned down at him.

'You? The Swede? It's the middle of the night.'

Ulfr looked over his shoulder. There was a noticeable change in the tone of the sky toward the eastern horizon.

'The morning is upon bakers, and shipwrights, and murderers.'

The guard seemed completely nonplussed by this, but Ulfr was a familiar enough sight that he gestured down to the gate below, which was opened moments later.

'Sveinsson?' the guard there said, surprising Ulfr by remembering his name.

'I need to see your master.'

'I suppose it's *possible* he's awake,' the guard began. 'Sometimes he—'

'I don't care if he's balls deep in his favourite woman,' Ulfr spat, surprising himself with his tone. He was not given to such Bjorn-like outbursts, but he was angry. The man looked to argue, but Ulfr rode his horse past and into the castle, dismounting not far from the gate and leaving the animal to wander.

Two guards overtook him, one motioning at him to stop and counselling patience, while the other ran ahead into the keep. Ulfr allowed himself to be brought to a halt at the keep's door. He wasn't sure it would improve his standing if he stormed into Hauteville's bedroom in a fit of rage, and so he allowed the man to keep him there while his friend roused the lord.

Serlo de Hauteville did not look at all happy as he appeared in the stairway five minutes later. His tunic was freshly thrown on, and he had the look of a man not yet ready to greet the world.

'What is the meaning of this?' he snapped, gesturing at Ulfr.

'You gave us permission to use the beach to build a ship,' Ulfr replied.

'Yes. In retrospect I might have made a different decision, but yes, I did. And I hope you are working well and fast, for the sooner you are off the beach and out of my lands, the better for everyone.'

'It will go smoother if you can keep your chain-shirted villains inside your walls.'

'What?' snarled Serlo, and there was a new anger in his voice, as well as uncertainty.

'One or more of your men searched my camp last night and killed two of mine.'

'Utter tripe.'

'It is not. An archer of some skill took my watchmen down before searching my camp.'

'Bandits. Or desperate locals.'

'No. This was the work of trained soldiers.'

Serlo's lip twitched. 'The castle gates are shut at dusk and not opened until dawn, and that is under normal circumstances. At the moment, they are shut most of the time. How do you suggest my men came to your camp? A climb and a swim, perhaps? Shall I have their armour checked for the smell of pond weed to locate the criminal?'

It was said with light words, but the meaning was anything but. Hauteville was furious. So, too, was Ulfr.

'You know as well as I that there are men of your garrison outside the walls. Some live in the village. Some guard the harbours, others in watchtowers on the roads. And I'll wager they rotate on a daily basis. No, this was the work of *your* men, Hauteville. It gives me no joy to level such an accusation, but I will not lose good men to opportunistic greed.'

'What are they after, Northman?' snapped Serlo. 'Caulk fibre or split timbers?'

'I am here to tell you one thing, Hauteville. We must stay now until our work is done, and then we will be gone without delay. But in the meantime, speak to your men. Tell them to stay away from the beach until we are gone. The next man I find skulking around the work site and prying into our business, I will nail to a fucking post like your White Christ and stand him upright on the beach for all to see.'

Hauteville's eyes veritably bulged with anger and shock, but before he could bluster into a reply, Ulfr turned and walked away, reaching his horse and pulling himself up into the saddle.

'It is in their blood,' the shipwright called across to the angry nobleman. 'You are only five generations down from sons of Odin like us. Their blood – *your* blood – sings songs of battle, of beach raids, of taking slaves and chests of Hacksilver. But the difference is that we of the old ways follow our jarl, and when he tells us no, we do not. Tell your men no, Serlo de Hauteville, if you be a jarl yourself.'

He turned and rode away, ignoring the tirade of haranguing that followed him from the angry nobleman. He seethed all the way back. He'd had a plan to speak to the men on the beach and bring them all together, making it more secure, suggesting better pay for the labourers if they were willing to start standing watches, but as he left, he decided that was simply not going to be enough. They were one week into an eight-week build, and in those seven days alone, they had gone from having a reasonable working relationship with the lord of Pirou and his people, to being cold and distant, with levelled threats. It might not take much more to push them into conflict, and that would be bad, especially with most of the Wolves gone east with the duke.

He passed the farm to see Mariot, still tired, barely risen, yawning as she did her first rounds of the property for the day, and gave her a half-hearted wave. She returned it, but he was gone already, bearing down on the beach and the work site there. As he rode, he could feel determination hardening in his heart, and when he reached the edge of the dunes and looked down across the long slope of sand at the construction site and all the Wolves and workers, he had three new ideas ready.

He rode his horse to the edge of the camp and vaulted from it, leaving the animal to go about its own business while he strode purposefully into the thick of it, where every man was gathered, waiting, many with bleak or angry faces, aware of what had happened. He ignored many halted questions and barged his way through the crowd like a ship through a high wave, until he reached the cradle in which lay the keel and its first few strakes.

'We have a problem,' he announced, as he clambered up to the viewpoint high on the new ship's keel.

There was a general murmur of acceptance of this fact. It was hard to deny. He gritted his teeth and asked Odin for wisdom in this. These were people from the lands of Pirou, but none were specifically Serlo de Hauteville's men, in that any street hawker or coppersmith in Miklagarðr was a Byzantine, but few were really the emperor's men. He had to hope he could buy more loyalty from them than they felt they owed their own lord.

'There are men hereabouts who do not trust us, who think we are carrying treasures, or who are working for enemies. I believe that all of you, from Wolves who have been with us since the revolt of Maniakes, all the way to workers from Fulquerville who have taken our coin for two months' labour, are aware that we are no enemies of the lord de Hauteville, and that we are no hoarders of secret wealth. We have gold, but we have enough simply to survive and to build the ship we need to move on. Once we have this ship built, we will be gone from this place, and there will be no more trouble.'

This was greeted by generally affirmative sounds. The light was starting to change, the sun influencing the colour of the sky at last. Dawn was on its way.

'I have three proposals. Were Halfdan Loki-born here, it would be his place to make such decisions, for he is our jarl, but without him, it must come to me. So I have plans. The first is for our defence, and to prevent a repeat of what happened last night.'

He let this sink in. No one, he was sure, was keen on the idea that enemies might pick off their watchmen and ransack the camp. He had their attention, and he could more or less feel that they were on his side – for now.

'I intend to take one day out from the work on this ship. Today. We have two score timbers, which are unsuitable for our work and are due to be collected and returned to the lumber yards of Coutances. I intend, instead, to keep them. Today, every hand in this camp, including my own, will dig trenches, cut timbers, bind ropes, and combine the three to pull a palisade into place all around this site. I want a strong timber wall around the shipyard, with walkways in the form of small fighting platforms. There will be one gate, facing inland. I have no intention of letting men steal into our camp again. If they wish to repeat their crime, they will have to do so as an army, not as thieves in the night. It is my belief that in one single day we can raise such a defence and protect ourselves, for I will also seek out fresh timbers. There are many I turned down for ship construction that would be more than adequate for a palisade.'

'Who will man it?' asked one of the Wolves, an Apulian. 'There are six of us now, and that leaves little time for sleep or work.'

Ulfr nodded. 'I will come to that. But first, my second point. We work now from sunrise to sunset, with a break for a meal. You are all paid well by shipwright standards. But I am willing to pay more. Much more. Speed becomes ever more important. A man needs eight hours of sleep, and thanks to the light this close to winter, twelve hours a day are in darkness. That means we are spending four hours a day when we could be working either waking up or eating dinner and trying to get to sleep. I realise that working sixteen hours a day, four of them in the dark, and eating on the job, is a harsh schedule. I know, for I have done it myself. But by my calculation, for every three days we work this new schedule, we have done an extra day for free. Two extra days a week. Think how fast the ship could rise.'

There was some consternation about this among the crowd, and so Ulfr, praying Halfdan would approve, and would see it from his point of view, held up his hands. 'This is why I propose to double the wage of every man here. Think on it – double the pay for four extra hours a day? Now tell me this is not possible.'

This was greeted by a general surge of positivity. They were already being paid well, after all. Double their wages, and these men would make in two months what they could normally hope for in a year. He waited for the hubbub to die down once more. He had them. The last one was something of a gamble, but it was a neat solution, if it worked.

'Lastly, we are the Wolves of Odin,' he shouted.

This earned a rumble of distrust from the entirely Christian workforce.

'We have your White Christ followers among us, including those around me now. But we are men of the North. Raiders and traders, sailors of the whale road. Yet until this vessel is finished we have no ship, and constant betrayal and war have robbed us of many of our fellows. So I say this.' He took a deep breath. 'I see many strong arms here. Strong arms that wield a tree axe or lift a timber. But such a strong arm just as easily guides an oar. I see men of fierce pride and men of action, whose strength would be lost among the armoured cattle of the lords of this land. Each of you carries the ice and rock of the North in your blood and bones. Each of you, but for an accident of birth, could have been Wolves.'

He'd laid the groundwork. Some of them were already thinking ahead, some with almost hungry expressions.

'Our company has taken men on from Rus lands, from the great city of Miklagarðr in the south, from the Hauteville knights in Apulia. It matters not where they came from, they are now Wolves. Should any of you feel that, when this ship is complete, it would be better to sail away in it in search of fame and riches than to return to poor service of a rich, fat lord, I will find a place at an oar for every man who can pull it in time. And any man who signs on to the ship owns a piece of it. That is how it works.'

There was a mixed murmur. A little less positive than he'd hoped, but perhaps that was better. They wouldn't have room for every man, after all. But those who felt moved to accept would work all the harder to achieve their goals, and could be taken into the watch rotas while construction continued.

'Think upon it while we work today to protect our future.'

As he dropped down from the cradle once more, leaving them all to discuss their plans, Farlof hurried across.

'These are shipwrights and labourers, not warriors. I doubt any among them has ever swung an axe or a sword.'

'Then that is something else we will need to look at. I will source weapons for all our people, chain shirts and helms, too, if I can. And you and the others will train the new men to use them. Frankly, as long as they can row an oar without collision, that will do for me until we are free of this place.'

Farlof nodded, not entirely convinced, but Ulfr was content he had done what he could. Trouble was brewing, and fast, and if he could not only produce a ship in record time, but crew her as well, then he would have achieved the impossible, and even their jarl could have done no better.

Now, time to begin.

Chapter 15

Ulfr approached the gates of Pirou with men at each shoulder. It had been eight days since he'd last visited, and he would have liked nothing more than to have stayed well clear of the castle for good, but the presence of the wounded Geoffroi, and of imprisoned Beatrix, had preyed on his mind sufficiently that he'd girded his loins for another visit. Beatrix was in some ways his responsibility, and Geoffroi was an ally of the Wolves, and both languished under control of an enemy. Had the lord of Pirou's army been just a little smaller, Ulfr might have been tempted to go in with axe in hand and break them out, though he also acknowledged that this was a very Ketil plan – which was to say, insane.

It had been a tense week. There had been no contact between the castle and the beach shipyard, no exchange even of words between Hauteville's men and those within the newly defended beach stockade. With just the one day's interruption to construct the palisade, they had doubled their efforts on the ship, which was truly taking shape.

It would most certainly be the fastest-built ship he had ever begun, and possibly the fastest ship *anyone* had ever built, but then he had more manpower than most shipwrights could hope for, ready-cut timbers, all the equipment in advance and unlimited funds. The dwarves, shipbuilding for Loki, could not have done better.

Even as he rode, whenever he closed his eyes he could see it there on the beach, already almost a ship. The shell was near complete, barring the last few strakes on each side, and already the ribbing was going in to support the hull. Everyone involved was exhausted, for sure, but that did not seem to be hampering their work, and Ulfr did not think that was just a case of the money, although their pay *was* impressive. It was also the sheer joy and satisfaction of watching their construction take shape, something only a craftsman could ever understand. These men had spent their lives mostly repairing old ships or building small fishing boats. Only a precious few, including the shipwright from Fulquerville, had ever helped build a ship of war, and even then it had been as part of a large shipyard, just one piece of the machine. This was a work of craft in which they could all take pride. It was a proper longship, worthy of Freyja's attention.

It was a dragon boat.

And he'd named it, in his heart. She was the *Sea Dragon*. There was no other choice. At times this week he'd found himself walking around it at night, when the work had ended, muttering the name as he looked at her sleek lines and imagining the decoration he would eventually carve into her delicate timbers.

If things went on at the pace they had been, then the main construction would be done within another week, that being a complete hull with all the internals. She would be essentially seaworthy, and there would be just the ancillary work to take care of. Then would be mast, oars, sail, steering oar and so on, but probably not the figurehead and sternpost. Clearly, they were important to any ship's identity, but equally clearly a ship could sail without them, and time was becoming more pressing with every passing day. There would be one more week of hull work, and then a couple of days of pulling everything together. They already had a timber selected for the mast.

The gates of Pirou castle were closed. This was the first time Ulfr had approached them without their standing open and his being waved in without a challenge. He felt a tightening of his chest. Tension was building, and everyone could feel it. The one time this week they *almost* had interaction with Hauteville had been when the Norman had taken it upon himself to ride to the beach with a small party of guards. He'd only come as far as the high dunes, where he had reined in and looked down at the work on the beach, surrounded by its defensive palisade, a fortress of foreigners within his domain. He'd said nothing before turning and riding away, but the clear impression was 'hurry up and finish and get off my beach.' Closed gates spoke volumes.

'I seek admittance,' Ulfr shouted up at the wall.

'For what purpose?'

That was new. Pirou had always been welcoming, even if that welcome had been strained of late. That was not the Northern way. Even enemies could be gracious hosts, as fabled Audun had found when he visited the King of Norway with his bear. It seemed that the rules of hospitality had been diluted with the generations these people had spent away from the North.

'To speak to friends,' he answered the guard. 'To Sir Geoffroi and the lady Beatrix.'

'Wait there.' Short. Curt. Unfriendly.

There was a long pause as discussions took place inside the castle, and finally the man returned to his place above the gate. 'Permission is granted to speak to Sir Geoffroi.'

Not Beatrix.

Ulfr's eyes narrowed as the gate opened. He rode forth to the castle, with a Wolf at each shoulder, across the bridge and into the great wide oval bailey of the fortress. Something cold touched his nose and he looked up, expecting rain. He did not want rain. Rain was the bane of anyone working with wood and canvas. But autumn had begun the slide into winter, and it was becoming less clement all the time. They'd had two showers already that week, and the temperature was plummeting to the extent that they'd all bought extra blankets and burned fires late into the night.

This was not rain, though. As he looked up, another flake drifted down, lazily, to land on his arm.

Snow.

Damn it.

But at least it would be a light shower, and brief. A man brought up where Ulfr had been, in the icy North, knew snow well, like a childhood friend, and he could take one sniff, one look, and say with reasonable confidence that it would snow for perhaps an hour, and light enough not to lie. But it was a worrying warning sign that more was to come, and that the weather was truly on the turn. And if ever there was a bad time for even a veteran ship's pilot to take a new and untested vessel out to sea in a hurry, it would be in winter storms. The time was coming for sacrifices and gifts to the gods.

He bit down on his worry. Such concerns were for when the ship was *finished*; there were other worries to concentrate on before then. He felt sharply the absence of the others. Halfdan would be able to make the critical decisions that would see them steer through all this with little trouble, especially with his Loki-born luck. Gunnhild would know what was happening, and would be able to see their course ahead and help guide the jarl. Leif would be full of useful knowledge and titbits, even here where he was a stranger, so clever was he. And Bjorn and Ketil were a great comfort to have around when there was the ongoing threat of violence, which it very much felt there was.

As they came to a halt, he turned to the men with him: Erik, a Varangian who'd been with them since the sands on the south coast of Italy, and Richold, one of Thurstan's Normans from Apulia.

'Erik, stay with the horses. Don't let the guards take them away and stable them. Stay out in the open, and keep your eyes wide for any trouble. If anything happens I want to be able to get on this horse and be gone in heartbeats, all right?'

Erik nodded, and as the other two dismounted he took the reins and kept their horses together without ever himself leaving the saddle. All around, Pirou's guards were watching them with barely disguised malice.

On foot, with Richold – a man who had once served another Hauteville a world away – at his side, he reached toward a passing servant.

'You. Thrall. Where is the knight Geoffroi to be found?'

The bow-backed man pointed to one of the low wooden buildings at the far side of the compound, and again Ulfr's eyes narrowed in suspicion as he nodded his thanks and turned, making for that place. Geoffroi was a nobleman himself, a jarl of his own land, albeit a small one compared with Serlo de Hauteville. When Halfdan, and then William, had come to Pirou, space for them had been made in the keep. It had to mean something that Geoffroi was being kept in a separate building far away. Was it a lack of trust? Was it more a form of imprisonment than hospitality? The rules of the host were truly lost in this place.

Approaching the building, Ulfr noted no guards on the door, so they were not prisoners per se. He rapped on the timbers, and someone bade him enter. He did so to find that the place was little more than a cottage, too homely to be intentional guest quarters. To Ulfr's eye, it looked to be the residence of one of the free karls who worked in the castle, a man of position, but not a noble – perhaps a craftsman, or even a priest. Whoever it was had been turfed out to make room for Geoffroi and his companion.

Geoffroi sat by a fireplace that roared with golden life, painstakingly painting a design on one of those Norman teardrop shields. His brush made neat lines down the edge; he did not look up from his work. The other man who'd arrived with him lay in a cot to one side. He was awake, but sallow and unwell-looking, as though the weapon that had wounded him had borne elf poison.

'Master Ulfr of the Wolves,' Geoffroi said, still concentrating on his work.

'You are doing an excellent job,' Ulfr said, noting the neat-ness of the work.

'Thank you. At home, someone would have done this for me. But while I languish here, I have made use of my time repairing our armour and building and painting replacement shields. I have the feeling I will need them soon enough.'

Clearly the unease was getting to Geoffroi, too, then. Ulfr wondered for a moment what to say. This was when Gunnhild, or Halfdan, or even Leif would be in their element. Ulfr had sensed that he needed to visit the man, but now that he was there, he couldn't quite say why. Except that the man was a good, honourable one, and that he was clearly as uncomfortable in the current circumstances as the Wolves, and that made them kin of a sort. He chewed his lip for a moment, wondering how best to start.

'There is trouble brewing in Pirou,' Ulfr said.

Geoffroi stopped his painting and looked up, finally. 'Oh?'

Ulfr frowned. There was no surprise in the man's tone. More of a question, perhaps, as to how *Ulfr* knew of such things, away on his secluded beach.

'The lord Serlo tolerates our presence at best,' the shipwright explained. 'He wants us gone. I wonder how long we have before his tolerance drains away and he decides to *make* us gone.' They were not the honeyed words of a jarl or a skald – but then, he was a plain man.

Geoffroi nodded. 'Despite our differences, Ulfr of the Wolves, I suspect we sail in the same boat, there. But we are both stuck. You have an unfinished ship, and cannot leave until you complete it. I have a wounded friend here, who deserves all my care, and I cannot leave until he is well enough to travel.' The man sagged a little. 'Then there is the question of to where I would travel. My home is within the domain of the rebel Cotentin, and I cannot say for certain whether they remain loyal to me or whether it now hosts a rebel garrison. Perhaps the only place I will find aid is in Falaise with the duke.'

Ulfr nodded, thinking far ahead. 'Is Falaise on a river?'

Geoffroi gave him a knowing smile. 'Not one large enough for a ship to navigate. The nearest navigable river would be the

Orne, through somewhere like Clécy, if your ship had a shallow enough beam.'

'How far is that from Falaise?'

'Ten miles or so, I reckon.'

Ulfr nodded. That would do.

'But the journey there along the coast would take you past many ports held by rebel lords. It will not be an easy journey.'

Ulfr shrugged. 'My jarl is in Falaise, your duke is in Falaise. Your friend cannot ride, but I'd wager he could lie in a ship.'

'You offer me a way out?' Geoffroi said, brows raised.

'I do. And you will be valuable, for you know the coast where I do not.'

'I'm not sure Serlo will be so happy to let me go. We have been moved here to keep us out of the way, I think, but also safe and contained. I have seen new men arriving in Pirou for days now. The garrison here has almost doubled, and some of the new men are not wearing Hauteville colours – are not wearing *any* colours, in fact.'

'Mercenaries?' Ulfr asked.

'Or men of another faction who wish to keep their identity hidden. I fear Serlo de Hauteville is playing a dangerous game. He may not be a rebel lord himself, but I wonder whether he teeters. Allegiance to William is not looking very favourable at the moment, with the duke trapped in Falaise. Unless he can gather a huge amount of support, the rebellion looks too strong to oppose.'

Ulfr thought about this. Was that why Beatrix remained at Pirou? She was betrothed to the lord of Eu, who was, from what Ulfr remembered, a staunch supporter of the duke. If Serlo was having second thoughts about his alliances, it would make sense not to send his sister to her betrothed, but to keep her as a valuable piece in the game of politics.

'We need to leave Pirou before Serlo turns on the duke,' he said, flatly. 'The moment he joins the rebels openly, we become the enemy, rather than merely an inconvenience. You should join us at the beach.'

Geoffroi shook his head. 'Not yet. Thank you for the offer, but for now we are better here. Joining you at the beach would put Hauteville on the alert, I think. And every day we wait, Brenier here gets a little stronger, and your ship is a little closer to ready.'

Ulfr nodded. 'I have to see Beatrix.'

'You will not be permitted.'

'I'm going to do it anyway. Get well. Get prepared. Watch Hauteville and his men, and be ready.'

As Geoffroi nodded his agreement and returned to his painting, Ulfr left the building. Richold, at his shoulder, coughed lightly. 'Can we trust him?'

'Insofar as I trust anyone in the land, I trust him. Out in the land of the Georgians they have a saying that "my enemy's enemy must be my friend".'

Now that Geoffroi had mentioned it, as Ulfr looked about Pirou castle the increased number of men was indeed apparent, and many were in plain hauberks with unpainted shields. It seemed likely Serlo de Hauteville was preparing to make his move, for he was building his strength ready. If, as seemed inevitable, he declared his support for the rebellion, he would have sufficient power to claim a leading role in it, alongside men like Cotentin and Bessin. Time was running out. Ulfr could almost see the sand draining through the hourglass, counting down to the time when anyone who had a connection to the duke became the enemy.

'Stay in the open,' he said to his companion as they crossed the short stretch of open ground between the buildings where Geoffroi and Beatrix were being housed. 'If anyone comes, delay as best you can.'

'You're pushing this, Ulfr,' the man warned.

He knew he was. He'd been given permission to visit Geof-froi, but not Beatrix. He had to hope she was in the same room in which he'd found her last time. There was no guard, of course, for the house was locked from the outside, and so

Ulfr could not enter. Instead, he walked around the far side and approached the shuttered window to her solar, the room in which he'd spoken to her a couple of weeks earlier.

'Lady Beatrix?' he hissed through the closed shutters.

There was no reply, and so he rapped lightly on the timbers and repeated his call, slightly louder, lips pressed to the gap between timbers. He stood there for a moment, the light snow continuing to settle in his hair, gradually soaking him, and finally a voice called in reply.

'Hello?'

'It's me, Ulfr. How are you faring?'

'I'm a comfortable prisoner,' came the reply.

'Your brother wavers in his allegiance to the duke.'

'I'm sure. He will always do what looks best for him and the family at any time. The duke is young, unstable, and not popular.'

'My people are with the duke, and the time is coming when we will have to leave in a hurry. Our ship will be ready in a little over a week, I think, unless disaster strikes.'

'Good luck to you, then, Ulfr the Swede.'

'Come with us.'

'What?'

'You've run away from your family more than once. Why not again?'

'Ulfr, I am a prisoner.'

'We will come for you. When the time is right. When we can.'

He could almost feel the resigned sag through the shutters. 'I will not escape again, Ulfr. And if you attempt to take me, you will then fail in your own escape. I am done now. I am but Serlo's token to use in his game.'

'You could—'

'Go,' she interrupted.

'We cannot leave you here,' Ulfr said to the shutters, but as he listened for a reply that did not come, he was somehow sure she had gone, leaving the room. He sighed. She did not deserve this. As he rounded the corner, back to where Richold waited, he clenched his teeth. He was determined. He felt sure that if Gunnhild were here, she would see their threads woven together – Ulfr and the Wolves, Beatrix and Geoffroi. That they would leave Pirou and the increasingly untrustworthy Serlo de Hauteville behind.

Four men in chain hauberks with the colours of Hauteville were approaching across the grass. As they reached the two visitors, one of them threw out an accusatory finger.

'What were you doing?'

'Going for a piss,' Ulfr replied, lip wrinkling. He was angry, and when he got angry, which was not often, he tended toward the confrontational.

The man glared at him, but apparently had no argument against this. After an irritated pause, the guard grunted. 'There are latrines for that, Northerner.'

'I was desperate,' Ulfr replied, and then turned and walked past them, being sure to bump into the man's shoulder insolently on the way.

As Richold fell in beside Ulfr, he hissed, 'You're spoiling for a fight.'

'The man pissed me off.'

'Spoiling for a fight when you're surrounded in an enemy castle with odds of a hundred to one is stupid.'

Ulfr knew that. He was irritated, but he also knew that. The pair hurried across the open grass and to where Erik waited with their horses. The four guards were following them across the open bailey, keeping their distance, but the air of menace was palpable. Reaching Erik, they grasped their reins and pulled themselves up into the saddle.

'Let's go,' Ulfr said to the others, and led them through the gatehouse, fearing that at any moment those timber gates might shut, closing them in. They did not, and it was with a great sense of relief that Ulfr crossed the moat and returned to the open countryside.

'This way,' he said, turning left toward the north.

The others frowned, but followed, this being a longer route back to the beach. A short ride brought them to the village of Pirou, where there was ancillary work being done for the ship. Like all good longships, this new vessel had no need of iron, for the whole ship was formed from split timbers, pegged with treenails and sealed with caulk, but he'd retained the village blacksmith anyway, for other reasons. As they approached, to the echo of hammer on anvil and the column of black smoke belching from the forge roof, Ulfr smiled. Three axes hung on timber pegs outside, freshly made though yet to be sharpened, and a number of iron plates the size of a man's palm were stacked on a table. He'd thought to check with the smith on his progress, but progress was clear from just a glance outside.

He'd needed nothing metal for the ship. The crew, on the other hand, was a different matter. He had plenty of men, and each of them would need equipping. At first he'd thought to source chain shirts and good swords, but it seemed, with a little prying, that in this time of unrest, with all the lords of this land busy consolidating their forces, arms and armour were as hard to acquire as warships.

He'd then spoken to the smith. The man was no sword worker or armourer, of course – those were different, special-ised skills – and the man simply did not have the time to manufacture steel rings to work into shirts anyway. But his skills were sufficient for certain things. He had built a career out of making tools and utensils for the locals and patching old metal-work. As such, his ability to make an axe was unquestioned, and so Ulfr had set the man to making axes – good, large, solid axes such as a man could wield in war. In addition, the man had admitted that armour was beyond his skill, but many a poor man gone to war had found good protection by simply sewing metal plates to a leather tunic, enough to turn a sword. So, Ulfr had also set him to work making such plates. Additionally, the man had told Ulfr that though he had no experience with constructing shields, a shield boss should be easy enough, and so he would work on a number of them, to which Ulfr could add the timbers in time. Clearly, the smith was progressing well, just from what was on display at the front, and so Ulfr decided not to disturb him, and instead rode on to find the carpenter at his shop on the edge of the village. There, he dismounted with his companions, tying their horses to a rail and entering the workshop.

The carpenter had been put to work making certain things that needed the skill of a craftsman. The steering oar was one such item, and the man had been given that task at the very beginning, as well as the curved and reinforced block for the strake, where the steering oar would be attached. The mast-step, too, and the rakke, and other parts that took a carpenter's skill to get right.

Ulfr was pleased, as he stepped inside, to see the progress on display. The steering oar was complete, standing against a side wall, perfectly formed. The mast-step, too, was ready, sitting on a bench. Other parts he could see around the place in various stages of completion. All was going well.

The carpenter was at work in a back room, but as he paused in some noisy task he clearly heard the three men in the outer room and emerged through the door, blinking away sawdust and wiping his hands on his smock, dust settling all around him. The man smiled with recognition, and nodded a greeting.

'Come to check on progress?'

Ulfr nodded. 'That, and another question. A thought occurs to me.'

'Oh?'

'In a good old longship, the rowers sit on their sea chests. It has always been this way. In the *Sea Wolf* we did precisely that, but since we lost the ship in Miklagarðr we have been sailing in Byzantine ships. Their galleys do not leave room for sea chests. They have oar benches. It only occurred to me last night that few among our new crew will have their own sea chest, and so it might be advantageous for us to adopt the Byzantine idea and fit out the new ship with oar benches. They would only have to be simple plank benches, but the idea is new to me, and so I'm not sure how they would be fitted to the hull. We have plenty of suitable timbers at the beach, and I can set men to cutting them and constructing them, but it would be useful if you could have a look at the ship, tell us how to fit them, and then walk us through the first one. Do you think you could find time?'

The carpenter sucked air through his teeth and nodded, tucking his thumbs in his belt. 'It's an easy enough job. I think I can see how they would be fitted, but I'll come and have a look. I'm just working on a project for someone else for the afternoon, but when I stop in an hour or so and get back to your steerboard fittings, I'll come to the beach. I wanted to have a look at your sheer strake anyway, to see how my work will fit.'

Ulfr nodded, thanked the man, and they left the shop once more, noting that the light snow shower seemed to have ended, much to everyone's relief. He was mostly satisfied; he was a little irked that the man was devoting time to other projects, considering how much Ulfr was paying him, but at least he was concentrating on their work and making good progress. As they mounted up, Richold frowned.

'What's a sea chest?'

'Comes from the days of raiding and trading.' Ulfr smiled as they turned their mounts and moved out into the countryside once more. 'Each man has his own share of all booty, and each man keeps it in his own chest. That way there is never any argument about who owns what. But we lost our sea chests with the *Sea Wolf*. In fact, we lost most of the crew, too. I think that perhaps in these days of change, the time of the sea chest is past.'

That was a bleak thought. Another part of the old world slipping away...

The man nodded, and the trio began the three-quarter-mile ride to the beach. The conversation varied as they rode, until suddenly Erik hissed for them to hush, throwing out a finger.

'Look.'

Ahead, five men sat on horses directly in their path. Even from this distance, Ulfr could see the glittering of chain shirts and steel helmets in the winter light. He had been in Pirou long enough to know that there was no garrison to be found in the area, the nearest places that normally sported warriors being the castle or the harbour at Fulquerville. For men to be here, on the road, boded ill.

They could only be here for Ulfr, and the chances of this being a friendly visit were very small. He looked first to Erik, and then to Richold. With tremendous lack of foresight, the three men had ridden for the castle and their meetings in just tunics and trousers, with cloaks thrown over the top for warmth. They had their weapons with them, but they were unarmoured, while the five men waiting for them on the road were clad from knee to crown in steel and wielding long swords. Trained warriors, well armoured, and outnumbering the Wolves five to three.

'What now?' Richold muttered, his right hand reaching to the sword at his side.

That was a good question. Again, had the others been here, they would probably have thought differently. Halfdan would have some wily plan that would see them either past without a fight, or victorious with one. Gunnhild would find a way. Bjorn and Ketil would probably laugh that five men, no matter how armoured, were hardly even worth the contest. Ulfr was less heroic, more pragmatic. They were three men, unarmoured. The enemy were five, prepared for war. The contest would be trouble. There was a chance they could manage a win, but it would be costly if they did. If they survived it, there would probably be only one or two left to ride back to the beach, and even that much was uncertain.

'We need to avoid a fight.'

'You're sure?' Erik asked, gripping his axe.

'We need every man now at the ship. I don't want to lose another body, and we're outnumbered and out-armed. Be ready to ride hard when I say.'

The two men nodded. They didn't like the idea of flight, but Ulfr was right. There was a good chance at least one of them would die if they fought. Instead, they continued along the road at their leisurely pace, with low, murmured conversation.

Ulfr could see the farm track leading off, perhaps twenty paces this side of the five men who blocked the road. He knew every farm in the area, from his negotiations with them over supplies, and he could picture in his mind every field and gate between here and the beach. The farmers might be irritated with him, but they'd get over it, knowing how much he was paying them for all their supplies.

'Good morning,' Ulfr called to the five men in his best Norman dialect.

There was no reply, which further signalled ill intent, yet Ulfr rode casually. He kept his voice low as he addressed the other two.

'The farm road off to the left. Ready?'

As he neared the riders, who readied their swords with malice, Ulfr suddenly shouted 'Now,' and kicked his horse into speed, veering off the road and onto the farm track. Behind him, Erik and Richold reacted instantly, and in moments the three men were galloping as fast as they could away from the main road. Behind them there were shouts of anger and surprise as the five men fumbled to get their horses moving before turning onto the road in their wake.

The surprise had been enough to buy Ulfr and his friends plenty of time, and they were way ahead of the five Norman warriors, who were only just on the track as Ulfr led the others between two barns, jumping a low gate into a field of sheep, who scattered at the high-speed intrusion.

'Who were they?' Erik asked as they rode.

'Mercenaries, I think, but in the pay of Hauteville. We are fast outstaying our welcome. Come on.'

And they rode across fields and between hedges, as though Hel herself was grasping at their horses' tails. It was a massive relief to Ulfr when he saw the dunes hove into view, and beyond them the palisade around the beach site.

'To arms,' he bellowed as they crested the dunes and raced toward the gate, which stood open when ordinary work was going on. At his call, men all across the camp stopped whatever they were working on and ran to the encircling palisade, lifting either swords or axes or makeshift weapons or tools. In heart-beats, Ulfr and the others were racing through the gate, and heavy, stocky workers were pushing them closed and dropping the bar.

Shaking with the effort, Ulfr dropped from his horse and ran, clambering up the slope, to the walkway at the gate. The armoured riders had stopped at the dunes and were looking down at the beach. They stayed there for a short time, and then turned and disappeared.

'Our time is almost up,' Ulfr gasped. 'No one leaves the compound unarmoured now, and never less than half a dozen men at a time. Got that?'

There was a chorus of affirmative murmurs, and the men began to drift back to work.

Ulfr watched the empty crest of the dunes for some time. Pirou was becoming more perilous by the day.

Chapter 16

The blacksmith's cart bounced and jerked across the rough dunes in the icy winds that blew up the beach, it's owner's face ruddy with an expression that Ulfr could only label 'worried'. The vehicle finally reached the flatter sand and stopped leaping about so, settling into a rhythmic sway as it approached the camp gate. There, Farlof waited, impatient, twitching. Ulfr knew how he felt, and looked around at the work.

It was, needless to say, slow going.

Of the many workers he had at the site, perhaps half were labouring away to finish the ship. It was nearly there, following another solid week. So close... but now this.

Work had begun as usual before dawn, the men performing their tasks by torchlight in the cold night air, but with a diminished workforce. Whereas every night for weeks, since Ulfr's changes, the men who lived locally had come to the camp gate in time to join their fellows who stayed in the beach camp overnight, this morning they had not turned up. It was a bad sign, the second of the day. On rising from his tent that morning, he'd opened the flap to see a cat of midnight black striding purposefully across the camp, and though he'd spat after it to remove the power of the curse it had left him with a bad feeling that seemed destined to be borne out. A few workers failing to arrive could be put down to bad luck or laziness, but half the force said something entirely different. The surviving workforce had worked much of the day since then, and now, by mid-afternoon, he was noticing the difference in speed.

With luck, the smith would have news. As the cart passed through the gate, Farlof and his man closed it once more, for no one was taking chances these days.

Men hurried over and started to unload the axes, the steel plates, shield bosses and knives that the man had made over the past week. Ulfr watched with a sinking feeling as he crossed and joined Farlof next to the vehicle's bench, looking up at the smith.

'You could get none?'

He'd not really expected success, but he'd been hopeful. The smith had claimed to have a friend in the castle who could slip him half a dozen shirts of good chain from the stores for a small fee, and the smith was in and out of the castle on a semi-regular basis, so his visit there would not be suspicious. Moreover, rumour had it that Serlo de Hauteville himself had left the castle with a small group of riders four days earlier; his absence should make such transactions at least possible. Half a dozen chain shirts would have been very useful.

The man shook his head. 'No chance today. Never seen the castle so busy.'

Ulfr felt the hairs rise on his neck, alertness flooding him at this news. 'Tell me.'

'Lord de Hauteville has returned, during the night. He's got a guest with him, too.'

'Go on.'

'The lord de Cotentin is in Pirou, and he's brought a force of cavalry. The castle is flooded with knights. It's like an army. There's so many of them they're even camped outside the moat, too.'

Ulfr and Farlof exchanged a look. Both men were well aware of just how much their own danger had just increased, but Ulfr also thought on Geoffroi and his friend, trapped in the castle, recuperating. Geoffroi had already set himself against Cotentin. If the visitor learned that the knight was there, things could become very nasty very quickly.

'There is more,' the smith said, his expression bleak. 'Your workers from the villages have been rounded up. They are being kept in the camp outside the castle, and they've been given spears and shields. I think they've been drafted into the lord's army. I left the castle as fast as I could before someone took away my cart and stuck a spear in my hand.'

Ulfr felt his spirits sink further. He would not get those workers back. Hauteville had them, and he wouldn't let them go. Worse, though, was the news that the rebels were building an army. That could only mean they were openly moving against Duke William, which would also mean against Halfdan and the others.

'We're out of time,' the shipwright said.

'What?'

'They're preparing to launch an attack. And Serlo de Hauteville knows that we and the Wolves support the duke. Even if we changed our allegiance now, he would never believe us. We are Cotentin's enemies, and if Serlo has raised a rebel flag, then we are his enemies, too. They prepare to march east and deal with the duke, but they won't leave us on the beach behind them. They'll have to finish us first.'

Farlof nodded, and Ulfr turned back to the smith. 'It will be dangerous to go back to your home. You are welcome to take shelter within our defences.'

The man shook his head. 'No. They will come here first. I go to stay with my brother near Avranches until this is over. I wish you luck, Ulfr Sveinsson. I am sorry I have no better tidings for you.'

As soon as they had finished unloading the smith's wares, the man gave them a sad salute and turned his vehicle slowly, digging deep ruts in the sand, and trundled back through the gate, changing direction from his arrival path, instead angling south, crossing the dunes and heading away from Pirou entirely.

Farlof closed the gate and then crossed back to Ulfr. 'What do we do?'

The shipwright was chewing his lip, deep in thought. 'Come with me.'

With Farlof at his heel, he scurried across the sand to the ship. If he could only have four or five more days...

She was nearly done. The sheer strakes had been added, the whole shell constructed and caulked. The steering oar had been fitted, using the specially constructed blocks the local carpenter had made for them, though for now it was in a raised position, not dropped into place. All the ribs and the keelson were in, and the crossbeams that acted both as an extra strengthening and as the benches for rowers were in place, though some had not been fitted and finished. There was as yet no mast, no sail, no prow or sternpost, no oars, and no decoration to any of the timbers. Most importantly, nothing had yet been tested. Ulfr was pleased with the work they had all done, and with the job they'd all achieved, but he'd not had the time and opportunity to check every strake, every treenail, every inch of caulking. Without a day to give the ship a full check, there was always the possibility the vessel would be pushed out into the waves where it would immediately spring a dozen leaks and sink forever. It was rather more than a simple risk.

But...

'She *should* be seaworthy.'

'*What?*' Farlof breathed, looking back and forth along the ship.

'As long as all the work has been done exactly as I ordered, the ship should be seaworthy. She lacks finishing touches.'

'Like a mast. Sail. Oars.'

'A lot. But a ship can be rowed without a mast and sail. A stern and prow post can be made in due course. For now, what matters is whether she floats, and she should.'

'You're not seriously suggesting that we put to sea now?'

'I'm suggesting that if we stay here, we're all going to die. I'd rather put my life in the hands of Ægir and Ran – and in my own skill – than trust to the goodwill and mercy of the lords Hauteville and Cotentin.'

There was nothing Farlof could say in argument to that. He was still shaking his head, though. 'What if she sinks?'

'Then we drown.'

'Comforting words, Ulfr.'

'Listen, it's too late in the day for the rebels to come and deal with us now. We should be safe until tomorrow. But I would be very surprised if Hauteville and his army do not come with the dawn. And at dawn, the tide will be at its highest, within twenty yards of the palisade. That is our time to put to sea.'

'So it will become a race, at dawn, between the tide and Hauteville.'

'Something like that, yes. But it gives us the rest of the afternoon and the night to play with, and that solves three problems.'

'Oh?'

'Firstly, it gives us time to do some last-moment checks. There is no point in starting any new part of the work. Next was to be the mast, but we have neither the time to finish it, nor a sail to raise on it, so we abandon the mast for now and trust to oars. While we still have light, get the workers split into two parties, one large, one small. The smaller one can finish fitting the crossbeams so that they are sturdy and comfortable. The larger group needs to go round and check every last treenail and every last inch of caulking, making sure there are no leaks or cracks. That way the ship is as ready as we can make her.'

'It does not fill me with confidence.'

'But it is better than nothing. Secondly, once the sun goes down and such examination and work is no longer possible, we should also be safe from prying eyes. I have no doubt that Hauteville has someone watching us at all times. There are fishing boats not far out to sea every day who could report back, and I am sure I have seen figures in the dunes this past week, watching the camp. Hauteville has been keeping a careful eye on us. But when it gets dark, and they are blinded to our work, we can begin. The gold needs to be unearthed then and moved into the ship, along with everything we need for the journey. Load her up under cover of darkness, but be as subtle as you can, for we may still be observed, and we don't want to give Hauteville any reason to move on us early. We need the morning tide, else we'll be portaging the ship across a very long beach.'

'You keep saying *we*, with all this. Where are *you*, Ulfr?'

'That's the third thing,' the shipwright said with a fierce smile. 'That gives me half a day to get us oars.'

'And how will you do that?'

'With a little bit of stealth, a little bit of violence, and a lot of luck.'

Farlof gave a dark chuckle. 'You sound like the jarl now.'

'Good, I'll need his Loki cunning.' He turned to the others and pointed at Erik and Richold. 'You two. Come with me.' He looked back at Farlof. 'Good luck. Make sure she's seaworthy and load her up. With Odin's will, Hauteville won't realise we're preparing and won't come until it's light. We'll be back before dawn with oars, or we won't be back at all, in which case we're all fucked.'

'You're full of encouraging words today.'

Ulfr gave his friend a wry smile, and then, with the other two Wolves, crossed to where the horses were kept tethered among the only area of scrubby dry grass within the compound. He swiftly saddled one, while the others did the same, and then, moments later, was riding out through the gate once more.

'Where are we going?' Erik asked as they left the camp, bursting into fresh life under Farlof's commands, riding across the sand below the line of the dunes.

'To find oars. We leave on the morning tide.'

This brought startled looks from both of them, and Richold's brow lined with concern. 'Is she seaworthy?'

'You should know – you built her.' At his increasing worry, Ulfr grinned. 'The others are checking her over today and then loading her in the dark. There's no time to get the mast ready and we have no sail, so if we want to leave the beach at all, we're going to need oars.'

'I thought there were no oars to be found?'

'Not without pissing off their owner. But the ones I'm looking at, their owner is Serlo de Hauteville and his skippers, and I can't see damaging our relationship with him making things any worse.'

'So what's the plan?' Erik asked.

'I don't have one. Not yet. The oars will be somewhere in Fulquerville. They were being stored ready for one of Hauteville's ships. If we're lucky, they're still in storage and we can find them, thieve them, and get away back to the beach. If we're unlucky, the enemy ship will already have been fitted with them.'

'And then?'

'And then thievery might have to involve some violence, too.'

He kept quiet on his fears. If Serlo de Hauteville was so ready for war that he'd openly brought a rebel baron to his castle and they'd mustered an army, there was a damn good chance that he'd had all his ships mustered, too, which would mean those oars were aboard an enemy vessel. That could be a lot of trouble. And if they were *really* unlucky, Hauteville had already sent his fleet ahead, around the coast, heading for the duke's harbours in the east, in which case Fulquerville might well be empty of both ships *and* oars.

The four miles to the river mouth was ridden in silence, and Ulfr could feel the tension emanating from the others, just as he could feel it in himself. No matter what the others on the beach managed, if the three of them could not manage to find oars then they were going nowhere in the morning, and Hauteville would come and finish them all off. Ulfr had good men, and quite a growing force, but many were as yet untested in a fight, while the rebel lords had a trained, professional army at their fingertips.

He looked up, trying to spot the ravens in the steel-grey sky, but of Huginn and Muninn he could see nothing. Perhaps even Hrafnaguð, Odin the Raven God, was blind to their peril today. Was it the curse work of that damned black cat? Silently he vowed a gift to the Allfather if the great god would help them until dawn.

There were, in his opinion, maybe two hours of daylight left, this close to true winter. On the beach the others would be working hard to check the caulking before the light was too low to do so, but for Ulfr, things were working the other way. He could not make his full move until the light was gone. On the bright side, he had kept his eyes and ears open as they left the camp, and he'd not seen a sign of anyone watching him leave. Likely whatever guard or thrall Hauteville had set watching the camp had got bored by then, and his attention had wandered. Whatever the case, no one had followed them along the coast, or at least as far as Ulfr could tell.

The familiar sight of Fulquerville came into view. It was past high tide by some time, and the water was receding, with low tide expected before midnight. There was still sufficient water for the more shallow-beamed vessels in the harbour to bob around, but those with a deep keel were already resting at odd angles in the sand.

Ulfr felt his heart pounding with the tension as they neared the wide tidal harbour, anticipating disaster. He felt failure looming at the sight of only shallow fishing vessels and was gripped with the fear that he'd been right to worry that the baron's ships had already sailed.

Then the warships came into view, and relief thundered through his veins like the storms of Thor. The two warships that had been berthed for weeks were still present, while two more had arrived, one clearly very new, brought in from another port somewhere along the coast. In that moment, in his head, Ulfr ran a calculation. Sixty miles lay between Pirou and the duke's fortress at Falaise, which could only be where the rebel army was bound. A fast force could cover the distance in a couple of days, and a reasonable army in three or four, but if they needed siege engines and wagon trains, which seemed likely, they would be moving no more than ten miles a day, as Ulfr was painfully aware from their slow wagon journey from Apulia in the summer.

So it would be six days before the rebel army reached Falaise. From his discussions with Beatrix, Ulfr could safely estimate the coastal route to the duke's local harbours at a little over twice that distance, but ships moved faster. Unless the weather was set against them, and presuming their skippers and crews were all competent, Hauteville's ships could reach their destination in two or three days. Of course they were not gone yet, for Hauteville would not want his ships in danger for days before he and the army arrived. The ships would be setting off in a matter of two or three days, probably, in order to arrive at the same time as the army.

They still had a chance. If the ships were here, then so were oars.

At his signal, they reined in by the nearest building, keeping as much out of sight as possible, peering off into the harbour. He examined the four ships. Unless his eyes deceived him, he could see that three of them had their oars shipped neatly, while the fourth, the nice new warship, seemed to have no oars at all. It had come under sail, and had not yet been fitted out. The gods were being kind to Ulfr this day. Perhaps Odin was watching after all.

There was, of course, no activity in the harbour's ship-building area, for all the men who worked there were either in Ulfr's beach compound, checking over the new ship's caulking, or holding a spear in Hauteville's camp, armed for a war against the duke. The only activity he could see was men loading the ships, and those men appeared to be the sailors.

Plans began to form in his head. If the oars were not on the ship, then they could only really logically be in the storehouses

238

of the shipyard area, where he'd been prying the first time he came here. Those buildings were at the seaward edge of the harbour, while the warships were berthed further up the channel, in the heart of the village area. If the oars were stored there, the three Wolves would have to retrieve them from those buildings.

They would need twenty oars – ten for each side – which the new ship had been designed to take. Ulfr had mentally calculated that each horse could carry seven oars strapped to it the four miles back to the beach site. Of course, what he hadn't thought of was the logistics of moving the oars to the horses, and what would happen if they were discovered. If they had the horses near the warehouses, then they would need to ride loaded down with long, heavy oars all the way past the warships, across the river, and then back along the south side of the harbour before they could even leave Fulquerville. That was just asking for trouble. But then, if they left the horses at the southern edge, they would have to lug seven oars each that same route by hand, just to reach the horses.

Clearly, the horses were out.

'Here's what we're going to do,' he said, pointing to illustrate his words. 'The oars are almost certainly stored in one of those large buildings on the far side, near the sea. That's their shipbuilding stores, and one of the ships is still lacking oars. But I was wrong in thinking we could get them away on the horses. So here's the plan. While Erik and I secure the oars, Richold will sneak down to the shore near the buildings. From here I can see a small rowing boat, maybe a four- or six-person one. It's high and dry right now, so it's in easy reach. Richold, you need to get to that boat and drag it down to the water's edge. Erik and I will bring the oars and load up, and then we'll push out to sea and *row* home with our prize.'

The others stared at him as though he were mad.

'You want to steal oars *and* a boat?' Erik hissed.

'And look at those waves,' Richold murmured, pointing out to sea. 'You want to row back in that?'

'I am more at home on the waves than on a horse.' Ulfr grinned. 'We get those oars in the boat and I'll get you home with them. That I promise. And with two of us rowing, we'll move fast. And,' he chuckled, 'we won't be short of oars to row home with.'

The other two were shaking their heads, but Ulfr had it all set in his head. As long as nothing went wrong, this would work. Retreating from the water's edge, they moved inland, around the back of the village area, toward the crossing of the river a little further up, and there they waited for an hour until the light began to fade.

Once gloom had settled across the land, the three men rode across the shallow river and, instead of moving along the river front, they circled around behind the buildings. The village was slightly busy, figures moving about their evening business, finishing up for the day, heading to or from the tavern, and so they would stay away from open ground. Once behind the village, unseen, Ulfr gestured for the others to tie up the animals by a small copse close to a barn and wait there. The village would need to be considerably quieter for their business to go ahead.

They waited there in the ever increasing dark, and every now and then Ulfr would scurry across the open grass, dip between the houses and glance around the harbour, each time admitting, grudgingly, that the place was still too busy for such a theft. Gradually, as midnight came, the figures around the village disappeared into their houses or aboard the ships, and the visible population thinned until it petered out to nothing. Finally, Ulfr decided they were good.

The three men abandoned their horses, leaving them to roam, while they crept between the buildings in the increasing darkness. Lights glowed here and there in the village, and, as they reached the harbour side and peered left and right, carefully, before emerging, they could still see lights aboard the warships. The skippers and their crews remained aboard, so close to the time of departure for war; there was no one clearly visible on the harbour side, though.

Taking a breath, ready for trouble, hand on the haft of his axe, Ulfr led the other two out from between the buildings, where they walked through the village in the black of night, as though they were taking a stroll, trying not to attract undue attention.

There were two warehouses above the empty slipway. Ulfr sucked his teeth as they approached, trying to decide how best to approach this.

He gestured to Erik. 'You take the nearest. I'll take the furthest. If you find the oars, come and get me straight away.' Then, to Richold, 'You know what to do.'

As they neared the buildings, the Varangian veered off to the left, approaching the nearest warehouse, drawing a sax as he went. There were no lights on in the buildings, but that was no guarantee of a lack of danger, especially when the day had started with such an omen of ill luck. Ulfr moved toward the second building, while Richold scurried onwards, making for the boat that was their only realistic escape option.

The shipwright drew his axe as he neared the building. Something was telling him that danger lay ahead; he could feel it in the air like a draugr hovering over him, menacing. The warehouse had three entrances, just like its twin: a huge double door above the slipway from which goods could be moved in and out to the work area; a second, similarly huge entrance on the landward side, where wagons could offload their goods for storage; and a small door in the side, facing out to sea. Ulfr thought about it, and reasoned that the larger doors were probably always barred from the inside, just as the sheds had been back in Sigtun, for they were only opened while goods were being loaded or unloaded. That meant that the only reasonable approach would be the small door, and so it was for this one that Ulfr made.

He reached the door, creeping the last few paces, and listened carefully. He could hear nothing but the lap of distant waves, the hooting of an owl in the trees behind the houses and the gentle murmur of the people back along the harbour inland. Still, he could *feel* the danger, even if he could neither see nor hear it. His mind raced. If there was a guard in the place, he should be either asleep on duty and therefore audibly snoring, or sitting, bored. Bored men make noises, too – shuffling, tapping, humming. Very few men were ever so silent they could not be heard over the distant tide retreating.

If there was absolutely no noise, and yet he was sure there was someone here, then that person was deliberately making no noise. And if that was the case, then perhaps the watchman sensed danger, too.

He looked at the door. It opened inwards. There was a lock and a latch. If there was a lock, the door was probably simply kept locked, and never barred from the inside. There would be no point. But locks could only hold under so much strain. The man inside, if he was anticipating trouble, was probably just on the other side of the timber. Ulfr imagined he could hear the man breathing.

He smiled and stepped close, then dragged a booted toe across the stonework, making a small sound. He then stopped and listened.

There.

He could just hear the faint sounds of careful movement inside. Right behind the door. Someone *was* listening. With a grin, Ulfr took three steps back, then ran and hit the door with his shoulder. He was a large man, with broad shoulders, and consequently brought a great deal of weight and momentum to the barge. He hit the door like a bull, the lock splintering with a sound that cut through the night sharply, the door itself slamming inwards, hard.

Ulfr was rewarded with success immediately. The man had been right behind the door, and the blow had sent him sprawling backwards, falling to the ground. He'd had a sword out, which clattered across the floor nearby, fallen from his grip.

The burly shipwright was on him before he could recover. Leaving the door clattering back against a shelf of stock, he dived for the stunned watchman, axe out. As he dropped onto the floored fellow he changed his grip, one hand on the butt of the axe, one near the bottom of the haft. Before the man could fight back, Ulfr had the axe haft pushed against his throat, while he pressed hard. He felt the crunch as pipes, bones and tendons broke under the assault, the man's face changing colour, eyes bulging and pinking where the blood vessels burst. He was making gagging sounds, unable to speak or breathe. Even when the sounds stopped and the body fell still, the shipwright held the axe in place for a count of thirty to be sure.

He looked at the Norman. He'd been a warrior, doing his job. He deserved a chance. Ulfr reached out and collected the fallen sword, bringing it back to the man's hand and wrapping the fingers around it, for the possibility that Odin's maidens would come.

Then he rose swiftly and ducked back out through the door, up to the street and down to the slipway. There was no sign of increased activity, and so his assault on the warehouse door had apparently gone unnoticed, thankfully. He dipped back inside and hurried this way and that. It was exceedingly hard to identify anything in the dark, and he was starting to think he needed a lamp, which might attract undue attention, when he found what he was looking for by the simple expedient of falling over them.

The oars were in a pile close to the slipway doors. Quickly dropping to a crouch, he used his fingers to examine them, counting as he went. There were plenty − more than twenty, anyway − and they were a good length. Grinning at his success, he rose and hurried over to the door, then ducked around to the far side, to the other warehouse.

The small door stood open, yet undamaged, and a body lay in the open doorway, throat cut, in a huge pool of glistening dark liquid. Ulfr stepped over the mess and into the gloom, putting away his axe as he went.

'Erik?' he hissed.

'Ulfr? I've found them.'

Ulfr blinked. 'Me too.'

'Two lots? They were holding out on us. What now?'

'We take five from here, the rest from the other warehouse. It's nearer to the boat, and we'll have to do four trips. They'll be heavy, but with one of us at each end we should be able to carry five easy enough.'

They counted out five oars and lifted them with a grunt. Ulfr tucked them under his armpit, using both hands in a circle around them, fingers knitted, and with Erik doing the same they carried the first load out through the door. As yet there seemed to be no alarm raised, and they took the most concealed route around the building, then scurried with their prize across the sand to where Richold was holding a small rowing boat at the water's edge.

'Well done.' The man grinned as the pair dropped their first load in the boat and then turned and ran back to the stores.

For speed, this time they went to the nearest shed and picked up five of the oars Ulfr had found, repeating the process. With ten in the boat, they turned and ran back for their third load. It was as they emerged with the final five that they heard a warning hiss from Richold, who was pointing wildly inland. They ran, abandoning subtlety, and dropped the last load into the boat with a clatter. As they began to push the vessel further out into the water, the sea lapping around their calves, Ulfr looked back across the harbour. Men on board the warships were shouting and waving, and other figures were pounding along the riverside.

'Quick,' he grunted, and they jumped into the boat as carefully as they could.

By unspoken agreement, Ulfr and Erik, as the two most muscular, took a pair of oars and thrust them through rowlocks and out into the water. It took a matter of heartbeats for them to find their rhythm, and by the time figures were running down the beach after them they were sufficiently far out into the water to be out of reach. An archer arrived and loosed a couple of desultory arrows across the sea at them, but they both fell well short, and by this time the two Northmen were pulling on the oars with the strength and skill of professional sailors.

They had done it. They were fleeing Fulquerville, without pursuit, with a boat full of oars.

They just had to get back and then launch the ship before Hauteville arrived with his army.

Chapter 17

It *was* a hard journey, even Ulfr had to admit. Once away from the safety of the harbour, the winter sea was extremely choppy, and it was hard to make headway. Behind them, for some time, they could see urgent activity in the harbour, but no one followed them out. The ships couldn't do so because of the low tide, and no one else there was brave – or perhaps stupid – enough to test a small rowing boat on the open water.

He lost track of time, but would estimate they were in the water, struggling south along the coast, for more than three hours, possibly nearer four. At one point the current pulled them far enough out to sea that they briefly lost sight of land, but through sheer effort they managed to angle back in. It helped that as they began to approach the Pirou area the tide was coming in, and the currents changed.

They were all grateful when the shape of the new ship surrounded by its palisade came into view, a vague shape in the dark lit only by dots of golden light, for the campfires burned all night now that winter cold had come.

As the boat finally beached, the three sailors heaved great sighs of relief. Looking up, they saw the changes made in the camp during their absence. An entire section of palisade nearest the sea had been removed, forming a large opening between ship and water, and therefore an easy access for the three travellers. Ulfr approved. He'd been planning to do that next anyway. They would need the freedom when the water was up, and there was no longer any real value to their defence. If the rebel army came, a palisade wouldn't change things much.

Workers came hurrying down the beach to them, grinning. For a moment Ulfr was worried. What if observers up in the dunes saw this? But then they might have seen the boat arrive anyway. Everything was a race, the time for subtlety more or less over.

'You did it.' Farlof laughed as he approached, men running past and grabbing oars from the rowing boat then ferrying them back up to the ship.

'You doubted me?' Ulfr smiled, jokingly.

'With this? Yes. How many?'

'Twenty.'

'Then we have all we need. We worked all night,' Farlof reported. 'We found a couple of dubious patches, but everything now has been re-caulked if it needed it, all the rowing positions are in place, everything is stowed on board, the steering oar is ready to drop into position and fasten, and we've put the unfinished mast aboard. I figure that if we survive to leave the beach then we'll probably find somewhere we can finish the work.'

Ulfr nodded. 'You've done well then, my friend.' He looked up, then back. 'I reckon the sun will start to show in about three hours. By then the tide will be close enough that we should be able to launch. There is nothing of great use we can do in three hours, but it would be best to keep the men busy anyway. Better not to have time to dwell on what is coming with the dawn.'

Farlof nodded. 'I have an idea. I'll assign everyone a bench, so that the whole crew knows where to go the moment we launch, and while we wait for the tide I'll get them in their places practising their oar-strokes. They've done some work on it, but now we've got actual oars, and the closer their timing, the better it will be for everyone.'

'Good. And while you're at it, load four spare long spars of timber.'

Ulfr left them to it. He was tired. It seemed an age since he'd had any reasonable sleep, and he'd spent the past few hours struggling against an unruly sea in a small boat. He let them carry off the last of the oars, then pulled the small rowing boat up further onto the sand and took his axe to it, holing it in three places, just so there was no chance of anyone attempting pursuit in it.

There was one job he needed to do yet, now that he had time. He'd named the ship, which was good, for to name a thing was to give it power, and *Sea Dragon* was a good, powerful name. But he knew the secrets as all good craftsmen, and he knew the reason that the *Sea Wolf* had been such a powerful, impressive ship was not just her construction, but his carefully worked designs that gave her extra speed and stealth; for just as names had power, so did runes and images. He'd not had time to work the new ship with such things yet, and taking her out untested without any precautions seemed foolish.

As such, as Farlof had the assembled men settled into the ship, he retrieved a chisel and mallet and moved to the prow of the ship. There, he painstakingly carved on each side, below where the figurehead would go, an М, the *ehwaz* rune of the Older World, imbuing the ship with the spirit of speed, progress and travel. This done to a quality of his satisfaction, he moved to the stern to where the steering oar was fitted, and here he carefully carved Ⱶ, the *kaun* rune of the Younger World, imbuing the steersman's place with inspiration and ingenuity. It was a small thing, but it was a start, and it would make a difference.

What work could be done completed, Ulfr climbed to the top of the dunes, carefully, looking this way and that for any figure left observing them. He saw no one and so emerged into the open, looking away into the distance. Twinkling lights marked the location of the castle, busy even through the night with the preparations for a campaign. He half expected to see an army surging across the grass in between, but nothing came as yet.

Returning to the camp, he spent a while watching the oar practice. They were a lot better than he'd expected, but they had a way to go, and still, in truth, had yet to practise with water giving them resistance. There were, he noted, enough of them that there was a man on each oar, with eight standing watching, and they were just the ones who'd signed on for the ship. The other workers were clustered at the far side, looking nervous, with no part to play.

It was time to start getting things moving, he reckoned. It could be as long as two hours before the water was high enough for an easy launch, but for a slightly earlier one with a little more work, an hour away at most – hopefully before both the sun and the lord de Hauteville put in an appearance. He crossed to the ship and climbed the frame to the sternpost, where he waved to get everyone's attention. Once there was silence, he looked about him.

'We all know what's coming, and it would be better for all of us if we were gone before the lord of Pirou arrives. As such, I intend an early launch. I want to be on the water when the sun shows. Here is what we will do. A small ship such as this can be moved across land with portage. It is a simple thing, but hard, gruelling work. Look to the ports in the upper strakes through which the oars will spring. The ship is narrow and sharp, at just thirteen feet wide, while the oars we have are eighteen-foot oars. This means that they can be pushed through the ports, right across the ship and out the other side, with two and a half feet of timber protruding. The other ten oars can remain shipped inside. The ship's hull has a shallow beam at just four feet from keel to oar port. This means that men at each oar can grasp two and a half feet of wood and lift the ship from the ground and carry her.'

There was a collective groan at this revelation. Even for twenty strong men, the ship would be extremely heavy. Ulfr recognised this, but he also knew the ugly truth of the long term. If they could not manage portage, then they would never make a longship crew.

'There are other ways, but with the time we have, this is what we can do, and we shall do it. The waterline is currently maybe eighty feet from the camp. That's just under two ship-lengths. If we wait for the water to come to us, we run a higher risk of meeting Hauteville. We can achieve extra speed in our portage, as those without an oar position can put their shoulders to the prow and stern and help lift and move, including myself and Farlof.'

He turned to the gathered locals who would be staying behind. 'You have my thanks for all you have done, and for your loyalty throughout.' He fished around by his feet and drew out four bags of coins, which he threw to the group. 'This is a small bonus by way of my gratitude. I do not expect you to stay, for you will find yourself in your lord's bad favour, but I would ask that you swiftly dismantle the cradle as we lift the ship. A few hammer blows at the critical pegs marked with chalk should be sufficient. Then you can leave, scatter, go home, find somewhere to hide and wait out the war.'

There was a murmur of gratitude, and Ulfr was happy that they had earned it, and there was no need to put them at further risk.

'All right,' he shouted. 'Let's run through the oars, lift the ship and watch the cradle vanish beneath us.'

He and Farlof dashed around giving directions, and the twenty rowers slid ten oars through the ship, leaving the rest inside, then put their shoulders to the protruding lengths of timber. Ulfr could hear panicked groans as men tried to lift sporadically, only to find no movement at all in the massive weight. Daft. They should realise it had to be a collective effort. The other eight men were positioned four at each end, where they gripped the keel and prepared to help take the weight.

The local workers hurried forward with large mallets and positioned themselves where they could knock out the pegs that held the frame together, collapsing it beneath the ship.

All was ready remarkably fast. While last checks were made, Ulfr once more climbed the dunes and looked east. Though it should be hard to tell, he was willing to bet that there were more lights and more movement at the castle than last time. Something was happening. He'd been right to start the launch early.

Back down to the beach, he shot a look at Farlof that suggested they needed to move fast. Orders were given, and then a countdown of five began.

At three, Ulfr cupped his hands to his mouth and shouted, 'Take the weight.'

There was a huge chorus of cursing, moaning and shouts as every shoulder and hand gripped and lifted. Ulfr was satisfied to see, despite the negativity, the whole ship rise almost a foot from the cradle.

'Brace yourselves,' he called as Farlof shouted 'Two.'

At 'one', the workers swung their hammers and the entire cradle beneath the ship collapsed in a splintered heap. There was a fresh round of cursing then, partially from those who'd not been pulling their weight and were suddenly forced to, but also from those whose legs took glancing blows from falling timbers and flying pegs.

They had it, though. The ship was held at shoulder height.

'Forward,' Ulfr bellowed, and gestured to Farlof.

His friend ran forth and took a place at the prow, adding his own shoulder to the lift, and Ulfr did the same at the sternpost. Slowly, with a steady chorus of swearing, the ship inched forward, leaving the pile of timber and moving with inexorable slowness toward the advancing tide.

Their task complete, the local workers called their thanks and their wishes of good luck, and then disappeared, melting away across the beach into the night, which was now starting to change shade, gradually lightening.

The first trouble happened less than half a ship-length away. Someone swore and let go sharply, and the sudden pressure of added weight caused a cascade effect as others let go. The ship dropped, and it was only through sheer strength of muscle and of will that those who remained managed somehow to take the strain and stop the ship crashing back to the beach. It might not have damaged her, but she was still so new. All it would take was for fresh caulking to come loose, and suddenly they would be putting to sea in a colander.

Farlof delivered a series of blistering insults at the man, who, chastened and red-cheeked, blew on his sore hands and grabbed once more, lifting. Then they were moving again. Finally, after what felt like weeks of travel, they had moved more than a ship-length away from the ruins of the cradle, and Ulfr, aware that this was a new and untested crew being asked to do one of the hardest things a crew could do, relented. He gave the orders that the ship be lowered to the sand. She was standing at the gap in the stockade, and men were keeping her balanced and upright without having to lift. Everyone would get a few minutes of rest before they tried the second leg and actually reached the water with her.

Leaving Farlof to the work, Ulfr took the opportunity to run back and check on the situation once more. The sky was definitely changing shade all the time; it was a way off properly light, but details were visible out across the fields as he reached the top of the dunes.

His heart caught in his mouth as he looked east. There was a mass of humanity around the base of the castle. The rebel army of the lords de Cotentin and de Hauteville was on the move, and he doubted they would go anywhere else to begin with but to the beach. He found himself wondering how the barons had so anticipated his early launch as to leave the castle early themselves – and then he saw it.

Two horses pounding across the fields in his direction, halfway between the castle and the beach.

Shit.

He turned and looked down across the beach to where his crew were having a breather, the new ship still short of the water.

'Farlof! Get them moving. The rebels are coming.'

It did not require his friend giving orders this time. Everyone down there had heard the news, and none of them were in any hurry to meet the lord Serlo de Hauteville again. In moments the ship was being lifted and slowly moved forward. Ulfr knew he should be down there helping, but he suspected he knew what was happening here, and that took precedence right now.

As the two horses came ever closer and the world became ever lighter, he saw that the mounts did indeed carry the very people he'd suspected, though not in the order he'd anticipated. Geoffroi rode ahead, wearing his war gear, ready for a fight. Behind him came not his injured friend with a passenger, but rather the other way around. Beatrix de Hauteville rode astride, like a man, the wounded Norman soldier behind her, arms wrapped around her waist.

Ulfr looked up beyond them. The army was most definitely moving their way, and at speed. They had left the infantry, just horsemen pounding across the turf, chasing down the three fugitives and expecting to catch the shipwright and his men on the beach into the bargain.

He waved to make sure he got the two riders' attention, and in what felt like mere moments the pair were reining in sweating mounts at the edge of the dunes.

'Well met, Ulfr Sveinsson,' Geoffroi shouted, holding up a hand. 'My companion and I wondered if there might be a spare place or two on your ship.'

Ulfr laughed. 'Always for a brave man. Welcome, Geoffroi. The ship is moving already.'

The Norman dismounted and crossed to the other horse, helping his wounded friend down. The pair of them bowed respectful heads to Beatrix, and then began to move past Ulfr, staggering down the sandy dunes, making for the beach and the work there. Ulfr crossed to the other horse and reached up a hand to help Beatrix down.

'Sadly, the sea will not welcome me today,' she said.

He frowned. 'What?'

'I came to help Geoffroi with his friend. And now I will help you, Ulfr of the Northmen. Take your ship and put to sea, and kiss the waves for me.'

He shook his head. 'You can come. We have room.'

'No, Ulfr. I have a different war to fight, and this one in my own family. Fear not for me. I will not be harmed. I am too valuable a treasure to damage.'

Ulfr was still shaking his head, but she had clearly made up her mind, for she turned the horse and reached down, pulling a sword from a scabbard slung on the saddle. He stared and she turned once more, just briefly, with the strangest smile.

'I will buy you what time I can. Put to sea, Ulfr.'

And then she was gone. She kicked her horse to speed, letting out a roar of belligerent fury that would give Bjorn a run for his money, and charged across the turf, sword levelled, roaring defiance as she charged the army of her brother head-long.

He looked back. The ship was almost in the water. The men were achieving the seemingly impossible, driven by the necessity of survival. He should help, but somehow he could not let Beatrix do this without someone watching – without a witness who could sing songs of her glory in the mead halls. She raced across the farmland, roaring like a warrior, and he was struck then that no one had ever actually told him what a Valkyrjur should actually look like, but right now if he had to describe the warrior handmaidens of Odin, by all the gods, he would be describing Beatrix.

And it worked. She charged the rebel army, and as the two met it was the mass cavalry of the barons who veered off, peeling away to avoid contact with her. Their charge across the fields ended for a time, as they raced off to the sides, unsure of what to do, for there could be no doubt that Hauteville was bellowing orders that his sister was not to be harmed, yet she was charging back and forth, attempting to slam a blade into any man she could reach.

He gave her a sad smile, oddly certain that, though he would never see her again, she would be all right. Life was not done with a woman of her quality yet. He turned his back, asking Odin to watch over her, despite her adherence to the White Christ.

She had bought them precious time; now they needed to make sure it had been worthwhile. He turned, scrambling back down the dunes, and pounded across the beach, kicking up sprays of sand in his wake as he bore down on the ship. She was at the water, but they hadn't lowered her yet. Farlof was ready to walk her out until they were neck deep to be sure, good man that he was.

By the time Ulfr was closing on the vessel the whole ship was in the water, the men at the prow waist deep, those at the back just at ankle depth. He ran to the stern and put his shoulder to it, heaving onwards. Slowly they moved out into the water, and he felt every inch of tide was a saviour reaching up to help him to freedom. The water touched his knees, and he could hear the approaching army, the shouts back across the fields just beyond the dunes. He wondered for a moment how Beatrix had fared with her brother – but he had to put her from his mind. She was right. She was far too valuable as a potential political bride to be allowed to be damaged, and so she would be all right in the long run, though it was extremely possible that Serlo would take it out on her in his anger, regardless. Not all punishments were lethal or left lasting marks.

Forgetting her with some difficulty, he continued to heave, feeling the water slopping up around his thighs. As it touched his belt, he heard the first cries of alarm from behind. The vanguard of the rebel army had reached the dunes.

'Drop her,' he bellowed, and prayed that there was enough water to take her weight.

Every man along the hull let go, and the ship slapped down into the water just as the first glow of light began to play across the dunes behind them, highlighting the six riders up there who were gesticulating, pointing at the ship out across the beach.

It was still a race. They were thigh deep in the ice-cold water, but a horse could manage that, too, and it would take them precious time to get moving.

'Climb in,' he shouted, even as he watched the ship rock once or twice and then settle.

There was enough water for her shallow beam. At his urging, the half a dozen men at the back heaved and gave the floating vessel just the tiniest bit of momentum, allowing her to gain a few extra inches of water as the men climbed aboard and added weight. He almost panicked then, worrying that he'd misjudged it. The keel touched the seabed for a moment, but then it was moving once more, heading out to sea. He watched as the last few men piled aboard, and then finally there was just Ulfr at the stern, stomach deep.

He looked back. Horsemen were pounding across the wide expanse of sand toward them, and there was still time for trouble. Then, hands were reaching down from the ship, grabbing his wrists, pulling him aboard.

Ulfr was the last man in the ship, and he realised then that he was the only real sailor among them. Farlof had done a few stints in Byzantine galleys, but not a single man had rowed or crewed a longship before. They were milling about, uncertain of the next move, and so he tried to put away all thoughts of what was happening outside the ship.

'Pull the oars back across so that they are level above the water. Run out the other ten through the ports you've cleared and do the same with them – all oars horizontal, above the water.'

As they began to work, he ran across to the steering oar. She was still lifted and tied, but he feared that dropping it might simply land it in the sand where it would act more as an anchor than a steering board. He called over one of the unoccupied men and handed him a knife.

'The moment you think the water is deep enough to take the length of that steering oar, cut the line and drop it in, then angle it straight out to sea. Got it?'

The man – staring, worried – nodded.

Ulfr ran forward, pointing to other unoccupied men. Perhaps it was useful to have spare men who were not required at the oars after all. He found four of them, and then gestured to the four long timbers he'd ordered brought aboard at the last moment.

'Get astern. Grip them tight and push them down into the water, into the sand. Punt us forward. Give us any extra momentum you can.'

The men grabbed the timbers and ran. Apart from him and Farlof, and Geoffroi and his man, who were collapsed near the bow, only three men were unoccupied. He waved at them.

'You need to move across the whole ship. Examine every board and every peg. Look for any leaks. If you find one, report back to me.

That was it. Everyone had a job. Everyone except Farlof, but he was useful just moving around helping people and giving commands. Ulfr hurried back to the stern, where the four men were heaving with their poles against the sand, helping drive them forward. They were moving deeper all the time, and the tide was still coming in, giving them added safety.

The lead riders had reined in at the water's edge, but he could see others coming up behind them, and this wasn't over, for orders were being given out. He heard Farlof giving the order to dip oars, and a moment later there was a horribly arrhythmic clatter and splash as twenty inexpert rowers failed spectacularly to achieve unison. There were two cries of pain as oars collided, knocking back against their owners. Ulfr winced. Such things could break ribs. At least they had spare oarsmen.

Farlof was on it, and his cursing and snarled orders had their effect. There were two more half-hearted failed attempts, but on the fourth stroke, the oars disappeared into the water with an almost perfect unified splash. Still, there were failures as they rose and turned and then clattered and splashed here and there back into the water, but by the time they'd had eight or nine strokes, the oars were moving in pretty good time.

The ship was cutting out to sea.

Next to Ulfr there was another splash as the steering oar was dropped into the water. His joy at the thought that they were at sea at last was curtailed by a blood-curdling scream from his right. He turned, sharply, to see one of the men who'd been punting them away had dropped his timber and was slumped over the stern, a long spear already falling away, covered in blood, thrown by a rider who'd ridden out into the waves. Others were coming, too, and it looked as though archers were arriving. Ulfr felt a grim satisfaction as a second thrown spear fell short, splashing into the water behind them. That was it. They were out of reach, and by the time archers got anywhere near the water the ship would be too far out to reach. They were at sea, and every oar stroke took them further from danger.

He gestured to the man with the steering oar. 'Keep us straight until you can barely see the horses on the shore, then give me a shout and we'll start our turn north.'

Leaving the nervous-looking man to his work, Ulfr moved forward, noting with some satisfaction that the oarsmen seemed to have achieved a basic rhythm. He didn't know how long they'd manage to keep it up, but for now it would carry them out of danger and even out of sight of Pirou, thank Odin.

Back in the bow, he approached Geoffroi.

'I am glad you escaped. Where can we take you? I assume you are not here for a life on the waves?'

The knight chuckled in a tired voice. 'I cannot say that is not tempting, but no. I have duties. I shall not stay in the Cotentin, for the rebels now control the peninsula, possibly including my own lands. I will make for Falaise and the duke, and lend my sword to his cause. I am leaping to the assumption that Falaise is where you, too, are bound, for that is where your jarl will be found.'

Ulfr nodded. 'We will get as close as we can to Falaise. This Clécy place of which you spoke. From there we can rescue Halfdan and the others, and you can rejoin your duke. During our journey, I am hoping that you will be able to help navigate, for you will know these shores better than anyone here.'

Geoffroi nodded.

The sun chose that moment to burst free of the horizon. Though it was still bitterly cold, the day looked set to be a dry one, and the winter sun blazed with golden glory across Nordmandi.

'I have a gift for you,' came a voice, and Ulfr turned to see Farlof behind him.

'Oh?'

'Some weeks ago, I heard you talking to yourself.'

He reached into the bags and goods stowed near the prow and found a large sack, which clearly weighed a great deal from the strain that showed on his face as he lifted it. Whatever was in it was a good three feet long and a foot both wide and thick. Farlof held it sideways across his hands, as though he were offering a sword. Frowning, Ulfr reached down. As he took it, his friend removed the sack.

'Gods,' Ulfr said in a breathless tone as he looked down at what slid free of the cover. The dragon's head was carved with immense skill, and touched up with black, yellow and red paint, giving it a fearsome appearance. It was an old-fashioned design, like the ship's prows of his forefathers, like the great dragon boats that had sailed from fjord and isle to raid on the rich coastlines of the east for fifty generations.

'I heard you call her the *Sea Dragon*,' Farlof explained.

Ulfr could only nod. He wasn't entirely sure he could trust his voice. It was rare that emotion claimed and floored him, but this was one such moment.

'When...?' he managed.

'I hired the carpenter at Pirou to do it, privately.'

Ulfr smiled, thinking back over his visit there, when the man had come out of some back room, claiming to be working on a private project. The sneaky bastards. The *wonderful* sneaky bastards. A name gave power. Runes gave power. But *this* would give the *Sea Dragon* more power than anything. This completed her.

The danger on the beach entirely forgotten as they cut ever further out into the water, Ulfr and Farlof lifted the dragon's head and fitted it to the prow post. It would need to be pegged in, but just looking at it, standing there, proud, sent Ulfr's heart soaring.

They were free. They were heading north with the *Sea Dragon*.

He'd done it.

Chapter 18

The sun dawned on a new world for the Wolves of Odin.

For Ulfr it was a return to an older time, of longships and the icy whitecaps of the seas south of his home, of the sound of oars and weary men, of creaking timbers and crying gulls, of the freedom a man can only know in the embrace of the whale road.

For Farlof, it was the world of his forefathers that he himself had never truly experienced. He was a Northman to the core, come south to serve among the Rus in the Byzantine Emperor's guard and then sent west to fight in Italy, but he had spent most of his life on land. What time he'd had on the water had been in the slow, heavy war galleys of the Byzantines, with their fire-belchers and their multiple oar banks. He had never known the simplicity of a swift-lined raider with a complement of men small enough to be brothers.

For the others, it was *truly* new. Most of them were workers in the harbour of Fulquerville or local labourers from Pirou who had taken Ulfr's offer as the chance for a new life without the drudgery of serfdom in Nordmandi. They might yet regret their decision, as the sheer effort of sailing a longship on the open ocean seeped into their bones, and maybe the uncertainty of their future, too; but for now, despite the weariness and effort, they were in high spirits at the opening of a world of adventure. Ulfr was willing to bet that after a few weeks, once their muscles had built and the rhythm and pace of the whale road had claimed them, none of them would want to go back to their land-bound world of tedium and cruelty.

A new world under a cold winter sun, as the waves slapped against the side of the ship and the oars rose and fell, rose and fell, rose and fell, now in a reasonable rhythm, the best part of an hour away from the beach at Pirou.

They had escaped capture or death at the hands of the rebel barons, and they had a new ship with a new crew, hungry for possibility. True, the ship was unfinished, and at the first real opportunity Ulfr intended to spend two or three days ashore as they finished the mast and found a sail to raise upon it and save the arms of the crew, but even unfinished, she was a thing of beauty.

He knew that it would be a year before he was done with her. Apart from the actual ship parts that were required for any reasonable voyage, she would need a sternpost; the crew would all need shields that could be slotted into place along the sheer strake, and, more than anything, she needed to be made to feel like *their* ship. The *Sea Wolf* had been carved with intricate and ancient designs, and the same would be true in time of the *Sea Dragon*. It would be an ongoing work whenever they were not actively at sea.

'Ship oars. Rest for quarter of an hour,' he bellowed between cupped hands, drawing a cheer from the rowers, who must be close to exhaustion, this being their first ever voyage at the oars.

Farlof and Geoffroi wandered along the ship to meet him at the stern, where he had taken over the steering oar from the new man. All along the way men cheered them and grinned. Rarely had a ship ever seen such good humour.

'What is the long-term plan?' Farlof asked as he settled in to lean against the rail.

Ulfr shrugged. 'We sail the coastline until we reach the river that Geoffroi told me about, then sail inland as far as it's navigable. Then we need to stop and move across land and make contact with Halfdan and the others at Falaise. There, Geoffroi will join his duke, but I presume the rest of us will return to the *Sea Dragon* and make our way to the sea.'

'And after that?'

'This is the jarl's call, but I think we shall be bound for homelands. We still have unfinished business with Harðráði and our stolen ship – and with the priest Hjalmvigi,' he added in a dark tone that those who were not in Georgia with the bloody jarl and his rabid priest would never understand.

'But you have a *new* ship?' Geoffroi said.

'The *Sea Wolf* is ours, too. My last great ship. If you had a gold coin and someone took it from you, would you shrug and forget it, because you knew you had another gold coin?'

'Point taken,' smiled the Norman.

'What can you tell us of the journey to come?'

Geoffroi scrubbed his short hair with a rough hand. 'Probably not enough to help, to be honest. Normally there are plenty of good harbours to put in to, and the coast is clear of pirates these days. There are various small hazards, from sandbanks and submerged rocks to cliffs and surprise currents, but those I know well enough to see us through. The problem is that everything is changing.'

'Because of the rebellion against the duke?'

'Quite. Harbours that I know to be friendly will probably now be closed. Places that are the usual anchorage of traders will probably be filled with warships instead. And while there are still no pirates, now there will be ships of the rebel barons, which may well be worse for us. My homeland is on the north tip of the Cotentin. I cannot say for certain what has happened there since I left and my own lord rebelled, but it may be that it remains untouched, in which case we will find friends there. Whatever the case, there will be two or three coastal villages between here and the river where I will be welcome. All we need is to make it to one of them, and we can pause there long enough for you to finish your mast and purchase a sail. After that, things will become easier.'

Ulfr smiled. 'Good. That all sounds as well as could be hoped.'

'Uh… Skipper?' called a voice from further forward.

Ulfr looked past his friends and saw one of the new men at the prow alternately waving at him and pointing off toward the coast ahead. He looked in that direction and his breath caught in his throat. *That* was something he'd not taken into account. A little short of an hour out from Pirou's beach, they were about to pass Fulquerville on their way north. He cursed, chiding himself for having overlooked the most blatant of dangers. It was fully high tide, and what they had done in the harbour that night would be be known to all. It came as no surprise, then, to see three warships moving across the tidal harbour toward the open water, angling to intercept the *Sea Dragon*.

Some darkly humorous part of him chuckled at the fact that there were three, the fourth unable to pursue thanks to the fact that the *Sea Dragon* was using their oars to get away. Still, it was not enough to make him laugh openly right now.

Once again, he felt keenly the absence of his friends – Halfdan with his luck, Leif with his knowledge, Gunnhild with her certainty, and Ketil and Bjorn with their promise of violent victory in almost any circumstances. But there was nothing for it. It came down to him. He was the skipper and in absolute command, and so the onus of saving their collective hides was entirely on him.

Three to one. All three were bigger ships, and all three had sails. That meant that outrunning them would rely on the strength of the oarsmen's arms, and they were already tired. Running would not save them, even though the *Sea Dragon* could be the faster ship by far when she was finished.

He thought back on what he'd seen of them in the harbour. They were really very similar to an old-fashioned longship, just a bit larger and of slightly differing construction. That meant that they would not have great weapons of war fitted on board, as the Byzantines had. They would rely instead on boarding their enemies and overwhelming them in the old manner. They might have archers, mind, and that made a great deal of difference.

He remembered, with a further sinking in the pit of his stomach, the warriors he'd seen aboard them. Like almost all these Norman soldiers, they were killers. With the love of war of an ancient Northman, combined with a hunger to prove themselves and to conquer, they had become violence incarnate. Then he looked at his crew. They were mostly manual labourers or the men of a shipwright. A little over half of them were armed, with axes mostly, and seven wore tunics of leather sewn with metal plates. Few had helmets, even fewer chain shirts. And of them, who had any experience at war? The answer to that was a bleak one: Ulfr, Farlof, Geoffroi and his wounded companion, two Apulian Wolves and two Varangian ones. Of a crew currently of thirty-two, eight had any skill in combat, and one of those was too badly wounded to fight.

So not only was running away almost certainly a death sentence, so was any attempt to fight them. That left only something sneaky – and that, really, was Halfdan's role.

He found himself cursing again as he ran through it all.

'We're in trouble,' Farlof summarised.

'Yes. They outnumber us, and us being without a sail means they can outrun us, and as things stand they can easily outfight us. Halfdan and Gunnhild would have a solution, but I have not.'

'This ship has a shallow beam, yes?' Geoffroi said thoughtfully.

Ulfr nodded. 'Very.'

'I doubt those three ships are anywhere near as shallow?'

Ulfr thought back, picturing them at low tide in the harbour, leaning at an angle in the sand. He nodded. 'Much deeper, I'd say.'

'Can we get ahead of them?'

Ulfr looked along the coast. The enemy ships were only just emerging from the harbour. The skippers were utilising sail, saving their oars for the attack. He did not even need to look up or around to sense that the wind was a north-westerly, which made their decision foolish. They would be struggling to use the wind, and the further north the *Sea Dragon* managed, the worse that struggle would be. So it all depended on the oarsmen.

He cupped his hands again. 'The ships of Hauteville are coming for us,' he bellowed, which cut through the good-natured murmur across the vessel and silenced the men with a solid air of nervousness. He took another breath. 'We cannot fight them, but if you are strong, and you can bend to oars once more, we can still beat them. How are your backs?'

There was a roar then, which surprised him. He'd half expected nerves to claim them, but somehow their new-found freedom on the waves had given them a confidence he'd not anticipated. He grinned.

'Are you men?'

A roar of affirmation.

'Or are you *Wolves*?' he bellowed, and this time the roar was deafening.

He had planned then to give the order, but he discovered, again to his surprise, that he had no need to. Someone among the crew, even as the roar died down, was already calling out a time beat, and the oars dropped into the water in time with that rhythm, the *Sea Dragon* surging forward with astonishing speed.

'Damn, she's fast,' Geoffroi breathed.

'I only build fast ships,' Ulfr replied. 'Some men prefer bulk, strength or capacity. I like speed.'

'And I like your thinking,' the Norman said. 'All right, here's what we do. There are three routes along the coast north of here, each defined by a series of sandbanks. The furthest west, out to sea, is the clearest, and any ship can ply it, but the waves will be high and cruel that far out, and it will take time to sail far enough out and back. The central route is the one used by most traffic, for it is clear for all but the deepest of keels, but it still takes time to sail far enough out and back. The inner channel is only used by small and very shallow fishing boats, for it is too dangerous, though it is also by far the fastest route north.'

'Hazards?' Ulfr grinned.

'The Lucky Banks – which are not – the low-port reef, and the rocks known as the Feet of God. Only a lunatic takes the inner channel, but it will easily gain a ship an hour or two on pursuit by either of the other routes.'

Ulfr laughed. 'And we have a beam so shallow that even small fishing boats would be envious.' He peered off ahead. 'How close to the shore?'

Geoffroi smiled. 'Angle for land now, aiming for the far side of the harbour, and I'll take the prow and call your route.'

The Norman rushed to the fore then and grasped the great carved dragon, peering into the spray. Ulfr angled as he was told, toward the shore to the north of Fulquerville, and watched with a frisson of nervous energy as the three vessels began to pick up speed out of the harbour. It was going to be close.

With every few yards they cut north, the three warships closed at a tangent, intending to cut them off. Then, just when Ulfr was thinking they would do it, the three ships furled their sails and the oars were run out. Moments later the warships of Serlo de Hauteville were surging forward, racing to beat the *Sea Dragon* to her planned route.

'Farlof!'

'Ulfr?'

'Double the oar strokes.'

His friend looked back with wide eyes. They were already going fast, a punishing pace for untrained rowers who were already tired. Any faster and they might just risk breaking their own oarsmen. But Ulfr held the man's gaze. If they didn't make it past the three ships, then nothing else would matter. Farlof seemed to realise this, nodded, and immediately bellowed out the new order, then began to stamp his foot loudly to create the new rhythm.

The noise from the oarsmen died away as every man saved his breath, bending all his effort to the work. Ulfr felt pride in his crew as the *Sea Dragon* lurched forward once more, a new pace sending her bouncing across the waves like a dream, despite the weariness of its inexperienced oarsmen.

He watched the coast angling toward the *Sea Dragon*, watched the three enemy ships desperately trying to stop them. He knew they were going to make it, as long as the rowers could keep up the pace. He paid attention to Geoffroi, who was waving and gesturing for a little more easterly. He changed the angle of the steering oar, and in moments they were cutting ever closer to the enemy.

It went on like that for mere minutes, though it felt like years to Ulfr. Changing the angle, watching the shore, marking their enemies. Then they were almost at the point of collision…

And then they were passing the danger. The *Sea Dragon* shot across the bow of the lead warship, just three ship-lengths ahead of it, raising an audible howl of anguish from the Norman crew. Then, in quick succession, they raced across the front of the second and third ships, closer to each one as they passed.

Behind them, as they raced for that dangerous inner channel, the three warships panicked. The lead ship, which they had passed first, decided there was no hope of following and raced out to sea, making for the middle channel – the clear one used by most sensible shipping. The last of the three seemed to decide that pursuit was fruitless and slowed, turning, preparing to make for the harbour once more. The middle ship, though, fell into pursuit. It turned as tightly as it could, veering so sharply that men tumbled and slid around the deck, trying to come about behind the *Sea Dragon*.

Ulfr's concentration shifted in an instant with that instinct of a born sailor. The threat of enemy vessels had been left behind, and their pursuit became a worry secondary to what lay in front of them. He had one eye on the coastal waters ahead, and the other on Geoffroi in the prow. It took only a dozen heartbeats into their new course for him to realise just how dangerous this route could be.

The Lucky Banks turned out to be sandbanks that formed a visible ridge during lower tides, but at high tide were submerged just below the water's surface, waiting to snag the keel, steering board and oars of any vessel foolish enough to come near. Ulfr saw five different places where the sand came close enough to the surface that even the *Sea Dragon* risked grounding, but with every twitch of a hand from Geoffroi, and every slight nudge in angle at the steering oar, they moved deftly between the obstacles, continuing to cut north all the time.

Looking back momentarily when the Norman signalled a stretch of clear water, Ulfr was impressed to see that the enemy warship was still on their trail, using their own movements as a guide to avoid running aground. It was doing impressively well. A quick glance in the other directions confirmed that the third vessel had returned to the harbour, and the one they had first encountered was out of sight, out to sea. They would soon be far behind. It was just this persistent pursuer who continued to threaten the *Sea Dragon*.

After perhaps two or three miles of the submerged menace, Ulfr was getting the hang of this coast, until suddenly Geoffroi threw out a series of urgent signals. The shipwright tried to follow them as swiftly as he could, bellowing for the right oars to back water, turning his steering oar madly, calling for Farlof, who hurried back and forth among the rowers, trying to keep them working as a team even as they were given differing instructions depending on which side of the ship they rowed.

The *Sea Dragon* lurched sharply to the right, dangerously so, and the crew bellowed out in fright and consternation as they struggled to stay in their benches, holding tight to their oars as the ship swayed wildly. Ulfr's eyes widened as he saw for what they'd been bound: a submerged reef or rocky shelf, only visible as white foam where the water slammed into it. Had they not turned sharply, they'd plainly have torn out the bottom of the *Sea Dragon* on it.

He was both irked at and grateful to Geoffroi. He felt that perhaps the Norman could have prepared them for it earlier, but on the other hand, he *had* saved them from hitting the thing.

Then, the reason for the last-moment move became clear. Even as the *Sea Dragon* began to pick up speed making east toward the shore, the ship following them had had too little time to react and lacked the skill and knowledge of the combination of Ulfr and Geoffroi. He watched with a great deal of satisfaction as the Hauteville warship ploughed into the reef, even as it tried to turn at the last moment. With a sound like a tree screaming, the timbers of the enemy ship tore and gave, breaking on the rocks.

They sailed on, turning a leisurely north once more at a signal from Geoffroi, and leaving behind the slowly disappearing wreckage of the warship on the rocks. By the time they left the low-port reef and passed among the Feet of God, Ulfr was starting to rather like the challenge of this place. These rocks were easier to deal with. They presented more of a challenge in terms of navigation, but at least they protruded from the surface and were readily visible.

An hour later they were clear of all the hazards and moving at a reasonably leisurely pace along the coast in a northerly direction. With Ulfr's blessing, Farlof eased the pace – without such immediate danger any more – allowing the men to rest a little. The most exhausted rowers were swapped out for those who'd not had a stint at the oars, and they moved on with increasing confidence. Some time in the early afternoon, they reached the tip of the Cotentin Peninsula, and followed the curve of the coastline as it turned east. The going became easier, the wind with them, the waves lighter with no submerged obstacles.

They sailed on for another hour, keeping the pace steady, watching the coast ahead and occasionally the open sea behind, warily. Twice, Ulfr thought he saw the shape of a Norman warship on the horizon behind them, but the winter clouds made the view hazy and uncertain at best, and he could not say for sure what it was.

It was around mid-afternoon when there was no longer any doubt. The shape of the enemy ship appeared unmistakably on the horizon, and had come closer – close enough to see it constantly. Ulfr had spent enough of his life in similar positions to be confident that while he could see the Norman ship, the reverse would not be true, for the enemy stood out black in a world of blue and grey, while the *Sea Dragon* would be lost to view against the ever-changing coastline. That would only hold true for so long, of course, until the enemy was too close to miss them.

Finally, as Ulfr was starting to worry about the predicament for which they were heading, Geoffroi called across to him.

'This headland marks the edge of my own territory. Watch now, and we will see whether they remain *my* lands or whether Neel de Cotentin has taken control of them.'

As they passed around the shallow headland, Ulfr looked ahead at a stretch of rocky shoreline that boded poorly for ships that came too close, rocks that led up to cliffs that towered some sixty feet above the water.

'Look,' Geoffroi said, voice tight but with a hint of victory. He pointed to the top of the cliffs, and Ulfr spotted a tower atop the great rocky outcrop, a squat stone construction, and above it, snapping in the wind, was a flag – two simple horizontal stripes, white over black.

'Yes?'

'My colours. I had hoped that my lands would be too minor for the lord de Cotentin to bother with for now. He has bigger problems and greater enemies than I. And if these lands are still mine, then we have friends here. Slow your rowers and watch the cliffs.'

Farlof gave the order, and the *Sea Dragon* moved to little more than a drift along the coast. Ulfr watched, not sure what he was looking for, yet he saw it half a heartbeat before the Norman pointed and said 'here'.

The cliffs folded inwards into a narrow defile. It was not deep, and any attempt to climb the sixty feet would be at best gruelling, but it struck Ulfr immediately as just about the right size to hold a longship. He looked at the rocky shoreline, where shelves of grey points sat just beneath the water's surface, yet at that defile they dropped away, almost mirroring the recess under the waves. The *Sea Dragon* could approach, with careful steering, and reach the cliffs without grounding on rocks, and with a little work could be pulled up and beached in the narrow, V-shaped cove.

He grinned. 'Farlof, have the oarsmen back water until we are still. Then we need to turn sharp and make for that defile. Once we're lined up, we move very slowly, so that I can adjust and prevent hitting any submerged rock.'

Farlof nodded and went about the work. The *Sea Dragon* slowed, and then gradually turned to point into that narrow cove. Over the next quarter of an hour, they moved slowly in between the narrow rocky shelves, with Ulfr making tiny, fractional adjustments with every two or three heartbeats, all the time with that distant Norman warship coming closer, growing larger on the horizon. Finally, the Wolves shipped oars and coasted the last twenty yards, coming to a halt just short of a narrow, gravel beach. There, they waited, swaying barely imperceptibly with the waves lapping against the rocks.

They could even hear the sound of the approaching Norman vessel now, and every Wolf held his breath as the ship approached, and then passed, willing them not to see the berthed ship in the narrow defile, but it seemed that the gods were with them. The Normans ploughed past without a glance in their direction.

Ulfr let out an explosive breath once they were far enough gone that not even the sound of their oars and shouts echoed back to the cove. They had made it. From here, it should not be too difficult to move from friendly haven to friendly haven all the way to Falaise, especially with the local coastal knowledge of Geoffroi to guide them.

'I think we're safe,' he said with a sigh of relief.

'You know what's better than a hideaway?' Geoffroi said with a smile.

'What?'

'A hideaway in my lands, with a sailmaker just a mile along the coast.'

Ulfr grinned. Today was getting better and better.

Part Four

ᚹᛟᛚᚠᛖᛋ ᛟᚠ ᛟᛞᛁᚾ

Rebellion

Cattle die.
Kinsmen die.
All men are mortal.
Words of praise will never perish,
nor a noble name.

On Renown from the *Hávamál*

Chapter 19

'You are a most curious priest,' Halfdan said, brow furrowed as he strode through the upper corridors of the duke's keep, his head rocking with that slight swimminess of just a little more wine than was good for him.

Beside him, the man in the long White Christ priest's robes, with the aquiline nose and the slicked-back receding hair – receded so far, in fact, that his tonsure might be entirely natural – gave him a smile and a bird-like chuckle.

'How so?'

'I have met priests of your nailed god often in my travels. They range in their personality. I have met those who were so desperate to make every man believe that they were willing to flay or burn a man to persuade him. Such men burned my village and killed my father,' he added darkly, remembering the hated Hjalmvigi. 'And I have met priests who were too important to care about those of us who cling to the true ways. Men who would rather talk to a wall than to sons of Odin and Loki. I have met those who hate, and those who ignore, those who thirst for conversion, and those who burn with the desire to kill all who do not believe. What I have never met is a genial priest.'

This made Archbishop Ælfric laugh out loud. 'Oh, you poor deluded pagan. *Genial?* Back in Angle-land, there are men who think I am the Devil incarnate, who think me proud and violent, and wicked, and dangerous.' He gave Halfdan a sidelong wink. 'I *am*, of course, *all* those things. But only among those who deserve it. In my home things are different, Halfdan of

Gotland. Half our island is still inhabited by pagans and heretics, clinging to ungodly ways in their northern and western lairs, sacrificing and singing songs to demons long dead. If I had taken on the mantle of Jorvik with the intention of rooting out paganism and heresy, it would have taken the rest of my life without even managing to get as far as the old Roman wall. No, I leave the punishing of paganism to those men such as you describe – young, hungry, and at least slightly insane. For me, I am content in the knowledge that however much you enjoy your beer now, in the eternity of the hereafter you will burn forever, while I will look down on you from Heaven and tut like a kindly schoolmaster.'

Halfdan frowned. He hated talking to the oddly affable Archbishop of Jorvik, because half the time he couldn't tell whether the man was serious or mocking. Usually both, he suspected. Ælfric was a complicated man, yet oddly Halfdan couldn't help but like him. It helped that he was the first priest of the nailed god who had spoken to the jarl as an equal, of course.

'So this Emma,' he said. 'She is a queen in your land, yes?'

Ælfric nodded. 'Not *the* queen, but *a* queen. Her husband was king some years ago. I crowned the new king myself earlier this year, her son Edward. But he and the former queen are not on the best of terms. He has stripped his mother of all her property and wealth.'

'And you ask the duke to help her?'

The archbishop gave a strange smile. 'She is in a difficult position. Dispossessed in Angle-land, yet not overly popular here, despite being the duke's cousin. She has retreated to Bruggis, and so I am here to beseech her cousin on her behalf. I am rather rueful, however, over my timing. To choose a time of rebellion to visit shows a distinct lack of foresight, I fear.'

Halfdan nodded as they returned to their rooms. The castle was rather quiet at this late hour, so long after the feast was finished. Most of the attendees had been abed for at least two hours, including the duke. Halfdan, however, had ended up in conversation with a small group of men, drinking the best wine on offer in surprising quantities. It seemed that one of the qualifications to become a bishop was a prodigious capacity for strong drink. Ælfric hardly seemed affected.

The archbishop was only one of the men who had attended the feast that had been thrown to test the support of the eastern barons. Forty-seven invitations had been issued to men of title, land and the Church, and twenty-six had attended, which left a worryingly large number of likely rebels. For Halfdan, the gathering had had an unexpected side effect. Naturally, for men of international politics, occasionally various conversations had turned to foreign lands, and the jarl had heard some baron mention Jarisleif of Kiev. That had pricked his ears, and he'd drifted into that conversation as it was something pertinent to the Wolves.

That had been when he'd heard the most important news since Miklagarðr. At the same time that the Wolves had been battling their way across Apulia, the thief Harðráði had returned to Kiev and married Jarisleif's daughter, Ellisif. The thief remained for now in Kiev, which meant that the *Sea Wolf* would also be there, but it was said that he gathered support to come west once more, for in addition to his claim to the Norse throne his marriage put him in the royal line of the Swedes.

Everything had fallen into place that evening. Gunnhild had said there was some connection between the duke and Harðráði, and whatever it was, by sheer accident during a feast, Halfdan had heard exactly what he had hoped to hear. He was energised, and a little drunk, but mostly excited. He had what they had sought: information as to their prey. Better still, a little steering of the conversation had brought fresh insight.

Olof of the Swedes was long gone, dead even before Halfdan and his friends had reached Georgia, succeeded by his son Onund, once a companion of Jarl Yngvar, and worse — or possibly better, Halfdan had yet to decide — the hated priest

Hjalmvigi had become Onund's personal confessor. It seemed that Halfdan's enemies were re-emerging, gathering in the north. They might be powerful men – the glorious but untrustworthy Harðráði, as heir to numerous thrones, and the priest, against whom Halfdan had sworn a new blood oath, as a royal advisor – but Halfdan was a powerful man himself: veteran of wars, of the imperial guard, friend and protector to dukes and empresses.

A great conflict was coming.

Of course, that brought with it a somewhat unwanted memory: a dream of himself standing as Loki, on a bleak, blasted hillside, watching the great guardian of Bifrost, Heimdallr, emerge from a doorway to face him under a blood-red sky.

Ragnarok.

The jarl, his wits slightly dulled by the wine, realised that his mind had wandered as they walked, and that Ælfric had been speaking to him unheard all this time.

'...and so there has to be some peaceful solution between the king and his mother. Though I have troubles enough in Jorvik.'

Halfdan gave a non-committal grunt and nodded, hoping that it appeared he had been listening.

'If I cannot put my own house in order in the North, how can I hope to persuade King Edward to do the same. It is a problem. But for now, it is a secondary problem.'

The jarl continued to nod, lost, wondering what he had missed.

'Some problems have to wait,' he said sagely, hoping that fitted in with whatever they were talking about.

'Are you invested in this war, my God-denying friend?'

That was rather a good question, and one he needed to discuss with Gunnhild. Did they really have to stay now? He couldn't see what difference it might make to him and the Wolves whether the duke won or lost. Was it any of their business?

His uncertainty must have shown, for Ælfric gave him a sly smile. 'Yes, I think that I, too, would like to find a fast ship for home before the fighting truly begins.'

'I think the duke will win,' Halfdan said suddenly, rather surprising himself.

'Oh? He racks up enemies at an impressive rate. He is hopelessly outnumbered now, and it remains to be seen whether the King of France will have anything to do with him. Henri might just as easily throw in his lot with the barons. His relationship with William has rarely been good, and he might stand to gain a great deal in the region if the duke falls. Do you have some demon-delivered wisdom that escapes me, Gotlander?'

Halfdan grunted. He was starting to get sick of this whole 'demon' thing of which the archbishop was so fond, but the man seemed to say it in such a light-hearted tone it did not come across as insulting.

'William will win, I think. He is desperate, and desperate men are capable of things that evade those with more to lose. He is clever, beyond the ken of most Normans, and that, I think, will see him drag the French in on his side. He is ruthless to the core, and so where others would baulk at doing the unthinkable in order to win, the duke will not. And perhaps, most of all, he is lucky.'

'Luck is more important than power or prestige?'

Halfdan snorted. 'Of course. Luck is the most powerful thing in all the worlds. Loki, time and again, sets himself against the greatest gods of *Ásgarð* and *Vanaheim*, and is it not his cunning and luck that sees him survive until the end of time? Who else but a lucky god could stand against both Thor and Odin?'

'It makes my skin crawl to hear your words, Halfdan of Gotland.' The archbishop gave a strange smile and stretched. 'It may be that you are right. But whether he wins or loses, there will be a war to scourge the Earth in the process, and I have no desire to become caught up in it. I must soon take my leave and return to the coast. Anyway,' he said, stopping and thumbing at the door they had reached, 'this is my chamber. Fare you well, and may God come to you in the night and drag your heathen carcass from the dark into the light.'

There, again, blistering wicked words, spoken with a half-smile and a light voice that made it somehow almost a joke. As Ælfric closed the door and left him alone in the corridor, Halfdan shook his head, hoping to shake some of the fuzziness from it. He wondered whether Gunnhild would still be up. Other Wolves were – Bjorn and Ketil were both down in the hall, engaged in stupid competitions with the duke's men, throwing axes and drinking beer. Leif and Anna had retired quite early. But Gunnhild and her sisters…

When had he started thinking of them like that?

He was still musing on that when he arrived at her door. He listened. He did not want to knock and disturb them if they were asleep, but the faint sound of murmuring came through the timbers, and so he rapped lightly.

'Come in, my jarl.'

It no longer came as any surprise that Gunnhild might know who it was, before word or sight, and so he pushed the door and entered the chamber.

'If Odin is an aspect of God,' Cassandra was saying, 'just as in the Holy Church, the Father, Son and Spirit are all one, then we can see so many parallels. Gunnhild, even your story of the three gods creating the first man and woman is but a mirror of the Trinity and the creation of Adam and Eve. The hanging on a tree is clearly an interpretation of the crucifixion, and your Valkyries are but the angels of the Lord.'

Gunnhild turned, fixing Cassandra with a withering look. 'Cease your prattle, girl,' she said with thin lips and narrowed eyes.

Cassandra looked ready to argue, and the ever-talkative Anna was clearly winding up to take part in the discussion, but as Halfdan cleared his throat, with a flick of her fingers Gunnhild dismissed her sisters and turned to the visitor.

'My jarl.'

'I have news of both Harðráði and Hjalmvigi,' he said, words tumbling out with the ease of the wine-loosened tongue.

She nodded as though she knew this already, which slightly annoyed him. 'Time is almost upon us,' she said.

'Almost? Gunnhild, Harðráði comes west as heir to two kingdoms. Hjalmvigi stands by the throne of the Swedes. The time is *now*.'

'No, Halfdan, it is not. You are not ready. Be patient.'

Normally, these days Halfdan knew better than to argue with the völva, but the wine had done its work.

'Gunnhild, this is not our war. We should leave before—'

'Leave how? Patience, young jarl. Ulfr Sveinsson builds you a ship, and even a month is far from up yet. We are not done here.'

'If we get caught up in the war—'

'Then it is as it should be. Threads are woven by the Norns, not by men.'

'Gunn—' he began afresh, but stopped, blinking, as she held up a silencing finger a couple of inches from his nose. 'I just think...' he started again, but her brow creased in irritation and she wagged her finger.

'Hush,' she hissed, and then looked up and about as though sensing something in the wind, even in her peaceful room.

'What is it?'

Suddenly he felt that twinge of anticipation, a slight itch in the Loki serpents on his arm, and without needing to will it, all the wine seemed to have drained from his system, the fog lifting.

'The duke needs you,' she said suddenly.

'I'll get my byrnie.'

'No time. Go now.'

Halfdan frowned, but the wine was no longer blanketing his wit, and the look on the völva's face brooked no argument. In two heartbeats he was out in the corridor again, pounding along it in his soft boots, unarmoured, yet as ever with the Alani short blade at his waist, balanced by a sax at the other hip. The duke was in danger, it appeared. And if there was no time for him to find his chain shirt, then there was certainly no time to find the other Wolves and call on them.

As he ran through silent, deserted corridors, heading for the duke's rooms, he paused momentarily at one of the keep windows. His mind was replaying the fall of the castle at Valognes and their desperate flight from the place, leading him to wonder whether he was facing a repeat of that troubled night. One glance outside suggested it was otherwise. He could see the duke's soldiers patrolling the walls, and there was no hint of trouble. This was something else, then, which was good, given that they were at William's seat of power and there was nowhere else really to run.

The bastard's suite of rooms stood on the uppermost floor, occupying the whole thing, and so there were always two men on guard at the doorway that led upstairs to those chambers. As Halfdan turned a corner and saw ahead an empty corridor, that doorway ominously unprotected, he knew that Gunnhild had been right. There was a true threat to the duke at this very moment. He hoped he was not too late as he ran closer, and, even as he closed on the doorway, he couldn't quite say *why* he hoped. Had he not been saying to Gunnhild that this was not their war?

Still, he slowed, making his pace light, calming his breathing, and closed on the doorway.

Still no guards.

He ducked around the door frame, just exposing one eye, peering into the gloomy staircase. It was dark, but there was enough of a glow from above to illustrate that it was empty. A quick glance down on instinct, and it did not take much to spot the blood spatter that spoke silently but eloquently of the guards' fate. He listened, holding his breath.

There were faint sounds from above – murmurs and scrapes, nothing readily identifiable. The urgency of this insisted itself upon him once more, and he began to climb, taking the stairs two steps at a time, trying to stay as quiet as possible while moving fast. He reasoned that if there was trouble in the duke's rooms and he couldn't hear much, then no one would easily hear Halfdan climbing the stairs. He reached the top in twelve bounds and leapt round the corner, weapons out, sax in one hand, sword in the other, ready to take down any enemy lurking there.

No enemy waited, blade in hand, but two bodies heaped by the side, coated in blood, answered the question as to where the guards had gone. Several facts struck him rapidly with just a glance at the pair. Firstly, the attacker or attackers had to be strong to drag armoured men up the stairs. Secondly, he or they had to have been considered a friend, or at least no threat, for both men had died from a blade drawn across their throats from close range. To get so close, the guards had to have allowed it. Lastly, the attacker – or the attackers – knew the layout of the place and what to do without being noticed, for to kill and drag bodies around could only be done if you knew you could do it unnoticed. That all combined to suggest someone who knew the castle, and the duke and his guards well, probably from within the duke's assembly.

Halfdan tried to recall the layout of the lower floors, but quickly realised that this one had to be different anyway. He'd never been up to the duke's rooms since they'd been here. He peered off ahead. A glow emerged from two sources. Slowly, he approached the first doorway, tense, weapons at the ready. There was no noise there, or at least only the crackling of a fire, which could in truth cover the slightest of noises. From the second doorway he could hear the sounds of a struggle. He ducked his head around the edge of the first door.

This was a guardroom, the accommodation for half a dozen of the duke's most senior and trusted men. For a moment, he frowned as he peered around the interior, for it appeared to be a scene of such normality it seemed odd in the circumstances. Then he realised that the three men at the table in the centre were not moving. There was no blood, but even from the doorway, he could see how they had died. All three were slumped in their chairs with glassy expressions, foamy drool at their lips. A half-full glass of wine sat on the table in front of one; his neighbour faced a glass lying on its side, the wine pooled on the surface and dripping onto the floor. The third glass lay broken on the floor close to its owner, wine puddled beneath his chair. A jug sat at the table's centre.

Once again, the work of a perceived friend.

In that moment, Halfdan's mind pieced together the sequence of events. Whoever it was had arrived at the bottom of the stairs with a jug of poisoned wine, had been granted admittance, had delivered it to the guardroom, and then retreated. While his victims drank their final drink in that room and choked out their lives, he returned to the bottom of the stairs, where he swiftly killed the two men with a knife to the neck, his attacks entirely unexpected and coming from behind. In two moves, the attacker had removed all the protection that lay between him and the duke's room.

One man, Halfdan decided as he stepped past the door and bore down on his destination. Two men would have put the guards on more alert. One man delivering wine after a feast could play the visiting friend card. Two could not.

Four more steps and Halfdan was at the next doorway, peering in. The room seemed empty for a moment. It was not furnished as richly as he'd expected, and in that moment he remembered William's room at Valognes. He'd had an antechamber full of men. It seemed the same here.

As he stepped inside, he could see the connecting door into the duke's personal chamber, firmly closed, and could hear clonks and grunts and growls from beyond it. A body lay before the door, and after more than two weeks at Falaise, even a stranger knew the shape of the Count of Crespon, William's right-hand man, the Seneschal of Nordmandi. Crespon had been present since their arrival, the first man to greet the duke upon his return, and probably the most trusted man in the land. He had died badly, his neck, arm and leg all rent and bloodied, his face mangled from a sword blow that had almost removed the lower jaw.

Halfdan felt a twitch that made his eyelid jump. This was treachery, and only when the traitor had reached the solid Count of Crespon had he been challenged. But Crespon's own sword, lying close to his hand, was also bloody, suggesting that he had succeeded at least in making his opponent pay for his death. Halfdan, aware that the attacker and the duke were in the next room, and probably alone in there, stepped over the body and pulled open the door.

The bedchamber was dimmer than the previous room, lit only by the guttering fireplace and a single candle, prepared for slumber, and it took Halfdan's eyes a few moments to adjust.

William was fighting for his life, but the jarl had to give him credit. The fifteen-year-old duke had been surprised by an attack from within, while unarmed and abed, yet he had managed somehow to get from the bed to a large ornate chair – more a throne than anything – and duck behind it. Better still, he had somehow managed to snatch a long iron candleholder, almost as tall as William himself, and was using it to jab and swing and hold his assailant at a distance that made it difficult to strike a blow.

He saw William register his arrival with the tiniest flick of an eye, but the lad was clever enough not to let his opponent realise, saying nothing. Despite Halfdan's having pulled open the door and stepped inside, the noise of the struggle was enough that the assailant, with his back to the door, had not heard the fresh intrusion. For critical moments, the man was unaware of Halfdan's presence.

He had but heartbeats to make his decision. In moments the man would become aware and turn, and then the fight would be more difficult. Halfdan lifted his sax and hurled it. It was not a well-balanced blade, and flipped and turned in the air, but his aim at least was true. The knife hit the attacker on the back of the head, pommel first. The man let out a yelp of pain, for even the pommel would hurt, and turned on a bloodied, wounded leg, wincing, free hand going to the back of his head.

Halfdan had not waited, though. The moment the sax had left his hand, he had started running, and by the time the attacker had fully turned to take in the new threat, the jarl was on him. He hit the man at full pelt, slamming him back into the chair, where he fell awkwardly on his wounded leg, trying to lift his long sword for a blow. Halfdan had the upper hand in more than one way, though. In addition to the surprise of his attack, while the Norman's heavy long sword was difficult to bring to bear in such close quarters, Halfdan's short blade was perfect for the circumstances. Even as the man struggled to push off his assailant and rise from the chair, Halfdan pulled his arm back and stabbed. He felt the tip of the sword press against the heavy cloth of the man's rich tunic, then felt the pressure ease as the garment's resistance caved, and the blade pressed down into flesh, burying itself in the man's organs just below his ribcage. The man gasped and twitched as Halfdan pulled himself back.

As the traitor continued to gasp in shock and pain, yet managed somehow to pull himself upright, the jarl took a single pace back and looked at his foe properly for the first time. He vaguely recognised the man. A new arrival at Falaise, he had only been there a day or two, joining them for the feast; one of William's perceived loyal lords.

The man staggered a step and miraculously managed to bring his long sword up ready to face his enemy, though as he did so, the wound in his cut leaked a sheet of blood and a small coil of intestine protruded, threatening to slip out.

The man was struggling, tears in his eyes, even as he prepared to fight. He would not survive, and he knew it. All he could do was fight to the last. Halfdan, recognising the pain the man was in, took another step back, forcing him to advance again. This time, as the blood sluiced afresh, that coil of gut did slide free, and the man, realising something was very wrong, reached down with his free hand and pushed it back in as he raised his sword.

Halfdan ducked away again, and the man lurched another step. More blood. Fingers failed to contain the coil as the wound opened up with the movement, and a further stretch of gut slid free.

The sword dipped, the pain and effort too much for the would-be assassin, and with no defence raised, Halfdan stepped forward, swinging his sword. It was not made for slashing and cutting, rather for stabbing, but its edge was kept keen anyway, and the blade slammed into the man's neck, cutting through muscle, tendon, cartilage and flesh. The blood sprayed, an artery severed. The man's sword fell, and Halfdan pulled back, then pressed forward again, this time driving his blade into the man's heart, sliding it hilt-deep between ribs.

The man took another step, gasped again, made a keening noise, and then fell to his knees, where he stayed a moment longer, the whining noise filling the room until he toppled face first to the flagged floor, dead.

Halfdan breathed deep and stepped over to one of the very expensive-looking wall-hangings, which he used to carefully clean his sword of gore before sheathing it. He then located his fallen sax and stooped to collect that, too.

By the time he was composed once more, William had replaced his candleholder and come out from the protection of his throne. He looked perfectly serene for a man who had so narrowly escaped death.

'It seems that inviting your enemies to dinner is a bad idea,' Halfdan murmured conversationally. 'Who could have guessed such a thing?'

William gave him a hard look. 'My men would not let someone untrusted get so close, Gotlander. This is William Montgommeri, Viscount de Hyèmes. He is one of my closest aides, one of the few men on whom I have relied since the start.'

'Then even those closest to you can no longer be trusted.'

The duke nodded, sighed and scrubbed his scalp. 'This will change things. That business at Valognes was an opening blow. This was meant to end things, but when my enemies discover that even my closest and most trusted cannot get close enough to kill me, they will not try again. This will be the end of knives in the dark, Halfdan. The next move will involve many swords, horses and machines of war.'

'We are here on the word of Gunnhild,' Halfdan said flatly. 'If war comes, do not count us among your army.'

William responded with a sly smile. 'As long as you are within these walls, you are part of it, my friend. Now go and pray to your demons, for there comes a storm on a biblical scale.'

Chapter 20

Halfdan hurried along the corridor amid the buzz of urgency. The news was all over the castle – and indeed the town, too. A rebel army was closing on Falaise. The duke's home was about to come under attack. William had called a council, and Halfdan had been invited as the leader of a mercenary unit in the castle, but he had first taken a side trip to Gunnhild's chamber. As he reached her open door, he swung in through it and gestured to her.

'Tell me the time is right to leave.'

She shook her head, and he felt his nerves jump. Time was very short, if they wanted to avoid being part of the duke's war.

'The enemy are coming, Gunnhild. If we don't leave before they arrive, we'll be trapped here, under siege. I don't think anyone wants that.'

Her gaze was filled with steel as she locked her eyes on his. 'Why do you make me repeat myself time and again, Halfdan. We are not done here. The white thread I saw bind to our weaving here I suspect is your new friend, the archbishop, and a dragon yet rears in our future.' She sighed, and her expression changed to one that a parent might wear while trying to explain necessity to a recalcitrant child. 'And simple practicality says we wait for Ulfr, unless you intend to leave without him?'

'Of course not,' Halfdan said, defensively. 'But we could ride for Pirou and join him there.'

'And if we miss him? If he has finished his work and sails for Falaise while we arrive at an empty Pirou? *Think*, Halfdan. All is as it must be. Accept your part in the weaving.'

It was Halfdan's turn to sigh and sag, nodding his acceptance. 'All right. But every day we stay now binds us to the duke and his cause and drags us deeper into this trouble. I just remember how we stayed too long at Miklagarðr and almost lost everything.'

'And I might remind you that it was you, not I, who kept us there.'

That shut him up. He could think of nothing to say that did not make him sound like a fool, and so he took his leave swiftly, and hurried back across the keep and down the stairs. The duke's hall was protected by his guards, but they stepped aside to allow him entrance. His visit to Gunnhild had made him late, and the council had begun without him. He listened as he crossed to a free seat at a table filled with barons and lords and priests.

'If we are besieged, we risk everything,' one of the lords was saying. 'Better to withdraw than be trapped. Rumour has it that the French king has turned sympathetic to your cause. I suspect Henri sees you as young enough to be malleable, controlled, while he will know that your enemies, should they take the throne, will be less so. Let us flee to the arms of Henri and safety.'

'Henri begins to favour me,' William replied in an acid tone, 'because I have offered him land and gold for his aid. Nothing more. And his army still gathers near our borders undecided, but until I have an agreement with him, sealed by the Church, I will not walk into his grasp, for there I may find myself more a prisoner than I could ever be to Cotentin and Bessin. No, I make my stand here, at my home. And when we fight them off, then we will have shown our strength and can ally with Henri on more level terms.'

He thumped the table with a balled fist in a warlike manner. Again, Halfdan was struck by how impressive he was for such a young man. He showed considerably more strength and gumption at all times than any of the others at the table.

'There is something to be said for the path of peace, however,' Archbishop Ælfric said in the silence that followed.

'Peace in captivity is not a thing to be sought, no matter how peaceful it might be,' the duke countered. 'And I am aware that your place here is peripheral at best. I imagine you would like nothing more than to leave, to flee back to your Angle-land. You are welcome to do so, good Archbishop, though I cannot supply you with escort or goods for your journey, nor can I guarantee you a ship for passage when you reach the coast. I'm sure you understand my position.'

Ælfric nodded sharply, and sat back. He had come to Falaise with the entourage of a senior churchman, from what Halfdan understood, but without a military escort. That had been provided on his landing in Nordmandi by the duke. Halfdan could imagine how reluctant the priest would be to leave Falaise and try the thirty-mile journey to the coast through potential hostile territory without a military escort.

'What of the enemy?' the duke asked. 'Their composition?'

'The colours of six enemy barons have been identified, my lord duke,' a noble said, leaning forward on the table and steepling his fingers. 'Mostly from the western regions, and including Cotentin and Bessin. Outlying pickets at Uxeium count their numbers at just under two thousand, including three hundred or so riders, two units of archers, and carts that carry siege engines, as well as the expected baggage train.'

'They mean business, then.'

'Quite, my lord duke.'

'I, on the other hand, have but six hundred men,' William countered, 'which is poor odds, admittedly, but I also have the strongest walls in the region. With a little care, we can hold Falaise almost indefinitely, and do not forget that winter is upon us. A besieging enemy will find no comfort or ease in the coming months. Frostbite and starvation will do half our work for us. No, I think a siege will actually work in our favour. We will hold, and we will break them by Christmas, whereupon

I will put my ultimatum to King Henri. When he sees our strength he will join with us, and then it will be *our* time. We will turn upon these rebels and bring them to heel.'

'We have supplies for two months stored in the castle, my lord duke,' another man put in.

'Not enough,' William replied swiftly. 'Though I intend to break my enemies by Christmas, only a fool would not prepare for longer. I want those supplies doubled, and every weapon, shield, hauberk, bow and arrow to be found in the area all brought into the castle. The enemy close rapidly, so there will be something of a race to bring in the supplies while we can.'

'And the town?' a senior priest put in.

'My Lord?'

'The people of Falaise, my lord duke?'

William straightened. 'I would love nothing more than to protect my people, but this is not the time for such considerations. Every mouth inside these walls that eats our supplies has to be attached to an arm that wields a sword. The people of Falaise will have to decide whether to stay and trust that the enemy will not wage a war against civilians, or to leave and seek safety elsewhere.'

'That is not a Christian approach,' the bishop admonished.

'But it is a *practical* one,' William replied archly. 'I will allow men of God to remain, for the preservation of our souls remains of importance, but every man will carry a cross or a weapon – or both – or they will leave.'

At a call from the duke, two men brought a huge map of the region and spread it across the table, the vellum rippling as it was smoothed out.

'Very well. Let us look at supply sources.'

Halfdan sat back and let the discussion wash over him. He held no real importance in this meeting, and no knowledge of the area anyway. He was silently musing over the possibility of getting a message to Ulfr back in Pirou when he became aware of a presence at his shoulder.

'What?'

'Why do you remain at Falaise?' Ælfric murmured.

'A question I have asked more than once myself. Gunnhild counsels patience. She is of the opinion that we are not ready to leave.' He turned a knowing smile on the archbishop. '*You*, of course, *are*.'

'Your friend Leif tells me that you have a ship.'

'We *will* have a ship,' Halfdan corrected him. 'Ulfr remained at Pirou, constructing a new longship. We wait for news.'

'And when you receive your news, you will leave?'

Halfdan nodded. He assumed so. He *hoped* so.

'Then when you leave, I ask for passage with you.'

'We do not know where we are going yet. It may be Daneland, or even back home.'

'If it is north of here, it is a step in the right direction.'

Halfdan shrugged. 'I see no reason why not. You have gold, of course?'

Ælfric chuckled. 'I can compensate you, yes.'

With that the archbishop returned to take part in the discussion. Halfdan simply sat silent and half-listened. Before long, lists had been drawn up and plans made. Halfdan accepted a part in the gathering of supplies. The Wolves numbered eleven in total, and every party being sent out was of six men with a cart, each set a village or two to rob of goods. Halfdan noted the name of the village assigned to them and its position on the map. The place was a few miles north-east, far from the direction of the approaching army, which suited him just fine. As they were finishing up, the duke put up a hand and waved Halfdan over.

'Your destination, Jarl Halfdan, is the village of Spanei.'

Halfdan nodded. He knew that.

'It lies just four miles away.'

Another nod.

'The village lies within the territory of Falaise, but is subject to two local religious houses: the abbey at Ouche and the priory of Perreriae. There will therefore be a tithe barn in the village filled with goods destined for the monks, as well as granaries for the village itself. We need grain, but taking the monks' goods will not be popular. You will have to be forceful, but also respectful and persuasive.'

Halfdan nodded again. It was clearly no accident that the duke had assigned that particular village to the only group in the castle who did not kneel to the nailed god.

Leaving the duke and his hall, Halfdan returned to his friends and assigned roles. He would take Bjorn and Ketil, Leif, Gunnhild and Thurstan to the village, while the others were to stay at Falaise and protect their interests there.

The adventurers convened in the bailey a short while later, where they were given a cart and horses, four of the party mounting the beasts, the other two climbing up into the cart. Everyone was kitted for war, with the exception of Gunnhild, who carried her staff; she was clad in her favourite green dress, her confidence an armour in itself.

The journey was chilly, but dry, the air crisp and the sky a pale grey as they rolled and clopped along the road from Falaise. The journey was not a long one, even with a cart slowing them, for the road was good, flat and well travelled, and their destination close. Reaching the edge of Spanei, Halfdan peered off ahead. The place was quiet, rural and pretty. Timber houses stretched out along five roads that led off variously to outlying farms or other villages, and the centre clustered around a pond, the ubiquitous White Christ church, and what could only be the tithe barn. It was the only structure in the village of a size to match the church, and was, in fact, slightly larger. A long, single-storey place of heavy stone with no windows, beneath a tiled apex roof, it was of a far higher quality than the houses around it. It lay close to the church, at the edge of a green graveyard, with one other house beside it, on the other side, the whole encircled by a low wall, with three gates, one allowing access to each building.

As they approached, Halfdan trotted ahead and dismounted, then pulled open the wide timber gate. He did not miss the nailed god cross carved into each leaf of the gate, marking the place as the property of priests. As he stepped aside and the cart rolled through into the yard between wall, barn and smaller building, the jarl looked about them. Troubled eyes were watching from doors and windows around the village, a dog barked from behind another gate, incessantly, and a pair of young children emerged from a garden, only to be grabbed by their mother and escorted back inside hurriedly. Presumably word of the approaching army had spread throughout the countryside, too. The nerves of the people of Spanei were tangible, a crackle in the air.

The cart approached the larger door in the barn's side and rumbled to a halt, its occupants climbing down, while Halfdan and Leif approached the door. The handles of the twin doors were secured with a chain of iron links, that itself held firm with a padlock that immediately fascinated Halfdan, for the main lock was formed of iron in the shape of a wolf.

If ever there had been an omen...

'Bjorn, can you open this without damaging the lock?'

The big man grunted, wandered over, and looked down. For a moment he fumbled in one of the big pouches at his belt, and then produced an iron spike as long as his hand.

'Where did you get that?'

The big albino shrugged. 'Dunno. I pick stuff up.'

And with that uninformative answer, he jammed the spike through the same link in the chain as the lock, then turned it and wedged the tip of the spike in the tiny gap between the doors. Halfdan watched in fascination as Bjorn took a step back, then drew his huge axe from his belt and readied it, reversed, the butt facing the lock.

He swung. Hard.

The iron butt of the axe slammed into the head of the spike with the force only Bjorn could manage, and the result was spectacular. Halfdan winced, realising he should have predicted this. The blow was indeed sufficient to drive the spike through the link, forcing it open so that the chain fell apart, slithering through the handles and falling, hitting the dusty ground just after the padlock, now also free.

The side effect, however, was that the spike had been driven deep between the two doors, followed by the reverse blow of the axe, and the area of the door handles exploded in a shower of broken timber and splinters, the doors jerking inwards.

'I said, just the chain,' Halfdan snapped, irritably.

'No,' Bjorn said with an air of confidence. 'You said "without damaging the lock". You never mentioned the doors. You need to be clearer.'

Halfdan sighed and crouched, sweeping up the wolf-shaped lock. What use it could ever be without the key, he did not know, but its very form seemed to be saying that the jarl should have it. Rising and slipping it into his pouch before fastening it, he pushed the doors wide and stepped inside. The place was huge and musty, with that smell that only hundreds of dry sacks of grain in an enclosed space can issue.

One glance told him that there was more grain than would fit on the cart. Still, they'd only been told to fill the cart, so that would be enough.

'Start loading up,' he called to the others.

Bjorn and Thurstan began lifting grain sacks and carrying them outside on their shoulders, dropping them into the cart, where Leif and Gunnhild would stack them carefully to best utilise the space. Halfdan glanced across to see Ketil moving toward that other house. As he did so, the house's door opened and a man emerged, stumbling out into the light of the yard.

'You can't take that,' he shouted.

Brave, Halfdan thought, given who he was shouting it at.

'Your duke, William of Nordmandi, has requisitioned this grain,' Leif called back from the cart.

'It's not his to take.'

'Nor is it yours,' Leif countered. 'This grain is for the monks. Yours is in granaries.'

'But when they come for their tithe and we cannot fulfil it, where do you think the shortfall will come from?'

Leif shrugged. 'It's a poor deal. You have my sympathy.'

'And children, who will starve. Put it back.'

'That cannot happen, I'm afraid.'

'I will fetch the priest. He will damn you all.'

'Do we look like we give a shit, old man?' Ketil said suddenly, close to the man, and took a single step forward.

Before Halfdan could shout an order to the contrary, the lanky Icelander threw a punch that landed dead centre in the man's face, sending him sprawling into the dust. Just to be sure, then, Ketil gave him a good kick in the side to make sure he stayed down. Behind Halfdan, the others resumed their work, ferrying sacks from the barn and stacking them in the cart. The local lay unconscious in the dirt, and Ketil crouched, looking him over, then rose with the man's purse in one hand and a reasonable quality sax in the other.

'Look at this?' he called, holding up the knife. 'What else is he hiding?' With that, the giant strode toward the house.

'Stop,' Halfdan called back. 'We're here for the grain.'

'And any weapons and armour we can find, from what I heard,' Ketil replied, as he disappeared through the man's door.

Halfdan bit his lip. Strictly speaking, that was true, though the general understanding was impounding the goods from stores and smiths, not ransacking the houses of commoners. But he knew better than to try and stop the Icelander. Ketil had calmed a lot since his little adventure in the east, and rarely leapt into trouble without thinking it through, but that Icelandic impulsiveness always lay just below the surface and would never be fully exorcised.

Halfdan left him to it, watching the ferrying of sacks to the rapidly filling cart.

That was when he heard the new noise.

Hooves. *Pounding* hooves, and those of several horses. He cocked his head, trying to isolate the sound from those in the yard, and decided they were coming from the other direction, off to the north. Hurrying across to the boundary wall, he leaned over it, beside the corner of the barn, looking past the church, along the shady, tree-lined street.

Half a dozen horsemen were coming their way. He couldn't see their colours yet, but they were armoured and with spears, and there was about their pace and their manner only threat. He turned.

'Stop. We have trouble.'

Bjorn and Thurstan paused in their work, halfway between door and cart, the latter dropping his sack, where it burst and started issuing a steady stream of grain with a hissing sound as the man drew his sword. Leif and Gunnhild stopped arranging sacks, picking up their weapons and turning to face the peri-meter wall.

Damn Ketil. The man was somewhere in the house, robbing the owner. Halfdan could probably shout loudly enough for the man to hear, but that would also undoubtedly alert the approaching riders. He fumed over the decision, but reasoned that these new men were probably coming for them. If they were riding for Falaise, surely they would be moving slower, saving their horses. They were riding hard, which meant riding to something urgent.

'Ready yourselves,' he called to the others, and then ducked below the line of the wall, crawling along it toward the gate. Thurstan stepped back into the darkness of the tithe barn's interior, while Bjorn ambled across to the cart, still carrying his sack.

The riders rounded the corner mere moments later. Halfdan couldn't see them from where he was, hidden below the wall, but he heard the six horses slow and then stop near the gate. There was a strange momentary silence, filled only by the shush of chain shirts, the jingling of harnesses and the breathing of horses, then finally a rider spoke, in thick Norman tones.

'Who are you?'

Leif was the one to respond – with his ear for accents, he had the best Norman speech of them all. 'Duke William of Falaise has called for supplies against a siege by rebels. This is now his grain.'

'No,' the rider said. 'This is the property of the Abbey of Saint-Évroult at Ouche. You will replace those sacks in the barn.'

'No,' Leif replied.

Halfdan heard spears being moved, grips changing. He left his sword sheathed, but pulled his sax free.

'Last warning,' the Norman called. 'We carry the authority of the Abbot of Ouche, who recognises no lord but God above, and his pope in Rome.'

'Fuck off,' called Bjorn dismissively, which made Halfdan smile. Some people never changed.

'You resist?' The man called.

'Up your shitter,' Bjorn said airily.

Halfdan braced himself, and half a dozen spears suddenly sailed out over the wall above his head. It was more of a warning volley than an attack, and four fell short, clattering across the yard. A fifth became tangled in the cart's rear wheel, and the sixth hit one of the grain sacks in the vehicle, causing an explosion of tiny granules as grain poured out into the cart base and then to the yard.

He heard the drawing of swords.

'Last chance,' the rider called.

'I thought your *last* warning was your last warning,' Leif called lightly.

At a cry from the leader, the horsemen rode through the gate, swords out, shields on arms, meaning true violence. Halfdan waited until the first five passed and then sprang from his hiding place. His arms went round the waist of the rearmost rider, behind his shield. While his left arm gripped the man tight, his right hand – blade held in a reverse grip – sought

301

that divide in the hem of a Norman hauberk that allowed an armoured man to sit astride a horse, and the blade slid up into the man's groin and upper thigh inside the chain protection. He stabbed three times in quick succession, not careful with his aim, for he was being dragged alongside the horse, but the blows were clearly enough, for he felt warm blood cascade over his hand in a torrent. The man gave a high-pitched shriek, and his sword fell as he let go of the reins, shook his shield free, and both his hands went to his ruined groin.

Halfdan let go of the man and fell away, staggering to stay upright, as the dying rider veered off to the corner of the yard, yelling in horror, blood sheeting down over his legs and the horse. He was done for; he would be gone in minutes.

Halfdan turned in time to see Bjorn throw his burden. A sack of grain is a very heavy thing, and the impromptu missile hit the lead rider full in the upper chest, slamming him back in the saddle. What happened as a result Halfdan was unsure, but there were bony cracks, and the man gave a mighty cry of pain and then lolled in the saddle at an unnatural angle, shield falling to his side, sword dropping from shaky hand.

Leif's throwing axe took another rider in the torso. The Norman chain hauberk was sufficient to stop the blade driving deep into his chest, but the sheer weight and power of the blow was sufficient to smash ribs even through the coat, and that rider was out of the fight in an instant. Another horseman had made the mistake of trying to round the cart to come at it from the other side, but as he passed the open doors of the barn, Thurstan, until then unnoticed, stepped into the open and swung in one move. His long Norman sword slammed across the rider's back as he passed, and the man slumped forward in his saddle, broken in an instant, his horse wandering off into a corner.

Two left, and that was about to narrow to one. A rider reached the side of the cart and swung with his sword, shield held up in front of him. Leif had to drop into the bed of the cart to avoid being struck, but Gunnhild simply leaned back casually, lifting her staff, double grip all at the top end, and then lanced out with it, suddenly and in a single blow. The butt of the staff hit the rider in the face – one weapon lengthy enough to reach him from the cart.

Halfdan was about to go for the last rider when some instinct stopped him. He looked past the man to see Bjorn, a towering mass of Thor-driven rage, leap from the cart, throwing himself at the remaining attacker. It was neither graceful, nor strategic. It was simply a mindless attack. The great, white-haired and pink-eyed monster hit the Norman in the saddle, and the pair went tumbling from the horse in a heap, the Norman's ankle broken by the stirrup as it was pulled from it.

Halfdan stopped paying attention then, for the man was doomed even before he landed, winded, on his back in the dirt, with a massive insane warrior crying violent curses atop him. The six riders were gone, swiftly, thanks largely to the surprise of half the Wolves being hidden.

Ketil chose that moment to emerge from the house with an armful of loot, from a pewter candlestick to a sharp-looking kitchen knife, the unconscious owner's wife following with harangues as she smacked him repeatedly with a twig broom.

'I *missed* it,' the Icelander complained as he emerged into the yard.

'That will teach you to leave us to the hard work while you loot the locals,' Halfdan said with a smirk.

Ketil, tired of his pursuit, suddenly turned, yelling 'Shut up, woman,' and hit the wife with the candlestick, resulting in half a dozen dropped pieces of loot and an unconscious woman.

Without needing to be told, Bjorn and Thurstan returned to ferrying grain sacks from the barn, while Gunnhild pushed the broken bag from the cart, roughly sweeping the worst spill away, and Ketil stowed his poor haul for the return journey. As Leif waited for the next sacks to arrive, Halfdan crossed to the clever Rus.

'This abbey… How far is it from here, d'you think?'

Leif shrugged. 'No idea.'

'But these men,' Halfdan replied, thinking back. 'They said, "This is the property of the Abbey of Saint-Évroult at Ouche," as though they were monks. Do the abbeys around here have soldiers of their own?'

'It's possible. Or another lord connected with the abbey sent them.'

'But whatever the case, we can safely assume they're not from this village.'

'I'd say so, yes.'

Halfdan looked at the six horses. They were not exhausted, but they were definitely weary, and more so than riding into a fight across a village warranted.

'I thought they were coming for us, but now I think I was wrong. They've come a distance, and they're riding in the direction of Falaise. Any lord who intends to stand under the duke's flag from this region is already at the castle?'

'I would say so, yes.'

'Then these are enemies, from another lord, coming to join the fight. The army from the west is not the only one. The duke may have badly miscalculated the odds.'

Leif said nothing, though his face spoke volumes. Halfdan turned to the cart.

'Load up those last sacks and then go. We ride back to Falaise, and as fast as we can.'

'Why?' Thurstan called, carrying another sack across from the barn.

'Because those riders weren't sent for us. They were the vanguard, scouts who just bumped into us on the way to attack Falaise. And if six men armed for war are coming, then there'll be plenty of others on their heels.'

At those words, efforts were doubled with this last journey. The sacks were thrown aboard and not even settled into place before Leif and Gunnhild were slapping the reins and getting the horse moving with encouraging calls. The cart rumbled out of the gate, picking up pace as it swung wildly into the road and turned for Falaise as fast as the beast could pull it. It would be exhausted, but it only had to make four miles and they would be safe. The others mounted up, and the jarl sent his friends ahead with the vehicle as they left the village, trundling out into the open road, heading south-west for the duke's fortress.

Halfdan, on the other hand, did not mount or leave. Instead, he spent precious moments grabbing the various bodies of fallen soldiers, and of the man and his wife, and dragging them into the tithe barn. This done, he went around the yard, grabbing the reins of the various milling Norman horses and led them, too, inside. Happy that all clear evidence of the scuffle was hidden, he closed up the tithe barn's doors and the door to the adjacent house, then led his horse out of the yard and closed the outer gates, with their little incised crosses, too. He looked over his handiwork. A near-empty grain sack blew and slithered around in the breeze, and the yard was a scattered patchwork of bloodstains and fallen grain, but anyone riding past with a purpose would probably not notice anything amiss. It was all he could do. A passing army would move on to Falaise at a steady pace, but if they knew they were close behind raiders with a cart full of supplies, they might well pick up their pace to intercept.

He caught up with the cart a mile from the village, and together they rode on for Falaise and what passed for safety.

It was only as they crossed the fields and moved into the edge of the town of Falaise that Halfdan, habitually looking over his shoulder every few minutes, saw the lead riders of the main enemy force emerge around a small woodland behind.

They had made it back, but they had brought war with them.

Chapter 21

Bjorn ambled over from the nearest stair, his huge bulk impressive in the morning sun. Halfdan could swear the entire castle wall trembled with each footstep. The man was scratching his groin with one hand as he walked and tossing a peach up in the air and catching it repeatedly with the other.

'Morning,' Halfdan murmured, taking his eyes from the army gathered below and turning to his big friend.

'My head hurts.'

'I'm not surprised. I think the garrison are starting to worry. They stockpiled wine and ale for months, and at the rate *you're* going, it'll be gone in weeks.'

Bjorn merely huffed as he came to a halt, and the two men turned and looked out once more. The enemy forces had been in place for six days. They had sealed in the castle, and then systematically emptied and looted the town, sending its populace away. Now, there was no connection between the duke's fortress and the outside world.

There had been no attack yet, though. It had taken the first two days for the two forces approaching from east and west to meet, plan, encamp and encircle the fortress, and then a further two days to clear out the town and gather the supplies they would need for the siege. The fifth day, the rain had come in immense waves, and everyone, inside the castle and out, had lurked indoors, watching despondently, with only unlucky guards out in the open, drenched on duty. By the end of the day, the rain had become sleet with the promise of coming snow, which had lightened the hearts of those trapped in the fortress, for they would be warm and well fed, while the besiegers would be cold and hungry. Such was warfare.

The sixth day had been dry, but with overhanging clouds filled with snow, waiting for the right moment to empty over the world. The attackers had made the most of the dry day, even though they sloshed through pools and puddles of slush as they worked. That day the machines of war were uncovered and unloaded from the wagons, set in position and prepared.

Then night had come, and with it two promises: one of impending snow, the other of impending violence.

The defensive forces of the Duke of Nordmandi had been divided up by William and his close advisors. The great castle of the duke was impressive – the walls of stone, with a great stone keep, stone gatehouse and chapel within, only the various ancillary buildings within the bailey constructed of timber. The southern wall was the most perilous, for the slope up to it was low and gentle, the approach a wide swathe of grass between wall and town. The east held the great gatehouse, a difficult proposition, but a natural target, and the west held high walls atop a steep slope, overlooked by the keep within, another dangerous approach. The north was the least concerning, for the walls there were as high as everywhere else, but they rested atop a steep slope, dotted with cliffs and high rocky crags that would deter all but the most determined attacker.

William had positioned his Normans largely to south, east and west, concentrating their number at the weaker south wall, where they had packed bags of sand behind the walls and braced them with timbers to apply extra strength against siege weapons. Two smaller Norman units had been assigned to the northern defences, one at each end, supporting the keep area and the gatehouse end, while Halfdan and his Wolves, not entirely trusted by many of William's advisors, had been given the centre of the wall, above the crags, where little was likely to happen. That had suited Halfdan fine, but had annoyed Bjorn, who'd spent days grumbling about everyone else getting all the fun.

'Will they come today?' the big albino mused, looking down at the army gathered a few hundred paces away from the base of the crags.

'I think so, but probably not here.' Bjorn looked unhappy, so Halfdan pointed to the great catapults. 'They might try and hit us with those, though.'

Bjorn huffed again. He couldn't tear the arm off a rock missile and beat it to death with the soggy end. As the two stood watching, a handful of archers stepped out from the front lines of the enemy, bows in hand and arrows nocked. They moved into place and aimed, pulling back the strings. Halfdan and Bjorn remained in place, only partly through personal daring. Over the past few days they'd learned from experience that even the best shots down there could only just get an arrow up here, and even then, with little accuracy.

A small flurry of shafts was released and hurtled toward them. Most clattered against the rocks below the wall, though one hit the wall itself before falling back, and one, miraculously, sailed over the battlemented rampart, hitting the stonework of a merlon with a clack and then falling at Bjorn's feet.

Halfdan, having ducked instinctively, rose once more to find the big warrior beside him staring down at the fallen arrow and muttering an anatomically unlikely curse. He then bent, collecting the missile, and walked to the parapet once more, leaning over.

'This is your arrow,' he shouted down at the archers. He then lifted the peach, still intact and untouched. '*This* is your *arse*.' He then proceeded to push the arrowhead into the peach. 'Think about *that*,' he bellowed, holding the pierced peach high, 'and *stop fucking shooting at me!*'

Halfdan grinned as the archers below retreated among their ranks.

Somewhere back across the castle, a horn blared out, three times in quick succession, and all faces along the wall turned inwards. A pennant was waving, and a call was being relayed all around the defences. The enemy were coming.

Halfdan turned and looked back down. Nothing was moving below the cliff. He turned once more, frowning, to look elsewhere. Banners were waving all over – in several positions on the dangerous south wall, near the gate to the east, and on the high wall to the west – each gathering men. Archers were nocking as they ran to position, ready to counter any assault. The enemy were clearly coming from all three approaches. But not the north.

He spun again, looking down.

'Why not here?' he muttered, as Ketil and Leif approached from one side at a run, Gunnhild and the others from the far side.

'Because this place is no fun,' Bjorn grumbled. 'Because we're in the one place there will be no attack.'

Halfdan nodded, though he was only half listening, and wasn't at all sure he agreed.

There was no real movement among the enemy ranks, yet he was sure things had changed. He focused, looking this way and that, and realised that the men were moving slowly, individually, forming in units here and there without it being immediately obvious from above. He realised then why the arrows had come.

'Those archers weren't random,' he hissed. 'They were to attract our attention so they could see what the wall's strength in men was. And the other three wall attacks… I think they're all decoys.'

'You think they'll come from the north?' Leif said in surprise. 'The hardest approach?'

'And therefore the one nobody expects, and the poorest defended one.'

Sure enough, as he looked back the units had changed again. Where the front had formerly been an unbroken line of archers, or bored men with spears leaning on shields, there were lightly armoured men among them in groups, with shields and swords out. And there, finally, Halfdan spotted a man with a huge coiled rope over his shoulder. A little careful observation and he found two more of them, almost hidden among their fellows.

'They're coming.'

'What are they waiting for?' Ketil asked.

'They want the other three sides occupied so no one can come to help here. Get ready for a fight.'

He watched as Bjorn made gleeful sounds nearby. He could hear the noises back across the castle changing as the anticipation of battle gave way to the actual action, each approach engaged in a fight to the death. Halfdan looked across the army. The siege engines at this side remained silent and unmanned. They were all catapults. No one could get a battering ram or a tower close enough to the walls to be of use on this side.

He almost jumped when the enemy began to move, so sudden was it. One moment the lines remained steady in place; the next, men were surging forward toward the steep slope below the Wolves. Halfdan was interested. The approach was difficult, steep, with only patchy cover, and at the end of the dangerous climb there was still a wall manned by defenders.

The groups knew what they were doing. Halfdan watched as the speediest raced up the lowest and flattest part of the slope and then disappeared from sight below a craggy outcrop. The other groups, four in total, each followed suit, only moving the first step of the approach, then moving into cover.

Halfdan turned to find Thurstan nearby and waved at him.

'Bring up the baskets.'

As the man nodded and started jabbing fingers at the others to come and help him, Bjorn narrowed his eyes at Halfdan. 'Throwing rocks is not fighting.'

'Only a fool lets an enemy get a foot in the door just so he's close enough to punch.'

This did not seem to particularly mollify the big albino, who grumbled off to help bring up the baskets full of rocks that sat close by every open stretch of wall.

'Not you,' he called to Ketil, who was turning to help. 'You have your bow?'

The Icelander nodded, pushing aside his cloak to reveal the weapon over his shoulder.

'Get an arrow ready. Pick off anyone you can.'

Ketil nodded, unslinging his bow, testing the string's tension and then unfastening the quiver at his side, sliding it into a better position and selecting an arrow. A cry of alarm rang across the castle, and Halfdan turned to see that, while the other attacks might be primarily decoys, they were also serious attempts. At the lower south wall, enemy archers were using fire arrows, which were coming over the parapet in clouds, occasionally striking a defender, though most were ducked behind cover. Soldiers were not their targets, though. The arrows were coming down among the timber buildings in the bailey, some hitting home. Already, thatched roofs had turned into infernos, some buildings belching black smoke as they burned.

Some in the castle had argued against William's plan to move the entire winter supplies into the lower level of the stone keep, instead of the outbuildings where grain and other such stuff was traditionally stored. Halfdan could imagine how they would not be arguing while the granaries and warehouses so recently emptied erupted in flames.

Back to the view from the wall. The enemy units down there were on the move again. They were being smart, hurrying almost horizontally at times, slowly zigzagging up the steep slope, moving from rock face to rock face and pausing each time, safe from view at the wall. Halfdan looked this way and that. They could get perhaps twenty paces from the wall that way before they were in open ground with no cover. Only a few small units were coming. He wondered why, and began to picture the coming events.

The enemy would do their best to get to the walls. Somehow, they intended to use the ropes to deal with the walls themselves and reach the walkway above. Then they hoped they had enough men to overwhelm the defenders, and they knew what they were facing, after that little archery stunt. He nodded to himself. The rest of the castle would then come to the north wall to help, but it would be too late. The enemy would have control of the wall, and the ropes would be long enough to reach the slope. Then more and more men would start to move as soon as the defenders on the wall were engaged. In theory, the whole siege could be over at the north wall on the first day of action.

But not now, for Halfdan had anticipated them, and he knew what they were up to. The only real failing point for the enemy was how they intended to use the ropes to crest the wall without falling foul of Halfdan and his men. First, though, was to remove their most valuable assets.

He waved at Ketil. 'Stop. Watch them carefully as they move. Find the ones carrying ropes and drop them.'

Ketil simply nodded and nocked another arrow, looking down, waiting for the next move below. Bjorn, Thurstan and the others were bringing the baskets of heavy boulders up and placing them every few paces along the wall walk.

Halfdan watched. The enemy were halfway up the slope, though a few had slowed and dropped back, and three bodies lay unmoving in the open with Ketil's arrows buried in them. He heard the Icelander hiss a promise to Odin, and a moment later an arrow thrummed from the wall down into the leading group moving from cliff to cliff. Halfdan couldn't resist a smile as the man carrying the huge coiled rope over his shoulder gave a sudden cry of pain and alarm. One hand went up to his face as he was thrown out of the line, tumbling away down twenty feet of steep slope, the rope flying free and uncoiling, slithering this way and that on the hillside.

He could feel the air of smugness settling around the Icelander even from where he stood.

The next movement came, groups zigzagging from rock to rock. Another arrow from Ketil, this time unfortunately missing the man with the rope, though it did strike the man beside him, who fell with a shout of alarm, clutching his shoulder.

They were getting closer and closer.

'Everyone take a stretch of wall as long as a man is tall,' Halfdan called to the others. 'Find a rock.'

Similar tactics were being employed by the Norman defenders to each side, further along the walls, but Halfdan had to concentrate on his own section for now. There were four units coming at their part of the walls, each with a rope. One such had already fallen, and though they had sent a man to collect the fallen rope, that had been a mistake. Ketil had simply put an arrow in the man sent to retrieve it before he even reached it. No further attempt had been made. That meant three more ropes coming, though he adjusted that as a second rope-bearer screamed, clutched at a buried arrow shaft and fell, tumbling back down the slope with his rope.

The enemy finally reached the highest crags where they could hide, and everything stopped for a moment. From here, they would be in the open, vulnerable. Then Halfdan heard the creak, and his eyes lifted, past the slope and across the gathered rebel forces, to the siege engines. While they had been concentrating on the approaching infantry, the Wolves had missed the men manning the artillery and preparing them. He watched as the catapults – six of them – reached their maximum tension.

'Down!' he shouted. 'Behind the walls.'

They did so, and a moment later there was an almighty crash as though the Jötnar were falling to earth, and the parapet shook as though Thor had struck it with his mighty hammer. Dust and mortar boiled up in a grey-white cloud, and flakes of stone flew over their ducked heads like a thousand rocky darts. One of the Apulian Wolves a little further along – damn it, but he *really* had to learn their names – bellowed in pain and reached up to the new bloody parting in his hair, where a flying shard had carved a deep line in his scalp.

The moment the barrage stopped, Halfdan yelled at the others to stay down, but rose sharply himself to look over the wall. The catapults had not been loosing at them the giant boulders which sat in heaps waiting, but baskets of rocks not unlike the ones Halfdan had on the walls. That was their intent – to remove the defenders or keep them pinned down so that they could not fight off the attack. Below, those four teams of men had braved all the falling rocks of their own barrage, holding their shields over their heads for protection. Even now, they were closing on the wall, only a few lying immobile with injuries from falling rocks.

His gaze rose to the artillery. Already the catapults were almost at full stretch once more, their crews working fast, shouting orders at one another. He could see two more baskets beside each weapon. This time, he remained standing as long as he dared as they released their shrapnel at the walls, while the men below crossed the last few paces with their shields up.

Halfdan dropped, only just in time, as fist-sized rocks swept through the air just above him, pounding against the battlements and sending more dust and mortar through the air in clouds.

By the time it had begun to clear, the assault had begun in earnest. A grapple clanked between the merlons over by Ketil, then slid and chinked into place, digging into stone and mortar as someone outside put weight on the rope. Even as Halfdan looked that way, he heard another land on the other side, and looked back to see the same happening there. At least there were only two. Without Ketil's arrows, there could have been four.

Over by the artillery, the final basket was being loaded into each catapult. This would take careful timing.

'Ketil? Thurstan? Use your saxes. Cut the ropes.'

The two men drew their short, sharp blades and rose, leaning out, going to work. Halfdan also looked out. Men were still tugging on the ropes, shields held above them, anticipating the third barrage. No one wanted to be climbing when that happened. Ketil and Thurstan were busy sawing through the ropes as fast as they could, though it was tough going.

He looked back at the siege engines, which were being ratcheted back into place.

'Drop when I say.'

He waited, listening to his friends sawing at the ropes furiously. The catapults were pulled fully back. Loaded. Shouts issued. Still, he waited. Then the weapons' arms were flung up, and the baskets flew into the air, covering half the distance to the walls before emptying of their stony contents.

'Now!' he bellowed, and Ketil and Thurstan disappeared along with their jarl behind the battlements just as the barrage struck. By the time the shards had stopped flying and the dust began to settle and Halfdan and the others had risen to look over the wall, the enemy were already on the ropes, starting to climb. Without needing to be told, the other two were already at work again, sawing at the ropes.

'Rocks now,' he bellowed to the others.

Everyone leaned out, looking down at the climbers and the gathered soldiers. Moments later, huge boulders were dropping on them. Those at the wall's base lifted their shields above them again, largely protecting them from the falling missiles. Those climbing were less lucky. Six were on the ropes already, and the top man at each climb took a rock straight to the head, screaming and falling away, the second man on Thurstan's rope similarly disappearing, injured.

More rocks, and another man fell, badly injured. Arguments had broken out below, none of those gathered in any hurry to be the next climber.

Then, Ketil gave a grunt of triumph. Halfdan glanced his way and could see that the rope there was about to give. He waved to the Icelander to stop cutting. Ketil frowned for a moment, then his mouth curved into a vicious grin, and he nodded. Halfdan had his Wolves concentrate their falling rocks on Thurstan's rope and the men gathered around it below, where they began to take a heavy toll.

Ketil, on the other hand, was making pretend sawing motions with his sax as more and more men began to climb that rope, unimpeded by falling rocks. Halfdan could see from the Icelander's face that he knew what to do, and so didn't bother with an order. Ketil waited until the top climber was almost close enough to touch, six more below him, hurrying to reach the top and to gain a foothold in the fortress, opening the door for the rest of the army.

Then the Icelander, with a laugh, gave the final cut, and the rope frayed, creaked and snapped. The rope and the climbers fell, smashing hard to the rocky slope, where those who lived through the fall with broken bones or bruises fell and rolled away down the slope. Hardly had Halfdan time to take in the whole scene before he heard the other rope give, and in moments the entire attack was retreating, all those groups who had climbed scampering and sliding and falling away back down the slope to safety. Just to be sure, the Wolves continued to throw stones, landing a few blows on the retreating rebels, the last man to fall doing so with one of Ketil's arrows in his calf. They watched, jeering, as the man pulled himself up to his feet with difficulty, limping away. Ketil was ready to put a second arrow into him, but Halfdan stood the Icelander down. Better to let the man live, wounded. That way he was useless in a fight, but still a drain on the enemy's supplies.

The other attacks to each side along the north wall had had marginally better success, the defenders not as prepared as the Wolves, but still they had not managed to crest the battlements, and the failure of their fellows at the centre of the wall had a predictable effect on their morale. In moments the other attacks were similarly retreating, pulling back to their own lines. The northern defences were clear once more. The cheer that went up all along the wall was premature, though. The assaults on the other walls were clearly still underway, and as the cheering faded Halfdan could see the catapults preparing once more, this time huge boulders being manhandled in their direction.

The enemy attack ended with men disappearing back among their own ranks, and by the time the other three attacks had faltered and failed almost an hour later, the true barrage had begun.

The Wolves were crouched behind the walls as massive rocks pounded the defences of Falaise, shaking the stonework as though it were but a flimsy wattle fence. Dust, mortar and fragments of stone were everywhere, while a fresh assault of fire arrows began at the far side of the castle, attempting to burn down anything combustible within. New crews of men with buckets were pulled together, and while Halfdan and his Wolves took shelter from the almost continual bombardment, men ran hither and thither in the bailey, hurling water from their buckets into the many new flames.

Noon came and went with nothing to mark it – even the apex of a watery winter sun they could not see through the iron-grey clouds. A light repast of barley bread and pork broth was delivered in bowls to all those on the walls, which they ate with no conversation or social engagement, and with the constant battering of artillery and swirling of dust.

That dust became less of an issue into the afternoon, but only because not long after their lunch the snow began, coming first in light, swirling eddies before settling into a steady fall, slanted south as the clouds blew in from the sea. The Wolves huddled behind their wall, protecting them from the worst of the blizzard, wrapped in their cloaks for warmth.

They accepted the snow willingly, despite their discomfort. Not only would it be so much worse for the besieging rebels in their tents and in the open, but it also made fire arrows impossible and nullified all attacks against the timber buildings within, helping to extinguish the last untouched flames.

The barrage continued for perhaps an hour, and then great covers made from ship's sails were dragged over each of the siege weapons to prevent the smaller, more delicate timbers from warping and the ropes from slackening at all, the wax already applied having protected them thus far.

The snow continued unabated for the afternoon, and only began to lighten and then fully peter out as the sun slid behind the western horizon and the gloom of evening came on. A brief flurry of fire arrows came once more, half an hour later, but the houses were so covered in snow and saturated by then that the attack was quickly proved futile and the enemy withdrew their archers.

Then, of course, the siege engines were uncovered, and a fresh barrage began in the gathering darkness. Someone came around the walls with a couple of twig brooms, and the drifted snow was brushed off to the ground below. Then someone brought out the ashes from the previous night's fires in the keep and spread them across every available path to allow the defenders a good grip as they walked, and to nullify the threat of the walls dangerously icing over.

Torches and braziers were lit all around the castle, as well as out among the rebels, great campfires growing there. Fireplaces inside the castle buildings were set and lit, black clouds belching up and out of smoke holes above.

Were it not for the pounding of rocks against the castle walls, it might almost have been peaceful. Men came round soon after with an evening meal, and Halfdan asked of them news of the other positions. It seemed that artillery was at work on every wall, the whole castle being pounded from all sides. The rebel lords knew their time to carry out the siege was short, and that winter would soon put an end to it, and so they were doing their very best to finish as swiftly as possible, even if that meant turning Falaise into a pile of rubble. The fortress, though, was of strong construction, and was holding up remarkably well to the battering.

It was, by Halfdan's estimation, close to midnight when a figure came wandering around the walls, head down and covered with a cloak's hood, shrugged deep into the wool for warmth. It came to a halt next to Halfdan, and when the head rose, he recognised the face of Archbishop Ælfric of Jorvik.

'You're out late.'

Ælfric shrugged. 'Though a man of God, I am not above lifting a mace and using it to crown the ungodly.' He chuckled.

'But here and now, I can be of little martial use. Besides, I am not sure how my king would view one of his archbishops going to war for a foreign duke. I have been wandering the castle's many ways and attempting to bring spiritual peace to those who suffer.'

Halfdan gave him a wry smile. 'And you even bring spiritual peace to the pagan?'

The archbishop's hand emerged from the folds of his cloak, gripping a bottle.

'I do, but the spirits I use are different.'

With a laugh, he handed the bottle to Halfdan, who took it, uncorked it and breathed in the acrid, strong aroma with delight.

'Thank you.'

'You are most welcome. It is the only one I could find, though, so you may have to share it with your men.'

Halfdan nodded. 'Not with Bjorn, though. One swig of his and half the bottle would go. It's quantity that matters to him, not quality.'

Another chuckle from Ælfric, though he swiftly became serious.

'So you truly intend to stay the course of this siege, Gotlander?'

Halfdan took a swig and smiled. 'As long as we must, and no longer. Gunnhild seems to think that we are not done here, though I think now that it is but a matter of waiting for Ulfr and his ship. I think I have found all I needed to know about the men I seek. But there is no point in fleeing into enemy controlled lands without a destination awaiting.'

'When you go, you will go suddenly, will you not? No farewells, no audience with Duke William.'

Halfdan nodded. 'I think so. We will go when the opportunity arises, and the window might be brief.'

'Then I must ask if I may stay with you, join your Wolves for our brief time here. I have no desire to fight another man's war among an army of heathens, but I would truly hate even more to miss my one opportunity to leave Falaise and get away.'

Halfdan laughed. 'How senior are archbishops in your nailed god church?'

'Very. There are only two in Angle-land.'

'So you must be rich.'

'I shall take that as an invitation.' The archbishop grinned. 'As long as I do not have to scribe your ungodly symbols on my person.'

'No, you don't.'

'Good,' sighed Ælfric, crouching beside him.

'We have *Gunnhild* to do that.'

Chapter 22

The low timber building was one of the few in the castle that remained entirely unharmed by either thrown stone or blazing arrow. Nestled up against the north wall atop that cliff, it was far enough from the other side of the castle to be out of the reach of the archers, but the angle below the walls also meant that all missiles hurled from this side went clean over the top.

Still, they could hear and feel the barrage continuing, as the castle wall reverberated to the blows of the catapults, every one sending a shower of dust down from the building's thatched roof.

The place had been a tanner's workshop, which was clear from the racks for stretching pelts, the bloodstained table and the runnels cut into everything, all leading to another stained drain that ran under the building's wall and through a small pipe in the ramparts out to the cliff side. Halfdan's gaze followed the drain, and he rolled his eyes as they met the hole in the wall to find Bjorn standing there, trousers open, pissing into the channel while humming a happy melody.

Everyone else stood around the room's edge, watching intently. The building's eleven occupants were silent, barring the spattering stream and gentle humming from Bjorn.

The Wolves – Halfdan, Bjorn, Ketil, Leif and Gunnhild, the five of them who had been together since the day they left Hedeby and sailed for Kiev. Rurik – for now, Halfdan had committed his name to memory – a man who had joined them on the beach in Italy during the revolt of Maniakes, a former Rus Varangian, but unquestionably one of the Wolves.

Solid Thurstan, who had left the uncertainty of Apulia with his Normans and had travelled alongside Halfdan and his friends for so long that when they had become part of the Wolves, it had seemed only natural. And, of course, two of those very same Apulian warriors – Abbe and Robert, he believed. And then, of course, Anna and Cassandra.

The Wolves of Odin.

They were only missing Ulfr and Farlof, and the six who had left with them.

How things had changed since Kiev, he mused to the eerie melody at the heart of the room. Of the eleven in this place, more than half prayed to the nailed god, yet here they were, part of Halfdan's *hirð*. Here they were, in fact, witnessing one of the most sacred moments of a believer in the old gods. In truth, Abbe and Robert looked more than a little uncomfortable, for they had never see this before, yet they were here, and they did not look away.

Halfdan had managed to persuade one of the units who ran around the bailey, extinguishing fires and fetching and carrying, to take their place on the wall for an hour while they ostensibly got a little indoor rest and warmth. In truth, they needed somewhere sheltered and hidden so that Gunnhild could walk with the Vanir.

Her song rose as it always had, like the lapping of waves against rocks in an incredibly swiftly rising tide, ever higher, always cresting, new, glorious and bleak, sad and eternal. But these days it had become so much more, with Cassandra and Anna joining their melodic tones to that of the völva, a rite as old as mankind, invoking the Seiðr and the companionship of Freyja, given heart and power by women who kissed the cross. It was truly a strange world.

As the völva slowly rose, her staff turning and whirling, Halfdan found himself thinking back over their time together, and over what their collective faiths meant. His youth had been steeped in the old ways, on an island that staunchly resisted the encroachment of the White Christ who had claimed most of the North. He had sworn a blood oath against Jarl Yngvar for killing his father and pulling down the Odin stone of their village in an attempt to stamp out the old ways for the king Olof.

But for all Yngvar's crimes, it had been the priest Hjalmvigi who had been behind them all, urging his master. And it had been Hjalmvigi, to the end of that year in the east, who had dominated Halfdan's life, his hated face becoming the face of all the nailed god men everywhere. Even though he had sailed in companionship with Leif, who had always been a Christian, Halfdan had not only clung to the old ways, but he had carried in his heart a burning hatred for the White Christ and his priests, who could not let the world live without them, who tore down sacred stones, and who killed good men because they remembered the power of Odin.

When, he wondered, had that begun to change? On arriving at Miklagarðr, the Wolves had hidden their true faiths and played the Christian for simple expediency. There, and beyond, all the way to that beach in Italy, he had met men who prayed to the nailed god, yet who were good men, still with the ice and rock of the North in their blood, who bonded together in brotherhood. And even though he had met another rabid priest, desperate to burn the 'heathen' in Acerenza, he had also met more good men in Apulia, Normans this time, who prayed to the nailed Christ yet joined that same brotherhood.

He'd not really thought about how comfortable he'd become around Christians until he'd met this archbishop, Ælfric, apparently one of the world's most important priests, yet a man who seemed content to accept Halfdan and his Wolves as a picturesque aberration in his world, something that he did not like or approve of, but could watch with fascination, like a scorpion.

The ritual's crescendo came at the same time as one of the most powerful strikes of boulder against wall. The whole building shook wildly as the three women reached the heights of their song and Gunnhild dropped like a hammer blow from the heavens, sinking into a crouch, her handful of bones and beads, coins and feathers and silver fragments scattering across the dirt before her.

'Tell me,' he breathed.

'The golden threads are gone from our weaving,' she said quietly. 'Gone *before* this night, even, gone their own way, in their own tapestries.'

'Harðráði,' Halfdan said, crestfallen.

He had been so hopeful. It had felt so close. That the duke and the thief might be connected had given him hope that they would soon find the man and the ship he had stolen. Yet it seemed things had changed. He did wonder, for one guilty little moment, how Gunnhild felt, given her own feelings for Harðráði. She had almost left the Wolves for him, and had defied even fate to stay with her jarl, after all.

'He is not gone forever,' she said, as though reading his thoughts, and with a certainty that at least reassured him a little. 'But that is in days to come. Your connection to the golden thread of the Byzantine Bear himself is not *severed*, just separated for a while longer. But the other golden thread that is William... I see it with us no more. Whatever our connection to the Lion of Nordmandi has been, we have done what we came to do. He is no longer your concern, my jarl.'

Halfdan thought back over the past few weeks. Things *had* changed. He had learned of Harðráði's new place at the court in Kiev, as heir to several kingdoms, all to the west, where he must surely be bound in the coming days. He knew where the man was, then, and he had an idea of the man's plans. *And* he knew of Hjalmvigi's role as chief priest to the new king of Swedes, Onund. *And* he had saved the life of the duke, an assassination attempt that could very well have changed *everything* in this land. Though the Bastard was outnumbered and besieged, William was confident that this siege was but the opening move in a war he felt he could win. Halfdan did not doubt for a moment that the duke would be triumphant. There was something about the Bastard Duke that spoke of great destiny. Had he been born two hundred years earlier, he would have been a great jarl himself – possibly the *greatest*.

Perhaps that was all they had needed, after all, to learn of Harðráði and Hjalmvigi, and to stop the duke dying before he could win his war. Was that what they had been waiting for? Could they leave?

He became aware that Gunnhild had been talking while he had gone off on his mental tangent, and was silent again, watching him with an irritated arched eyebrow.

'Sorry.'

'I still see the dragon,' she repeated patiently, 'but I think our time here is done. Watch for signs, for the white thread has bound to yours, my jarl. The priest will lead you to great things, and only through him can the Wolves ever hope to face Hjalmvigi and Harðráði and regain what was lost. We are besieged, but the path will become open, and the priest will lead the way.'

There was something more in her eyes that she didn't like. He could sense it. Something unsaid.

'What else?' Halfdan said.

She took a long, slow breath. 'Loki's chains weaken.'

Skies red as blood, shaking and booming, as though being torn apart. A black crack looming above him as he stood, sword in hand, watching his enemy emerge from the doorway of the stone hall. A tall man, in a glittering shirt of silver eyes shining almost gold in the reflected light of the dreadful sky; in his hands a sword that was the death of men and a beautiful and terrible horn.

Ragnarok…

Halfdan had to clench his fists to stop the trembling that began in his fingertips and threatened to engulf his body.

'We should return to the wall,' he said.

There were nods all round, some rather relieved ones from the Apulians, who'd not witnessed such a spectacle as this before. Halfdan sighed. Gunnhild had not been as clear as he'd hoped, with the exception of the part about Loki that he could have done without. He'd wanted to see a path laid out before him by the völva, a simple road he could follow that would take him to the *Sea Wolf* and its thief, and then to Hjalmvigi and vengeance. Instead, she had produced only nebulous notions, although at least they could move on.

Or they could have if they weren't trapped in a castle under siege...

At a nod from his jarl, Bjorn, who had finished his business and fastened his trousers once more, stepped across and opened the door, an arctic chill sweeping in with fresh flakes of snow in the air. Halfdan led the way, stepping out into the open, pulling up his cloak's hood against the light dusting of snow. With luck, the fresh fall would silence the siege engines once more, for they had been pounding the walls of Falaise for four solid days since the Wolves had fought off the assault on the northern approach.

As they left the room, he placed a hand on Gunnhild's arm.

'How are we to leave Falaise? And when?'

'When the signs tell us to.'

'But you said we could leave.'

'*Could* and *should* are not the same thing, Halfdan. We wait for Ulfr.'

Halfdan sighed with sagging shoulders. This was not the first time she had said that, but there were problems with such a thing. Even if Ulfr and the other seven men they had left at Pirou were free and healthy, even if they'd built a ship the likes of which Ran's daughters had never before witnessed, what use would they be at Falaise?

'Gunnhild, we're *thirty miles* or more from the sea and the duke's port at Diva. And have you seen the river here? It couldn't carry a toy boat. It's just a stream most of the way to the coast. How is Ulfr supposed to come to us? It makes no sense. He can only come as far as Diva, and we can't even guarantee that's not in rebel hands now. We have to make a break for it somehow ourselves and make for the coast.'

'No,' was her simple answer as she pulled free of his grip and walked on into the cold. Halfdan sighed yet again, and followed.

Ælfric of Jorvik stood beneath a half-ruined veranda outside a damaged smithy opposite, a small group of his attendants gathered around him, mostly lesser priest-people. The archbishop had refused to stay away, remaining with the Wolves throughout the siege, ready to leave at any moment, though he had drawn the line at actually attending a pagan ceremony, and had waited patiently in the cold.

'You can't bring them with you,' Halfdan said to the archbishop as the man emerged from the veranda with his entourage, to fall in beside them. He was taking out on them the irritability he felt after his conversation with Gunnhild, and he knew it.

'Oh?'

Halfdan bit his lip. In truth, that was just down to *him*. He didn't mind giving a lift to Ælfric, with whom he'd struck up an odd and very unlikely friendship over their time at Falaise, but he definitely drew the line at becoming a ferry service for nailed god priests in general.

He had no idea how they were going to leave. Gunnhild seemed insistent that Ulfr would come, and if so then it seemed undeniable that Ulfr had managed to build their new ship. There were so many unanswerable questions, though. He'd left eight of them in Pirou. Even with the best will in the world, it would be a struggle indeed for eight men to row even the smallest longship. Of course, perhaps he would be waiting for the rest of the Wolves, before starting to use the oars and relying on the sail. But where he would dock, and how they would meet up with him, were questions to which he really could find no answer. He was aware that the archbishop was patiently waiting for an explanation.

'Our ships... They are not merchant ships, with lots of hold space, or beds for guests. They are raiders and warships. There is only room for those who sail her.' He eyed the motley bunch following Ælfric, entirely composed of gangly youths, pale and thin-limbed, or small, wizened monks with their shaved heads and wrinkled parchment skin. 'Your people cannot row. They cannot come. That is all.'

The archbishop frowned. 'It is unseemly for a man in my position to travel so rudely. And you are asking me to place my personal safety in the hands of pagans on their warship.'

'Swap the ship for a castle wall, and you've been in that position for at least a week already,' Halfdan countered.

Ælfric's frown deepened. 'This we will discuss when the time comes. I can be quite generous, although I will concede that if left behind, a man of God will not be harmed by the other side when the fighting concludes.'

They were approaching the wall, and climbed the stairs, Halfdan leading the way and arriving at the top. The stones had stopped striking the walls at some point between house and wall, for the snow had become heavier once more. The soldier in charge of the unit that had been watching in their stead gave him a nervous look as they met.

'Anything happened?'

'They're pulling back,' the man said, though his voice did not carry confidence, 'and the artillery is being covered because of the snow.'

'Pulling back?' Halfdan said, crossing to the parapet and peering down.

It was true, though only marginally so. The enemy were still massed down there below the slope, gathered in their units around the castle, but the front lines had been withdrawn perhaps twenty paces. He drummed his fingers on the snow-encrusted battlements. *Why? What did it mean?*

If they had pulled back, then they were afraid of something from the walls, but neither the Wolves nor any of the duke's men had done anything new that might warrant such fear. And if *they* had not, then it could only be something of the enemy's doing.

His heart started to pound, and with a sense of impending dread he leaned out over the wall. He could see nothing down at the base. It was late afternoon in a snowstorm, the natural light already failing without being hidden behind huge, thick, boiling clouds and sheets of white. He could just about see the slope as a vaguely grey tableau, and could occasionally, between gusts, make out the patches of rocky cliff here and there. But just because he couldn't see something didn't mean it wasn't there.

'Shhh,' he called to the others on the wall.

Each of them was making a noise, from Bjorn's humming to Leif's foot-tapping keeping him moving and helping warm him, to Cassandra, Anna and Gunnhild's ongoing discussion, to Robert, rhythmically sliding his sword in and out of its scabbard an inch or so, to work out some tightness in the leather.

Piece by piece, the whole symphony of boredom ceased, leaving that rare, true silence, a stillness so complete that you can heard snowflakes landing.

Then Halfdan could hear it.

'Listen,' he hissed.

The others crossed to the wall carefully, cupping hands to ears.

The blows were being carefully struck so that they were truly arrhythmic, so that they did not leap to one's attention as a pattern, a man-made thing. They could almost be the sounds of wild animals. But they were not. They were the sounds of tools against mortar, dampened and almost hidden beneath the blanket of snow. Halfdan leaned back. Someone was chipping away the mortar at the base of the wall above the slope. And if the enemy lines had pulled back, that meant they anticipated the wall falling, which meant they hadn't just started it. They'd been doing it for some time.

He thought back over the past few hours. When he considered it, he realised that the siege machines had been hurling their stones to the left and right of this position, but not directly at it. Of course not, for they hardly wished to kill their own engineers who'd been working to collapse the wall. And the continual barrage of stones all around would have perfectly hidden the work of their picks until the snow had silenced the artillery. Then they had slowed and started to work in that arrhythmic way, without the cover of the smashing rocks.

He sucked on his teeth, drumming fingers on the snowy stonework. If they were allowed to continue, and the wall went, then only a rocky slope protected this approach. The castle would fall swiftly. Though on the surface it might not appear to be Halfdan's problem, even if the Wolves were planning to leave as soon as possible they had to deal with this.

'They're going to collapse the wall,' he hissed to the others. 'Get a rope.'

As silence fell again, he listened carefully. He could hear what appeared to be two picks at work, and only two, which made sense. Any more than two, and they would be hard to hide in the shadowy rocks at the base of the wall. He waited, still listening, until Leif and Thurstan reappeared with two coils of rope.

'Can't find one long enough,' the Rus explained, as Thurstan busied himself knotting the ends of the two coils together, then testing them for strength. Satisfied, he handed his coil to Halfdan, who waved to Bjorn and Ketil, by far the two largest men among the Wolves.

'Take the other end and brace yourselves,' he said as he looped the rope around his chest, making sure to leave sufficient breathing room, and then tied it as tight as he could. 'I need you to lower me, steadily, but fast. All right?'

The two men nodded. Ketil took the other coil from Leif, while Bjorn spat on his hands and then took the rope some eight feet from the knot at Halfdan's chest.

'Go with Loki's own luck,' Ketil said.

Bjorn simply farted and grinned.

Halfdan took a deep breath and climbed up onto the battlements. He'd never had a trouble with heights, and that had been tested more than once, on the high walls of Miklagarðr and on the abandoned roofs of Ginosa more recently, but somehow, standing in a howling gale, with icy snow slapping him in the face repeatedly, looking down into the monochrome world below that consisted of twenty feet of fortress wall and then perhaps sixty feet of steep slope with rocky cliffs, his stomach began to churn. Forcing down the queasiness, he turned, dropping to his knees on the battlements, arms gripping snow-covered merlons, and then lay down, belly cold on the stone as his legs slid out over the drop.

He pushed off.

For a moment, he felt a touch of panic that Bjorn had somehow forgotten what he was supposed to be doing, as he seemed to plummet without any kind of support. He managed not to yell, and then couldn't anyway as the rope snapped tight, anchored by the two great Northmen, and the breath was slammed out of his chest. Gasping, he swung this way and that for a few moments, recovering and trying to regain control. He managed to get a little swing going and pushed out away from the wall, then back, landing against the stone with the balls of his feet. His breath returned, and with it, his confidence.

He kicked again and swung away from the wall. To his relief, Bjorn and Ketil had got their act together, for as he swung out, the rope slowly extended and he slid almost his own height down the wall, reaching over halfway before his feet hit and he bounced once more. His confidence growing all the time as he worked, he reached down with his right hand and pulled his sax free, using only his left on the rope to steady himself. He had fretted for just the briefest moment over whether to use his sax or sword, but if he dropped a weapon he would probably lose it forever and, whereas he could easily replace the sax, the sword was truly one of a kind.

As he bounced out again he was still descending, and he could see the two men just below, working hard, hacking at the mortar between the stone blocks of the wall. Half a dozen blocks were missing already, and they were digging inwards. Fortunately, between the falling snow, and their own labour and the noise it made, they remained unaware of the danger descending from above.

Halfdan was, conversely, aware of everything, and so timed his next jump. He kicked out from the wall harder than before, swinging back some distance, just as Ketil and Bjorn dropped him the last six feet, but instead of landing, he swung back inwards with both feet out in front of him, spaced wide. He was rewarded, as planned, with a well-placed boot heel hard in the back of each of the two men hacking at the mortar. One yelped and fell forward, gripping his pick as he slammed against the stone and dropped to one side, trying to recover himself from the sudden, unexpected attack. The other folded up in an instant without a sound and toppled to the rough, stony ground, the tool falling from opening fingers. Even in that heartbeat, as he swung back again and dropped his feet to the ground, Halfdan realised that the impact had broken the second man's back. All well and good; that left only one. The other man pulled himself up and turned to face Halfdan, pickaxe in hand, face a grimaced mix of pain and anger. He bellowed something unintelligible in the blizzard, lost to the elements as the cloud of steam from his breath barely made it out.

Halfdan thanked Odin and Thor and Loki all for their part in his success. It was never a bad thing to acknowledge all the Æsir when great things happened, even if you weren't sure they had all played a part, for the gods could be both jealous and petty. He didn't bother with the Vanir, though. Freyja and her siblings were the province of Gunnhild, and he would assume that they were always happy as long as the völva seemed to be.

The man swung his pick with the expertise of a miner, not a warrior. Halfdan simply stepped closer, threw his arm in the way of the haft, taking a blow that would leave a bruise, and grabbed it with that hand, while the other came round, gleaming sax jutting from the fist. The blade slammed into the man's chest. Halfdan would normally, faced with such a situation, assume there was a chain shirt and strike for an area unlikely to be covered with protective armour. A man who had climbed this hill, though, and who worked as they did, had to be wearing only warm clothes. He'd been correct, for the sax slid easily between ribs, robbing the man of his next heartbeat, and then his life. The miner gave a horrified gasp and collapsed into Halfdan's arms. The jarl smiled a grimly victorious smile, and then heaved the man out and away across the slope, where he fell and rolled a way before coming to a halt beside a rock, black blood pumping out into the white world.

The sax was easy to clean, wiped in the snow three times and then on his trousers before being sheathed again. Then Halfdan paused. He looked up. The enemy might, possibly, have seen all this, though the odds were against it. And the moment the snow stopped, he'd be willing to bet that in a single minute the covers would be off the machines of war and rocks would start to fly again. Whatever the case, staying here was asking for trouble, and he realistically should try and climb back up, or jerk the rope and hope that Bjorn and Ketil realised that was the signal to pull him back in. But he also looked at the hole the men had already carved out in the short time they'd been working. It probably wouldn't be enough to put any strain on the wall as it was, without extra work, but then one well-placed rock from a catapult and they might just be able to capitalise on their damage.

He sighed. He didn't relish the idea of such hard and gruelling physical work, especially on a freezing exposed slope in a blizzard, watched by the enemy and within range of their archers and artillery. But he figured he didn't really have a choice. He couldn't do much about the mortar, of course, but even the stones on their own would both help support the courses above and make the location of their work very hard for catapults to find at a distance.

Consequently, singing an old song his father had sung when working at his lathe, Halfdan began looking around the slope nearby, finding the stones that had been cut out and pulled away, dusting them off of the coating of snow, and then hauling them with curses and sweat back to the wall. In a short time he had managed to locate what he believed to be all the missing blocks, and then set about the puzzle of fitting them back into place so that they were relatively snug, despite the lack of mortar. It was long and troublesome work, and more than once he had to remove several of the blocks and begin again to get it right.

Finally, he had only two blocks left to replace, though they were almost identical. He tried one in the lower of the two courses, but it did not fit. He then turned it end-on and tried again, still with no luck. Swapping it for the other block, he did the same, and then began to curse, realising that if neither block fitted, he'd gone wrong somewhere else, and would need to remove quite an area to test the other blocks. He was holding the last failure, sweating under the weight and the effort of building, when the voice spoke up just behind him.

'The furthest one on the left, I think. Two courses down.'

Halfdan turned sharply, sax leaping back out of its scabbard into his hand.

The barrel-chested man grinned at him as he pulled his pale grey cloak tighter, the material just the right colour to make the big shipwright barely visible in the blizzard.

'Ulfr?'

'I approve of men trying to learn a trade. Even kings and warriors should know how to build a ship, or shape a table leg, or skin a reindeer, or thatch a hut. But you did pick an odd time to learn your new skill.'

Halfdan looked down at the stone and laughed.

'I think the Lion of Nordmandi can take care of his own castle wall for now.'

Without another word, he dropped the stone, took three steps, and embraced the stoic, red-headed Wolf as though he'd thought to never see him again.

His eyes rose over Ulfr's shoulder, and it was with no small surprise that he recognised Geoffroi, the Norman from Valognes, and the man's friend.

Geoffroi gave him a fierce smile.

'Let me take it from here.'

Chapter 23

It took almost half an hour to get everyone moved. Halfdan had more cause than ever to be grateful for the snowfall that kept them obscured from the enemy positions, for rebel arrows would not have found it hard to pick a target.

While Halfdan and Ulfr had reworked the stones in the wall, and the solid shipwright, ever a practical man, had found small pebbles and lodged them between the larger stones in temporary place of mortar, Geoffroi and his friend had been hauled to the top of the wall by Bjorn and Ketil, where they helped the big albino and the tall Icelander anchor the rope. Then, the Wolves began to come down the rope and join the two men as they admired their handiwork. The wall would still be weaker here than elsewhere, but not nearly as weak as it had been, and it would be very hard to target by artillery, looking much the same as the rest of the rampart.

Gradually, the others had come to rest on the snowy slope. Leif, then Gunnhild, followed by her ever-present companions, Anna and Cassandra, then Thurstan, Rurik, Abbe and Robert, and then, close to the end, Ketil, Bjorn remaining at the top until the end. Second to last came Archbishop Ælfric, sliding down the height of the wall with some difficulty in his long robes, clutching his staff of office and coming to rest on the snow, looking exhausted.

Halfdan looked at him, frowning. 'You'll have to lose the cloak.'

Ælfric frowned, plucking at his chasuble with two fingers. 'It is freezing out here.'

'And your cloak is bright red. Hard to hide in snow. Take it off.'

Grumbling, the Saxon cleric shrugged off the crimson garment and, with it, unravelled a long strip of brightly coloured and gold-threaded silk. The former he let fall to the ground, though the latter he folded tight and tucked it into the belt that held his white ankle-length tunic tight. He pointed down at the red heap.

'If you only knew how much such robes cost.'

'Are they worth more than your life?' Halfdan said pointedly.

He looked up to see Bjorn sliding down the stone face, Geoffroi and his friend struggling to hold the rope atop the wall given the big man's massive weight. To save them what he could, Bjorn let go and dropped the last eight feet, almost falling as he hit the slippery slope, arms flailing comically as he kept his footing with difficulty. Ælfric turned sharply as the rope began to disappear upwards.

'My retinue!'

'I told you before that there wasn't room.'

The archbishop's eyes narrowed. 'I would make you swear upon the Holy Book to preserve my life and freedom, if such an oath were worth a wet fart to you people.'

That made Halfdan chuckle, especially given the wry smile that hovered on the edge of the man's face as he finished.

'You will be safer with us than *here*, believe me.'

'I do,' Ælfric replied earnestly, looking up at the wall and the now-disappeared rope.

Atop the rampart, Geoffroi and his companion leaned over the parapet and waved at them. 'Farewell and good luck. We will give you a quarter of an hour. God be with you.'

'I sincerely hope so,' the archbishop called back up, eyeing the pagans around him. Halfdan and the others called up their fond farewells. A quarter of an hour. The two Normans would stand vigil in the place of the Wolves for that time, and then hurry off to report their arrival to William and bring the damaged wall to the duke's attention. A quarter of an hour should allow sufficient time for the Wolves to be gone from the area before reinforcements came to the wall and discovered their absence. While there was no official agreement keeping the Wolves among the ducal forces, it seemed likely that William would be at best reluctant to let them leave.

With a last wave up at them, Halfdan turned. He saw genuine regret in Ulfr's eyes as the shipwright said his farewell and turned with the rest of them, and wondered what had happened back at Pirou. Whatever it was had forged a certain brotherhood between his friend and the two Normans, clearly. But either Ulfr had not thought to invite them to join the crew, or the Normans had turned down the offer, opting to remain and support their duke.

It was Gunnhild who led the first leg, taking the Wolves and their Saxon priest down to the first large rocky overhang, which would protect them from the worst of the snow and also make them very hard to spot from both above and below. The moment they were in the lee of the rocks, and in shelter, Halfdan grasped Ulfr by the shoulders with a wide grin.

'By Thor's mighty bollocks, it's good to see you, my friend. But how came you? We are thirty miles from the sea.'

Ulfr nodded. 'There we were lucky. My skill with steering oar and prow, combined with Geoffroi's knowledge of the coast and the region, made it possible. We have a new ship, my jarl. The *Sea Dragon* is almost as swift and almost as powerful as the *Sea Wolf*.'

Halfdan registered the name of their new ship, given in passing, with a smile, and turned to Gunnhild to see the satisfaction settle over her as the dragon in her vision became clear. He turned back as Ulfr continued.

'She sits in the last navigable stretch of a river at a place called Clécy, about ten miles from here. I left most of the crew with her, for safety.'

'Crew?'

'Long story. I'll tell you when we have time. For now, I have three men in a wood on the far side of the rebel force, and they have two carts and a number of horses. Enough for us to get back to the ship, and once we're off at speed downriver for the coast no one but Sleipnir could catch us.' He eyed the gathering at the base of the rock. 'Good job I brought carts. You seem to have picked up a priest.'

Halfdan laughed. 'Also a long story. But he's coming with us.'

'Going to be a crowded ship, but we'll manage. We need to keep moving, make use of the blizzard. We waited half a day out there for the weather to turn bad and give us the chance to get this close.'

The jarl nodded. 'Lead on.'

With that, Ulfr turned and began to move swiftly down the slope, slipping here and there, but keeping his footing with the sureness of a man born and bred in the rocky lands of the North. Halfdan followed, and the others came in his wake. In a turn of events that surprised the jarl, he saw the archbishop, shivering in only his tunic in the snow, slipping and almost falling as they descended the difficult slope, using his crook for stability. Suddenly it was Bjorn, of all people, who was next to Ælfric, grabbing him when he slipped and preventing him from falling. Halfdan made a mental note to check in to that later, for it seemed oddly out of character for the big man.

With care, and helping one another where necessary, the Wolves made their way down the slope, from craggy cliff to craggy cliff, slowly and silently descending to the flat ground below. The snow was still thick, coming down in a blanket, and had left a carpet half a foot deep on the grass. Ulfr had them stop at the bottom of the slope in the cover of the last jagged outcropping of rock that jutted, black, from the snow-covered long grass. There, they peered off into the snowstorm.

'That way,' Ulfr said finally, pointing off in a direction that looked, to Halfdan, just like all the others – a curtain of falling snow, with the indistinct shape of gathered men in the distance little more than a dark ribbon in the white.

'Are you sure?'

Ulfr gave his jarl a withering look. 'Who has navigated the whale road for more years than you have lived?'

Halfdan laughed. 'All right. That way it is. Lead on.'

Ulfr did just that, stepping out from the rock and pulling his cloak tight around him. As they moved closer to the enemy force, Halfdan started to see differences. The enemy were not one unbroken line of men surrounding the castle, as they had been earlier. With the onslaught of the weather, many units had been stood down and were taking shelter in tents or by fires, and the cordon around Falaise was maintained by small unlucky units left on guard, gathered in knots here and there, the gaps between them filled with picket positions of one or two men. It was one such picket for which they were making, the Wolves' position adequate to keep just enough falling snow between them and the units on either side to mask their movement.

At one point, Ulfr held up his hand to them, and they all stopped dead, silent in the falling white. The snow had lessened for just a moment, a freak wind sending it flurrying in various directions high up, and for just a few heartbeats, before the wind changed once more and the deluge returned, they were worryingly visible. Such was clear from the fact that Halfdan could then see a unit of archers not far off, and if *he* could see *them*, there was every chance *they* could see *him*.

Still, unmoving and silent, they must have blended in with the rocks and bushes that formed a mottled landscape with the snow, and by the time they were moving again, no alarm had gone up.

After what seemed an eternity, they were approaching the picket, and Halfdan's hand went to the hilt of his sword, wondering what Ulfr's plan might be to overwhelm the two men, before realising that no such move would be necessary after all.

The two pickets watched the castle ahead, but as they came close Halfdan could see the mute evidence of Ulfr's earlier passage, alongside the two Normans. One man was only upright because the spear he appeared to be holding was driven through his forearm, and he was propped against it, the butt wedged into the ground. The other appeared to be sitting on a tree stump, but the dark stain all down his front and in a puddle around his feet spoke eloquently of the cut throat he had suffered as the three men sneaked up behind him.

Another flurry of snow in fresh breezes caused the falling blanket of white to falter, and the whole group of escapees paused alongside the pickets, creating a shadowed tableau that from a distance could be mistaken for a small rebel unit in their rightful position. They remained there for what seemed hours. Halfdan saw Gunnhild looking up into the sky and followed suit. When he looked back down, her eyes were on him.

'The snowfall is ending. Very soon we will lose our cover, the enemy will come out of their tents, the siege engines will start again, and we will be caught in the middle of the enemy camp.'

Halfdan nodded, turning to Ulfr. 'How far?'

'Not far now.'

The shipwright looked up, as they had. The snowfall was increasing once more, though the clouds were higher and lighter, and inevitably it would soon be nowhere near as heavy as it had been. This would, they all realised, be the last cover they would get.

'Go,' Halfdan said, 'and move fast now. Follow Ulfr.'

The shipwright began to move at speed, hurrying through the ankle-deep snow, huddling in his cloak but with a hand on his axe. They followed, clustered together, and through the quickly diminishing downfall, Halfdan began to see more clearly the units to either side. For now they were unnoticed, for the enemy were intent on – if anything at all – the fortress ahead, not paying attention to unauthorised movement among their own forces. Occasionally, men glanced their way, but still no alarm went up. Dark shapes of warriors in the snow, moving among their own lines, could easily be mistaken for their own units assembling. It was all just a matter of time, though.

'Fuck,' Ulfr said in little more than a hiss, coming to a sudden halt.

Such a reaction from the usually stoic shipwright drew Halfdan's concern, and as he stumbled to a halt behind him, the jarl peered off ahead. He could see the shapes of men on horses, and other infantry, too, gathered near the edge of a wood. A man was giving orders, and Halfdan was about to ask the shipwright what was happening, when he realised the answer himself, for he recognised one of the figures.

Serlo de Hauteville, lord of Pirou, and brother of both Beatrix and Iron Arm. A man whom Duke William had welcomed into his own council, but who had watched the balance of power with the eye of a survivor and had in the end abandoned his duty and thrown in his lot with the rebels. Halfdan cursed. Ulfr had said their friends were in the woodland. Ahead was clearly that woodland, but Hauteville was there, too, and the Wolves were trapped among the enemy.

'What now?' Ulfr hissed. 'We need to get into those woods.'

Halfdan nodded, frowning, looking about him. They had all been at Pirou, and there was little chance the lord of that place would not recognise one of the Wolves who had escorted his sister north from Apulia. He counted up, quickly. There were nine riders and eight footmen with Hauteville. Eighteen altogether. With Ulfr, the Wolves leaving Falaise numbered twelve. Not encouraging odds, but with the element of surprise, they could be a lot more even. That element became clear as his gaze settled on the one man among them whom Hauteville would not know. His smile broke free as he gestured to the Archbishop of Jorvik.

'Ælfric?'

'Halfdan?'

'I need you to take the lead. Bluster and blather as we come close to those men. Buy us time before they are alert.'

The man looked doubtful for a moment, but resolve fell across him quickly. In leaving the castle, he had thrown in his lot with the Wolves, for good or for ill, and their survival meant his. He thought for a moment, and then nodded and struggled out ahead of them. He plodded off through the white with his staff in hand, making straight for the gathered group of riders.

Halfdan followed with Ulfr, and hissed back at the others, 'Weapons out. The moment they notice something wrong, or I shout, kill them all.'

And that was it. The Wolves of Odin, bristling with weapons, followed the shivering, half-dressed archbishop out across the snow in the last drifting flakes.

Just as the jarl had hoped, there was no sudden cry of alarm from the gathered Normans. The man leading the group took the majority of their attention, and he was a nailed god priest – a figure above suspicion, seemingly. Some of the riders, including Serlo de Hauteville himself, glanced at the Wolves following on, but they were armed and armoured men in the middle of an army of armed and armoured men, and with cloaks and amid the last snowfall their identity was not immediately clear.

'Father?' Hauteville called, confusing Halfdan for a moment, before he remembered that this was a term of respect for a Christian priest, and not just a familial relation.

'Thank the good Lord,' Ælfric shouted, relief filling his tone.

Hauteville stared at the man, frowning. Halfdan tensed as they neared. The Wolves each had a weapon in hand. As yet, none of the enemy had moved to draw a sword. The Loki serpents on his arm were tingling.

'I never thought I would escape Falaise alive,' the archbishop gasped. 'I took advantage of the blizzard. The duke's men never even…'

He needed to go no further. By that time, Ælfric was almost at arm's length from the lord of Pirou, the Wolves too close to the enemy to maintain a fiction any longer, and the riders had sensed something was wrong. Even as the archbishop's words tumbled out, one of the Pirou horsemen shouted a warning and drew his sword.

He never got any further. Leif's throwing axe hit him in the face, and he was robbed of senses and consciousness – if not his life – in an instant, lolling in the saddle, sword falling away. Ketil was the second to strike, his massive stride coming into play as he covered the remaining distance to another rider in three great steps, leaping with the last, his axe coming round in a wide swing and smashing into the man's side, breaking several ribs even through the chain hauberk he wore. The man cried out and doubled over, out of the fight.

The other Normans were drawing their own weapons, crying out with alarm and preparing to hold off the Wolves, but they were too late to do anything more than defend themselves. Bjorn swamped two of the infantry, dispatching one with a single axe blow that left a crumpled and dented head inside a crumpled and dented helmet, even as he grasped the other by the throat in one great, pale, meaty hand and lifted him from the ground.

The rest were piling in, Ulfr and Rurik with powerful axes, Thurstan, Abbe and Robert with swords. Gunnhild had her staff out and had already smacked a rider with it, the man reeling in his saddle and trying to push away the weapon long enough to draw his own sword, his head spinning from the blow. Even Cassandra and Anna were together keeping one of the footmen busy, the man struggling with the morality of fighting women, while they repeatedly battered him.

Halfdan turned to the one man in the gathering who mattered more than anyone, and found to his surprise that he wasn't there. Serlo de Hauteville's horse was stepping away, its rider struggling up from the snow, furious as he drew his sword. Halfdan caught the look of astonishment on Archbishop Ælfric's face as he lifted his crozier, the ornate top of which was broken from the blow he had landed on the lord of Pirou, unhorsing him.

'Finish them,' Halfdan called to his Wolves. 'Riders first. Stop them going for help.'

Even as his hirð did just that, Halfdan found himself facing Hauteville, the man's eyes slits in a face of pure anger as he shook the snow from his shoulders and braced himself, feet apart, sword in hand.

'So now you show your true colours,' the Norman spat. 'Mercenaries and thieves.'

Halfdan snorted. 'I hardly think a man who heaped praise on his jarl at the dinner table and barely waited for him to walk out of the door before betraying him and signing up with his enemies is in any position to sneer.'

Though Hauteville said nothing in reply, the look that crossed his face, momentarily interrupting the anger, made it clear that Halfdan's words had hit home. Serlo knew his own treachery, and the guilt was already gnawing at him.

'You will not escape,' he said, taking a step forward.

Halfdan looked about him. The Wolves had mounted a true surprise attack on these men and had overwhelmed most before they had even managed to draw a sword. Not a single rider had got away, and the last few men were fighting for their lives against the overwhelming force of Halfdan's hirð.

'I think we will,' he said, and then took the one step that put him within reach of the lord of Pirou.

Each man took in his opponent in that heartbeat. Both combatants wore chain shirts, Halfdan's a simple sleeved garment that came down to his hips, belted around the waist, Serlo's one of those great Norman affairs that reached to the wrist, with a square flap on the chest that could be pulled up in the form of a veil, the hem reaching below the knees, with a slit up the front, dividing it and making riding easier. Similarly, while Halfdan wielded his Alani blade, short and straight with an eagle carved into the hilt, Hauteville held a

345

long, heavy sword, tapering gently from a solid cross-guard, of the sort favoured by most warriors, Normans and Swedes alike. It was clear in an instant who was the heaviest armed and armoured, but that also meant that their fighting styles had been determined from the start.

Serlo came first, swinging that sword wide with impressive strength, gripping the hilt with both hands as the blade sliced through the air, coming round at diaphragm height. Halfdan had anticipated the blow, for he knew how limited the options were for a man with such a sword. As the blade swept round, instead of trying to parry it, which would likely fail, or leap out of the way, which would put him on the back foot, he stepped *into* the blow, inside the arc of the blade, slamming into Hauteville.

The sweeping blow met no target as the two men fell to the snowy ground, Halfdan atop his opponent. As he'd hoped, the fall knocked the breath from Hauteville, and the man's arms slammed out against the ground in a pose not unlike the White Christ Halfdan had seen on his cross in churches.

The jarl pulled back his sword hand, gripping that short, razor-sharp blade, ready to slam it down into the V-shape of the man's neck, above where his collarbones met, the only sizeable exposed patch of flesh. But before Halfdan could deliver the killing blow, Hauteville suddenly bucked, displaying more strength than Halfdan had expected, sending the jarl flying backwards, staggering to his feet. Halfdan was not to be stopped, though. Even as the Norman rose, long sword in hand, ready to come for another swing, Halfdan charged. Hauteville saw him coming and, anticipating a repeat strike, being driven to the ground once more, he ducked to the side.

Good – just as Halfdan had hoped. As the man stepped aside, the jarl threw himself down to the snowy ground, his sharp, short blade lancing out as he passed.

He took precious moments sliding to a stop in the snow, turning and clambering to his feet, but during that time he could hear his victory calling in the form of a shrill cry of agony from the lord of Pirou. As Halfdan settled into a steady stance once more, facing Hauteville, the Norman stopped bellowing, and began to pant as he forced down the pain and panic. He even managed to take a step on his good leg and drag forward the one that had had the hamstrings scythed through by the jarl's blade. He was having trouble staying upright, the left leg trembling and wobbling, threatening to give way at any moment, but still Hauteville glared at him, eyes coal-black, sword unwavering in his strong hand.

Halfdan had watched men suffer the wound that would end them more than once in his long life of war, and had seen wounds less than this drive a man to panic and flight. Not so, Serlo de Hauteville. If Halfdan had ever needed a reminder that the blood and bone of the men of this land was that same blood and bone that had defeated the monster Grendel, that had sailed the whale road in raiding ships and delighted in battle in a manner that would make Odin proud, he saw it in the struggling lord. The Normans were no longer Halfdan's people, but somewhere, deep down, there was the power of the North still in them.

'You're finished,' he said.

'Not while you breathe,' Hauteville replied, and, miraculously, managed another step without collapsing in a heap. Halfdan took a step himself. Hauteville was tottering, barely staying on his feet. He was close to overbalancing altogether, and Halfdan felt the weaving before him become clear. He smiled. He lowered his own blade and took one more step.

When Hauteville swung it was a mighty blow, meant to be the final one, the one that would end Halfdan and allow the Norman a satisfying revenge for his own disfigurement. But Halfdan was ready – that weaving of the Norns had shown him the way. As the huge blade swung, this time Halfdan dropped to a crouch, and the sword sliced through the air above his head, powerful enough that if it had struck him, it would have broken a dozen bones in his side. Instead, it met only air, and the momentum of the swing caused the inevitable. With only one stable leg holding him up, the swing sent Hauteville staggering three paces before falling to the ground.

This time, Halfdan did not give him time to recover. As Hauteville gasped with both effort and pain, struggling even to lift the heavy sword out of the deep snow, the jarl was on him, springing like a starved wolf on its stricken prey, reversing his grip on his weapon. His knee slammed into Hauteville's chest, knocking the breath from him once more, that big sword slamming back down into the snow. The tip of Halfdan's short blade found that V in the Norman's throat again, and this time he struck before his opponent could throw him or pull away. He drove the blade into the unprotected flesh and, unwilling to even allow a chance for Hauteville to survive, he added his other hand to the hilt, pushing down hard. The blade slid deep into Serlo de Hauteville's throat, keeping going until Halfdan felt it graze the spine and then meet the resistance of the frozen earth beneath the man.

He stopped there, his work done, and watched as the Norman's eyes widened, blinked, and then very, very slowly glazed and fell still. Even then, unwilling to leave anything to chance, he rose, leaning back, and watched Hauteville's chest for a long moment, making sure it neither rose nor fell, but lay still. Finally confident that his opponent was dead, Halfdan pulled his sword free with both hands and a great deal of difficulty. Then, trembling with both the effort and the cold, he rose, stepping back, away from the body lying spread-eagled in the snow.

Hauteville lay immobile, dead, that long sword in his hand. Halfdan looked down at him for a long moment, trying to decide how he felt about the man. He had been a strong warrior in life and had proved that right to the very end. He had the rock and ice of the North still in his bones. But he had betrayed his own jarl. He had broken an oath, and that was bad. Of course,

Halfdan mentally brushed aside his own oath-breaking when they had fled the Byzantine forces. That, of course, was *entirely* different…

No. Neither Odin nor Freyja would likely even look at Serlo de Hauteville for their great mead halls, as a traitor and a follower of the nailed god. But just in case, Halfdan decided to be sure. He bent once more and plucked the warrior's sword from his hand, casting it away, far from his reach.

Task complete, he rose once more and looked at the others.

Abbe was clutching his arm and cursing, though the blood-stains on the limb were small and not too alarming, and it did not appear that anything had been broken. Anna was nursing her face, which was black and purple around one eye and cheek where she had taken a blow from a chain-wrapped fist. But that seemed to be the grand total of the damage they'd taken, while Hauteville's small guard were dead, to a man.

He became aware that both Ulfr and Ælfric were waving frantically at him and pointing off to one side. As he recovered and turned that way, peering into the last few falling flakes, he realised that they had been spotted. The alarm had been raised. People were shouting and pointing their way.

He turned to the Wolves. They had to go, *now*.

'Ulfr, lead the way to your friends.' Then, to the others, 'Gather these horses. We need to move fast. Take the horses and leave the carts.'

This was it. They had to run before the rebel army began to hunt them down.

Chapter 24

The ride was fraught from the very beginning, and the only reason the Wolves managed to gain distance on their pursuers was the lack of enemy preparation. As Halfdan and the others pelted through the woodland after Ulfr, ignoring the thin branches whipping at them and the tangling undergrowth of the forest floor, the enemy were still huddled in their tents against the snow, unprepared for action. The jarl could hear the desperate calls and blasts, trying to pull together a force to pursue these men who had escaped Falaise. The Wolves led the horses, saving their strength for the ride to come, for it was easier to push through the woods on foot anyway.

'Why are we so important?' Anna gasped as they ran. 'Surely a dozen men and women escaping their clutches is hardly worth devoting such effort to?'

Halfdan turned to look over his shoulder at the small yet spirited Byzantine woman.

'They do not know who we are, yet, or what our purpose is. For all they know, we are messengers William has sent to reinforcements. They cannot let anyone escape Falaise, just in case.'

They mounted up swiftly, blessed with sufficient horses to carry everyone. Halfdan was almost overwhelmed to see Farlof, the trusty Varangian, along with four other of the Wolves there already. It almost felt as though the crew was whole again.

Soon...

They burst from the western edge of the woods on horse-back and began a breakneck ride, their route selected by Ulfr and Farlof, who had already traced the path from the ship to Falaise and could work out the reverse even in fresh snowfall.

They had at best a half-mile lead, with ten miles or more to ride, and even Halfdan, not the greatest of horsemen, knew what that meant. It came down not to the distance or their route, or planning; it came down to a simple equation. The endurance and speed of the Wolves' horses, combined with their skill in the saddle, against the same from the enemy. Half a mile was easy to make up.

They cantered across open fields, jumping irrigation ditches and skirting small copses and bushy hedges, always heading west, the shipwright confidently leading the way. Halfdan began to think that his worries had been unfounded, for by the time they had been travelling for perhaps half an hour – roughly halfway to their destination according to Ulfr – a glance over his shoulder in the clear air revealed riders in pursuit maybe half a mile back, having gained no distance on them.

Then things changed.

As they rounded the southern fringe of a densely packed forest, he spied movement off to the right, and, squinting into the grey, he could see a second group of riders bearing down on them, cutting across at a tangent. They were moving extraordinarily fast and looked certain to catch the Wolves.

'Look,' he bellowed, pointing off toward them.

Ulfr, just ahead, turned and followed his indication, face creasing into a frown.

'We have to go faster,' Halfdan shouted.

'No,' Farlof put in. 'We can't. We're going as fast as we can if we want the horses to make it ten miles. Any faster and you'll ruin it.' He looked across at the approaching men. 'They're killing their horses to catch us. We can't do the same.'

They rode on, Halfdan's heart pounding, watching the men. They were still closing, and it was clear they would reach the Wolves before the Wolves reached safety. He reasoned it out. The men chasing them had to have been commanded by someone with authority among the rebel leaders, and the man had realised that he might not catch them. He had therefore commanded a second unit to risk killing their own horses to catch them. There were maybe twenty riders over there, and eighteen of the Wolves, if he included Anna, Cassandra and the archbishop.

'Can we speed up for a *short* while?' he called.

'A mile,' Farlof conceded. 'No more, else we might not get there.'

'Then do it. Ride like Sleipnir with his eight legs for one mile.'

The Varangian gave the shout, and the Wolves picked up the pace, driving their tired horses from the steady canter they had maintained throughout the ride into a gallop.

Halfdan could feel the reluctance of his steed, could feel the sheer effort that was already beginning to sap his horse's strength as they pounded across the countryside. He glanced back and right. The enemy behind were keeping pace, more or less. The second group of riders attempting to cut them off were pushing as hard as they could, but they were suffering for it. Even as Halfdan glanced at them, trying to estimate distance, one of the riders fell out of the line, his horse collapsing beneath him. They might be animals bred and trained for war, but the Norman warrior was a heavy burden, chain-shirted to cuffs and shins, with helm and shield and spear. Those horses were being punished in the desperate attempt to stop the Wolves.

They kept up the gallop, but Halfdan knew it had to stop soon, and the frustration was almost overwhelming when Farlof bellowed the order to slow once more.

The jarl looked back again. The main pursuit had dropped a little further back, saving their horses as much as they dared. The intercepting unit were still coming on like diving seabirds, but even a glance told Halfdan that the speed was costing them dearly. There were at most a dozen riders coming, the rest having ridden their mounts to near death, and even as he watched, another animal fell.

'We need to slow to a trot,' Farlof shouted.

'No. We need to ride.'

The man fixed Halfdan with a stern look. 'If we do not rest them, my jarl, you will *walk* the last two miles.'

There was no arguing with that, and Halfdan gave a reluctant nod as the entire column slowed to a trot, allowing their horses a little time to recover.

'As soon as you think we dare, we need to speed again,' he said.

Farlof simply nodded.

Halfdan's hand went to his side, ready to draw his sword. Those eleven riders – ten, as the next fell away – were going to reach the Wolves. There would be a fight, but it had to be at high speed, for they couldn't afford to stop. The jarl blinked in surprise as an arrow suddenly whipped out from behind him, across the open ground, burying itself in the chest of the leading Norman horse. The front-runner fell, his horse injured, and the rider behind ploughed into him before he could jerk the reins and avoid the collision. In a heartbeat, the ten men had dropped to eight.

Halfdan turned to see Ketil and Leif riding side by side, the small Rus holding not only his own reins, but those of the Icelander's horse, too, keeping them on course while Ketil, free to use both hands, was busy nocking another arrow to his bow.

Halfdan was more than a little impressed. The shot had not been over any astounding distance, but from a moving horse it was stunning – only a year ago, the Icelander had been barely able to use a bow at all, fresh from the loss of an eye. His legendary skill seemed to have returned.

The second arrow missed, but that did not deter Ketil, and he nocked a third immediately as those remaining riders closed. This one plunged into the neck of a horse. The riders behind him made every effort to avoid a collision, but this cost them. They broke off pursuit momentarily to veer around the stricken animal, and in that moment two more horses staggered and collapsed from exhaustion. Five men remained, but the heart had gone out of them, and even before Ketil managed to sink an arrow shaft into another mount, they had broken off their desperate pursuit.

At a reluctant call from Farlof, the Wolves broke into a canter once more, and Halfdan could feel how unwilling his mount was. The animals had little left to give.

'How far?' he called.

'Three miles,' Ulfr shouted back. 'Maybe two,' he corrected himself as a narrow, shallow river came into view on their left, curving to meet them, with bush- and tree-lined banks. Then they were racing along the side of the flow, and Halfdan felt hope course through him.

'That's the river?'

'It is,' Ulfr confirmed. 'The Orne. And soon, the *Sea Dragon*.'

Halfdan looked back again. Still the enemy were in pursuit, but they were at least half a mile behind. The unit making to cut them off were finished, gone from view. Unless their own horses failed, they should make it.

Tension rising, they raced along the riverbank, across even, flat fields, and finally, as their pace ate another mile, Halfdan could see the river curving, coming around from their left and crossing ahead of them, bearing north toward a cluster of buildings sitting grey and uninviting in the winter air, smoke issuing from roofs.

Then...

A sail.

Halfdan felt his spirits soar. Another glance over his shoulder, and he could see the enemy were no closer. His horse was flagging, but they were almost there. Ahead, Ulfr kicked his own mount into speed, ignoring the rest of them, pulling ahead, and Halfdan could just hear him as he bore down on that sail and the ship beneath it.

'Cut the ropes. Get her moving,' he bellowed to someone on the ship.

Then the shipwright himself was leaping from his mount, even before it had fully stopped, hurtling across to the bank, where a small timber jetty that had seen far better days played host to a ship.

Halfdan marvelled as his own mount staggered to a walk, closing on the jetty. The ship was a thing of beauty. The same sleek, narrow lines as the *Sea Wolf*, perhaps a little smaller, but not much, built with the skill and precision he would only expect of Ulfr. A sail was already unfurled. There would be no hiding this ship, and Halfdan wondered how Ulfr had managed to sail her through such troubled rebel lands, given the bright red sail with its two golden lions, the banner of Duke William.

But other than that, it was a true longship in the old manner. There was even a figurehead carved in the form of an ancient dragon, the like of Fafnir. Ulfr had etched the first runes along the sheer strakes and begun the work of intricate carving, presumably during the quieter moments of his journey.

Halfdan had not been at all convinced that the shipwright, great as he was, could truly achieve completion of a vessel in such a short time, and yet there was the *Sea Dragon* in all its glory, not just a seaworthy ship, but a *hunter* – a work of art.

The second thing that made him boggle was the crew. Somehow, far from the six men he had left at Pirou, the new ship was fully crewed, a man at every oar, in sweat-soaked tunic and cloak, other men at the prow, the steering oar, hauling in ropes. He'd not seen such a number of men on his side since before Miklagarðr, before even Sasireti.

The others were arriving, their horses slowing, men and women leaping clear and hurrying down to the jetty. The ropes had been thrown clear and already the oars were being lifted, ready to push off and then begin their work. The river was narrow and shallow, and most ships would surely run aground or become stuck, but Ulfr knew his vessel.

Halfdan was the third to leap aboard from the dock, behind Ulfr and Farlof. The latter ran to the prow and started shouting orders to the crew like a man born to the whale road, while Ulfr crossed to the steering oar, the man controlling it relinquishing it readily. As Halfdan moved to the stern, the others began to jump aboard, Bjorn helping Archbishop Ælfric, who was struggling with his long tunic. Gunnhild joined him at the rear a moment later, the two of them watching the enemy horses bearing rapidly down upon them. It was still close.

Then they were being manoeuvred out into mid-flow, oars pushing against the jetty while others began to dip and turn the prow. Farlof gave a bellowed order, and the crew began a chant, an ancient rowing cadence that had to have come from Ulfr, for no one else on this ship would know such a song, sung long ago by great warriors of Odin as they brought iron and terror to the coasts of their enemies. The *Sea Dragon* suddenly surged forward like a great beast on the hunt, carving a path through the still, dark water, sending white waves to both shores in its passage.

The enemy caught up with them.

Even as the ship ploughed downstream, the first riders of their pursuit were there, riding along the bank, shouting, pointing, impotent, unable to do anything to reach their prey out in the water. Already some of the pursuers had stopped, reining in, knowing the futility of chasing any further.

A small group of riders continued to keep pace with them, one of them a nobleman. Halfdan recognised the colours, then the face, but it was Gunnhild who spoke to him first.

'See now, Neel, lord de Cotentin, what a true sea monster looks like. Return to your castle and have your tapestry finished.'

And then they were ahead. Somehow a gust of strong wind caught the sail and gave them extra speed, pushing them on through the water. Halfdan watched as the riders were left behind, slowly at first, then with pace, as the *Sea Dragon* picked up an impressive speed, racing through the town of Clécy, the riders finally stopping, their mounts exhausted. The rebel baron who had sought the duke's death at Valognes, had chased him and Halfdan and the others across the peninsula and to a dangerous tidal crossing, had sought them at Rigia, and who had trapped and attempted to break them at Falaise, had failed.

Somehow, as he watched that figure grow smaller until he and his horse were but a dot in the white, Halfdan knew that Cotentin was not destined for success. The duke – at a tender fifteen – had the mark of greatness, such an aura of power that there was no way these rebels would finish him. Falaise was but a step.

As they slid from Clécy out into the countryside once more, the river widened slightly, and the oars worked with the sail to give them an impressive pace that would carry them to the sea long before the rebel barons could get men anywhere near them.

They had done it. They were free.

Halfdan had been grateful for many things over the years but had never felt quite as grateful as he did at that moment. They were free to sail the whale road; they had a new ship, a new crew that Ulfr would tell him all about soon, plenty of gold remaining, and, best of all, he knew where Harðráði was, and had an idea of what the man planned – and he knew where the hated priest Hjalmvigi was, if not how he was going to get to him.

He relaxed.

He didn't realise that he'd actually dozed off, sitting propped beside the sternpost, until Ulfr shook him awake. He could smell the salt of seawater. Looking over the side, he could see they were still in Nordmandi, but the river was broad, deep and fast, and the smell and the cries of gulls made it clear that they were almost at the sea. He smiled at the shipwright as he stretched into wakefulness.

'How long?'

'Five hours. Gunnhild said none of you had slept in days, so we let you rest as long as we could, but now we approach the open sea, and there are decisions ahead that only a jarl can make. Speaking of which, your traveller wished to speak with you when you woke.'

It took Halfdan a few moments to realise that Ulfr meant Ælfric. He rose, noting that several of those who had ridden with him from Falaise were still asleep, Bjorn snoring like a bear with a head cold. He smiled and tottered across the ship between the unfamiliar faces of the new crew, to where the archbishop, clad in a borrowed cloak, stood at the prow, holding on tight as he peered off ahead. He turned at Halfdan's approach.

'Ah, the jarl returns.'

'Priest.'

'I need to go home.'

Halfdan nodded, thinking back to the map he'd seen in the castle at Falaise.

'Angle-land is just a few miles across the water. Consider it done.'

The man shook his head. 'I need to go *home*. To *Jorvik*, which is far in the north.'

Halfdan shook his head. 'We have business in the east. I can take you to your island, though.'

He became aware that they were not alone, and turned to see Gunnhild standing behind him, eyes bright.

'You can spare the time,' Ælfric said with a knowing smile. 'You seek two men, but the one who stole your ship is still in Rus lands, yet to come west, where you can meet him and reclaim what is yours. And your priest friend...'

'Yes?'

'I may be able to help you there.'

Halfdan flinched. He felt every sign at once: the Seiðr in the air; the itching of the Loki serpents on his arm; the sense of anticipation from the völva behind him. It was as though all the gods had stopped what they were doing and watched the exchange, possibly even the nailed god among them. The very air crackled.

'Tell me.'

'A man of the cloth derives all his power from the respect of his position. Your priest, who, from all you have said, is as wicked as a man can be, and may be a devil in God's Church, is the most powerful priest in your land, untouchable.'

'Yes?'

'What if he lost that position?'

Halfdan frowned. 'This can be done?'

'It is called excommunication. On behalf of God, the pope in Rome, and the Holy Church, as an archbishop it is within my power to call excommunication on any man below the rank of cardinal in Rome. It is no small matter. Excommunicated, your enemy would not only cease to be the most powerful priest in your land but would be stripped of everything. He would no longer be a priest at all. He would no longer be welcomed by the Church, no longer permitted into the temples of God, no longer able to attend Mass or any service, not granted the right of burial on sacred ground. He would be nothing. *Less* than nothing. Hated. Abhorred.'

Halfdan blinked.

'You can do this?'

'I can.'

'And you *would* do this?'

'In return for a favour.' Ælfric smiled.

'What?'

'Take me back to Jorvik. And there, you will remove a troublesome enemy for me. You remove my enemy for me, and I will do the same for you. Moreover, to sweeten the deal, I will offer you a bag of gold the weight of a man.'

'Any man?' Halfdan probed, avarice getting the better of him.

'Not your pale giant.' The archbishop chuckled.

Halfdan turned to Gunnhild. Without her confirmation, he could never strike such a deal. She kept his gaze for a long moment, and then smiled wolfishly and nodded.

Halfdan turned back to the archbishop. 'It would seem we have a deal.'

He grinned as his gaze rose from the man, over the prow. They were entering a broad harbour, and ahead, between stone piers, he could see the wide, grey whale road, Ran's daughters dancing as whitecaps on the rolling waves. He turned to Ulfr, at the other end of the ship. It seemed they were committed, and there was no need to hide anything from the crew.

'Set your course for the north of Angle-land, for a town called Jorvik.'

Ulfr, at the rear, nodded, guiding them toward the open waves.

Halfdan looked out ahead.

All things seemed to be coming together. One more favour, and then vengeance would be theirs.

Jorvik.

Of small sands;
Of small seas,
small minds are made.
Not all men
are matched in wisdom.
The imperfect are easy to find.

On Spirit from the *Hávamál*

Historical Note

This book was written partly to tell the story of what the Wolves' part in the history of the Duchy of Normandy might be, and partly to explore the character of Ulfr and of Viking ships and shipbuilding. First, though, the Normans.

In Britain, we tend to compartmentalise our invaders. I remember my history lessons being at times almost a dizzying blur of successive invasions. There were the Romans, of course, and I tend to focus on them, myself. And then, during what are often called the Dark Ages, there were the Jutes, the Saxons, the Angles, the Danes, the Vikings and then the Normans. What we largely miss by separating out these invaders is that many of them were very much the same people, or variations on a theme. The Danes were Vikings. The Jutes, Angles and Saxons were all peoples from modern Denmark or Baltic Germany, and were close enough to Vikings in many ways that by the time you'd argued the difference, they'd have punched you in the face, burned your monastery and run away with your money and children.

And then there's the Normans. We in Britain definitely see the Normans as different from the Vikings, and yet they were perhaps the closest connected of all. The Normans had only been in France for five generations between Rollo arriving on his dragon ship and bellowing about Odin, and William the Bastard fighting for his dukedom against the rebels. Five generations is not that long. The only real difference between Halfdan and William (aside from religion) is that William's people had been in Normandy long enough to have assimilated some language and habits from the Frankish peoples. It would be doing a disservice to the Normans not to give them some credit, mind. In those five generations, they had developed socially, linguistically, religiously, politically and in many other ways, into a distinct people. But that distinct people was still surprisingly close to Viking in many ways.

So to some extent, after their time in the south, the Wolves are almost on home ground now, or at least familiar enough that they can relate.

Normandy had undergone several periods of aggressive expansion by the early 1040s, carving out a nation that the French and Burgundians would have loved to see the back of, and then annexing the Cotentin Peninsula from the Bretons. There had been an unbroken line of dukes, but suddenly, with Robert's death, only an illegitimate son remained. William inherited his title and lands at an age so young he was probably seen as little more than an inconvenience by powerful lords. Yet he held on, he secured his throne, he survived a number of assassination attempts (lovingly portrayed herein), and finally, in 1047 (sadly a little after the scope of this novel) he led an army against a much larger rebel force at the battle of Val-ès-Dunes, and in doing so defeated them and secured his power for good. For your edification, be consoled that the rebel lords Neel de Cotentin and Ranulf de Bessin, along with many other powerful rebels, met their end at Val-ès-Dunes trying to bring down the duke and his new ally, the King of France.

Let us examine the story I have told, then, with this background in mind.

I suspect I have little to clarify from Part One of the book, which takes place mostly on the road with a last section at Pirou (of which more will follow in relation to Part Three).

The attack at Valognes is recorded in sources, though I have played with it a little. The original comes across as considerably more fantastical than my more prosaic version. I used a number of sources for the background to this novel, including Duncan's

The Dukes of Normandy, but the main source for this part, and the one that gives the best view of the rebellion itself is *The Conspiracy of the Norman Barons Against William the Bastard, Duke of Normandy* by Charles Edmond Prudent Le Cointe. Catchy, eh?

This work is the best source, and tells us of that first attempt on the duke at Valognes. In Le Cointe's work, we are told that the conspiracy was born at Bayeux between four lords: Neel de Cotentin, Ranulf de Bayeux (Viscount de Bessin), Grimoult du Plessis and Hamon (or Hammond) 'of the Teeth!' de Evrecy, Thorigny and Creully. Le Cointe tells us that the four rebel barons came to Valognes to deal with William, and that on the night of the deed they prepared in a local house, where they were overheard by a fool called Gallet, who happened to be favoured by William, and who ran to the castle, raising the alarm in time for William to escape their clutches. The fool then held off the enemy and saved the duke, and William fled alone, crossing the tidal river and finding aid at the house of Hubert de Ryes, who led the enemy away and saved him. This is, of course, chivalric high adventure, and very unlikely to bear any resemblance to what *actually* happened. I suspect my version is probably actually closer to the truth than the sources, for all of its being fiction. The movements after their meeting with Hubert are my own interpretation, including a fight among the ruins of Vieux-la-Romaine. It is, in our sources, the attempt on William's life at Valognes that triggers the full-scale revolt of the barons.

Of Ulfr's shipbuilding in Part Three, I have been forced to make leaps in logic and judgement in many ways. Firstly in the construction technique. Much of what I describe comes from the Oseberg and Gokstad ships, which are considerably earlier, dated to the ninth century. By the time of the eleventh century, things had moved on in the world of shipbuilding. I have nodded to the changing times of Norse ships with the realisation that their first ship would have had the oarsmen seated on their own sea chests in old-fashioned Viking style, while now they are installing oar benches. But I hope you will forgive me my anachronisms, for there is a purpose. Ulfr is old-fashioned. He is building an old-fashioned ship in an old-fashioned way, and so it seems appropriate to have the techniques solidly anchored in an earlier century. Also, I have sped up production. Normally, of course, it would take a lot longer to create such a ship. However, when studies are made of Viking ship creation, there is always an assumption as to the level of effort and manpower that can be applied. A traditional longship's construction begins with the shipwright walking the forests and choosing the trees for his ship, long before they are even cut and shaped. Given that Ulfr has ready-made parts, a vast workforce, and unlimited funds, I was forced to extrapolate as best I could how much faster work could be completed. The result here is not, I believe, outside the bounds of reason, for all its impressive speed. After all, the ship was not *entirely* finished!

A quick note before we move on, on the lords and locations in the Cotentin. Firstly, the castle at Pirou remains, though the place that can now be visited is a much later construction on the same spot. A stone castle with a moat has replaced the timber palisade of early Norman days. But Pirou is a real place, as is Pirou Plage, where Ulfr built his ship. The place was indeed built to guard two small tidal harbours. I have used old names for them, but the one to the north from which Ulfr steals the oars is now Saint-Germain-sur-Ay, while the southern one is at Geffosses. My descriptions will not match up to their current visibility, for much has changed on the coast in a thousand years. The hazards that lie along that coast, which Ulfr braves in his new ship, are based on descriptions and maps of the local coastline in the eighteenth and nineteenth centuries, the central clear channel named the Passage de la Déroule, the three hazards I name marked on maps as Banc Feli, Basses de Portbail, and Rochers de Taillepieds. The narrow defile where Ulfr rides out pursuit lies on the rocky north coast of the peninsula, just to the west of Le Landemer. My descriptions of Valognes, where the hunt is planned and the first attempt on the duke's life takes place, are largely conjectural, based on other surviving Norman fortresses of the early eleventh century. Of the Valognes of William's time, nothing remains. Even the medieval castle that followed was later demolished, barring one tower, which fell to bombing in World War II.

That Serlo de Hauteville, senior brother of the family, was part of the rebellion against William is again conjectural. However, Serlo's date of death is not confirmed, and he is not named among the many companions of the duke during the invasion of England in 1066, just two decades later, which suggests that he did not enjoy favour or prominence in Normandy by then. I have killed Serlo off here, in the last chapters of the book, in the winter of 1043. Various sources give Serlo's year of death as anywhere between 1027 and 1035, and yet he is also recorded as having inherited the family estate on his father's death in 1041, and so an earlier date of demise seems unlikely, barring some kind of zombie activity. Thus I have him on record as alive in 1041, but unrecorded by 1066, and so I am unrepentant in placing his demise in 1043 at the hands of the Wolves.

I have left Beatrix's fate outside the scope of this novel. Be assured that Serlo did let her live, for she ended up married twice, the first time to that very Armand de Mortain. The second may well be one Geoffroi di Conversano, who had been a companion of the other Hautevilles in Apulia. I have been vague in this, much like the sources. It is complex, as is so much in this era. The counts of Mortain and Eu remained William's supporters, and so Beatrix must have fallen on her feet in the end.

Moving on to the final part of the tale, the siege I have described at Falaise is not recorded in texts, though the sources are scanty and tend to leap about and concentrate on the more peculiar events. William's activity after the attempt on his life at Valognes and the outbreak of the rebellion, and his bringing on side of the French King and making the rebels pay for their actions are touch and go. The attempted assassination in his room there, which I have portrayed, comes from Duncan, though in that source it is the seneschal's lieutenant who saves William, and the event takes place at Le Vaudreuil. I have conflated events for ease of description. Once again, the sources of this era and region are extremely vague, often contradictory, at best suspicious, and jump about, missing huge, important sections. The tithe barn at the village (now known as Épaney) still exists, as does the church, and it was, as described, subject to the monks of Ouche and Perrières.

As you may have already surmised, just as I introduced Beatrix in *Iron and Gold* as a hook to drag the Wolves into this new story, the presence of the Archbishop of Jorvik (York) at Falaise is clearly a link to what is to come in book five. There is no record of Ælfric being in Normandy, but then his movements between his part in the crowning of Edward the Confessor in the spring of 1043 and his death in 1051 are unrecorded. The former queen, Edward's mother, is known to history as Emma of Normandy! She had blood ties to the dukes of Normandy, and when Edward stripped her of her wealth we know that she fled abroad to Bruges, not to Normandy, but she had ties to the archbishop, and there is no reason he could not have been used by her as an intermediary with her distant family. Certainly, she had her goods returned to her in due course.

So that brings us to the end of the fourth book in the series. With two books remaining in my plan, you will already have more than an inkling where the next one, at least, is set.

Halfdan and his friends have, in their journeys, lost almost everything, and yet now they have regained most of it, with an eye to settling the remaining scores, and have gained, to boot. They have some fame and infamy, great tales for the mead halls of their dotage, and a small fortune in gold, not to mention a new ship and a new crew.

Heaven help the enemies of Archbishop Ælfric.

See you in book five: *Loki Unbound*.

Simon Turney
April 2023

Glossary

Aesir – one of the two groups of Viking gods, including Thor, Odin, Loki and Tyr

Berserkr (pl. berserkir) – lit. 'bear shirts'. The berserkers of Viking fame who were overtaken by battle madness in the name of Odin

Draugr (pl. draugar) – the zombie-like restless dead, occupying graves and guarding their treasure jealously

Dromon – a Byzantine warship powered by sails or by banks of oars akin to the Roman trireme or Ottoman galley

Excubitores – an elite Byzantine regiment with an origin as imperial bodyguards, by this time part of the garrison of Constantinople

Freyja – the most powerful goddess of the Vanir, whose realm includes magic, fertility, war and the gathering of the slain to her land of Fólkvangr

Gotlander – one of the three peoples of modern Sweden, the Goths occupied the island of Gotland

Holmgang – an official, ritual form of duel between two opponents

Jarl – a noble of power (the derivation of the English 'earl') who receives fealty from all free men of a region

Karl – a free man. Neither a noble, nor a slave

Katepan – regional governor of the Byzantine empire

Loki – a trickster god, a shape-shifter, who is destined to fight alongside the giants against the other gods at the end of days

Miklagarðr – Viking name for Constantinople, the capital of the Byzantine Empire, now Istanbul

Mjǫllnir – Thor's hammer

Norns – the female entities who control the fates of both men and gods

Odin – most powerful of the Aesir, the chief god and father of Thor, who gave an eye in return for wisdom and who has twin ravens and twin wolves, and an eight-legged horse

Ragnarok – the end of the universe, including a great battle between gods, giants, monsters and the slain who have been gathered by Odin and Freyja

Rakke – A Viking version of a mast parrel, the sliding wooden collar by which a yard or spar is held to a mast in such a way that it may be hoisted or lowered

Rus – the descendants of the Vikings who settled Kiev and Novgorod and areas of Belarus and Ukraine, from whom the name Russian derives (Rusland)

Sax – a short sword or long knife of Germanic origin, known to the Saxons as the seax

Seiðr – a form of magic that flows around men and gods, which can be used and understood by few, the source of divination

Svear – one of the three peoples of modern Sweden, the Svears occupied the northern regions of Sweden, around Uppsala

'Tafl – a Viking board game akin to chess or go, where one player has to bring his jarl piece to the edge of the board

Theotokos [Pammakaristos] – lit. 'Mother of God'. Greek terms of Mary, mother of Jesus

Thor – son of Odin, the god of thunder, one of the most powerful of the Aesir

Thrall – a slave with no will beyond that of his master, often a captive of war

Valknut – a symbol of interlocked triangles believed to bind an object or person to Odin